The Sweetest Thing

Fiona Shaw

Virago

A *Virago* Book

Published by Virago Press 2004
First published in Great Britain by Virago Press 2003

Copyright © Fiona Shaw 2003

The moral right of the author has been asserted

A CIP catalogue record for this book
is available from the British Library

ISBN 1 84408 045 5

Typeset in Garamond by M Rules
Printed and bound in Great Britain by Clays Ltd, St Ives plc

Virago Press
An imprint of
Time Warner Books UK
Brettenham House
Lancaster Place
London WC2E 7EN

www.virago.co.uk

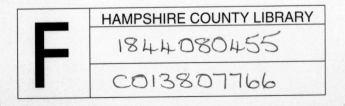

For Hugh Haughton

HARRIET

I was all of sixteen, the first time I met him. I know when it was because we'd come in to York for the Martinmas Fair. We'd it planned a long time and we'd done it, though if we'd known just what we'd done, we'd never have left the fishes.

So Martinmas makes it November. And I recall it was that cold I was ready to scream. I think maybe he thought I was going to do something foolish. I didn't think it then, but I do now, now that I know how much he fears things.

Of course I wasn't going to do something foolish. I've never been one with that kind of courage. But I was leaning hard against the bridge on Fossgate, looking.

It might have had to do with food. Nothing grander. There isn't anything grander when you're hungry. I've a vague rec-ollection there was something caught in the ice and I was maybe thinking the ice'd be like the salt we used in winter for the fish back home, and it'd have kept it fresh, whatever it was that was dead in there that day, if I could only fetch it in.

They skinned dogs and cats and all sorts round there and they'd pay you something for near on anything that had once drawn breath.

Sixteen had seemed like the great age in September and that's when we'd decided, Mary and me. We wanted to see something else than the sea.

We were flither-lasses and the ones that were best at it, like us, were stronger than the men even. I could lift the most, but it was Mary riled the lads, bragging as how she could better them.

First we'd to find the bait, and then gathering, and you'd to be shrewd for that, to know where was best. We'd fill our creels with limpets and mussels, cover them with weed, saddle them to our backs and get home.

I've missed the sea ever since, though Mary would think me daft if I could tell her that, because she was a city girl from her first breath of it.

Our plan was to go to the city and get ourselves work and a little room in a lodging house together. And after a time we'd both have sweethearts who might be in a factory or apprenticed, or salesmen better, or even clerks – that was Mary, she always dreamed higher. And we'd both get married, and live next door to each other and have one of them new houses with a proper privy of your own. I can still see it if I shut my eyes hard.

So then I said it to me dad, just light, not meaning it much in me voice.

And he said, 'You must be bloody joking an' if I ketch you so much as looking at the trains, I'll have yer guts in that tray with the fish.'

So he didn't think it was a good idea, and now I'd say he had a point, he knew more than he was telling. But he didn't tell, he just bawled me out, and Mary's dad the same.

She was the one that got the fares together, but I think even she was nervous the day we left, though she'd never let on to anyone.

So I was on the bridge in November, broad daylight, when suddenly there's this gentleman leaning next to me, and he's staring, or I think he is, down at where my hands are, all chapped with cold. He says, 'Good day,' and I'm thinking hey-ho here we go, and who knows, I was hungry enough an' all.

'Good day,' he goes, so I say the same back, then crack up laughing at the sound of it. But he's such a look on his face that I stop right off.

'I were looking to see if it were owt to sell,' I say, pointing my head at the water and he looks at me and I can see he doesn't know what the blazes I'm on about.

Anyway, we get chatting and he wants to know all about where I come from. All sorts about how we'd climb down the cliff, how heavy was the rope, did we wear skirts for it, did anyone ever fall, and how heavy the creel was, and when did we catch bait, and when not, and did we mend nets, and was it hard on the hands. And especially about how strong we all were. So I was soon wondering what on earth he was about, because who in their right mind wants to know about flither-lasses.

Now, he's all dressed up in this warm coat and this tall hat and gloves and I can't help it but I'm shivering. So I tell him I must go, I've to get on, though in truth I've nowhere to get on to, but maybe it'll be warmer somewhere else, and he looks at the ground in this odd way.

'I'd like a portrait of you,' he says and his voice is faltery. 'Would you accompany me to the photographer's? There's one just five minutes' walk from here.'

I don't know what stops me going, but something does, though I wish I had now and maybe things wouldn't have

gone as they did. But probably they would have done any
road. And then he looks so crestfallen, for all his polite
bowing, that I tell him I could come later, tomorrow, so long
as I can bring my friend.

Mary and me, we'd been friends a while. We didn't start that
way, more like pike and pilchard first off and I'll not be needing to say which for which. But there was a day that changed
it. It was winter and the men were long-line fishing, my dad
out for the day in his coble with my brother Daniel and
coming back in after dark, his beard gone to ice and my job to
bring him a bowl by the fire, and he'd hunch over while I held
it and watched the ice melt, drip, drip, drip, till the bowl had
a puddle. And meanwhile my mam'd be holding Daniel's
hands, chafing them just so and him wincing, gritting his
teeth not to make a sound while they warmed.

It were dangerous in the winter. The sea liked to take a
man now and then, like the dragon in the story. It had been
my Uncle Joseph the year before, out of my dad's boat, and
that's why Daniel had started in, younger than he would've
otherwise. Mam and Dad fought over that and it's the one
time I heard Dad bested. Even so, Daniel started.

Dad never shed a tear, but the day of the funeral, and them
carrying Joseph, his face was so fierce, his cheek hard up
against the corner of the coffin, if I'd been the dragon I'd have
shook. Except the sea-dragon never does, and you've just to get
on with it.

Bait is women's work. There's plenty else we've to do, but
first off it's our job to cover the hooks, hundreds of them, each
with its own creature. That first winter of our friendship,
Mary and mine, the bait was scarce and there'd been fights on
the scars with those from the next village. So we'd put a stake
in the cliff and hang a rope from it. Then all you'd to do was
gather in your petticoats like breeches, with a pair of strings at

the knee, and go down the rope, hand over hand. For at the bottom were limpets, kissing the rocks as best they could, but no match for our knives. The rope was easier work than the traipsing and the brawling.

Coming up, we'd sit on the ledge near the top as often as not, and whistle out to the ships at sea, our baskets full beside us. So this day I was whistling with Lizzie, another lass, and everyone's up from the beach below. The mist is coming in and it's cold sitting still, so we set off up. But at the top, I'm sure I hear a cry. Lizzie doesn't, so we stop and see if it comes again. There's no sound and she shakes her head.

'There's nowt down there, and I a'n't going to ketch me death of pneumonie.'

But I don't feel easy. 'I'm going back,' I say.

Lizzie's shivering, and she just hitches her basket and walks off. The mist's coming in fast, like it does, but I swing down quickly. Back on the scar, I can't see further than my own boots. The water's close by, I can hear the waves breaking over the pools. 'Helloo,' I call, my hand still on the rope, because I'm certain Lizzie's right now, and all I heard was a bird. 'Helloo.' I'm several steps up the cliff when she calls again.

'I'm down,' I think she says.

Slithering about in the covered pools, I find the voice. It's Mary. She's not one I know well. She's sat on a bit of rock, fiddling, so far as I can see, with this clutch of shells. Making patterns when the water's rising.

'What is it, Mary?' I say. She doesn't speak. 'Are you hurt?' I ask. She shakes her head and all the while the tide's coming up. 'Swim, can you?' I ask, as a joke. She doesn't get it, just shakes her head. The mizzle's getting heavy and now I'm starting to shake like Lizzie. 'Well, come on then, girl, let's get out of the way of the water,' I say and put my hand out to help her up. I'm strong, one of the strongest, but she's a dead weight, and I lose it for a moment.

'Christ's sake, Mary, do you want to drown? Help me, can't you.'

She doesn't do much and I still have to carry her to the rope. I tie her to it, whispering all the while what I'm going to do, speaking soft, patting her hair every now and then, because I can see now what's up. Then I set off myself, hand over hand, to the first ledge. Once I'm there, I call down to her, though I can see nowt, and start to pull.

It's the hardest pull I've ever done and my arms are yelling and my lungs heaving and I'm nearly thinking I must break and let go, when she's there with me, staring like as if she's in another place, as I find out afterwards she very nearly is.

That's how we get up, ledge to ledge, first me, then her, and all the while the weather close about and nobody to help.

I know her house, and half-carry, half-drag her there. All the while she's said not a word. Only when I'm off to go and her mam's wondering what the hell's been going, Mary says, so as only I can hear, 'Thanks,' and touches my shoulder.

That was it after. There was no one else.

She'd got scared down there, scared rigid, that's what it was, the biggest daredevil in that place. And she got hell for it after. Her mam and dad first of all, and then just everyone else. She never told what happened, kept her silence, but it was a bad one there, it left her high and dry. She couldn't do the work. Not only the rope. She wouldn't go near the water.

Mary's mam was well known for cuffing about. She'd get a bit in her and take it out on her children, Mary's brother Jamie especially, as he couldn't look after himself so well. She wasn't the only one, but she had a cruel tongue, and the drink didn't soften it. So right from the first off of me knowing her,

Mary was planning her escape and it didn't take long before I was to go too. To start with just the idea, but in the end, in the months before, it was to be for real.

We'd left first off, before the gulls had started up even, and we had eggs on the train. Those two things I remember as if it were yesterday. Our walking to the station and all the while me thinking I'd hear my dad's voice behind and that'd be that. And then the eggs. I don't know where she'd got them from, but Mary had them wrapped in one bit of paper, and a pinch of salt in another. Two each. There was a message on one egg, a piece of paper, and she read it and said in this little voice, 'How'd he know?', but she didn't say it to me, and then she put it somewhere safe and when she thought I couldn't see, she rubbed her eyes clear.

I put my shells out of the window, threw them out at the sheep, which didn't even lift their heads. Mary made patterns with hers, cracking the shells into pieces and fixing them in different shapes, until I'd had enough and said to her to stop making messes, and she laughed.

We got ourselves hired. It was so easy. Too easy and I'd have known better if I'd been anything more than I was back then. A woman hired me for a maid of all work, and I was to start tomorrow. Mrs Hough she gave herself as. She'd a place I could sleep in the kitchen and I could go there tonight if I wished, which was when it broke on me that come tomorrow we'd be separated, me and Mary, and not just a street apart, but maybe miles, in this huge city.

So I said I couldn't come tonight but that I'd be there first off tomorrow and Mrs Hough said to be sure that it was, and we left it at that. Mary thought Mrs Hough smelt strange, but I said it was still the fish in her nostrils, and besides she hadn't asked for my character, like they do in the stories, and, since I hadn't got one, I was glad of the work.

Mary got work just as easily. She was sniffy about being a maid, and ended up laundress to a Mrs Hutton with a laugh like a screech owl, who said she'd no room in her house, all the beds being taken by other girls, but she'd give us an address of a friend with a lodging house.

The city was nothing like I'd imagined. For a start, the noise was so different. I was used to the sea. Back home, when there was a storm on, you'd come inside with your ears aching, burning from the wind and you'd still have the roar in your head from the waves. But coming out of the train, we came into a din of words. I was ready for it, I thought, after all I'd been on a train before, been in Scarborough station a couple of times. But this was something else. So much steam I couldn't see my feet at first, and then all these people shouting and talking and walking, walking fast, and in the middle of it, me and Mary. I didn't know which way to look, but Mary didn't look around at all, just walked on as if she knew where she was going. Like she'd been here before, which I knew she hadn't.

And then it was strange to see the sky so high up. I'd to crane my head right back to catch a glimpse. And then so much of the place wasn't grand in the least, for all there were so many buildings and a church in every corner.

We watched the animals being bought and sold and we watched the hirings, and as the dark dropped, they lit the paraffin lights and we watched them on the merry-go-round. Just as I was dog-tired with watching and with the day, Mary was treated to a ride by this lad we had to run away from after. That's what she could always do. I'd be weary, or cold, or hungry, and so would she, and from somewhere she'd do something to make us laugh, or sometimes cry.

So we were standing puffed and giggling behind a tent, and Mary exclaiming that she never could see why the boys bothered her so, when a strange lady came up. Strange to me then, I mean, not after. But I thought her dressed queerly, in a black dress and funny bonnet.

'Would you be thirsty for anything,' she asked.

Not being sure whether she meant something to drink, so whether I had caught her meaning, I bobbed a curtsy to be polite and Mary giggled. She told us there was cheap coffee to be had just down the way, and why didn't she show us.

She took us into this place that was a hall and then into a room with coffee urns and pastry things at one end and a sign propped against the table with the prices. There were some others in here, all sipping at their cups and chomping pies and there must have been four more ladies like our one, each with her bonnet and black dress. I was halfway down towards the table when Mary called me out. 'Come on,' she said and without waiting she was striding, like she couldn't get out fast enough.

I said my first angry words to Mary then. I was cold and hungry and thirsty and it looked safe in there. I pulled her round by the shoulder.

'What did you do that for? Why did you march out?'

I don't recollect her answer but it would have been short. And something in it would have been the same as the answer she gave ever after, though she didn't know then what they were. That those people didn't really care for any except their own damn souls and they gave her the creeps. She'd a hard tongue on her for things like this, but then sometimes it seemed she could always see straight in, catch what they were up to, when I'd be still stood standing.

I don't remember much of our first night in York. We did find the lodging house, and if I'd had the money and if I hadn't been so tired, I'd have been back home quicker than the spit on water. It was close on the river, in a court off a lane so narrow you couldn't have got a cart up. We couldn't see what we were walking on, but from the smell of the place we could guess well enough.

There was a privy, a coal shed and a pigsty in the court and in one corner there were some children playing, or fighting. They were all over us in an instant, their fingers swarming across our clothes like the summer flies on fish that won't lift even when you swipe. They smelt too, and their clothes looked more pieces of rag than anything else. Their fingers were hard and prying and they only left off when Mary knocked at the door.

A woman came to it, a short, broad-shouldered angry-looking woman with an apron round that'd seen a lot of life. Mary was shaking a little, on account of the river so near by – she never could bear water again – and she'd gone pale as milk. The woman gave her this long look, and when we asked, she said we could stay the night, just the one, and that out of the goodness of her heart, and it'd be nine pence for the two of us, which was more money than I'd ever thought I'd pay for sleep, and tomorrow we must take ourselves elsewhere. They'd had enough of sickness round here for several lifetimes, she said, giving Mary another look.

She walked us across the yard and she had this funny walk, like her legs had grown different from each other. She handed us a stub of candle and some matches and said, 'That'll be a ha'penny,' and pointed her lantern at some steps set up against the coal shed.

We near on ran up them, so desperate by now to lie down, to escape the smells that made my stomach rise, and the children with their hands and the big woman and just to sleep. Inside the room was a pallet of straw with a cruddy blanket and a cracked pot. So we lay down in all our things and cuddled for warmth and slept our first night in the city.

We parted with a kiss and a promise to meet the next Sunday at the market cross at noon. She was to go to her new work and

I to mine. After the night we'd passed, I was pleased to be off and away to a job. The house was only ten minutes' walk and I was there in good time to be let in to the scullery by Mrs Hough, who turned out to be the cook, not the lady. She showed me my sleeping place at the back of the kitchen, 'Though you'll not be doing much of that,' she warned, but even so it was warm and snug compared to the place I'd just been.

It wasn't my fault I lost my job. I was used to hard work, but what the lady had me doing would've broke a horse. I was happy doing the dirty work, making up fires, getting in coal, drudging and blackleading, I knew how to do all that, it was what my mother had taught me at home. But then the bell would ring and I'd to be quick and tidy myself, wash hands and face and run up to see to the missis. I'd have to be clean and nice and waiting at table, then be back to scouring pans and helping the cook and the next it'd be running errands to the butcher and the baker and then it'd be serving tea and so on, never ending, forever changing aprons and worrying about my hair. I wasn't used to it, couldn't get the hang. I was used to salt, so washing soda wasn't so bad. But it was all the washing off and getting dirty and washing off again that did for my hands, and by the end of the week they were sore.

The missis never lost her smile. I reckon she thought she was good to me, but I'd never treat anyone like that. Anyway, it was a big house for one maid to clean and that maid me, and after two weeks and not a day's holiday and never the chance to meet Mary, I knew something was up with my right hand. It didn't just hurt, it'd gone puffy, and there was a cut that kept on oozing, not a lot, just a bit. Mrs Hough did what she could with a poultice at night, but it kept on and got so bad I couldn't bear to have her touch it.

Mrs Hough knew a woman over Fulford way who was good with this kind of thing, so I went and asked for a half holiday, to rest up my hand and get it mended. I'd learnt how to knock and wait just so, and how far to come in to the room, and how to curtsy and I did it all and then I asked.

The missis stared at me, still smiling her neat smile, and then shook her head.

'You can't just take your leave when you wish, you know.' Then she went on about how much she was teaching me and I oughtn't to be ungrateful and I'd been lucky to find such a nice establishment and some houses they'd take all kinds of advantage. I'd have liked to tell her all I could do if it came to clambering down the cliff, or flithering, or mending the yards of nets and the ripped places where the fish had fought. But I didn't. I didn't have the push for it, now I was here in the city and away from the sea. I only waited to explain again, that it was on account of my hand and that it wasn't getting better, but she wouldn't let me. Just ordered me out and said she'd have tea at four.

My hand was throbbing, and a thin red line was moving like a snake up beyond my wrist. I was hot that night and by morning the missis had changed her mind. She had me out, two weeks' wages minus a day, and blathering all this about country girls and diseases they brought. I don't know why I kept my tongue, maybe it was the fever made me act strange, but I let off to Mrs Hough, who nodded and 'there there'd' while she sponged me down, and then she got me to the Fulford woman, I don't know how, who, for most of my wages, gave me a bed and food and dressed my hand. After a few days I was well enough to leave.

In all this time I hadn't clapped eyes on Mary. For all I knew she might have gone home, but I doubted it. The road seemed very long as I walked back into the city. I went past the barracks quick as I could, because my mother had always warned me about soldiers, though there hadn't been much danger on the beach, and after twenty minutes I reached the cattle market.

More than anything had, the sound of the cows made me want home and if it hadn't been for Mary, I'd have gone. I came in through Fishergate postern and went to find the laundry.

Mary had got herself a room off Walmgate, not far from the laundry. When I turned up, we struck a bargain with the landlady. I could stay there too if I cleaned out the fires, got in the water and minded the children of an evening now and then, till my hand was better enough and I could find another job. Mrs O'Leary was a widow. Young and a widow. She did slop work, making shirts for the soldiers. Her husband had never had his health since coming over the water some years before and he'd been working out in the chicory fields till they did for him. Later, when we knew each other better, she'd tell me, thank God he went when he did and left her with only three or else what would she be now.

For a Roman she had a sound humour and sometimes on a Sunday she'd have me fetch a jug of beer and we three would have a high old time, though I'd mainly pour mine into Mary's cup, having little taste for it.

The room wasn't much to write home about, which was just as well since Mary was the writing one of the two of us, and she wasn't about to do it. She gave me a great bow when she showed it me which made it seem not so bad. She'd stuffed some rags round the window to keep down the draught. There was a little fireplace, but getting in coal by the handful, you'd to pay way over what my dad could get a ton for back home, and we hadn't any left by the end of the week.

'Nice brickwork,' she said, pointing to a place where you could see straight through the laths.

'They build them sturdy in York,' I said.

'Saves us a walk though,' Mary answered. 'No need to get off to the beach to get cold at least.'

'So which side are you having?' I asked.

'Not sides,' she said. 'Tipple-toe.'

End-to-end on the mattress, I got well used to Mary's feet, poor things that they were. Her boots didn't do much against the damp of the laundry, but we hadn't the money to get them seen to. Back home, it was my dad's job and he'd spend an hour, two hours, every night, plucking at a needle, or patching, with his salty rough fingers. I think it was the patching more than anything else made him so sour, after he'd had a day on the water, and he could be cruel as ice with his needle if you weren't careful.

The cold was different in the city and Mary felt it, though she'd never done so back home. So we'd wrap up as best we could in the bits of blanket, our shawls round our heads and I'd hold her feet, all chafed and sore, as a bit of comfort.

She said it was the life of a crab in that laundry, and if it weren't for the other girls, who had good tongues in them and made her laugh, she'd have given it up. As for me, maybe it was the best thing, getting that bad hand in the end.

So it was about a week on from me coming to the room, and my hand was near enough good again, when I met the gentleman on the bridge. I'd to wait the rest of the day till Mary came back, all pale and done in with work and I thought she must see I'd something to say, but she was that tired, it was all she could do to take off her boots, and that with my help. She wouldn't have noticed if I'd grown two heads before she'd had a sit and a bite to eat.

It never did to tell Mary owt on an empty stomach, or at least not too empty, so I waited on till she'd eaten. There wasn't much, just some bread with a scratch of dripping and a strip of bacon as relish that I'd fried so carefully to be sure it didn't burn.

'You not eating?' Mary asked, and I pretended I'd done so earlier. She nodded, but she knew I'd not. 'Well, at least drink your tea then,' she said, 'or you'll never get big and strong like me,' which was by way of a joke since I was the bigger. Anyway, that set her off talking about some of the other girls in the laundry. There was Annie with the cough who'd not be long there, but off to the Workhouse soon, and Jane who'd come in that day with this new trimming on her hat and Mary didn't know how she could've bought it seeing as she'd to hand over her wage to her mother and everyone knew she hadn't a spare penny. I wanted to know how were Connie and Hannah who had young men, and Mary said she had it from another girl that Connie's young man was not to be relied upon. So then I took and told her of the man I'd met on the bridge, and what he'd asked and would she come?

Mary's got a tongue on her and for all she was tired, she wouldn't leave off about 'my gentleman'. She teased me till we were in a scrat and I'd have thumped her if we'd been wading rockpools. But she said she'd come along.

The next day I met Mary after her work. It was already dark. I'd got us a pie each and she wolfed hers and half of mine. We didn't know our luck back home, with plenty to eat and most of it not fish. Now we were always hungry and with me still not with a job, there was only what Mary had got.

It was raining by the time we got to Coney Street and I could see him waiting under the gaslight, looking like he thought we might not come, standing stock-still in the middle of all the people rushing to be out of the weather. He bowed to us both and took us in a door and up we clattered, up these stairs in our heavy boots and we were in this warm little room with some chairs and the walls all covered with pictures. Mr Ransome – I'd learnt his name by now – asked us to wait a minute and disappeared all solemn up some more stairs.

We looked at the pictures, all sorts, but mostly people not like us.

'Look at her, Hal,' Mary laughed, nudging me. She pointed to a fat lady in a posh dress, then to another where you could tell the man's stood on a box for his height. There was one, of a frail little fellow, she thought looked just like her brother Jamie. It was him she missed most from home, and I could tell the seeing of the picture made her sad.

There were that many pictures, I soon got dull with looking and sat down and just waited, but Mary couldn't get enough, and she was running her finger round the shapes people made, and putting her hands up in front of her eyes, boxing them in with her fingers.

Mr Ransome came back with another man. 'Mr Benbow,' he introduced him. He didn't introduce us. Mr Benbow was right slick in fancy trousers and waistcoat and next to him, Mr Ransome, in his black, looked dowdy. He bowed low down and said something like 'Gratified.' I didn't like him, but Mary was all eyes.

He took us up the next stairs and we were in a room with glass in half the roof, the rain running down it, then he and Mr Ransome left. The room was full of things out of place. Chairs and baskets, a fancy table with a bit of lace, a settee and a velvet stool, costumes hung up like Punch and Judy without their man to move them, fishing nets and statues, even a stile and a gate with some carpets hung over, and there was a door, just standing to one side, opening to nothing. There were screens propped against the wall with pictures painted on. One was in a wood and one was by the sea, but not like the sea at home. There was a posh parlour on another. Mary ran about, touching things. She was excited, but I knew she was trying it on too. She lifted the lid on a piano and ran her hand down the keys, played a twiddle.

'Where'd you learn that?' I asked.

She shrugged, didn't answer. 'It's out of tune,' she said.

A lady came in. At least she was dressed like a lady. She started arranging things, fixing this big picture of the sea which she had on rollers across the wall, searching in the corner till she came out with these big baskets. Mary was still fiddling at the piano and the lady came over, put her hand over Mary's to shush her.

'Mr Ransome would like you to dress in some garments he's brought.'

'The piano is out of tune,' Mary said. She didn't like this lady. And then she said, 'I don't believe we've been introduced,' in a voice I'd not heard before.

The lady ignored her. 'You're to change here. There's a screen. It's perfectly private,' she said.

'What clothes? Why not as we are?' asked Mary.

'Fishergirl clothes, I believe. They're perfectly genuine.'

'Flither-lasses, not fishergirls. And you don't need to tell us whether they're real or no,' Mary said. 'They were next to birthday suits for us, weren't they Hal?'

It was a queer one, putting on those things, the kirtles, mine red and Mary's blue, and the jersey sleeves and a bonnet apiece with a cushion for the load. We already had on the boots, but we'd even to change our stockings for he wanted us in black and we both had on brown, and I couldn't see how you'd tell in the photograph. The baskets the lady had found weren't right, too shallow and too wide, but still it were strange to be dressed in it all again.

'Think what would they say if they could see us now,' Mary said. She was standing in front of a big mirror, all gold and carving round the edge, and bending, down and up, and reaching out her hand towards the glass and then reaching into the basket. She looked daft.

'What are you doing?' I said. I didn't like to think of them back home seeing us here.

'Practising. He'll want us to pretend, won't he?' She stopped in a moment, thank God, and did a little curtsy. 'We've only been gone the fortnight, is it?'

'Ay. You can't have forgotten that quick.'

Then Mary got the giggles, and then I did.

The lady must have told Mr Ransome and Mr Benbow they could come back in. They were talking and didn't even look at us first off. Only when Mary coughed and tapped her foot, then Mr Ransome looked up. He gave this smile when he saw us as made me pleased I was dressed in this get-up. Mr Benbow didn't smile and the lady, standing behind, gave Mary a frown, though Mary didn't see it.

'How do we look, Mr Ransome? Quite the real thing?' Mary was using the new voice again. She did a twirl, making her skirts fly out. They brushed Mr Benbow's legs and he moved away from her. Mr Ransome didn't answer, didn't even seem to notice. He was moving things about, pushing this board with rocks painted on so it stood side-on to the sea, pulling a net out of a box, like a magician with his hat, unfolding it. I could see he'd not handled nets much, he was making a pig's ear of it, and I went and showed him how.

So we got it draped, like you'd never see it for real, but I didn't say that to him. But Mary spoke.

'Oh Mr Ransome, you've got it just right,' she said. 'You must have watched us all at work, have you?'

I gave her a stare, but she'd turned her shoulder, so she didn't see me, and she didn't see Mr Benbow. He was looking at her like he'd only just noticed her, like my dad would look at a rare fish turned up in his nets.

Mr Ransome didn't answer her. Just straightened up, turned round and, fishing in his pocket, brought out some pieces of string.

'If you could just tie up the skirts as you do on the beach, we can proceed,' he said.

Mary'd sat herself down on the settee and made as if she were unwilling to get up.

'Come along now, girl,' Mr Benbow said to her. But when she turned to him and she were angry, he winked at her, gave her a little smile I wasn't supposed to have seen.

Mr Ransome fixed us, Mary standing, me kneeling. She was to put a basket on her head, and I was just to put my hands on my lap. He was very particular about our hands, wanted them to be clearly seen, and I did my best to oblige. He asked us some things while he was at it, wanting to know why we'd come to the city, and I did my best to tell him, and Mary was flippant with her answer to make him not believe her, telling him it was to be rid of the sea, though I knew she told the truth.

Mr Benbow was getting the camera ready, with the lady hovering about behind. The camera was sat on something that looked like a grand plant stand, the wood shiny and with brass corners. The camera was polished wood, front and back, mahogany Mary told me later, and in the middle there was a great black bellows, just like they used to have in the fireplace in the Crab and Bottle. I'd never had my portrait taken and I couldn't make out how the contraption would get me, because for all it had a glass eye staring, it was just a contraption of wood and brass and leather.

Then Mr Benbow was ready, a huge black bat, his voice coming out from under the cape telling us to be still until he said.

We had to stay like that for ages. Because of the rain and the poor light, Mr Benbow explained. My leg was itching but I didn't move, and Mary started to sing a rhyme between her teeth.

In Dublin's fair city, where the girls are so pretty,
I first set my eyes on sweet Molly Malone . . .

Then Mr Benbow's arm jerked a string and he said we could move. The rhyme was one of my favourites, so I started up too, while Mr Benbow clattered about with his machinery.

> As she wheels her wheelbarrow through streets broad
>   and narrow,
> Crying 'Cockles and Mussels, alive, alive-oh.'

And when we'd finished we came all over with the giggles and if they hadn't known not, they might have thought we'd been a jug too many at the beer.

The two men left and we got changed and the lady was rushing us so, wanting us out, that we left the clothes in a heap.

'They look sad there,' I said, thinking of our old lives.

'Good riddance,' Mary said.

The lady had rolled up the sea and was tidying the bits in a corner of the room, her back to us. Mary walked across to the camera, which stood all grand on its own, and lifted the black cloth. 'Give us a dance or something,' she said, and stuck her head under.

So I did a bit of a jig and Mary's voice came out all muffled and laughing as she looked.

'You're topsy-turvy, Hal, your legs are in the air,' which was as much as she had time to say because then the lady saw what she was up to and she fair skittered over the floor, still holding a net, and tugged Mary out.

'Get out of here,' she stormed. 'Nothing but trouble,' and so on, all the while pushing Mary towards the stairs and Mary was so surprised that she let her and she'd have been out on the street if the gentlemen hadn't come back in.

Mr Benbow coaxed the lady off, calling her Muriel and telling her not to worry while she blathered at him, and then she stomped off down the stairs and he turned to Mary.

Mr Ransome just stood there, like he didn't know what to do. Suddenly I was weary with it all and I sat down on the floor and thought how lovely it would be to be in amongst the painted trees on the board at the side. When Mr Ransome approached, I started up, but he patted me on the head.

'No, sit child.' And something in his voice stopped me protesting that I wasn't one. He brought up a chair and sat beside me.

'Here's payment for your time,' he said, and handed me some coins. I looked at them. There was two shillings. I started to thank him and he shook his head. 'It's payment for a service, and only what I think proper,' he said. 'No more, no less. But I have something else to say, if you will allow me.'

Then he said he had cousins and the cousins had a factory. I must have looked like I didn't rightly know what he was talking of, because he explained.

'Wetherby's Cocoa Works. It's close by the river and they use girls to pack. The wage is fair and they're good men. They'd take you on, if I asked them.'

'And Mary?'

'No. Not Mary. Mary is not . . . He has space only for one girl, and Mary has work, hasn't she?'

It wasn't so hard telling Mary about the job because she had news of her own.

'Benbow wants me back, and he'll pay me two shillings a go, just me.'

'What, as a flither-lass again?'

We were walking fast down Walmgate. It was cold, but also it didn't do to dawdle in this part of town or the police would have your names down quicker than a monkey's finger.

'Maybe. All those costumes, who knows? But he didn't let on to that woman. It's to be our secret.'

I didn't think anything of it then, except as something to celebrate. We could eat, and get our shoes mended, and maybe even, if it all went off well, I'd have a new bonnet and we'd go to the fair, come Christmas.

Two mornings later I went to the factory. There was a smell of cocoa that made my mouth water, so strong that I'd never have believed then that I'd cease to smell it so soon. A girl was waiting for me called Elsie. She took me into this big hall first, us and hundreds of others, and we sat on chairs, girls on one side, all dressed in bleached Holland pinafores like Elsie, and men on the other, most in white aprons, their caps on their laps.

'Assembly,' she whispered.

'What?' I said, but she put her finger to her lips. Everyone had gone quiet, and now I could hear the doors being locked.

A man was standing on a platform at the front. He was dressed in the same kind of dark suit as Mr Ransome and I could tell he was one of the cousins. He opened a big book on a stand and started to read. His voice was quiet, and yet I was sure that even those at the very back could hear all he said, like it or no.

'Blessed is the man that walketh not in the counsel of the ungodly, nor standeth in the way of sinners, nor sitteth in the seat of the scornful . . .'

I didn't know the words, except that they must be the Bible. In the minutes he spoke, I drifted till I was back on the cliff, watching the sea and the current lines, and his voice was the voice of the waves, until I returned and he had almost finished.

'. . . prosperity is a thing that the Lord does not scorn. So let us go out and work hard and fair and prosper.' As he nodded to us all, there was the sound of the doors being unlocked and then everyone stood to leave.

It was this man who interviewed me. He was looking out the window when I was sent in, and when he turned around and saw me, he made an odd noise in his throat, a kind of squawk, as if I'd said something that surprised him, though all I'd done was stand, head up and still as stone. Then he said something as made no sense, so I put it from my head then, though I'd reason to remember it some months later.

'So like her . . .' he said, and then he checked himself and took hold of his chair and sat down.

Close up his likeness to Mr Ransome was plain as day. Though this man's movements were quick to Mr Ransome's slower ones, and though Mr Ransome was clean-shaven and this man bearded, both had blue eyes and dark hair and the same high forehead. He sat at a great desk, his hands flat on the blotter, in a room up ever so many stairs. In the middle of the floor was a trapdoor and I could hear scratchy noises and men's voices through it.

Once he'd sat down, there was something too calm about Mr Wetherby, for that was his name, too still, as though he'd forgotten he had a body. Only the forefinger on one hand did differently. It kept tap-tapping, very lightly, as if it was trying to show me something. He stared at me very hard, my hair, my hands, my clothes, and then told me I would do and who could he apply to for a character. I thought it was all up then, since my old missis wouldn't give me the time of day, let alone a character.

'I'm sorry sir, but I was ill with my hand and . . .'

'Let me see it,' he said, so I laid it on the table. He didn't touch it, just looked. 'Given that I've heard good words of you from Mr Ransome . . .' Then he nodded and went on and told me what my work would be and what my pay. The fore-woman, Mrs Flint, would give me my uniform which I was to keep at the factory and wash weekly, and she would tell me the regulations of the place.

'You may keep your name, there not being another Harriet in our employ. It is my custom, if there is more than one, to rename a person. We expect you to conduct yourself at Wetherby's with the same fairness we endeavour to treat you with. Have you anything to ask?'

As we went out, he lifted the trapdoor and spoke to someone underneath and passed him a letter. I glimpsed a man, sitting at his high stool, nodding, before Mr Wetherby shut the lid on him. He had nice eyes.

Elsie took me all round the factory, excepting one set of rooms.

'The brothers,' she said, 'that's Mr William who you saw, and the other's Mr Caleb, like us to know where everything goes on, feel part of things. Except for the Superior Cocoa Rooms.' Then she dropped her voice to a whisper. 'They say there are only three keys to those rooms, the brothers having two of them and another as we never see having the third. What goes on in there is a secret. The men who work there, it's down on their contracts not to tell anyone.'

'Why?' I asked.

Elsie looked at me very solemn. 'Spies,' she said. 'From other men's factories. They want the recipe and they'll stop at nothing. They say there's a secret machine for the cocoa that Mr William went across the water to buy, to a foreign place but not France. And they put things in, or maybe it's take 'em out, that nobody else must know about.'

It sounded to me like she'd been told some steep ones, but I was the new girl here and I knew I'd best keep my trap shut. So I just nodded. Then she took me down the stairs.

The storehouse was in the cellar. It was a cold place with thick cobwebs at the gratings and piled to the roof with great brown lumpy bags which she said were cocoa beans.

'Right across the world they come,' she told me. 'It says so on the bags. Then we climbed the stairs, up and up, till we were at the top. There was a man there kneeling by a door which opened into air and as we passed him, he reached out into the sky and I wanted to stop him, thinking he'd fall, but he pulled in a bag like the ones in the cellar, unclipped it from a rope and gave the rope a tug.

Then Elsie showed me the roasting room with the big ovens going round and the men sweating already and shovelling in coke and on down to a room from which was coming an almighty clatter.

'We get the husks off in here,' Elsie shouted. 'Kibbling-mills they're called, and then we sell the husks off to the Irish. They'll eat them,' she said laughing, 'and what's left is called the nibs. We make the cocoa from them.'

We went down and down, looking in all the rooms, where there were machines for squashing beans and heating and making a dozen different kinds of cocoa, and chocolate, and creams, and men stirring and pouring and lifting and cutting, till we were back nearly on the ground again. It all seems second nature to me now, but that day I was dizzy with all I'd seen and later, when Mary was asking, I couldn't remember almost anything, except the man reaching into air, and dreaming on the cliff and the sea, and Mary didn't like that kind of talk.

The packing rooms were very clean. Cleaner than any-where, excepting maybe our kitchen back home after my mam had done a real scrub. They were full of girls, fifty or more, which seemed a vast crowd to me. All were so busy, they didn't even look up when I walked by. Some were weighing the cocoa, lifting it out of great barrels with such a smooth move-ment of their scoop that barely a dusting was lost, and pouring it into the scales where they might add a shake here and remove a bit there. Then others tipped it into a mould already lined with a paper and then with one neat move, pulled down the plunger to squash the cocoa so that each packet would match its fellows. A third group removed the packet and pasted down the ends while another group pasted on labels. There must have been a dozen different labels, Elsie made them out for me: Homeopathic Cocoa, Granulated Cocoa, Best Soluble Cocoa, Pearl Soluble Cocoa, Iceland Moss Cocoa, whatever that was. Finally, the last group were busy sorting the packets into crates of different sizes, reading off sheets, before the crates were pushed towards a small door at the far end of the second room.

'Through there's the gravity slope,' Elsie told me. 'It makes a great slide, but take care never to be caught or it's . . .' and she drew a finger across her throat. We peeked through the small door and watched as a man slid a crate down a long ramp to the room below.

'It must be fun,' I whispered.

'It is,' Elsie said.

'Elsie!' The woman's voice wasn't loud, but it made us both jump, she'd come up so soft. She was standing behind us, hands on hips but her face not saying anything. Her face, come to that, was odd. It was too smooth, so I couldn't tell if she was twenty or forty, and, it didn't show anything on it. She had on the Holland pinafore like the rest, but whereas the girls were all bare-headed, she had on a funny little white cap, puffed up above which sat on her blond hair like a sugar bun. I knew this must be Mrs Flint.

'Mr William said to show her round,' Elsie said, not looking the woman in the eye.

'And what could she possibly need with the gravity slope? Or the roasting rooms, or the storerooms, for that matter. I presume you've seen the works, the time it's taken?' Elsie nodded. 'This time I'm going to raise it with Mr William, the labour wasted just for one new girl, one paster, the lowest of the lot . . .'

'Yes ma'am,' whispered Elsie.

'. . . If he knew how you abuse it . . .'

'Ma'am, we didn't,' Elsie said in a shrill voice, 'did we, Harriet?' I shook my head slightly. 'We only—'

Mrs Flint interrupted. 'And why would I believe her? I've only met her this past minute and have no idea whether she's likely for the work. Nobody asked me.' Then she looked at me and her eyes looked black. 'How did you come to be here, girl?'

I didn't know what to say, opening my mouth like a fish out of water, though this Mrs Flint was someone I knew. I'd not seen her before, but I could tell she was like my dad. They'd both of them hit at you because the mood was on, though she'd do it with her tongue and he'd do it with whatever sharp thing he had to hand – a cleaning knife or a fork, or even once the fire poker. Dad didn't need the drink to begin it either, and he'd do it without saying a word, so as you'd never know quite if something was going to come at your head. The trouble was his brimful of fury that he carried about and there wasn't a thing we could do about that.

I was rescued from Mrs Flint by a noise behind, which made her whip around and away. A girl had spilt some cocoa powder. I didn't hear what she said, she never raised her voice, but when she'd finished, the girl's shoulders were heaving in silence.

'Come on, Harriet, quick now and I'll show you what you'll be doing.'

Elsie had me stand at the end of a table where girls were pasting down the cocoa packets and she showed me how to make up the paste.

'That's your job today,' she said. 'You're to make sure their bowls are never empty, and when the dinner break comes, you're to scrape all the paste into one bowl and wash the others. Then cover the full bowl with a scrap piece of paper so it doesn't harden, and then you're free to eat your dinner. I overheard Mr William says that girls who have duties in the dinner hour should take extra time at the end, but don't try it or Mrs Flint will have . . .' and she drew her finger across her neck again, which I could see was one of her favourites.

She gave me a pinafore and I set to. The work looked easy and it wasn't heavy, but by the time the bell for dinner was rung, my pinafore had splodges of paste all over and my hands were sticky and thick with it. There wasn't to be any talking during work hours, though some of the girls had asked me my name in whispers and given me theirs, but there had been no time or chance for any more talk. Elsie showed me how to wash the bowls and with her help I was done in ten minutes and we joined the others in the big hall with our dinner pails.

Elsie showed me off a bit – the new girl and the only one as had been a flither-lass. None but one of 'em had seen the sea before and they were all on at me to describe it, and then to know why I'd leave it for the city.

'But you got Mrs Flint in a white anger, Harriet,' said a tall pale girl. 'It makes her real cross when anything's done without her word, even if it's Mr Wetherby as decides.'

'So, how did you get the work, then?' asked another.

I didn't want to tell these girls about Mr Ransome any more than I did Mrs Flint. So I made as if I hadn't heard and asked another question.

'How come she's Mrs Flint? Is she married?'

Everyone wanted to answer that one, telling me no she wasn't, but they'd heard tell how she had a sweetheart once and she drove him off. Which was no surprise, because who'd have her?

'My brother says he knows she's not all there, if you know what I mean,' said the tall girl. I didn't know what she meant, but everyone else was nodding, so I stayed quiet.

'Just you wait till the next girl goes off to be married,' said Elsie. 'She always gives 'em hell then, for the week of notice they've to work. She's like a wild animal . . .'

'. . . Except she never raises her voice and she never touches nobody,' said the tall girl.

Another girl nodded. 'Ay, I'd much rather me mam shouting and clouting than Mrs Flint any day.'

Then they started on about the men they thought she was soft on, and how sad it was at her age, for she must be well beyond her thirtieth year, and how she never had a good word for anybody, not the masters and not the girls until too soon the hour was gone and we were back in the packing room.

By the end of the day I'd got the hang of the paste, but I was sick of the smell and of the touch of the cocoa powder in the air.

'What's cocoa like?' I asked Elsie as we left.

'It's like heaven,' she said. 'But you won't get any from there,' and she nodded back at the factory. 'Nor the chocolate and that's even better. They pay you not to take it. It's called pledge money. And anyway you're not allowed to bring any cocoa or chocolate in, even if you got it somewhere else.'

I was that tired when I got back to Mrs O'Leary's, I'd half a thought of going to bed till Mary came in. But Mrs O'Leary had made us a special supper to celebrate with slices of ham and I hadn't the heart to disappoint her. So I sat in the kitchen while she got tea for the children, and told her all I'd seen.

'It sounds like a good place,' she said, 'but a bit strange, with the morning prayer. What are they?'

'What do you mean, what are they?'

'You know, before we came over to England, there was terrible hunger in Ireland?' I nodded, because even in the village we'd heard something of all the Irish coming over, starving and desperate. 'Well, there were some that helped us, and chief among them were these strange ones they call Quakers. They talked like your man in the factory and they gave us soup and food and clothes, though they were the wrong lot.'

'They may be, I don't know,' I said. 'I don't rightly care as long as it's a job.'

Mary wasn't back till the lamps were long lit and the children in bed. Mrs O'Leary went out for some beer and I tried to tell Mary of my work, but she was in a strange mood and wouldn't hear me out. There was Mrs O'Leary's bag of bits on the table – scraps of old clothes and bits of wool for patching and darning. Mary tugged them out and was spreading the lot of them on the table, making pictures with the bits of cotton and calico, and the wool around the edges. After she tired of this and heaped it all back into the bag, she kept laughing or turning her shoulder to the scrap of mirror on the mantelpiece. It was like she was somewhere else, and even the thought of ham didn't bring her back.

'Seen nice Mr Ransome, have you?' she said, rolling her eyes.

'No,' I said. 'It's his cousins' business, Wetherby's Cocoa Works. One of them spoke to me at the start, he does with all the girls . . .'

'I've made some pennies today, too,' she said, 'and it wasn't by scrubbing somebody else's smalls.'

'Oh,' I said, tired now of her way.

'So, don't you want to know how?'

SAMUEL

Although ultimately it was the girl that stopped me, the little bridge that humped up and over the Foss was a favourite of mine. It arched over the foetid water in the quarter of the city to which my fellow Quakers came only to do good works. They would have looked askance at my lingering there, though by the time I met the girl, this thought no longer deterred me.

Even before I reached the bridge I knew that the girl leaning there was not from the city. Though she was dressed no differently from others, there was something about her posture that spoke of a life begun elsewhere. A gentleman looks a strange beast in these impoverished parts, unless he is clearly about some business or other. But the angle of the girl's head, as she stared into the horrid water, and her profile, made me careless of the world's opinion, and I approached her slowly along Fossgate, turning over in my mind how I should address her to set her at her ease.

When she stood up tall, just one hand resting now against the bridge's parapet, I saw she was perhaps only an inch below me in height, and her carriage and the broadness of her shoulders made her seem taller. She held her shoulders back and her head up, unlike the girls native to the city, and this, I learnt, was because of her life till now as a fishergirl, outdoors and upright, braced against the wind, a heavy basket balanced upon her head. Given this, one would have thought that her complexion would have been ruddy and coarse, burned by wind and sun and rain. But the skin on her cheek had a bloom coloured only to the palest brown, which made her seem exotic, standing so erect amongst the bleached city faces passing by, her strong fingers spread as though for balance on the rough pale stone.

That first day, I did not notice the full sweep of the freckles scattered over the bridge of her nose and across the curve of her cheekbones. They would become more prominent in the months ahead as her colouring paled, though she never has entirely lost the colour of her first life. But I did notice a small mole just above her upper lip which made her, in my eyes, entirely beautiful.

Her eyes looked brown that day, though in the months to come they were often grey. But what captivated me was the stillness of her gaze, a quality of attention I have rarely seen in anyone else. In fact, the only person I could immediately have named would have been my sister Grace. This girl did not look down in embarrassment while I talked, like so many others, nor let her glance flit about as though something more exciting was to come into view. When I came to know her better, there were occasions when she seemed altogether absent, to have heard nothing of what one had been saying, and one might have to repeat it all. But that is a separate thing.

I do not think she knew her own looks when I first met her, and once I had met her friend Mary, I saw that this was because Mary knew hers so well. As though Mary had taken for herself the whole stage. But I loved Harriet, which is the girl's name, I loved her from the first for that very ignorance.

I have never regarded our meeting that day on the bridge as anything other than providential. Since I cannot confide such thoughts to anyone close to me, I have kept them secret, at least for the time being.

She was only a young girl and I hesitated, as I had done before and would do afterwards, at the impropriety of my addressing her. But God sees my motives even if Man cannot, and that is good enough for me.

My visits to my sister in the Haven were frequent at that time and it was a pleasure that often offset the pain of my task, as I walked to and from it, through Walmgate and on – sometimes on my horse, but more often on foot – to watch, and occasionally to speak to, the girls of that poor part of our city. I have often regretted the fear I seem to occasion in children. For the most part, they run at the sight of me. Harriet told me much later that it had to do with my carriage, though she had another word for it. I scared them, she said, with the way I wore my coat and hat. I laughed at her words, but it made me sad. Sometimes older girls have been the same and it's been all I could do to coax them, as one might coax a wild animal, and persuade them to stay a moment.

She, on the other hand, was untouched by any such fear and, but for her friend, I might have thought it due to a life lived till then in a remote place where the labour was simple and unsophisticated, an elemental existence. But her friend Mary came from the same place and she had not the same mind in any one thing as Harriet.

I had learnt much from the butterfly collecting I had done as a child, and then at school, about the principles of classification and it was now, at the time that I met Harriet, that I decided to make a portfolio of working women, to have them photographed in their natural working clothes and, when possible, with the tools of their trade. I would mount each portrait and caption it carefully, stating where and when I had met her, her name and her profession. Also, where she originated from and how long she had been at her work, with her date of birth if known. I had taken a few photographs myself and I would start my collection with these. But I knew that I had not the physical strength, nor the talent, to pursue this project on the scale I now wished to. The photographs I took *en plein air* were of too poor a quality and I had to employ the resources of a professional.

So much was changing that I wished to capture these girls before their trade disappeared, or was altered out of all recognition by machinery or new prohibitory laws or some such.

So I approached John Benbow.

Benbow. The commanding feature of this man, beside which the size of his nose, the height of his forehead, and the slight stoop to his shoulder are all forgotten, is his stare. His eyes have the most extraordinary shade of green, like the green in the stem of one of Mother's orchids. They give him the look of someone who knows already what you have to say and who is waiting, quite courteously, for you to say it. Set in such a pale skin as he has, they appear almost to burn, so that it is no wonder that the girls in his classes live in awe, if not in fear, of him.

As I say, not long after meeting Harriet, a week or so, for I believe the project was nearly hatched in my brain before I knew I had it there, I approached him with the proposition that he act as my photographer in recording working girls, and offered to pay him handsomely for the trouble of doing so. Our classes for such girls were going well, and because of this and our shared curiosity in evolution and scientific development, I assumed there would be more for him than simple professional interest in such an undertaking, as there was for me. He considered my proposition for a matter of twenty seconds, and agreed to it, adding certain provisos to do with discretion and time of day.

What he actually thought of my project, he did not say. He made a remark at the time I did not understand, something about how close we two were after all, despite appearances. But when I asked him to explain himself, he declared it was nothing important and no more was said.

I knew a few things by now about the lives of the girls I met on the streets. I knew that you could clean your teeth with coal dust, and colour your toes with blacking to hide the holes in your shoes. That it was better to bury a baby in a box than have him buried on the parish. I knew that cobwebs pressed to a wound stopped bleeding and that a heated onion cured earache. I knew that 'East or West, Home is Best' and that 'God is Master of This House'. I knew how hungry the girls always were and how proud, and that you could get faded fruit off a barrow late at night very cheap if you hadn't too fussy a stomach. I even heard once how my own cousin William had put tar on some of his factory walls to stop the courting couples who liked to gather there, and that more than one girl had had her only dress ruined and no money for another.

Most of all, I knew what the girls did to earn their precious shillings. There were all sorts: costermongers, scullions, maids-of-all-work, dustgirls, factory girls, milkgirls, slop-workers, needlewomen, fisherlasses and sackgirls. All of these I had photographed in the costume of their work and all with some tool of their trade. So the costermongers had their baskets of cabbages and the needlewomen their piece of fabric. The milk-girls stood proudly with their yokes across their strong shoulders and shiny pails hanging, and the sackgirls sat beside a pile of sacks, their hands resting on their laps like two pieces of red meat.

How little I truly knew then, when I thought I knew so much. I would discover that this knowledge stood for nothing when I needed to understand a girl's heart.

It was Harriet's hands that moved me most when first we met, and always with these girls, more than their faces or the raggedness of their clothes, it was their hands. Their hands which had been to places I could barely imagine, which had performed tasks that would make the Quaker girls at Meeting shudder. Even those hands that were so coarsened, so reddened and roughened with work, the skin splitting, the nails chipped, callouses making a harsh terrain of the palms, even those hands were beautiful.

And I, who had never known manual labour, could only look, and wonder at their work. So I'd encourage them to keep their hands visible for the photograph, and even on occasion roll up their sleeves or adjust their position, finding myself strangely moved when I did so, to show them off more fully before Benbow took the photograph. I am sure the girls thought me a droll and strange creature, and maybe I am. It is true to say that I am more moved by a dustgirl sitting on the floor than by any gorgeous lady that might brush past me on the street.

In the months that followed our agreement, Benbow made photographs of many dozens of girls, and I mounted them in the albums I had purchased. They were handsome volumes, bound in shiny calf with a tooled spine and marbled edges and end papers, with labels in red leather saying 'Ransome Collection', and the volume number. With them I also kept the black diary I had had since I was a boy. Although I no longer wrote in this diary regularly, very occasionally I would add some detail of a girl's life or person that seemed especially interesting, so that this had grown, over all the years, into a treasure trove into which I could delve. I rarely did, but at least I knew it to be there for the reading, should I wish.

The portfolio grew rapidly and I found a place for the volumes in a cupboard in my bedroom to which I only held the key. I still did not know what I would do with them, once the work was completed, though chief amongst my thoughts was the idea, inchoate but persistent, that somehow they could be put to use in improving the lot of working women. Though another thought, as powerful as the first, was that I would simply keep them there, a precious archive I could return to in future years. I did not think this thought directly, nor stop to consider what this returning might consist of. But I held it in the back of my mind alongside those other thoughts I did not like to look upon directly, such as the notion I could not fully push from my head, that no heaven would ever take Mother in and so there was no heaven.

Then, on the day I met Harriet, I thought Benbow a good man. Now I know goodness to be a more complex virtue, and I would still call him good, though my fellow Quakers would disagree if they knew of him what I know. I have always known him to be brave.

The photograph Benbow took that first time is still dearer to me than any other thing I own, though I have taken a liberty I know Harriet would grieve at, in cutting it to fit my own heart. I keep it safe in the pages of my Bible.

When I visited Benbow next, the two girls were already pinned to his parlour wall. I hadn't expected this, because they are, after all, nothing more and nothing less than what they are – which is lasses not ladies. Indeed, it gave me quite a turn to come upon them like that, stuck between a lady with a lap-dog and a courting couple encircled by a garland of roses, her engagement ring and his splendid fob watch prominent, their amour, I'm sad to say, rather less so. How proud I felt to see the strong figure of my 'flither-lass', so great a contrast to all the coddled forms around her.

'Pretty, aren't they?' Those were Benbow's words to me. Innocuous, you might think, and it was only much later that I felt their full weight. That day I gave, I believe, just a curt nod and preceded him up the stairs.

The year before we had begun some classes for working girls, on the model of those we already had for young men. These were initially only in reading and writing. However, to everybody's surprise but my own, some of the girls had proved already so able, that we were contemplating further studies. Some mathematics, a little Latin, and Benbow wished to introduce them to some scientific principles. We had met on this day to discuss this further.

We sat in the desk corner of his studio, the light pouring in now through the glass roof and lighting up most strangely the painted scenes propped against the parlour table and the piano. He served the most exquisite coffee in fine china cups and we discussed Darwin and Huxley. Our views were not so far apart, though I was, I am, a Quaker, and he an Anglican freethinker. At least that is what he told me, though in truth he must be close to an atheist.

Benbow had for me also a list of the girls he proposed to have in his class: Ann Jones, servantmaid; Charlotte Norris, seamstress; Lucy Riley, waitress; Kate Shearer, tobacconist; Emma Milnes, domestic servant; Rose Canford, clerk; Mary Bourne, laundress.

'I know all but the last,' I said. 'Is she new to the classes?' He nodded, with a small smile I understand better now. 'And you are sure she is able?'

'She is very keen,' he said. Perhaps if I had known then what I know now, I would have wished to strike her from the list, though I hope not. It is not given to many girls to rise above their sex and perhaps there must always be a heavy price to pay in doing so.

Before leaving, I bought another copy of my fishergirls from Benbow, the flither-lasses they called themselves, for I wished to have a second to keep by me, now that I had pasted the first into the new album.

My life at this time was a strange one, taking something of a chrysalid form. I had, for many years, been at the mercy of an invalid constitution that had kept me to my bed for months at a time. Although this had limited my life, the one substantial benefit it had brought to me was to free me largely from the duties of my financial inheritance. It meant that during my frequent periods of indisposition, I was unable to involve myself in the tannery business I had inherited from my father, and the responsibilities of the tannery manager had increased over the years to incorporate those that would usually have fallen to me. There were years in which I didn't visit the tannery, which bore my name, being called Ransome's, more than three times.

Though this state of affairs would not have suited many, and I am acquainted with no other Quakers who could have borne it, and though I knew it worried my cousin William, it suited me very well. I was rarely called upon for my judgement, rarely obliged to attend a meeting.

The cocoa factory was another thing. It is true to say that my history at Ransome's Tannery was uncomfortable. I had never, since boyhood, been able to stomach the place, and certainly Wetherby's Cocoa Works produced an altogether sweeter product. But it was not what was made that lured me there, so much as those who made it, or some of them. The tannery employed only men, whereas the female population of the Cocoa Works had increased twenty-fold in the last ten years and it was quite something to stand in the hall as the bell went and be immersed briefly in the tide of feminine bodies, their firm arms and flushed cheeks, their voices calling to one another, their strong hands. And now my fishergirl, Harriet, was to be working there too.

In the previous months my long indisposition had begun to lift, I do not know why, and so I found myself with more of a life on my hands than I as yet knew how to fill.

Perhaps if it had not been for my mother, I might properly have done something with my new-found liberty. I had then a particular interest in those newly liberated slave territories of the American Confederacy and thought for a short time of travelling to see how the Negroes' lives had altered, my natural scepticism causing me to suspect that less had changed than that nation would have us believe. However, my mother had grown accustomed to her son and it would have been too great a cruelty to deprive her of her customary habits in her final years. So I restricted my efforts to my home city, in which there were, and still are, manifold possibilities for change.

I had lately directed my efforts, in concerted form, towards a charitable institution that was receiving much by way of obstruction in the city. It was a Home, though some might dispute the word, for Unfortunate Young Women and their offspring. Its doors were always open and they never turned a body away, which is more than could be said for that benighted institution, the workhouse. One might have thought that the citizens of York would welcome a place doing such unwelcome work. But we never thank those who place our sins before us, and besides the Home was Roman Catholic.

Even so, word of the nuns' work travelled fast. It wasn't long before they opened their door one morning to find a swaddled bundle on the cold flags. The mother, unable either to keep the baby or to enter the place herself, had left him as best she could, wrapped in rags against the night air. That baby, though chilled by its night exposure, recovered. But the second time this happened, the tiny form was quite cold and no amount of tenderness could return to it its scrap of life. So after this the nuns took to leaving a baby's cradle on the porch at night, fresh-made with warm coverings and, every so often, in the morning they would find it filled, the covers tucked carefully round.

It had been brought to my notice that attacks had been made recently on this place. One night the cradle was removed, and later found nearby, all hacked to pieces as though a demon had been at it. Laundry had been stolen from within the garden, and bricks thrown at windows. Worse, tradesmen had been persuaded – I can imagine how – not to call and financial subscribers (for the place survived through charity) had withdrawn promised sums.

I was determined to do something to help the Home and I had thought I would have Mother's support. But when I broached the subject, I discovered quickly that it affected her too closely for tolerance and I must look elsewhere for counsel. Fortunately, there were others of my mind within the Meeting, younger Friends in the main, and these I spoke to. It cost us much in labour and coin, but the Home did not close and a cradle remained in the porch. I need not say more on this now. The Home will find its place in my story later.

It was a matter of some weeks rather than days before I had the opportunity of contacting Harriet again and I had been very busy in the meantime. But a particular task took me early one morning in the New Year to my cousins' factory. I needed my cousin William's signature on some document relating to my mother's financial affairs and since he was leaving that day for Paris, it was important I caught him before his departure. There was little point in trying to see Caleb, for he would be locked deep in his chemical ponderings.

William couldn't immediately attend to my business, as it was the time at which the factory gathered in assembly for prayer and Bible reading. Instead, he requested that I accompany him to the hall. I have a great reluctance towards appearing before crowds. Even at Meeting, which of all places is one of those most familiar to me, the sight of so many all together ties my thoughts and locks my tongue. I am not one of those Friends who reach towards public office, now such things are possible, though I admire greatly those who do. I like only to work in private, my left hand not seeing what my right, and so forth. So I declined his request and contented myself with a seat in his office.

'I should have liked you to have seen them all, Samuel,' he said on his return, 'heads bowed, humble before the Lord.'

I began to say again what he already knew, but he prevented me, saying that God enables different men in different ways.

I didn't ask him about Harriet. There would have been nothing improper in such a question – I had, after all, provided her with an introduction to his Works and it was therefore natural that I should want to discover how she got on – but I felt that he might not have fully understood my motive. So I had written a small note while the factory was at assembly and left it for delivery on the clerk's desk in the room below. Not knowing in which department the girl worked, I had had to be content with placing her name on the envelope.

'Rachel is well?' I asked. 'And the children? John?'

William nodded. 'Thank you, they are all well and John quite recovered. I never thought I would regret the day the boy was not naughty, but Rachel tells me he is up to his old mischief again, for which I thank God.'

'And the cocoa?'

'Slightly delayed.' William shook his head as though to dislodge some irritating pressure. 'Only temporarily.'

I had asked the question out of courtesy, for I found it hard to become excited about a beverage. But William had never been one to notice other people's indifference.

'Caleb is less sure than I. Not of the product, which we both know to be unparalleled within this country. But of how best to sell it.'

'This is a new cocoa, which you wish to sell?'

So engrossed was he by the burning question, that he failed to be amazed by my ignorance, and merely answered me.

'We have been making it a while, but we are the only ones to be doing so. In this country, that is. They have it in Holland, of course, and so it is imported here. But there is not another cocoa manufacturer within this country who can produce what we have within these very walls.'

'How so?'

'It is a question of process. We acquired a press from the Dutch, and with this we are now making the first unadulterated and alkalized cocoa within Britain.'

'But Caleb is unsure of something?'

'Caleb is a scientist. He understands the movement of liquids within glass. I am a man of business. I understand the movement of products within grocers' shops.'

'And you are sure that Wetherby's is the first to produce such a thing?'

'I have taken the steps necessary to be sure. There is still nobody near us.'

William stared at the floor so hard that my eyes followed his, but all I could see was the grain of the wood, dipping in places where years of wear had worn it down.

'We'll find our way in this', he said finally. 'But is there nothing more I can do for you,' he asked, 'now that you are fully recovered? You know you've only to say the word and there'd be a place for you here. I know you will never involve yourself more closely in the tannery, Caleb is taken up with his potions entirely, and it will be seven years or more till young John is of an age to start.'

'I'm always much obliged to you,' I answered, 'but it would go hard with Mother were I to change my habits now. I fear I have no talent for business, and I have concerns in the city I would be loath to give up on.'

We had had this conversation before, and each time I was surprised to see that it produced in my calm cousin a considerable agitation. Perhaps not visible to the stranger's eye, it was glaring to me, who had been brought up so close to him. Taking a coin from his pocket, he began to rub it forcefully between his fingers as though there were something to erase. He found it impossible to understand that, although I had been more than happy to provide the capital for he and his brother Caleb to purchase the Cocoa Works, I wished to have no part in the running of the business. In truth, even beyond the need to keep Wetherby's as a family business, William didn't think it quite manly to be living a life like mine. I was a Director, after all, and ought to behave like one.

'Do you not think,' he said, 'that both your mother and those concerns you speak of in the city would go on well enough without you?'

'I think, with the help of God, that each must decide for himself what he had best do with his life,' I said.

He nodded and replaced the coin in his pocket. Then he walked across to the window and leaned on the sill, staring out.

I could hear the clerks in the room below. My note would have been discovered by now, and the envelope with its unfamiliar hand passed around, no doubt, from one man to another. Perhaps even now it was being taken out of the office and down the stairs and on its way to Harriet. I felt a small flurry in my stomach at the thought, and then a noise returned me to my place in my cousin William's office.

William still stood with his back to me, his index finger tapping on the window sill, but he had muttered something, more at the glass than to me, it seemed. I begged him to repeat his words for I hadn't caught them and at this he turned back to me, his face screwed and angry. 'I asked,' he growled, 'after your sister. How is she?'

This took me aback and it was a moment before I answered. It had been some considerable time since he had made mention of her.

'She is as always,' I said finally.

'And can you not say her name?' Still he spoke in a growl.

I walked across to him, for the man was visibly shaking, and placed my hand on his shoulder. 'William, Grace is as well as she can be. The care for her is kind and she wants for nothing. At least for nothing that she can have.'

'Do you see her?'

'I do, as ever.'

'And does your mother?'

'No.'

'Why not?'

'Cousin, you know why. It was found not to be advisable. Please, let it rest. You are tormenting yourself.'

As quickly as his fever had risen, did it fall. But when he was again seated in his great chair, next to his desk, atop his thriving factory, where beneath him so many laboured so efficiently, so productively for his grand enterprise, I could only feel pity for the man. For the thing he had wanted more than any, he could not have and it must always be so.

He did not detain me longer, barely looking at my papers before adding his signature. Only as I was taking my leave, and my hand was in his, did he say, 'It is best to be busy, Samuel. Better to have no time to think.'

I was halfway down the stairs when a bell sounded, and the instant it was quiet, another bell, and another, till all around me, in distant places, I could hear the echo of the first. Then they stopped and the building seemed to pause before the doors opened and, like a great flood, they emerged. So many girls.

They rushed about me as though I was not there, and I stood my ground, like a man inside a swarm of bees who can stand still and not be stung. Or perhaps they were more like butterflies since all were moving and in every direction and it was hard to see any one properly. All I could see were scraps of arm, of neck, of hair, tight-braided, of hands, like wings in the air, moving, gesturing, some still sticky with their morning's work, and the swish of their pinafores and their urgent voices. The sweet smell of cocoa was thick upon them, an odour, as I would discover, that haunted their persons hours after they had left the place.

Though I looked hard, I could not see Harriet. I had only met her on the two occasions, but I would have known at a glance, and even in the throng, the turn of her head, the cut of her profile. But still the sight of all these others was comforting. So when the rush had abated, I made my way out and back into the more familiar sea of the city.

Lunch, fortunately, was taken up with Mother's news. Her orchids had arrived and she had ordered the poor kitchenmaid to stand attendance over them until she could see to them herself. This caused so great an excitement in Mother that she had not her usual gimlet eye for my state. I was agitated beyond reason by the thought of my letter to Harriet and knew my face to be flushed. Usually this would be cause enough for Mother to order me to my room, and broths and poultices would invariably follow. But today she remarked only that my appetite was poor before returning to the subject of her plants.

'I must be sure John cleans the glasshouse properly and ask him to order wood chip, and gravel. I am considering a new sprinkling system. James Backhouse is to come and discuss it.'

As a child, I could not pretend to be interested in Mother's talk of plants and flowers and she would have found my pallid responses hard to tolerate if it had not been for Grace's passion, for Grace had always loved Mother's exotic blooms. And now for Grace, when almost all else had fallen away, it was the flush of veins on some rare specimen, raised beneath her glass with all the care in the world, that brought back to her fingers the tender touch and to her voice the softer note that otherwise seemed so much hidden, suppressed by her trouble.

'You see, Samuel, how the flower has climbed out from the leaves.'

'Isn't that what most flowers do?' I might reply, never very good at saying the right thing. Then she'd groan and speak slowly, as though parsing for a child.

'But the leaves are like lances, and the flower has done well to pull free.'

'The colour is very fine,' I'd say, searching for easier ground and my sister would, on a good day, regard me as though I were some species of idiot and on a bad one as though I might at any moment make a charge on her life.

It was strange to me, that my sister had chosen the same form of admiration as my mother, given the history they had between them. But unlike them I didn't, I don't like orchids. They have too predatory an air. And I have made my study that of human beauty, pulling free when it can of the sharp leaves of desperate poverty. I cannot be moved by plant life.

The warmth of Mother's glasshouse always took me by surprise. Mother had on her gardening smock, which gave her a delusory air of bucolic calm. She was unpacking her booty. Straw was strewn about the floor and a dozen pots sat on the table, their shapes of slender green breaking the air.

'Have you any plants you could spare?' I asked her. 'I could take them with me on my next visit. She'd be very pleased.'

'And would you say they were from me?' There was the faintest hint of uncertainty in Mother's voice.

'Would you wish me to?'

'She would know.' Mother's face set stern again. 'When do you next visit?'

'Well, I hadn't planned till next week.'

'It must be sooner. It will suit the plants better.'

I nodded and turned to leave. I had my hand on the door when she spoke again.

'I believe Benbow called.'

This was my mother's way of expressing disapproval, to delay mention of it till I had nearly gone. There was nothing my mother could have put her finger on about Benbow, and it was not that he was no Friend. She knew nothing of him but his calling card and yet she distrusted him.

Benbow gave me the excuse I needed to walk into the city again that afternoon. It had struck me, during the talk of orchids, that Harriet might enjoy a trip. My letter had made no such suggestion, had merely hoped that she found her new job satisfactory, that her health was good, and mentioned that I would be crossing the bridge on Fossgate at a particular time on a particular day. But now I decided that, should we meet, I would suggest a visit to the circus, maybe, or the theatre, though the difference in our station would make the latter more awkward.

'Samuel!' I was leaving the house, but Mother's voice was urgent. 'Samuel!' she called again. I returned to the glasshouse. 'You are going out.' I nodded. 'For what?'

'I have a class to give. I'll be back for supper.'

Mother said nothing, but her frown was on my back all the way down Bootham and only with the thought of Harriet and of my plan to see her again, did I manage to lift the weight of it.

HARRIET

Mary came back one night with the picture of us took at Mr Benbow's. Us as flither-lasses. It seemed an age ago, all that, and Mr Ransome in his dark coat. We'd had Christmas come and gone and the weather still bitter as sin and me as quick now as any other girl in the Cocoa Packing Room and Mary doing well and coming home with ribbons and bows and fancy goods. She was still working in the laundry, still cooking funny stories of the other girls. She wouldn't say much about Mr Benbow and his pictures, even though I knew he was taking them of her, but she let things slip here and there and that gave the game away.

I'd catch her putting her fingers to her eyes, making a square out of them, the way she'd done that day we were in the studio, like she was trying to see something – a bit of the street, or a kid with a stick, or even the wash jug on the chest of drawers. But the time I asked her what she was looking at, she just said, 'Oh, nothing.'

She'd promised to bring back some of the pictures he'd taken to show me, but I'd believe it when I saw it. She must have been doing what he wanted because he were paying her better than she'd ever make with her arms to the elbows in a tub of soda, but I did wonder what it was, that he should be so nice to a working girl with no manners and an edge to her tongue. It'd be fair to say I had my suspicions even back then, but it'd be a long while before I owned up to them.

'Mr Benbow sends his apologies,' she said, 'for it being so long since it was took.'

I looked at it. It mustn't have been much over a couple of months, but it felt a world away.

'It doesn't look real,' I said.

'It isn't the best either,' she said. 'He'd have done better if he'd . . .' but she stopped when she saw my face. A girl, even if it was Mary, going on like she could tell the man his job. 'Well, it isn't, is it?' she said. 'It isn't real.'

'No, I know, but . . .'

'Anyway, that's what they like,' she said.

'Who?'

'Them as pays for 'em.'

'But Mr Ransome paid for it.'

Mary gave me one of her looks, the one that says you don't know your head from your whatsit. 'He paid for the first,' she said, 'but he's not the only one as likes little flither-lasses, now is he?'

'He's a good man.'

'So have you seen him since?' Mary asked. I shook my head. '*I* have,' she said. 'In the studio, with a girl as looked like he'd picked her right out of the gutter . . .'

'Probably he had,' I said

'And he had her picture took, too.' If she was trying to wind my spring, she'd not manage with him.

'So where's the harm?' I said.

'I thought you might be jealous,' Mary said, 'that you weren't his only sweet girl.'

Mary had taken to knowing things since she'd been going to the classes. Now when she was home, which wasn't much, if she wasn't getting herself up smart, and she'd more than a pinch to the cheeks to use now, she was practising something or other, or she was round next door to borrow Mr Jackson's old newspaper, which he thought strange enough, but so long as she brought it back, being as they cut it into squares for wiping.

'Funny what we wipe our arses with,' Mary said.

'We don't,' I said, because Mrs O'Leary didn't get a paper, being a woman and not being able to read. 'We wipe them with . . .'

'I know what we wipe *ours* with. There's no need to be vulgar,' Mary said sharply. A bit rich, coming from her I thought, but didn't say. She'd got funny like that those past weeks. Some things she'd say and I'd be thinking it was to shock, and I wouldn't be, though Mrs O'Leary was. But when I looked at her and her saying them, she wasn't even knowing she was doing it. And then there were other things, dead ordinary things that we'd always said, and she was getting touched about them.

'Anyway, are you going to show it to the girls at work?' She was making peace.

'Maybe. But then . . .'

'What?'

'I'd have to explain. About how come I got the picture and . . .'

'No you don't. You don't have to tell nobody nothing that you don't want to.' Which she didn't. I knew that. Ever since the day she'd got scared and I'd taken her up the cliff, she'd kept her own to herself. Even with me. But I'm done up different

and I can't help myself for the telling. At least I couldn't then.
I've my own secrets now, too.

Mornings I was up before first light and kept a speed with
the chores because the cold was vicious. When the fire was on the
go, I'd nip to check the clock on St Denys's at the end of
the street and then I was back to wake Mary.

If I'd the time, I'd walk by the river on my way to the Cocoa
Works, over Ouse Bridge and then up North Street. It wasn't
properly on my way and added a good few minutes so I didn't
do it if I were short. Because once I was by the water, the brown
tug and shine of it, and all the business of the boats and the
barges, I couldn't make myself hurry, and me late would have
been all Mrs Flint would have wanted to fuel her war against
me. The path by the Ouse was muddy, even with the frost so
hard it was scorching the stones, but I'd galoshes and I could
splash with the best of them if I were in the mood and still have
my boots clean for my work. The galoshes were too big, but
they were given me free with my job, so I'd no complaints.

The morning I was taking in the picture, the day was clear
and the air so cold, it cut like vinegar at the back of my throat.
On the track beside the Ouse the puddles had been frozen a
week or more and most were smashed by now, their clear glass
gritted into white, and muddied. But there was one I found in
the ditch that was like a rockpool gone still. Grass blades and
a spider and bubbles of air fixed under the cold eye of the ice.
I put my finger to it until the cold was like a pain. I could have
put my heel to it after, but I didn't.

It was dinner time before I could show the girls my picture,
but it was worth the wait, they were all oohing and aahing,
like Mary and me were some trapeze men or ladies with beards
or something.

Jane, whose eyes were so wide you'd think the world
amazed, asked if it were the real sea behind, which I took as

meaning she's never seen the real sea or she'd have known better. But I told her no, it's just a bit of paint and she nodded like I'd spoken something wise.

'You're wearing trousers,' someone else said, and then the others were saying it too, but nicely, like it was my joke.

'It's the skirt. You pull it up and between your legs,' I said.

'Get away,' Elsie said and the others joined in. 'You're having us on.' 'You never do,' till, to shush them, I said, 'Shall I show you?' and they were all at me to do it. So I did. I gathered up the hinder part of my Holland pinafore, tugging it between my legs, making more of a meal of it for the laugh and this got the girls roaring. 'And then you pin it up and tie strings round the knees so it stays,' I finished off and I was standing, legs spread and swaggering, one hand clutching my skirt, one hand to my head to balance the basket full of limpets, which is the flithers of our name, when it was dead quiet of a sudden and the girls in front of me divided, like Moses and his sea that Mr William read us about once, and there was Mrs Flint. Flint in name and flint in all else.

She didn't say anything straight off, just stared at me as I pulled down my skirts, brushing them off like as if there were some specks, but there weren't, and by the time I straightened up, Elsie, Jane and all the others had slipped away like so many rabbits.

Somehow the picture was back in my hand again, and it might as well have been coloured red and smoking for the chance I had of keeping it from Mrs Flint. Still staring at me, she held out her hand, palm flat, for it.

Her face didn't change when she looked at it, only her cheeks and the top of her neck, where you could see above the collar, got a flush.

'I'll need to keep this and speak to Mr William,' she said, and I near bit my tongue, for Mary's voice in my head was answering her: 'Makes you jealous does it, you old prune?'

Then she nodded her head like to say: 'And you must take the consequences.'

The rest of the day the girls kept their distance, as if it was catching, what I'd got, and they were very sorry, but they didn't want it. Only Elsie didn't and I could have cried my thanks. Even Mrs Flint was near on kind, like she might be to someone on the way to the scaffold. And every time the door opened, we were all thinking it'd be for me, but it was only the lad about the weights, and once the clerk with the nice eyes about the Christmas boxes, and miserable though I was, I was sure he looked my way and smiled, which cheered me for a minute. But by the end of the day I was worn out, what with being a leper and a criminal and about to lose my job and all for a silly picture.

Elsie walked me home – she insisted – though she lived the other way in the Bedern, up near the Minster. She said she knew lots who were out in market gardens and she was sure I could do that, especially since I was well used to hard work. But you'd to be up very early and it was quite a walk to get there, though sometimes you could catch a lift on a cart. Or else there was the glassworks and that was already my end of town. But when I asked her what they've to do, she was a bit shy of telling and I knew it couldn't be very nice.

'D'you not think there's a chance they'll keep me?' I asked.

She shook her head. 'Not if Mrs Flint has asked for you to go. They always take her part. She goes to their church, the Quaker place, so they believe her over us.'

'But I've done nothing wrong,' I said. 'Only had a picture taken. And what's more, but you must promise not to tell . . .'

'I promise on my mother's soul,' Elsie said, putting her hand up into the dark as if her mother's soul was hanging there, which I suppose it might've been since her mother was dead. Anyway, she was serious, so I told her.

'That picture's because of one of them. It was him as asked me to go in and get it took, me and Mary, and then it was him as got me the job at Wetherby's, him being a cousin of the masters.'

Elsie was dead impressed, I could tell, because she didn't have anything to say for ages.

'And that's all . . .' she began, then stopped. She took a breath and then asked in a rush: 'He didn't ask you for nothing else?'

Soon as she'd said it, I could see how it must look. But I told her no, and that I hadn't thought on that, but that he didn't seem like the type, which made her laugh. And though I was to lose my job tomorrow and nothing to go to and no good word with me again, I laughed with her. We laughed all the way through the market in Parliament Street and the stalls nearly all packed up and the little kids scavenging bits of this and that, them and the cats. Elsie got us hot potatoes from the man with one leg with his stall on the market cross, so hot she burned her tongue and did a mad dance, tongue out, till I thought I'd die from the stitch in my side. Then we were on down Pavement and our noses to the window of the posh grocers with its piles of coffee beans and sugar and tins with bright labels and boxes of our cocoa of course. Elsie licked her tongue against the glass, cooling it from the potato and that brought out one of the little lad apprentices and he shushed us away with a wink. We walked down Fossgate and past the bridge where I first met Mr Ransome, but I didn't tell that to Elsie, until we were at my street.

Back home, Mrs O'Leary was troubled by Paul, her youngest, and his cold. She asked me to keep him still while she dressed him in a vest of lard and brown paper. So I held him firm and whispered a story my ma used to whisper me, of a brave sailor and a storm, and took his mind off the smell, which was making me retch, while Mrs O'Leary's stitches flew till he was all done up and there he'd stay for the winter. And then, when the winkleseller rang his bell at the end of the street, I was off and bought tuppence to cheer the little lad but also for the taste of the salt and the sight of the shell, though I should have been saving not spending with tomorrow to come.

I didn't mention my carry-on to Mrs O'Leary. Not to her, nor to Mary later. Might as well wait till it's happened, I told myself, but it was the first thing like that I'd not told Mary. The first thing I kept as a secret. Even when she climbed into bed and I felt her breath against my toes, even then, when her closeness was an urge to tell, I was quiet. Only, by my hand on her ankle, taking my comfort as I could.

I got the call from Mr William first thing the next day, by which time I'd done so much worrying I was beyond caring. Lots of the girls threw me nice looks and some, out of Mrs Flint's eye, gave me the thumbs' up. But I knew they didn't any of them think to see me again.

I climbed the steep stairs for the second time and stood at the open door. Mr William sat at his desk. Talking and sitting across from him, writing things down, close by the door, was the clerk with the nice eyes I saw that first day. They didn't notice me, so I stood to one side and waited. I had all day after all.

From where I was standing, I could see the young man's writing. He was putting down shapes I'd never learnt in my alphabet. Long slashes and dots and curves, but none of them from the ABC. I listened to hear if Mr William was speaking funny and that might have explained it. But Mr William was talking English. I was standing only a few yards from him and could hear every word since he was taking no trouble to lower his voice. All I could see of him was his arm and hand on the desk. He had a piece of paper on the blotter, a picture I recog-nised only too well, and while he was speaking, he was fitting it in snug, first to one corner of the blotter and then to the next, absently, in the way you do when you're thinking on something else. I don't remember who the letters were to, but I heard enough later that these might or might not have been the ones.

'Dear Mr Bailey,' Mr Wetherby was saying, 'Thank you for your information regarding Taylors' kibbling techniques and the recipes for their Spanish chocolate and Soluble Cocoa. I enclose £3 – in payment as agreed and beg to remind you that any more information of similarly high quality will receive similar remuneration. Yours, William Wetherby.'

He instructed that this be sent to the Mile End Road, London, which seemed a funny name for a road and then he was on to another one. This was to a Mr Dawber thanking him for information about Fry's moulding department and paying him so much, and then there was a third one and I began to wonder how long I was to wait to get this over with. This third asked a Mr Cloony to make up both samples included and see whether he could identify the difference in taste. That Mr Caleb Wetherby had been thinking the Van Houten's cocoa had to have cinnamon in it while he, Mr William Wetherby, was more inclined towards cassia. But so far they'd had no luck in reproducing it.

Mr William paused after this letter and the clerk stopped making his shapes and he lifted his head up and saw me. We couldn't have been looking at each other over a few seconds, but I knew that moment that I'd have to see him again, and him me. I didn't go wobbly at the knees, like they do in Mary's sixpenny romances, and my head wasn't spinning, nor my heart throbbing. In fact I felt just the same and I was still waiting to lose my job, but just as I know the tide will rise and then fall, so I knew we'd have to meet again.

'Come in, Harriet.' Mr William's voice was the same as always. He didn't sound angry and for a second, till I saw his face, I wondered was he going to let me stay. My clerk left and Mr William shut the door behind him.

He came straight to the point.

'Mrs Flint found you with this in the dining room yesterday.' He picked the picture off the blotter and held it between his thumb and forefinger like it were something dirty. 'She said you were engaged in showing it off to a number of other girls.'

I nodded, but didn't say anything, not seeing as there was anything that needed saying. He went on.

'I don't consider it proper that girls in my factory parade themselves in this way. Dressing in borrowed clothes, feigning to something, having your image taken so that who knows what kind of person can purchase a copy. Again he stopped and I held my tongue again. 'I'm disappointed in you, Harriet,' he said. 'I have looked in my records and see that Mr Ransome gave you a warm testimonial, in good faith I have no doubt, and you have let him down as well as Wetherby's. Have you anything to say before you leave?'

I'd rather he'd been angry than disappointed, I'd like to have said, but didn't. Instead I told him only that I weren't pretending, for I had been a flither-lass all my life before and saw nothing wrong in putting on the clothes once more. And that the gentleman who wished me to dress in those things had no thought of anything improper and to have suggested so was to do him an injustice. I couldn't bring myself to tell Mr William that it was his cousin who was the gentleman, for where would be the use in that, so then I was quiet and looked at my hands and waited for my dismissal.

For what seemed like an age, I stood like that, and he sat in his chair with my picture on the blotter and he didn't speak. I could hear the clerks in the room below. The one with the nice eyes would be there, making something out of his strange marks. Maybe it'd be him who copied out my going into some great red book: Harriet Brewer, dismissed after one month for . . . I looked up at Mr William. He was staring at my face so hard, I couldn't help but put a hand to my cheeks thinking there must be something there. A smut maybe.

'Sit down,' he said.

I shook my head. 'No disrespect, sir, but I've a job to search for, so if you would . . .'

'Sit down!' he said again. He didn't raise his voice, but there was something in it, I was so taken aback, I sat.

'You've been honest with me about this affair, I believe, and I am inclined to think, on hearing your testimony, that dismissal would not be just.'

I didn't believe my ears and waited a moment for the kick. Then I wanted to whoop. But all I did was nod my head. Now my legs had gone to water and there was a jellyfish in my belly. I was just wondering whether he meant for me to say something when he started up talking again.

'I will make no mention of this business again. However, in return there is a task I will expect you to perform for Wetherby's. Something that will put to good use your evident talent for being photographed. Not now, but in the near future.'

This was the kick, I supposed, and I knew I'd to say yes, though I hadn't an idea what it could be, so I nodded and he told me to go. I knew that the others in the packing room would be left standing when they heard I'd still got my job and that of all the girls in York I was the luckiest that morning, and of all women, Mrs Flint would be the most bitter. And since there was no point worrying over Mr William's bargain, I put it from my head.

It wasn't long after this that I got the letter. I'd become a dab hand with box pasting by now, and I was midway through my count when I heard my name.

'Harriet!' I turned to see Mrs Flint holding a piece of paper at arm's length, and disappearing out of the door, my clerk.

'Has somebody shat on it?' Elsie whispered, because of the way she had it between her fingers, and I couldn't help the giggle. It was a letter, addressed to me and sealed.

'Notes are not to be delivered in work time. Notes are not to be delivered at all while you are at Wetherby's, and this is the second,' Mrs Flint said, and I thought she might tear it up, but she didn't. She threw it at me as if she were throwing a stone and I caught it swooping with my pasty hands. 'Take it to your peg and return directly. You'll make up the lost time during the dinner hour,' she said, her words like gravel. I wondered why she'd let me have it, and how long it'd be before she struck me with her fists.

The other girls were on at me to open it, but I kept it sealed until I was all the way back at Mrs O'Leary's. Then, safe and alone in my room, I tore the seal and it wasn't from the clerk at all, as I'd suspected, hoped even. It was from Mr Ransome.

Dear Harriet, It is now some two months since our meeting on the bridge, and I am hoping that you are well settled at Wetherby's. I do not wish to intervene further, merely to be reassured of your good health, and knowing no other way, have penned you this note. Circumstances demand that I pass by our little bridge on Saturday of next week, and if you should so happen to be there at about five, I would be pleased to hear of you. Yours respectfully, Samuel Ransome.

It took me an age just to make out some of the words, being unused to reading. In the end I'd to ask Mrs O'Leary's Ellen to read the longest ones, and when she asked me why I'd not got my letters properly since Mary had, I snapped at her. I was sorry the minute after, so then I'd to go and make it up and do what she'd begged me over and over, which was to show her how we used to climb the rope.

It made her laugh, me making out the actions.

I could never do it,' she said, and I said it was just as well, then, that they'd not be asking her, and then I swore her to secrecy about the note. It had been better asking her than Mary, for Mary'd told me more than once of her scorn for Mr Ransome and his kind.

'Interfering do-gooders, knowing best for others. They know nowt. And the Quakers are the worst.'

'Why?' I said.

'Too bloody quiet,' was all she'd say and I knew better than to ask more.

Elsie thought I was daft to meet him. 'You don't want to go messing with that sort, it'll only be trouble,' she said. And even when I told her he was very proper, she only said, 'It can't be. He's from there and you're from here and the two oughtn't to mix. Oil and water. Stick to your own,' and clamped her lips tight. But I'd an obligation I couldn't explain to her, and whatever Mary said, he seemed a good man.

When I got to the bridge, he was there waiting in his odd clothes and a bag in his hand that looked for all the world like a lady's carpet bag. I knew he'd come specially, whatever was said in the letter about circumstances. The day smelt almost of spring and after a week of rain it had caught us on the hop with being warm and there was a smell coming off the water below I couldn't rightly place and didn't rightly want to. Something rotting, rotting and breeding at once.

He bowed to me and touched his hand to the tall black hat, though he didn't lift it like they do in the novels. 'Harriet Brewer,' he said, as though I might not know my own name.

'Mr Ransome,' I said, bowing back and thinking how the girls at the factory would laugh if they could see me now.

'Shall we walk a little?'

We set off back down Walmgate at quite a pace and though I tried to keep a little behind, still I was glad of the dusk and the lamps not yet lit, because it wasn't what was right, for a gentleman and a girl to be out in this way.

He walked me right out of town and after a bit I wondered, had he forgotten that I'd just come from the factory and on my feet for hours. Though he said he was happy for the opportunity of some conversation, we didn't have more than two sentences and after about a quarter of an hour stepping briskly, we came to some gates and, set back a bit with bushes and whatnot in front, a big building. Mr Ransome held up the carpet bag, and there were leaves sprouting from the top.

'I have something to deliver. I won't be more than a few minutes,' he said.

'And I'm to wait here?' I said, thinking he'd ask me further in. But he only nodded, and was off with his long, flat-footed step.

The building wasn't a house – or at least not a home – but I couldn't see what it was. There was a sign at the gate, but we were past too fast for me to make it out. Maybe it was a hotel, a very quiet one. Or a school. Betty in the Cocoa Packing Room had been to a school that had a thousand children. But all that grass and the daffodils by the trees didn't look like a school, and it hadn't the two entrances Betty told about, one for the boys and the other for the girls. I'd ask him what it was when he returned. It was getting cold, and without the walking to warm me I was starting to feel the chill. I leaned against the sign and hummed and stared out at the road. Standing there on my own, it didn't feel strange, but ordinary. With the light dropping and nothing to look at, nothing but the shape of a dog, limping a bit, making its way along, the other side of the road.

The dog was going along like dogs do, stopping and starting, keeping its nose sharp for any scrap to eat and I was watching, trying to see which foot gave the limp, when there was this strange noise behind me. I'd heard the same sound years back, when I'd got too close to a calf and its mother had rushed me, roaring. I turned and there was nothing, not a cow nor anything else. Then suddenly there was this noise again and a creature, a woman it was, came running at us.

Me and the dog ran down the road, the dog hop-legging it just as fast as I was, and both of us stopping under a tree like we were in something together. Then the dog went on, all dignified, hop-hopping, and I walked slowly back up to the strange house, looking out for the creature, who seemed to have gone, and wondering what Mr Ransome could be up to.

He was waiting for me by the notice and though I couldn't see in the near dark, I'd have guessed there was a blush to his neck.

'Did you . . . Were you . . . You're out of breath?' He was embarrassed all right, and before I could stop myself, I was downright angry with him, something I'd never done before, never had the opportunity, not to someone like him, a gentleman.

'You've had me stood out here waiting for an age after a long day's work and it's cold and I just got attacked by some crazy thing that rushed at me roaring.'

'I am very sorry for your fright,' he said. He put his hand on my shoulder, though at first it was my neck he touched which gave me a shiver, and with a firmer hand than I'd have thought he possessed, he had me chivvied quick back towards the big building and we were in at a side door and through into a bare room, where just a table with an old red oilcloth and four chairs stood and the gas just lit and still smoky. 'I'm going to get some tea. Stay here. Nobody will come in.'

By the time he was back I'd had it right up, being treated like this, all hole in wall. So I asked him, 'What is this place?' saying I'd go soon with all this rushing about and nobody to see us business.

He nodded and didn't say anything for a bit, looking across at the window, though you couldn't see a thing out of it now. I saw him properly for the first time over that table. His hair was still black, but it was making for the back of his head already, though he couldn't have been much beyond his thirtieth year and he'd an odd kind of a baby face, even with the dark makings of his beard, with his pouty little mouth and chubby cheeks. His eyes were large and blue and they looked at you like a dog does, trusting you without a reason to.

'I'll go,' I said again, threatening, and made as if to get up, which forced him on at last.

'It's called The Haven and my sister lives here,' he said. 'I am visiting her today; I visit her every week. She's been here since she was eighteen, over ten years now.'

'She's not married then,' I said, not knowing what quite he was telling me.

He shook his head slowly. 'No, nor ever likely to be. This is a home for those . . . those whose mental faculties make them unable to care for themselves. If you understand me.'

I nodded, because I did. There'd been a lad back home. The eldest son he'd been, which drove his dad to drink the men said. The women thought it a poor excuse for a bevvy, and what of his mam, since it was she that cared for him, right from his first day to his last. I heard the whole story in the end off Mary. This lad, anyway, he was a strange one. Older than me by some years, I knew him like we all did. He was this great tall fellow, never been out on the boats, and soft-skinned, and that handsome sometimes you'd forget what he was, or wasn't.

So often he'd be there, always in the same place, always stood against the wall of his home, barefoot and with this old blanket about him, watching the village go off about its business, which was fish one way or the other. One hand about the neck, keeping the blanket close, when it was cold, which most times it was, and the same in the heat. And his other hand would be on the wall, fingers spread like a starfish over the whitewash, always moving, like they were searching for something, but they never found it. His mam used to bring out his dinner to him there, only try to fetch him in at night and even then we'd often hear his cries, sounding like as if she were trying to murder him, though she loved him more than all her others.

Then he disappeared. He wasn't there with his starfish hand and his eyes following you and his funny noises, and he wasn't there the next day, or the next, and his mam wasn't saying anything, not looking for him, not weeping, with a face like someone had ripped the guts from her. But I heard my mam talking to my dad and him saying he wouldn't hold it against a soul for what happened, and her saying, but his own flesh and blood and how it'd be the death of his mother. And it was, for she died not a month after he'd gone wherever he had.

So I knew what Mr Ransome's sister might be. 'She's mad then,' I said, but he shook his head again. 'Well, what's she doing here?' I asked, but he didn't properly answer me that day. I pointed at the teapot. 'It'll be stewed if I don't pour it out,' I said.

The tea was very good. And there was buttered bread, too, in thin slices.

'My sister isn't mad like that person you saw. I think she's more sad than mad.'

'So she'll go home. When she's less sad,' I said.

But he shook his head and said how his mother felt this to be for the best, had done all these years, and how anyway now she'd be ill-suited to the world beyond, and I wondered what he was doing, with me here, and I asked him. He reached across the table then, and covered my hands with his. His hands were hot and dry. 'Perhaps I am sorry for bringing you,' he said.

'Perhaps you will be, if you don't take your hands off me,' I said, and he looked at them as if they didn't belong.

'Tell me about yourself,' he said, and I knew I should ask to go home now, but there was still buttered bread on the plate, the room was warm and though he was a strange one, I didn't think he'd try anything on. So I told him about the factory, though not about the photograph and that, and answered his questions as well as I could. He had such a pile of them and I remembered how he'd done this that first day on the bridge. Where did the girls put their wet things in the mornings? Was I one of the tallest? Did you need to be strong for the work? What about my hands? Had the other girls done other kinds of work too? Dirty work? Factory work? Did any suffer varicose veins? He'd heard they could be a problem, even for the younger factory workers. Had my life in the rockpools made my fingers nimble?

'Gathering the flithers, my fingers were so cold most of the time, they might have been a string of sausages for the difference it made,' I told him, thinking he'd smile, but he only nodded his head and then was off asking something else and I was answering him but wondering too why he wanted to know all this and why I wasn't . . . I didn't know the word. Not scared, but how come it wasn't stranger. Mary would have thought it strange. Elsie too.

'Do you ask the other girls this stuff?' I said.

He poured us both some more tea and I took another piece of bread which I must have ate very fast.

'You're hungry,' he said, like it was a great thing to see, putting the plate of bread in front of me, and then he left the room.

It was the barest room he'd got us in, nothing, not even a scrap of decoration, on the walls. Only two pieces of paper pinned up, one with writing, the other with a plan of something. I got up to look at them. On the first it said at the top, KEYS, and then there were names, and I could make out Mr Ransome's in the middle. On the other piece of paper was a drawing with lines curving round and then meeting other lines and numbers and arrows. At the top this one said DRAINS.

Mr Ransome came back with a feast. A plate of cold meat, chutney, some old shrunken apples, which were dense and sweet, more bread and a jug of milk.

'Please, eat all you want,' he said. So I did, and still he hadn't answered my question, but went on staring at the red oilcloth as if it was all written there, what he needed to know. It was black outside and there was no curtain at the window, so I could see all our room lit up in the glass like a mirror. Me and him sat behind the table, the tea things and the food, and the two pieces of paper pinned on the wall.

'You go to Mr Benbow's with other girls,' I said. 'Mary's seen you there, and them in their work clothes, not dressed up special like we were. She says sometimes they're really mucky.'

'Yes,' he said. 'I want a record of them, of the girls, I mean. Of the time,' he added.

This made no sense to me.

'Mary says I shouldn't trust you,' I tell him. 'She says you shouldn't trust a gentleman with so much as a fart.'

If he was offended by my words, then he didn't show it, but I wished he was. He was too odd for a gentleman talking to a factory girl. It wasn't natural. All he did then was look down at the tablecloth, his brow knitted, these broad creases cutting across.

'I must go now, else Mrs O'Leary'll be sending out after me, not home yet,' I said.

He looked about to say something, but then swallowed it and stood. It was dark as pitch outside and I stumbled on the uneven ground so that he offered me his arm, at least until I could see more clearly, and equally, be seen. He saw me to Walmgate Bar and, not because I was sorry for him and not because I was afraid, but some other reason I couldn't say, I agreed to meet him again, but I knew I'd not tell Mary.

SAMUEL

I knew, when I was a boy, that it was important to collect. My father read journals. He followed the proceedings of the Geological Society and the Royal Society and the Zoological Society, which my mother tolerated. And he tried to interest his only son in these matters, which my mother did not tolerate.

My father would tell me of the important men, Lyell and Lamarck, Grant and Darwin, who were collecting things and he would explain how the laws of God's universe were being rewritten. The men with their cases and trays and tanks of fossils and beetles and locusts and dull little birds and strange vegetable creatures that lived on the sea's floor. And I wasn't quite sure what he meant, but it seemed a wonderful thing nevertheless, that all this could be achieved by collecting, and so I became a collector too.

First, when I was still quite young, it was butterflies. So, directly the air was warm enough, after the April colds, I'd take my cousin William out to stand for a day with glass jars and nets and notebooks. It wasn't that I made him stand. More that he preferred the standing to the pursuit.

Being cousins and nearly of the same age, William and I were often in one another's company. But this connection of blood and our Quaker inheritance were all, are still all, we could be said to have in common.

He had no liking for the outdoors and perhaps I used my few extra months of age to persuade him more often than I should to my ventures. So, in the way of these things, it would habitually be him that got his feet wet in a boggy patch, or his head swiped by a branch, or his arms stung by nettles. And even when I'd filled our jars with every colour of the rainbow, even later when I'd got them all displayed, the velvet wings pinned out wide, all their beauty clear to see, still he took no pleasure in the creatures and could find nothing in them to set his mind to wonder.

'You know the Lord placed them there,' he'd say to me, 'the butterflies and the beetles and the nettles. What need have you to lift them out and pin them up? The Lord suggests we consider the lilies, not pick them and dissect them.'

'Perhaps it is on account of your knee you feel this,' I might say, because he had scraped it, or it might be on account of the bee sting, or the mud on his shoes, because there was always something, and it was perhaps a malicious observation, but it always seemed to me that he managed to take the Lord as his advocate in our arguments, and I think that has never changed.

It was perhaps only his great admiration for my father's business head that kept William as my reluctant companion on these expeditions. He would listen bored but respectful at the dinner table when my father gave out his opinions of the latest book of science, until my mother silenced him. She detested what she spoke of as Father's 'hobbies' and once I overheard her shouting at him.

It wasn't that I was eavesdropping, for the door had to be gone past, but it may be that I slowed my step when I heard my name uttered.

'If you would have Samuel grow up in this way, questioning at such a young age all that is put before him, then who is to say where it will end . . .'

'Dear,' my father interrupted, and I wondered at his courage, 'it won't undo God, only make his ways more impressive. Complexity is part of his grandeur.'

But my mother wasn't asking for his reassurance.

'And what of our daughter?' she said. 'Who is still a small child, and a female, and who admires you excessively? All of them, William too, sitting there, their good food growing cold on their plates, while you chatter on with your absurdities. Wondering why it is birds have different size beaks, when any nursery child could tell you it is so they can share out God's food without strife, the one eating the seed and the other the worm.'

I am sure William would have agreed with my mother, though his admiration of my father would have prevented him saying so. He was tolerant of his uncle as he never has been of me, and, as I have already said, this was on account of his uncle's skill in business.

My father, David Ransome, was a tanner, like his father and grandfather before him. More accurately he was the proprietor of a large establishment, and of its profitable trade.

Tanning, as I was to discover, is a malodorous and dirty business, though being the owner, my father need never have gone near the works. But it was a point of principle for him, at least once in the week, to spend a morning in his yards and sheds.

We knew these mornings, Grace and I, because of Father's clothes and Mother's mood. Father would sit down to breakfast in tannery clothes. These were blue flannel trousers and jacket, a coarse linen shirt and clogs, though he would keep the clogs in a bag with his apron until later. Mother would sit opposite as usual and she never said a word, but we knew she was angry. When we bowed our heads for the grace we could feel her fury leach into the silence.

My father seemed not to notice. He would eat his breakfast as he always did, asking Grace and I, each in turn, if we would pass him butter, or marmalade, or salt. Then he would rise and take his leave. Although he was a fine horseman, he always walked there, clattering on the cobbles like any labourer in his clogs.

'It is a fine sound, this clatter,' he said to me once, 'can you not hear the music of it?' and I could.

Though Mother did not eat breakfast, she always sat with us at the table. The maid would bring her a tray with cup and saucer, a jug of hot water and a sprig of rosemary on a small plate, or in the warmer months a sprig of mint. On days when Father was to visit the works, she would dip the herb sprig with such ferocity, we children knew that to say a word on anything was to risk the slice of her tongue. And yet, though Father seemed in so many ways to accede to Mother, in this matter he was immovable, and unperturbed by her disapproval.

Father was so thoroughly acquainted with the processes, which turned a bloody pelt into the finest morocco, that he would often take a turn at the trade. He believed in his own way that one ought never to ask another man to do that which one was not prepared to do oneself. So each week he'd make his way to the works and walk in, unannounced. Then he'd go across to a man busy about his business, and, with unrefusable courtesy, ask to relieve him of his task.

So he might spend a half hour sleeking a soaked hide, pressing the water from it with the 'sleeker', which is a great wooden paddle. Or he'd borrow a 'flesher' from a currier and stroke down the hide, stretched on its frame, drawing the two-handled broad blade down the skin in a great sweep, paring from it the last vestiges of flesh. If the hide was from a large beast, he would raise the blade high above his head and finish down by his ankles, reminding me more of the infidel at prayer my mother had described than the English Quaker he was.

He might even join the yardmen and busy himself in drawing the hides from their pits of pigeon and dog dung, or from the bark where they'd lie a full twelvemonth, lifting them high with a hooked pole to see how they were going.

He'd come back home stinking and exhilarated.

'Just going to wash,' he'd call, and Nellie, our maid, would already have the water ready in the kitchen, and the special towel. We'd hear him oftentimes humming as he scrubbed the animal smells from his skin, though he always stopped before coming through the kitchen door because Mother didn't like it.

The first time Father took me to the tannery, I thought I should die. It was my eleventh birthday and I had come in to breakfast to find two packages in brown paper beside my place. Mother was in bed with a bad head and sent a note with her birthday greeting saying she would be down at lunch.

The first package contained my own, smaller pair of blue flannel trousers, linen shirt and apron. And in the second package was a pair of clogs. Father's eyes were bright and he barely allowed me the time to eat before I was chivvied upstairs to change.

I came down proudly. This was a day I had been waiting for. I'd even discussed it with William, though conscious in this respect of the disparity in our positions. My father was a wealthy man, whose trade could be measured by the leather in men's shoes and the shine on their saddles. William's father was not. He owned his own grocery business, but things had gone badly for him. He had kept the business going, but only by borrowing money from my father on more than one occasion. Both William and I knew this, though I think neither could have said when we had been told. When the time came, William would take up his apprenticeship in the place whether he wished it or no.

'Quick now,' Father said when I came down in my new garments, my trousers rolled twice and my sleeves hitched, for Father had bought the clothes with room for growth.

'But what about Mother?' I said, before catching Father's expression. He had his eyes lowered, abashed. 'She doesn't know, does she?' I said.

He shook his head. 'Time enough for that,' he said. 'No man should mind dirtying his hands. It's the spirit that God looks to.'

You could smell the tannery before you saw it. A vile smell, composed, as I soon learnt, of rotting animal flesh, quick lime, mounds of mouldering animal horn, greening in the autumn damp, and, over it all, the acrid odour of animal excrement, a smell which bit into your nostrils and made your eyes water.

We walked down a street towards the river, a pretty street with old houses and front railings. Then, close to the water the houses stopped and Father was looking at me proudly. In front of us was a cluster of buildings, all of them blackened. Tall wooden windowless buildings, and sheds, and piles and heaps around them and flies everywhere. The smell was so strong, it coated the back of my mouth.

'Here we are,' said Father, his voice sharp with excitement.

Down the side of the largest of the buildings was a passage and this opened out into a wide yard. On this first day and always after, I never saw this yard but that I felt myself to be in a twilight time, when things might not be as they seem. Half a dozen men were stirring at the black oozy liquid that filled the half-dozen dark pits cut into the ground. Not stirring, in fact, but heaving great poles about, causing the water to boil and curdle. The men were dressed in clothes that looked, at first, no more than rags, but I learnt later that the holes were burnt in them not by time and wear, but by the lime they used to take the hair off the hides. Piles of bark, the size of small buildings, were heaped around the yard, and mounds of parings, from the hides, ready to be removed by the glue makers.

'Stay close, Samuel,' Father said. 'Don't want you falling in.' He said it by way of a joke, to reassure. But it was all my body needed. This merest suggestion set my stomach trembling and then my head was spinning, and there was a roaring in my ears, and if one of the men hadn't caught me, I would have fainted right into one of them.

I came round a moment later and my stomach took over where my head had left off, and I vomited until I was heaving on air.

Father stood beside me, his face concerned. When there ceased to be any substance to my retching, he took me inside one of the blackened buildings, guiding me with an arm around my waist, tenderly, gently, in a way that evoked some early feeling in me, almost like a taste in my mouth, and I was glad I'd been ill, to have Father tend me like this.

'Sit down. I've some business to transact, then we'll be off home.'

He spent a quarter of an hour in conversation with the foreman, before taking just a short turn with a sleeker. It was the first time I'd ever seen him bend his body like this to a task, and when he was done he came over to me, his brow bright with sweat, his eyes bright with pleasure.

'Come, Samuel,' he said, and we left and walked home.

I had wondered if he'd be angry at my body's failure of nerve. But he was not. Rather, he seemed contented with the morning.

'So now you have seen the source of our prosperity, Samuel,' he said. 'A messy business, but very profitable.'

I nodded. My body was limp, my head ached. 'And you needn't worry about your nausea,' he went on. 'It's what every apprentice does in his first week. It's like sea-sickness. You'll get used to it.'

But I did not get used to it and I came to dread it. On the fifth day each week Mother would lie abed, not appearing for breakfast, and each week, dressed in our blue, Father and I would walk to the tannery. Though he never said so, Father longed for me to take a turn with the sleeker or the hooked pole. But unlike the apprentices, I never outgrew my disgust. And each week, I was as faint and as sick as I had been the first, so that the foreman took to having a bucket left ready for my visit, and I rarely had the strength for my schooling in the second half of the day.

Even so, with quiet persistence, Father showed me a little more of the business each time, till I could have told any man how to make leather, and how to be sure of your prices, buying and selling. And visit by visit my horror grew that this was to be my future, so that I envied my sister and what seemed to me then to be her freedom.

Grace, my younger sister, was doubly named. First Grace because she had been granted by God when my parents had long thought I was to be their only one. And second because it was only by God's grace and by the skin of her teeth that Mother survived her daughter's birth at all. That's what my father told me when I asked. I would never have asked Mother.

When I was shown the crib, I was told I peeped over, stared in and shouted, 'Monkey!' Then ran away, furious. And when

Father asked me what was wrong, I beat at him with my fists and asked where was my sister.

My sister was born a tiny, wizened creature, with long fingernails, a mop of dark hair and a will to live. In her first months she sucked the wet nurse dry, and she grew up into a beautiful, chubby, curly-headed little girl with an insatiable appetite for exploring and little regard for the limits of her gender.

Grace was always a wonder to me because she never minded Mother's severity, though she would pay a heavy price for this when she was grown.

'Silence until five,' Mother would say at lunch, both week-days and weekends, for the afternoon hours were the hours of her resting. And we were expected to stay quiet in our rooms, and then to play with no noise in the garden. I found this easy, with my books and journal and butterflies. But for Grace, Mother's injunction was impossible. She was a different crea-ture. Her spirit needed air and movement. It was a wild thing that chafed and strutted in our solemn, dark house in York.

Grace had no wish to school her mind to the alphabet, nor her hand to making neat shapes in her copying book for the governess. The dresses she had to wear, miniatures of Mother's but for the corsets, had her roped and trussed. She hated their dark colours and would beg ribbons and any pretty pieces she could of the maids. She'd wear these wrapped about her wrists, pinned to her bodice, plaited into her hair, only to tug them off and stuff them up her sleeve on hearing Mother's footsteps.

Often in the afternoon I'd be sitting at my books, or writ-ing my journal – written for Father's inspection each First Day evening – and there'd be the faintest knock on my door. I'd open it, and Grace would be standing there, diminutive, eager.

'Come and see, Sam,' she'd say, and she'd have something in her palm – a dead spider, or some flower petals or an owl's pellet. Or else she'd grasp my hand and, barely allowing me the time to cap my pen or close my books, she'd tug me to some treasure she'd found, or made.

Perhaps Mother found it hard, having a child like Grace beside a child like me. Because although I loved to be outside, collecting my butterflies, or working at some other task, I took no pleasure then in roaming and I rarely came back muddy. Whereas Grace was always getting up to larks.

It's one of the earliest of Grace's special places that I recall best. I was in the garden, sketching, and she mustn't have been more than a handful of years old, when she took hold of my index finger.

'Come and see, Sam,' she said as always and we walked down the garden till we were almost out of sight of the house. She let go of my finger to clamber through a rhododendron bush on hands and knees, then around a bed of nettles until we came clear into a patch of high wild grass, far beyond the reach of the gardener's shears.

Grace had made a tunnel through, and now she slithered along it, the shiny dark satin of her dress easing her progress. I followed, struggling to keep my lumpen body, for so it seemed beside hers, from destroying her secret way.

At the end of the tunnel was a circle of flattened grass, and here Grace put her arms out proudly, the queen of all she surveyed.

'My perfick place,' she said, and despite the dress, she reminded me of a leveret in its form.

'It's wonderful, Grace,' I said, but she didn't need my praise. She knew what it was.

As she grew up, she went on making these dens and hidey holes, her 'perfick places' as we still called them, and they grew with her, becoming more sophisticated, more elaborate. She often showed them to me, though not always, for once, in the midst of my own pursuits, I came upon one that I had never seen. And after a time she didn't need me to show them to. She had found someone else.

Grace told me not long ago that that garden became her heaven and her hell.

'I understand the heaven,' I told her. 'But not the hell.'

'It is where Mother and I came closest,' she said, 'and it is where she let me go.'

I was standing on a terrace in The Haven, looking down at the gardens busy with people. And Grace, she was crouched, huddled more, in the doorway, unwilling, or unable, to step further out.

The sun was low, making even the smallest gestures – the pruning of a rose, or the turning of a page – into vast pantomime shadow shapes.

Grace turned away from the spectacle.

'The flowers,' she said, her voice so low I had to ask her to say it again.

'The flowers?' I said.

'I think she couldn't forgive me for the flowers,' she said.

My confusion must have showed, because she spelt it out for me then.

'Because I love them as much. I made my places, you remember, in the midst of the things she loved, out of the things she most loved. That is where she found me on that day.'

'But she must have been proud of you for that. And now your articles . . .'

'She might have loved me, but she hated me instead.'

'And yet she never wanted to be climbing among the bushes or . . .'

Grace interrupted me. 'No, but that's not it. My passion was for the same thing, and so she felt, she feels, I have made hers bad because of mine.'

'But you are, you have made yourself a botanist. And she . . .' I paused, because so much suddenly seemed to hang for Grace upon this. 'And she, well, she is not interested in the science. She likes them as impeccable beauty. God's most delicate wonder, she will say often. Never to touch.'

'Yes, Sam. Never to touch. And what did I do? I touched, and more. And afterwards? Afterwards she never wanted to enter the garden again. I know. Even before I was taken here, I saw it. I shut her in. That is what she feels, and so she hates me. And now she gives her interest to the rarest and most delicate of flowers and she raises them inside her house, inside her glass house. She raises them as a rebuke to me. So that you will come here and tell me the news and say, "Oh, Mother has nurtured the rarest of rare orchids," because it will be a rebuke to me, and it is.'

Mother never liked Grace. Even when Grace was small, Mother punished her more severely than she needed to. There had been a child who had died. A little girl, Anne, born just a year after me. When I was four and she three, we were both ill with influenza. I recovered, and she did not. The only memory I have of Anne is of a face opposite mine in a perambulator. Nothing more.

Grace was born less than a year later, and Mother disliked her from birth. Already by the time she died, Anne was a child eager especially to please her mother, and like Mother, she was particular and tidy in her dress, and unusually fastidious in her manners for one so young. Grace was none of these things, and Mother never forgave her for it.

Mother punished Grace for not being the dead child, and Father was powerless to prevent her doing so. I would say now that he felt somehow responsible, guilty even, for Anne's death, though there is nothing he could have done to prevent it. And Mother blamed him, too, as though a proper paterfamilias would not let such a thing occur.

I am sure Mother believed her severity to be a necessary part of Grace's moral education. But it has been clear to me since childhood that Mother simply could not bear Grace for being alive. For if Anne had lived, Grace would never have been born. And Grace proved no replacement.

There was a rule, that each person was to bring down their chamber pot in the morning. Grace and I knew, from other children at Meeting, even from William whose family had only one maid of all work, compared to our half dozen staff, that this was not the usual practice. We knew it was on account of our mother, and, when Grace was very small, there were many times I would return for her pot.

So we left them each day, covered, in a long, pungent line, just beside the servants' door. From Father's down to Grace's little pot, like the bowls of porridge in *Goldilocks and the Three Bears*. Then they would be emptied and returned to our rooms by the scullery maid.

But one morning, Grace didn't bring hers down. She wasn't very big, perhaps seven years old. She hadn't forgotten, but she didn't want to do it. And when Mother heard, she ordered Nellie to strap the pot to Grace's back.

'You may walk outside with it for the hour,' Mother told her.

Nellie did as she was told, put a peck of a kiss on the top of Grace's head and sent her out into the garden. Grace was a tortoise on hind legs, but skipping and hopping, at which Mother frowned. So Mother ordered her onto the road.

'She must learn humility,' she said, and for a long hour Grace was made to walk up and down outside our house, her head held high in small defiance at the stares from other children and the whispered asides of neighbours.

I believe Mother punished Grace for not being like her. That's what it amounted to, the shutting outside, or inside, or the hours Grace was set to memorising Bible verses, or sewing

'God is Love' in fine needlepoint. And maybe it was not in her secret garden places, but during one of these times, in the reciting of a Gospel or shut up in the dark of the broom cupboard, that Grace found her companion.

As for me, I was thoroughly a schoolboy by this time and, in the main, not witness to these events. Since Grace never said a word, I heard what was happening only from Nellie. And barely a day goes by but that I wonder, if I'd been more at home, whether I could have prevented what occurred later.

HARRIET

It was summer now and Elsie and me, we were walking part way home together as we did, and gossiping. There was lots to catch up on because I'd been moved rooms at Wetherby's on account of Mrs Flint's temper. She'd have been the death of me, or her, if I'd stayed put, so I'd been moved to Mrs Horner's Room which is the Creams. Strawberry, Vanilla, Coffee, Blackberry, Orange, Rose, you name it, Wetherby's would make a Chocolate Cream from it.

Anyway, there was this smell as we came over Ouse Bridge. It was dung of some sort, but not any I knew. I was wrinkling my nostrils, wanting to walk faster, but Elsie stopped near a shadowy heap and peered at it. Then she turned to me, excited.

'That horse must've eaten something queer, poor bugger,' I said, but she shook her head.

'It's the circus,' she said. 'That's elephant dung.'

'Elephant! Get away,' I said. 'What're they doing with elephants on Ouse Bridge?'

Elsie turned to me, her eyes bright under the gaslight. 'They'll all have been along here. Elephants and lions and monkeys, and tumblers and clowns and trapeze ladies, and great wagons with them dressed up to be mermaids and Rule Britannia and all.'

'Mermaids,' I said.

'Ay. And so many horses with plumes and brass and all lifting their feet right high.'

We'd reached our corner, where she'd to go to the left and I to the right.

'You've not been, have you?' she said.

'No,' I said. 'There was one used to come to a village a few miles off, but we didn't go. Mary did once, snuck off. But she said it weren't up to much. A couple of horses and a clown so weary he couldn't barely keep his eyes open, and summat they said was a lion, but Mary said it were that old and that faded, a sheep might have mauled it.'

'Well, tell her to come to this one then. She'll not come out of it sneering, I promise, not even Mary.'

'Don't be so cross. I'm only telling what she told me.'

'Anyway, you're coming to this one. You'll never believe it.'

'They bring some strange stuff out of the sea in the nets, I'll tell you,' I said, a touch huffy at always being the green one.

'Not so strange as what they have in their cages,' said Elsie, 'you wait and see.'

Elsie's words made me think of a man as used to come to our village, not often, maybe once or twice in the year, and he'd have a handcart with these big boxes and a dog. Winter or summer, he always wore a great black coat with pockets all over and a tall stovepipe hat, and he was clean-shaven, which was a rarer thing then than it is now in a full-grown man, and a rare thing indeed in our village. He'd set himself up outside the Crab and Bottle and wait for enough to gather, Mr Grandison the landlord always supplying his wants happily enough with the crowd he brought. And when the crowd was nearing a size, the man would strap cymbals to his knees, a drum to his shoulders and sticks to his elbows and play tunes on his concertina that got the dog to howling. Then he'd say this funny rhyme I still have the last lines of in my head. They're maybe not quite right, but near enough:

> So pay your penny and make your prayer
> And don't be fooled by what you see,
> They know you've only come to stare,
> But two can play at thee and me.

And as he said this last line, he'd point at some person in the crowd and then open the biggest of his boxes and inside would be something alive, mostly some animal, but once it were a little woman. A girl you'd have thought except she weren't, and much littler even than I was then. And that person in the crowd he'd chosen, though he'd just pointed a finger and knew nowt about them, would shrink back as if he might have put a curse on them.

Then he'd bring out his ticket book and write off the tick-ets, one for each penny and if you wanted more than one look, you'd to buy two tickets. Sometimes I'd get to see, and sometimes not, and some of the things I saw, they've hunted through my dreams since.

Mary was home that evening and I asked her if she remem-bered the man with the cart and the boxes.

'Ay,' she said. 'It was more than once I'd a mind to escape with him.'

'How d'you know he'd have let you?'

'Oh, he'd have let me.'

'So what stopped you?'

Mary shrugged. 'Didn't like his eyes. Didn't like his eyes and didn't like his coat. It could've hid all sorts.'

'I should be flattered, I suppose, that you chose me over him, then. Even if it was only on account of a coat.'

Mary looked at me sharply, like she didn't know if maybe I wasn't joking. I kept my face still as I could, eyes on my darning needle, in and out, catching at the hole in my stocking, until she knelt right down, petticoats in the dust, and chucked me under the chin. I grinned then and she made as if to swipe me round the head, grinning too.

'You're a dark one, Hal,' she said.

'We're going to the circus on Saturday,' I said then and made it a question to her.

She shook her head. 'I can't. I've an appointment.'

'On a Saturday night?' I said and because right then I was fed up with skirting around, 'An appointment?'

She nodded. 'Work.'

'Not laundry work,' I said, and she gave me this small smile.

Maybe I knew from the first what Mary was up to. I'd say that I did, or thought I did.

'Well,' I said, 'so it'll be just me and Elsie then.'

It was further out that way than I'd walked before, through Micklegate Bar and along the Mount with its tall houses and, suddenly, down the hill and we were on the edge of the Knavesmire. 'It's where they used to do the hanging, off to one side,' Elsie told me. But now it was only the races. I'd never have dreamt there was such a place, like a green ocean, so close to the city. The circus was put up to one side, a great tent in different colours and all around it caravans and horses and small fires burning.

Elsie thought I was putting it on, and we'd paid our money, that I didn't want to see the animals in their cages, or the Bearded Lady, or the Serpent Man.

'I don't like the smell,' I said, fishing for an excuse.

'But it's the Menagerie,' she said, 'it's part of it. Besides, you've been dunking around with fish for years and they've more of a whiff than a dog's arse.' She was cross, as cross as I'd ever seen her, but I wasn't going to change my mind.

'I'll wait for you here,' I said. So she went alone, tossing her shoulder, and I stood on the edge of the golden light, stamping my boots against the cold and watching the hawkers and the crowd.

A man with a hat and red waistcoat was banging a gong and yelling to people to 'Roll Up,' which they were trying to do, queuing for their tickets, and there was a clown acting very sad and then creeping up on someone and making as if to be them. He'd stand behind them and do all they did, just so.

I saw him do it to this woman and everybody laughing and she not knowing why, and when she turned and saw him, he snatched a kiss. And then it was this little boy who was hopping, one foot to the other, like he needed to go, and the clown set up hopping too, still with his face so sad. And when the boy caught sight of him, he pretended to take a piss against the tent and the man with the tall hat came and walloped him and he ran off and the crowd calling 'Ohh' in sympathy. But he was back the next minute and then he nearly caught it proper.

Standing a bit apart was this man, smartly dressed with a big coat and a fancy hat. He had his back to me, looking towards the city, and seemed like he was waiting for someone. There was something about him I'd seen somewhere else. Even from behind you could tell he thought a bit about himself. He had this cigar he was smoking. I knew he was because the clown was smoking one too, flicking it just as if it were really there. Then the gentleman must have started to pick his nose because there was the clown picking his, just the same, in this calm way like he might be in the privacy of his own house. I was one of the first to notice because of where I was stood, but once other people started to see them, the gentleman and the clown, both with their fingers rummaging, the laugh spread like a wind until, at last, the gentleman turned to see what all was going on.

Soon as he turned, I saw it was Mr Benbow and I wondered how I'd not known him before. My heart beat faster at the thought that he might see me laughing at him, and remember where he'd seen me before. But he was so mad at the clown, his hands making fists and eyes glaring and mouth working into shapes, he'd no time to notice further and anyway I slipped further into the shadow.

It seemed an age before Elsie came out. And when she came she'd caught herself a pretty fish indeed. He had his hand round her waist already and she was laughing loud and throwing back her head though he wasn't more than a boy.

He didn't look to be as old as me, his skin was so smooth and his body like a willow. Standing in my shadow, I watched them, Elsie searching through the crowd, and then I came and joined them.

Elsie's pretty fish, whose name was Bert, was a boon, for she was so busy with him, she didn't bother herself with me. 'This is Harriet and she's not seen a circus before,' she said by way of introduction. 'Oh, ay,' said Bert, and that was that.

We found places on the tuppenny benches quite high up, but we could see it all. The air was such a mix of smoke and sawdust and strange smells, I didn't dare fill my lungs at first and took shallow breaths. There was a fair din around us, and people getting settled, but when the drum began, such a hush came over, and then a bang and some smoke and into the ring came these horses galloping, their tails tied with ribbons and feathers from their manes, and running in after them the riders who leapt on their backs while they galloped, and the riders stood up and did a little play of love while still the horses galloped round, only sometimes making a figure of eight, or going two and two, to the left and to the right.

Then there were acrobats, and after them the elephants, great dusty creatures with small sad eyes. The elephant man, in his funny spangled trousers, had them standing up on boxes, and catching each other's tails, and waving their trunks to his wand, and everyone but me clapped and cheered.

It was the lions and hoops and the man with the big whip that did for me. Elsie was happy. Each lion roar and she was snuggled further into Bert's arms. She didn't need me there. But I'd had enough of animals doing people's things and I whispered her something she'd not have heard, but no matter, and stumbled across people's legs to the steps. It were a sight to look back on, all those faces, mouths part way open, so many together, they put me in mind of my trays of creams, lined up row on row to be boxed and sent off.

I was halfway down the steps when somebody tapped me on my shoulder and brought me up in my tracks. Thinking it was him I'd seen earlier with the cigar, I didn't turn about, but it was a different voice spoke my name.

'Harriet, is it?'

I turned then. It was my clerk from the factory. Him with the nice eyes.

'You leaving?' he asked, and I nodded yes, thinking that he must've remembered my name from Mr William's office.

'I'll come with you,' he said, and it seemed obvious he should.

We got down near the ringside and the two shilling seats and the clowns were out again, one with a petticoat round him, and a monkey dressed as a baby in a perambulator.

'Oh, now you stay put in there, good babby, good babby,' the petticoat clown was shouting, loud enough so even Elsie and her Bert could hear if they were still listening at all. And the monkey, as it'd been taught, soon as he said that, was out of there, its nappy trailing, and across the sawdust and straight up a rope. And the clown ran over, beating at his chest and making this loud wail. 'Oh no, oh no, coom back, babby,' he shouted, mopping his eyes with his petticoat, and running at the rope in his long flappy shoes and the monkey climbing higher and higher. 'Coom back.'

We were nearly to the entrance and all this still going on behind, when there was a shriek that went through my bones. I turned around so suddenly I caught my clerk in the chest with my elbow. The monkey was down from the rope and he'd set himself onto a lady's lap and was tugging at the feathers in her hat. She'd a face I knew better even than my own.

'Mary!' I said loud, the word coming out before I could stop it. But no one heard except the clerk.

Mr Benbow was on one side of her, but on her other side, and with his arm about her shoulders like she was his, was a strange fellow in a checked waistcoat and broad cravat and he'd eyes for nothing else, not the monkey, not the clowns, for nothing but her.

They had the monkey off her in a second, Mr Benbow laughing fit to split and the checked waistcoat saying something not so nice to the clown, or so it looked from his face. Then the clown tipped his hat to Mary and wheeled his perambulator away and the crowd was back roaring and calling to him, but all I could see was Mary and this odd smile on her and the waistcoat man bending over her like I knew she'd hate.

We were walking back into the city and it was easy there beside him, as if we'd known each other for years.

'Do you think . . .' I stopped, not knowing how to put my mind, then started in again, nodding my head towards them. 'Do you think that man and her with the monkey, do you think they might be courting?' I knew as I spoke how daft it sounded, but I thought maybe the clerk would say yes just to be polite. But he shook his head.

'Do you know her, then?' he said, and I wondered how he knew.

I nodded, which he must have felt rather than seen in the dark. 'We came to York together.'

'Did she know you were going to the circus tonight?' he asked.

'Yes, and she said she couldn't come on account of an appointment.'

'An appointment,' he said.

'I know the man on her other side,' I said. 'That's Mr Benbow, he took my picture. But I don't know the one with his arm on her.'

We reached Micklegate Bar with me still worrying over Mary and the man, when the clerk stopped right under it, with the smell of piss on the stone.

'Well, if they were courting, then my name's not Thomas Newcome,' he said.

'That's your name, is it? Thomas Newcome?' I said.

He nodded and turned to me, holding out his hand. 'Pleased to meet you, Harriet . . .'

'Harriet Brewer. Pleased to meet you, too, Thomas Newcome.' And we shook, our cold hands warming for a moment and him looking at me so long I thought maybe he'd asked me a question and I'd not answered him.

'Now, it won't be an appointment, but will you walk out with me tomorrow?' he said, and I nodded, wishing we could touch hands again, touch anything.

'You'll be all right home?' he said, like it was something he felt he ought to, and I laughed and so did he.

'I'll be off then,' he said, and I nodded again, and he was gone.

I stood about a bit after. His lodgings were back the way we'd come, so I watched him walk off past the Windmill Inn till the dark had him. It was a sharp night, clear, the stars bright, their pricking lights like promises. My breath made ghosts in the gaslight and I knew I'd be setting up for a chill if I was stopped there long.

It was something you knew too well, where I'd come from, what it was to be cold. All the different kinds of it. The dry cold and the wind flicking at your fingers, your cheeks, the insides of your ears however tight you pulled your scarf around you. And the foggy cold which laid itself across your skin like damp rags. And the wet cold of the sea so as your fingers and toes'd be red and scurfed where you'd to dry them with your skirts, the salt stinging in the cracks between and the backs of your hands, and your skirts like sandpaper on your skin.

We'd tell stories against the cold, Mary and me. Take our minds off of it. The girls all did, but the men didn't, which is maybe why they made more of the hard things, least that's how it looked to us. Though it wasn't so much stories Mary and me did as doing 'best of' and 'worst of'. First, one of us would say our best food and then the other, and then it'd be the worst of: food, ribbons, trees, names, beaches, times of year, girls, and always in the end boys.

'You're always one for the soft,' Mary'd tell me. 'How can you say Robbie Walton's your best? He wouldn't know how to tie a knot without his ma there holding both ends of the rope. You go with him, you'd have to show him what for before he knew what to do with . . .'

'Stop it, Mary,' I'd have to shout then, else she'd go on and on, and always there'd be gristle in her words so as you couldn't leave them, but they'd be back in your mind when you lay down at night. And them as she chose for her best, they'd be the hard nuts, the lads you'd not want to cross, the ones as looked at you long and didn't leave off. And now, in one go, I'd fallen for . . . well, he wasn't a hard one like Mary chose, but there wasn't a lot soft in him, though I'd find what there was and take it to me. I'd fallen off the edge, and no rope to hold to, dropped into something which took my breath away.

But I wasn't so much feeling cold now as numb, and that from the inside out, not the other way round, and it was more of a lurching thing, as made my hands and my feet and my belly, and other parts too, seem like they were cut off and in some other place where I could feel them more, not less. I leaned back against the city wall, putting my hands behind me, palms hard against the brick, knuckles pressed into my shawl. There were more people walking in to the city now. The circus must have finished.

I shut my eyes and imagined my fingers touching his neck, and then round to his brow, his hands, his face, his dry soft lips like the paper skin on a scallion. My hands fingering down his backbone, picking out each rib down to the top of his trousers, and round to the hardness of his stomach, feeling just the slight touch of hair, and then down just a half inch to the buttons on his fly. Now my heart was pounding and it was hard to get my breath, my belly flipping and tossing like a fish fresh out of water. I shook my head, opened my eyes, tried to get some air. He must be about the same age as Elsie's young man of the night, Bert, I thought to myself, but there wasn't much else alike. He was someone from another country.

'Thomas,' I said, just quiet, not so as anyone could hear going past. 'Thomas.'

I tipped my head back against the city wall, shut my eyes again, so as I must have looked like I'd had one over, but I didn't much care.

'Thomas,' I said, keeping his name nearly in my mouth,

tucking it in between my teeth, and then I couldn't help myself, I was talking to him, saying things I didn't know I'd got in there to say, things I'd have died if he'd guessed at three minutes ago when he was stood by me.

I don't know how long she'd been speaking to me, the woman. But I jumped when she put her hand on my arm.

'You all right, love?' she said. She must have been near enough my mother's age, and her face was worried.

I nodded.

'Only you look feverish, and you didn't hear me' she said. 'You'll catch your death stood there for long.'

She still had her hand on my arm, and I couldn't help myself, I shrugged it off, roughly maybe because she looked surprised, but I couldn't let it lie, not after my dreaming.

'I'm fine,' I said. 'I'll be off home now.' And I walked away before she could speak again.

I was exhausted when I got into bed, as if I'd been climbing cliffs not sitting under a circus tent. And perhaps it was because my body felt as if the skin had been peeled off, that I tried to have it out with Mary that night when she came in. I couldn't sleep, my thoughts rolling round like pebbles in the tug of tide, and I was on to her like a ferret, poor girl, when she came through the door, telling myself I was anxious for her, though I'd say now it was jealousy a bit, that she'd maybe had some of what I already knew I wanted with Thomas. She'd changed back into her ordinary clothes, but I could still smell the evening on her, her cologne mixed with cigar smoke, and I laid into her like I used to hear them talk on the quay of an evening.

'You didn't fool me, nor anybody else, Mary, with that outfit you were wearing. Your tits near to popping over, like a couple of little turnips, and anyway, I could see it wasn't made for you. It must have chafed you raw under the arms.'

Mary sat down on the bed and I thought she was going to blaze out. But she didn't speak in no more than a quiet voice.

'I used to wish I were a boy, Hal. Thought it'd be better to be wearing the britches than to be pulling up my skirts. And even after my fear came, even then I still wished. To be a boy in the boats facing the sea than at home with the women, mending and praying. Then I'd never have got afraid. But I wasn't a boy and I was afraid, so I just wrapped my wish around myself and held on to it. Until I first went into Mr Benbow's studio with you on that gloomy afternoon and my tummy rumbling with hunger and all those pictures on the wall.'

'And then what?' I said. 'You found there was something you could do that men couldn't, and that they'd pay you for it. That's it, isn't it, Mary? They're paying you. Is it for pictures, or is it more than that?'

I'd thought she might slap me when I said this, but she didn't. She looked at me like she was wondering how much to say, her fingers tugging at the frayed edge of the blanket.

'I like the photographs,' she said. 'And the studio. He's teaching me a lot, and not all like you'd imagine.'

Mary's calmness made my blood boil the worse, and I pulled the blanket out of her fingers and yelled at her.

'You don't know what I imagine, Mary Bourne. You've not a clue, because I never see you now, what with you spending all your time fancying yourself up for them with too many pennies and not enough bloody buttons on their trousers.'

'Is that what you think?' she said, still quiet, and now her quiet took the wind out of my sails. I didn't answer. She nodded, more to herself than to me. 'It is, isn't it,' and she shrugged. 'You're wrong, Hal. But let's not say it all out loud. There's Mrs O'Leary to think of,' she said, and tilted her head towards the wall.

Mary stood up and walked towards the window. She stood, facing me, her face falling in and out of the shadow of the candle.

'There's more to taking photographs than that shiny box,' she said. 'That's what Mr Benbow's showing me.'

'God, Mary,' I said, but she shook her head.

'I can't tell you, because it might never happen. You'll have to trust me on it. You used to say it about water. Don't you remember? How you'd love to catch it? The look of it, and you can't? But photographs catch things. And not just ladies as look like powder puffs and little boys in velvet. And not just girls in their dirt.'

I didn't know what she was on about, but I was too weary to go on any more.

'He paid me tonight,' she said.

'You mean the man in the waistcoat. Paid you to put his hands there, at the circus.'

'Yes.'

'And does he pay for your pictures too?'

'Yes. And it's all he gets.'

'More than enough,' I said.

'He gives as good as he gets,' Mary said, 'which is more than your bloody cocoa lot do.'

'They pay me for my work,' I said, 'and it's a fair wage.'

'I heard that they dock a penny from your wages every week to buy books for their bloody library. A penny! Whether you like it or not. You can't barely read, Hal, and I bet there's lots of other girls don't read at all, nor have any wish to. And then they come over all pious at the same time. Tell you it's for the good of your what?'

'Who told you that, anyway?'

Mary stretched back on the bed, so her head was right across my lap, her hair all stiff and smelling of something she'd put in earlier.

'Mr Benbow told me,' she said. 'It's true, ain't it?'

I stroked her sticky hair. 'Yes, but . . .'

Mary buried her face in the covers, and when she spoke, suddenly her voice sounded near to crying.

'Don't "but" me any more, Harriet. I'm too tired. Too tired with it all.'

We didn't neither of us say any more, but I helped her with her laces and brushing out her hair and then she slept and I watched over her and wondered how it was I'd fallen in love, and what would come of it, since I couldn't do a thing about it.

Thomas took to walking me to work, on the days when he hadn't to be there especially early. He'd be waiting at the end of my street, kicking a pebble, or, more likely, behind a book, for I quickly learned that he was a great reader. We'd have a little banter then, which got to be a habit.

'Well, fancy,' he'd say, 'good morning to you. D'you live in these parts?'

'And what's it to you?' I'd say.

'It might be owt and it might be nowt, but I'd heard there was a pretty girl, the sweetest thing hereabouts, and I was after walking her to her place of work.'

We'd carry on like that a while till one of us started laughing, and it were usually me. Then we'd set off at a brisk lick towards the river.

It was Mary pointed out he'd the same shape as the men back home. Stocky, strong-shouldered, though he'd only to lift a pen, not a net tumbling and weighty with fish. But I knew his shape very well without needing to be told it, even by Mary, and his eyes were like none I'd seen anywhere. Sometimes they'd seem near blue, but in the clear daylight of that first spring of ours they were green. Such a green, as put me in mind of I didn't know what. And he'd only to look at me, and me not thinking any particular thing, and there'd be this stab, low in my stomach, as if he'd hit me.

It seemed an odd thing, even in those first weeks, that I'd fallen so far and so fast for him, because he wasn't what I'd thought I'd fall for. For a start, he was older than me, it might have been five, it might have been ten years, I didn't know exactly till later. And then I'd thought I'd go for someone cheery, someone who'd have a laugh up his sleeve. But I'd gone for Thomas.

After a while, and no one else near along the river, I'd take his hand. Tug it out from his pocket and catch it between mine. It was a funny thing from the start with us, that he'd let me do things as he'd more likely knock another one down for, man or girl.

His hands were so soft. He'd calluses running along his fingers from the pen, but for the rest the skin was smooth. I'd lay it out, palm up, and make as if to read it. Long lines for life and for children, running my nail tip from his fingers to his wrist, making him groan sometimes, and then he'd seize my hand in his and lay his kisses on my fingers and I'd want him to eat them, take them in between his dry warm lips and never let them go.

We'd talk of anything those times. Of what we most liked about the winter, and what about the summer, of our favourite food and of our growing up. It was like I'd always done with Mary, and so different.

He'd a harder time to tell of, growing up on the streets from young and kept on the parish, so he said, but he didn't like to talk of it and always turned it to me, begging tales out of me till he knew the names of everyone I could think of back home and what I thought of them.

Sometimes we'd dream and talk of what we'd do if something happened like we found a sovereign on the ground. He'd a dream of travelling far, but my thinking didn't run further than my stomach.

'I'd have a feast in the summertime. Maybe in a field, or some big place, but not posh. And there'd be the longest tables, chairs, and starched white cloths on the tables and on the cloths, food. Beef and turkey and hams and suckling pig like in Mary's stories. And potatoes and beans and toma-toes . . .'

'And fish?'

I shook my head. 'No. No fish.'

So then Thomas and me were going steady. My first fellow and he'd turned out the one, no question. He wasn't the one I'd imagined, but now I'd met him, I couldn't think on anyone else.

But it shifted things a bit and not all of it were that easy because everybody else wasn't as pleased as me. Take Elsie. She went through men like sand. She'd pick them up and this time they'd be the one, it was love. They'd be out a few times and then she'd drop them. I'd ask her, 'What was it you didn't like?' and she'd shrug and tell me she didn't know and if I pressed her, she'd glare at me and give out it was his fingernails or that his hair was too straight, and I'd laugh.

'Too straight. I didn't know you'd a thing for curls,' but she didn't think that funny, telling me not to be so bloody smug and turning her back.

'I'm only having a laugh,' I'd say but she'd still huff and go on about it were all right for me with my clerk tucked into my skirts, but she'd be eighteen in October and still no fellow to call her own.

And then there was the problem with Mary, and that was that she'd a thing against Thomas.

'He's a hard one,' she'd tell me, 'he knows where he's headed and there's not a thing will stop him,' and I'd nod, because he was hard, with others. But not with me. Never with me.

'You're on his hook, a'n't you,' she said once. 'He can just pull you in, arm over arm, and you'll be there, your mouth open, lips caught, like some daft fish falling for our flithers.

'You've not felt it yet,' I answered her. 'Not felt what it's like. I can't help myself and I don't want to.' And she tossed her head and wouldn't speak.

But if it comes to that, he'd no great liking for her and so I'd hear it from the both of them about the other, till sometimes I'd clap my hands about my ears and hum, whichever of them it was.

'You're too much alike,' I'd say, and it was true, but it set them off again, till I held my tongue for the peace.

When Mary said she was moving out, I wasn't surprised. I'd been waiting for it. Her box had gone from under the bed the week before, the one she kept locked with a key in her bosom and thought I'd not noticed.

'I've a nice place offered,' she said

'Oh, ay,' I said, and the look she gave me. 'Will you be needing to give me the address or do I know it already?' I said.

'You know it, if you're not too grand to visit,' she said.

'You'll not be rid of me that easy,' I said.

For a bit then, in the last days, she got to being kind to everybody. I'd never thought she'd a place for guilt, but that was what it was. There were sweets for the children and butter and chocolates for Mrs O'Leary. Wetherby's Best Creams in a fancy box with flowers painted. We had a laugh as it might have been me as packed them. But the smell of them had me out of there. It was enough to live in at work, but my stomach turned over in Mrs O'Leary's kitchen.

Mary even brought back a bottle of sweet wine one night for which we'd no way to get the cork out but to break it on the step and some of the wine spill like blood. I'd no taste for beer, but I was drunk as a lord on the wine and swearing sweet nothings.

She told me I'd better be smartish round to her new rooms, she'd not speak to me else, and I asked did she think as they'd let me in and she answered she was her own master and she'd let in whoever she chose and I looked at her and she stared back at me.

So I said, 'Just so long as you know, then.'

And she said, 'I do, Hal, but don't go far off will you?'

And I told her it was only the wine giving her this mouth and anyway she was the one going.

'Needs must,' she said, and I said, 'Well, needs didn't have to before, did they, and why are you?' because I couldn't go on pretending I didn't care.

It was a hot evening and we were just in our slips and the bed was like our boat, with her one end and me the other. The street was quiet, it being that hour after the children were in and before the pubs shut up.

'He's not asked you to marry him then?' I said. Mary wasn't properly listening. She'd an itch and she was flapping about like a fish out of water to reach it, bending her arm like an acrobat to reach down her back.

'Sit still and I'll ease it for you,' I said. The skin between her shoulder blades was smooth and pale. I tried again with my question. 'Mr Benbow, he's not asked you to marry him?' and I thought of the man at the circus, the one as had his arm round her, like she was his. But I'd never said a word on him, and nor had she.

She laughed then. 'Mr Benbow? Oh no, he's not like that,' she said.

'Have I got the itch?' I asked. She nodded and I lay down on the bed, stared at the ceiling. The plaster was loose and in places I could see the laths above, like so many ribs. 'So what is he to you then? Is he just your boss?'

'Your feet are dirty,' she said and she took my big toe between her fingers. 'This little piggy went to market, and this little piggy stayed at home, and you'll never eat roast beef if you don't wash your feet and you'll never get home.'

'You don't want to go home,' I said.

'No,' she said and she squeezed my toe tight. 'No, I don't. And Mr Benbow. You don't know the half of him, Hal,' and I yelled out because she was hurting my toe. 'He'll likely do more good than a hundred of your po-faced cocoa-mongers, and he's taught me a lot about picture taking,' and she started on about light and shade, till I told her it was dull chat.

'It'll be your own fault if you don't see where I'm off to,' she said, 'if you'll not listen to me telling you,' but I said I couldn't see what shadows had to do with who she'd marry in the end.

'I'll change the subject then,' Mary said. 'Did you know he's all for ladies having the suffrage,' and she nodded her head sharp as if it was meant to settle something, except it didn't because I didn't know what she was talking of.

'What's suffrage when it's at home then?' I said.

Mary gave a yelp that was a laugh. 'It's voting, for the government. He thinks ladies should be able to do it like the men do.'

She was that solemn I couldn't help myself. 'They'll never do it like the men, Mary. They've not got all the bits.'

We near enough had an argument over it, and all beneath our breath on account of Mrs O'Leary asleep and the walls being so thin you could hear breathe near enough. It wasn't that I doubted her, but I didn't like Mr Benbow; hadn't liked him from that first afternoon in his studio. He was out for something with Mary and not the saving of her soul and she knew it but she wasn't telling me what.

'So it's on account of his do-gooding he wants you living in his studio, is it?' I said, and pulled my feet away and sat up, the bedstead cold and hard against my back. 'Come on, Mary, give me some credit.'

'There's a lot you don't know goes on there,' she said, 'and at least Mr Benbow knows what he's doing and he doesn't say it's otherwise. And he's got high hopes for me. He told me so.'

'I don't want to know,' I said.

'Not like some, not pretending. Not like your lot, getting your Thomas to do all the dirty work and not another penny in it for him. He might be making it out in his head, how he'll get the last inch and not them, but till then he's clerk and bloody doormat to those Wetherbys. Have you asked him about that? Mr Benbow's a good teacher. And at least he pays me my dues.'

I was in that much of a rage I thought I'd burst, and it was the worst thing I could think of that I said to her.

'And Jamie?' I said. 'What about Jamie?' I said. 'Going to tell him, are you? When you go back, all flush and doing everything for him. You going to tell him where it all came from?'

I wished I hadn't said it. The moment it was out I wished I hadn't and I'd have given over anything to take it back. Mary didn't speak, but something happened to her body, something like they'd taken all the bones out. She went soft and her shoulders curved down and her arms covered her belly as if she'd got a terrible wound. She didn't speak, but she looked at me and I didn't know what to look back. I hadn't anything I could look and I hadn't anything I could say.

He was the only one to get it that summer, which some in the village thought a miracle. He was a wee lad before, only four or five years old, but after the sickness he looked smaller. We weren't friends then, Mary and me, and I'd no notion of what it meant, that her brother Jamie had had the polio. He hadn't died from it, there'd been no small coffin and all the mothers with their lips set so and the men quiet in the pub, so he must be better, like my brother had been better from the measles after the time of my mam and dad being so worried. But he wasn't, nor ever would be.

Jamie's dad wasn't like mine. He was kind enough, though here was a son was never going to lay a line or stand him a pint after a good haul. He treated the boy like a thing that's to be coddled, like a pet, and never made mention of him to the other men, not even in his cups. But their mam was a different piece. She hated Jamie and if it hadn't been for Mary, the little lad wouldn't have lived out his first year after the illness.

They made a cart up for him, Mary and her older brother Ned. And one of them would pull it down the lane and along to the sea-break and he'd like to sit there and watch the sea, or sometimes in the summer they'd leave the cart propped where the women were mending the nets or so as he could watch the boats come in.

Ned was near enough grown and he was soon in the boats, so then, until she'd to go out flithering, it was down to Mary. We'd hear them coming first, the metal wheels dinning on the cobbles. Then there'd be Mary, tugging at her bit of rope, and then the cart and Jamie. He'd be sat all bundled up, even in the sun, one scrawny hand on the edge to steady himself, and each time I saw him I couldn't help but stare. The hump was that big on his little back, you could see it even with the blanket, and how his head looked to be stuck on to his shoulders odd.

All of him would be covered except his head and his hands which were shrivelled. Not shrivelled like my nan's hands which were grown lumpy now, though she still kept on with the knitting, and with the skin loose and brown marks on them the size of buttons, but shrivelled just as if somebody had sucked all the flesh out from the inside and robbed them of their colour, or sometimes left them a bit blue. And often

Mary, when they'd stopped, would take his hands between hers and hold them there and she'd have her head leaned close to his and she'd be whispering and he'd maybe smile or laugh.

Their mam couldn't stand it. Some said it was Jamie drove her to the drink, but Mary said she was at it before he was sick and all the sickness did was give her an excuse. She used to wallop Mary, and even Ned before he was too big, but she never seemed to hit Jamie. Maybe she feared it would kill him and then there'd be hell to pay – but she hated him every other way she could.

Often Mary would bring him to school and have him sit near to the stove and do some drawing, or just watch. It wasn't his brain was affected, but the teacher never tried to do owt with him and it was Mary taught him his letters. But sometimes their mam would keep him in – Mary said it was to punish her – and she'd come to school with her face sharp. It never did to cross her, but those times were the worst, for even then she'd a tongue could whip a cut quicker than any.

And when she was on to leave and come to the city and we were decided, Jamie it was that made Mary's going hard.

He must have been maybe twelve by now but he was still a tiny fellow and with his hump and his legs. He could haul himself about their place, but he could no more go out alone than he could fly. But if his body were so stumped and stooped, his face made up for it. It was sad to think such lovely eyes and such a handsome look, and hair black as coal and shiny like water on stone, were never going to get themselves a girl of their own.

One time I came looking for Mary and she was out. But her mam called me in and when I said I'd best be back home, pulled me on the arm till I'd no choice. So I stood across the room from her, and there was Jamie in a corner, half-leaning, half-crouching by the wall. She leant one arm on a chair to keep herself up and the chair screamed on the stone flags as it slid with the weight. 'Would you ever look at it,' she said and the air was strong to breathe even across the room, and she was pointing at Jamie. She spat at him then and I must have gasped or something, because she turned on me.

'Well, you take heed, girl and when you're grown don't let nothing cling on,' and she flung her arm at the poor boy away in the corner. 'Else it'll drag at you and take your life. Like this thing,' and she was maybe about to say more, or do more, when Mary came in.

Jamie never said a word, never lifted his head even, till he heard his sister. She saw us there and she knew, but she didn't speak to her mother, didn't even look at her. Just crossed the room and picked Jamie up in her strong arms and carried him out, and me following and her mother left in the kitchen and crying and her face flushed and her arm out for the jug.

Jamie wouldn't cry these times, but his face was like he'd gone away. There was nothing there and so Mary would have to bring him back. She'd a special voice and she'd coax him and tease him till he'd cry maybe, or laugh, and her with him.

She didn't tell him she was going, but he knew. She'd eggs for the train, a secret, but when she unwrapped them, there was a piece of paper with writing on it half-stuck to one, like someone had licked it and tamped it on. Mary picked it off and read it. She kept her eyes down, wouldn't look up. 'How'd he know?' she said and her voice was tiny, 'how'd he know?'

It was that piece of paper went with her everywhere, like the mark of a promise she had in her head, and maybe she thought Mr Benbow could help her with it, but I knew she was wrong.

The Monday I was called upstairs, the day was warm before we'd even got to work. We'd be dripping sweat into the Raspberry Creams by dinnertime.

Second Day assemblies – that was what he called Mondays – Mr William was in the habit of making a moral about new leaves or wise virgins. Something about the start of the week got him going. He reminded me of Mr Ransome these times, so maybe it was their funny religion, or maybe it was their family. I'd nudge Elsie when it got too daft. 'Here he goes,' I'd say and the bellies'd be growling and gurgling all about us, so loud it seemed a wonder Mr William didn't call for quiet, and the best thing was to find something else to do.

The girls did all sorts. Anna, who was in the Creams with me, would spend the time looking across at the men. She'd a list going and numbers one to ten and if you asked, she'd tell you. Elsie said she couldn't think the list was much use with Anna the plainest piece of pudding you ever saw.

There was another girl whose name I forget was knitting socks. She'd to do it under her apron and without Mrs Flint seeing, which seemed folly. But she never got caught. And another girl would catch a nap. There was a way she had, keeping her head tilted down like she were being especially holy. Elsie and me, we'd play water/scissors/paper, or I-spy.

Anyway, I remember what Mr William was saying that day because of what happened after. He was stood there like a post in his black clothes and saying the words like they were written for us lot sitting there, bleary-eyed, on a Monday morning in York.

It was already a hot day, as I said, but not so hot as to make a man's brow wet, not unless that man were busy about some hard labour. But Mr William, he was only reading from a book and he was dripping. Usually his voice was calm, smooth like a millpond. Today it had a shake.

'His Lord said unto him, Well done, good and faithful servant; thou hast been faithful over a few things, I will make thee ruler over many things: enter thou into the joy of thy Lord.' He wasn't coloured in the face, paler if anything than usual, and wiping his brow often and his handkerchief limp so you could've wrung it out. 'For unto every one that hath shall be given, and he shall have abundance: but from him that hath not shall be taken away even that which he hath.'

When he was done he nodded at us like he'd told us something we needed to know, and then he gave out his favourite words.

'Whatever thy hand findeth to do, do it with all thy might,' he said and so it was over and he was off the platform and out even before they'd our doors unlocked.

'Something's up,' I said.

'Well, anything'd be better than Mrs Flint on a Monday,' Elsie said.

It was an hour after and by the time the man found me, he was in a fluster.

'I've been bloody searching for you. Told you were a Creams girl but you weren't in there and they sent me to the Cocoa packing and that cow . . .'

'Mrs Flint,' I said.

'Good name for her. Anyway she wouldn't . . .'

'Well, you've got me now,' I said. 'What do you want?'

'It's not what I want, it's them upstairs as is doing the wanting and we'd best get a leg on it.'

He'd found me in the raspberries. I was still properly in the Creams Room, but they'd too many raspberries. Two weeks before it'd been strawberries, now it was raspberries. They hadn't thought to have so many so soon, but what with the sun there'd been these last weeks, there was more picked than they could manage and if they weren't sorted quick, they'd be rotted. So extra girls had been called in from other rooms to sort the fruit.

'Whoever wants a change from Creams, put up your hand,' they said, and a heap of us did, 'but if you don't like bugs, put it down,' and there were only four of us left. I wondered what the rest did at home when the bugs came down off the ceilings and out of the walls, like they did at Mrs O'Leary's.

The raspberries were for pastilles. And the strawberries, and cranberries and blackberries and redcurrants and blackcurrants. They'd even made elderberry flavour and orange marmalade flavour and Elsie told me last year they'd done tomato. We were sat at a long table, a line of us each side, all hands washed and ready and waiting for the fruit. Top and bottom of the table was a set of scales and an overlooker. After we'd sat some minutes, and in silence, lads brought in big baskets of fruit, and though it were something so different, I saw like a picture in front of the eyes the men back home lifting out the boxes of herrings all flashing silver and us waiting at the quay with our knives to scrape and salt them, and I could smell the fish and feel the cling of the fish scales.

The baskets were set one upon the other and we'd to line up and with a great metal scoop they'd fill each of us a tray to set before us on the table for the picking.

The room was gloomy, but the raspberries seemed to draw the light. They gleamed, and from them came this sweet smell, but so different from the turning sweetness of the Creams. We'd to rummage through the raspberries with our fingers and not bruise them, and pick out the bugs and the rotten fruit and drop them into a pot, and not eat a single berry or the overlookers would be on us. They were watching for any hand that made for the mouth, listening for any talk started.

Our fingers were stained red in moments, and rough and sticky with the bits and juice. It was like a torture not to lick them clean. Pretty soon the bugs were crawling out of the pots and so we had to squash them first, but that made a mess of the trays, or flick them back in as they were perched and wondering where to go next on the lip of the pot.

So when the man came for me, first I'd to wash up and straighten myself, though even after I'd scrubbed them, my fingers were stained pink and my nails scratchy with the hairs.

He took me up several flights of stairs to the door of a room and then, with a nod, he left me. There were men's voices inside, one Mr William's. I knocked, but nobody answered. I knocked harder. The voices were arguing. They hadn't heard me. I couldn't go in and I didn't like to hit the door again, but I couldn't return to the raspberries either. So I waited, and listened to the argument.

'But flowers have always worked fine,' a voice was saying. 'And alpine scenes, or kittens, or even children with hoops, or . . .'

'And they still will.' That was Mr William's voice. 'We're not getting rid of any children with hoops. But the times are changing and if we don't swim on top of the wave, we'll sink beneath it. Plenty of cocoa firms are going bust.'

'But sometimes it's better not to be right at the front. There are several I could name as good Quakers got their fingers more than a little burnt over the railways not so many years back,' said the first voice.

Mr William gave a snort. 'They were fortunate not to go down with Mr Hudson. They were fortunate not to be disowned. But this is quite different. There's nothing wrong with putting the picture of a girl on a chocolate box. Or a box of pastilles, because we'll have them out next, and surprise all the rest.'

'A pretty girl,' said the first voice. 'A real girl.'

'Well, there wouldn't be much point in putting on an ugly one,' said Mr William.

'Nobody else is doing it.'

'Nobody else in England can make cocoa like us now. We're the only ones can put on the posters, "Alkalised and Free from Adulteration", or the only ones audacious enough to, and we must be sure to put it in big letters.'

'They're long words for a poster.'

'That's the point.'

'As long as they can read it.'

'They can always look at the picture.'

'Could we not come up with something a bit more appealing?'

'That's what the girl is for. Look, it's your business to make the chocolates, and it's my business to sell them. That means knowing what everybody else is going to be selling, and knowing how our products sell best. I have Thomas . . .' Mr William's voice was rising and falling now, and I guessed he must be pacing about, for the words, just when I most needed to hear, were getting lost.

Thomas! I had my ear to the door but the other voice interrupted him.

'Don't tell me,' it said. 'I'd rather be in the dark. Only tell me that you're doing nothing you'd not be prepared to tell of in Meeting,' it said.

'Caleb, the sooner you're back in your laboratory the better, and let me see to my own conscience. Now, here's the dress for the tasting, the guests will arrive inside the hour, and I have the girl being brought up from downstairs.'

I took this for my signal. So I put my fist to the door again and fair hammered it. Now they heard me and Mr William called out, 'Come.'

Elsie had taught me how to curtsy. She'd learnt to when she were in service, which she'd stuck at a year, it being what her mother had done till she married, and then she'd given it up as a bad lot. So when I'd shut the door, I curtsied like she'd shown me.

On one side of the room was a table with a dress laid out like a dark ghost. Next to it were a collar and a pinny, all white, and something that must be a cap, heaped and flounced.

On the other side of the room was Mr Caleb, though he didn't see me at first. He'd his back to the door, fiddling with something on a high sideboard. But Mr William gave me a smile. 'Caleb, here is Harriet,' he said.

Mr Caleb turned towards me, his eyes going first to my feet and then slowly travelling upwards.

He was a small man with a round face and spectacles and dark hair that grew from his head in tight curls. He bore little resemblance I could see to Mr William except in a nervous movement both had, which was the tapping of a finger. Where Mr William was dressed in his usual dark suit, Mr Caleb wore a white coat reaching about to his knees and covered with marks and spills. His trousers looked dusty and his shoes scuffed. All this I saw in the time it took him to look from my feet to my head.

He looked astonished when he saw my face, and turned and looked at Mr William, and Mr William nodded to him. All this had me mystified. But then he looked at me again and held out his hand.

'Thank you for coming, Harriet,' he said. 'Please excuse me, for a moment I thought you someone else.' So we shook hands, which I looked forward to telling Elsie of.

'Pink fingers,' he said, pointing.

'Raspberries, sir' I said and he nodded. 'Ah yes.' He pulled a chair over from the side of the room, and made a sign to me to sit.

Mr William did the talking. Mr Caleb got himself comfy, leaned against the sideboard, fiddled with the urn of water set there, and listened. Once or twice he looked to be about to say something, but then he seemed to think better of it.

'Harriet, it is time for you to perform the first part of the task I mentioned earlier in the year. Do you remember?'

I nodded.

'The photographic task, sir' I said.

'That is part of the larger plan, and we will explain it to you later, when it is necessary to do so. But for now,' he pointed to the dress, 'we'd like you to act as waitress. Some gentlemen will be here shortly to taste cocoa and it would be appropriate if a female performed the honours with the jug.'

There was nothing needed saying, so I nodded again. Mr William was picking up the dress, when Mr Caleb spoke.

'We're assuming you have tasted our cocoa?' he said, looking from me to Mr William. I shook my head and he frowned. 'It's not right for her to act the hostess if she's never tasted the cocoa, William,' he said. Then he turned to me. 'You must have a cup before everyone arrives. A hostess must be able to vouch for her pot.' He turned to Mr William. 'Thomas could have it ready for when she's changed.'

'I'll call him,' Mr William said, and he handed me the dress, then left the room.

'How long have you worked here for?' Mr Caleb asked me.

'Seven months or so,' I said.

'And is it for reasons of taste that you have never tasted Wetherby's cocoa?'

'No, money. I can't afford it,' I said, and not wanting to sound complaining, added, 'But that's quite usual. Not so many of the girls have, unless they've a sweetheart with a fuller pocket.'

'And have you a sweetheart?' Mr Caleb said. I didn't want them to know it was Thomas, and besides it wasn't their business, so I ducked my head and pretended to be shy.

I got the dress on fine. I even managed the hooks and eyes by myself, like one of those contortionists with my arms twisted under and round and over. And I could do the pinny and the collar. But the cap. I'd never seen its like before and it had me floundered. I opened the door to let them know I was done and Mr Caleb was the first back. He looked me up and down.

'Good. And the cap?'

'I can't manage it by myself. I'll need somebody else to pin it.'

He looked behind him and gave a little nod. 'Well, I'll do it, but promise not to tell my brother. He'd not approve.' So Mr Caleb pinned it for me and only a moment after Mr William came in and carrying a steaming cup of cocoa.

If only Mary were here, I thought then. To see these two, one pinning on my cap and the other bringing me cocoa. She'll not believe me when I tell her. And then I remembered she wasn't coming home to ours any more and my spirits fell a little.

I wasn't looking forward to the cocoa that much, because I'd had enough of the smell, what with working in the thick of it these months. But the taste made me feel different. It wasn't like any other drinks I'd had, not like tea, nor even like coffee, which I'd tried once. It was thick on my tongue and a bit gritty in my throat, but so sweet I wished I could have held it there for longer, like pleasure made into something liquid. It had been in my nostrils for so long that sometimes I'd almost thought I'd tasted it, but now I knew that the smell was nothing like, compared with the feel of it in my mouth.

Mr Caleb's voice made me start. He was laughing. 'She'll do very well for the pictures, won't she William. Just feed her a cup of cocoa and get Benbow snapping.'

Mr Benbow's name made me start, but then Thomas came in to announce that the first of the guests was here and I forgot about it. Thomas gave me a little look, his mouth tweaked in a smile, and he busied himself bringing in chairs and checking the urn, which had begun to steam.

It was Thomas they asked to show me what I was to do.

There was a starched cloth with 'Wetherby's' made out in red thread, to go over the counter, and ten cups were to be laid out on top. Each was to have an exact measure of cocoa powder and I was to be weighing this out, using the scales and the small lead weight he showed me, while the guests were arriving. When Mr William gave the signal, I was to measure the hot water into the small jug, exactly so much, and then fill each cup. Put a teaspoon, stood up, in each one, set it on a saucer, and bob's your uncle.

After they'd taken several sips – these sips were the proper 'tasters' – then the guests would add sugar, each to his own. And they'd probably take refills and here I was to be sure and give them a fresh cup and saucer or else the cocoa residue from the first would unbalance the measure of cocoa in the second.

'Did you used to do this job?' I asked him. He nodded. 'Bet you didn't have to wear the cap,' I said and he smiled. Then he stood himself opposite the cocoa table, hands behind his back, and watched me.

It was just the same as playing mother with the tea, only with a bit more care as to the measuring. Back home, Mam would make up the tea in Dad's pint pot and he'd drink it and she'd take the last part. Then she'd wash the leaves over for a second brew and that'd be our chance, though it were little more than coloured water by then.

I stood there as the guests came in, all men in heavy suits, and I made them their cocoa, and I watched as they slurped and gurgled and said important things to Mr William, who nodded, and to Mr Caleb, who wrote things in a big green book. They all took a second cup and most a third. Finally, with much taking out of watches from waistcoats and grave nodding, they left.

'You can change,' Mr William said, 'and Thomas will return you to the raspberries. The costume was adequate, I think,' he added, turning to Mr Caleb.

'The costume was adequate,' Mr Caleb said, nodding, 'and the girl was more than adequate.' He winked at me. 'Thank you, Harriet. We'll keep the caps simple if we can in the future, eh?' And the brothers left the room.

SAMUEL

It had been three years since Father first took me to the tannery. Each fifth day, instead of making my walk to school, I would put on the trousers and coarse shirt and clogs and accompany him there. And still each fifth day I would spend the time hunched over a bucket because of my sensitive stomach, for that was how Father referred to it, rebelling in the only way it knew at the foul odours that assaulted me.

Perhaps it was because I had started to grow, or maybe my constitution was already wearied by the weekly assault, but sometime halfway through my thirteenth year these visits began to leave me unwell. I was not able to shake off the tannery smells and sights from my person and would often find myself incapacitated for two or even three days afterwards, obliged to stay home from school. I am quite a large-boned man today, full-fleshed, but when I was thirteen, with my aetiolated limbs and pale complexion, I resembled more some

plant left too long in the dark, which reaches with all its
energy towards the light. And my visits to the tannery merely
exacerbated this.

One fifth day I had only just seated myself at the breakfast table, dressed in my tannery clothes, when Mother came
in.

'He is not going,' she said. 'He is not going today, nor any
other day.'

Father had the appearance of one who has had the wind
knocked from him, and in the first silence after Mother's
words it was only Grace who ventured to speak.

'Then may I go?' she said. 'I have not Samuel's constitution.'

Mother pursed her lips at this, and Father was able only to
shake his head. As for me, I was unsure whether I felt elation
or despair, for I knew too well how much rested for both my
parents upon my visits to the tannery.

'Our son is not thriving,' Mother went on, much as if I'd
been one of her special plants, 'and the cause is clear.'

'But he will inherit the tannery,' my father said. 'It is an
honest business and he must—'

Mother interrupted. 'He must grow into manhood with a
sound constitution,' she said, and she picked a piece of toast
from the rack, as if this put an end to the discussion.

It was this that at last provoked Father to anger, and though
I hated my visits to the tannery with every fibre of my being,
my sympathies were with him.

'I think perhaps you do not understand,' he said. 'The
tannery is Samuel's future, and his past. And Grace's. It's the
family business; it's what we live off. You may not like it but
all this,' and he gestured to us, to the room, to the toast rack
and silver teapot, to the furniture, 'all this comes from my
stinking tannery. And if it hadn't been for Ransome's tannery,
you wouldn't have become my wife, Quaker or no. It is what

I have to bequeath. And it must be properly managed to thrive.'

I had never heard Father raise his voice before, never heard him angry with even the maids, and certainly never with Mother. I was scared, but she seemed unperturbed.

'Well, then you must train a manager,' she said, 'for it will not be Samuel who does the managing. And as for what you have to bequeath . . .' She left the sentence unfinished, an accusation, and stood up and left.

The three of us remaining sat in silence, till Grace, with her characteristic and terrifying audacity, reached across the corner of the table and picked up Mother's untouched square of toast.

'Don't know how Mother does on so little,' she said and buttered and ate it and left the room. Father was too crushed to rebuke her, and after a little he too rose. I made as if to rise with him, but he gestured me down. Mother had won and I would never again wear my tannery clothes.

I sat on at the table, unsure what to do, till Grace, my elfin sister, returned. She was elfin not in her size, for she had become a tall girl, her arms and hands and legs made strong in all her play out of doors, but in her gestures. And this by contrast with our mother, whose body was of such small proportion, but whose movements had a gravitas that often scared me when I was young.

Grace took me by the hand and led me from the table, leaving the breakfast silver and crockery, the cold litter of my parents' argument, for the maids to remove and wash ready for tomorrow's breakfast.

'Come and see, Sam,' Grace said and made me smile. This was her way and she tugged my fingers just as she had when she was barely more than a baby. We walked together into the garden and she took me far down, where I had not been for many months, and we sat together on the branch of an old cedar tree.

'But you know that Mother has me now,' I said, and neither of us made any reply.

If I were to say that Harriet Brewer became my muse, it would be to speak the truth. But I never set her up, like the Israelites and the golden calf, to replace my God. Only, for me, she made His glory shine brighter. Still, I knew that if the Elders were ever to learn of my preoccupation, that it would go very hard with me, whatever the truth. And the truth was, that my meeting with Harriet and the events after came not out of a sudden infatuation, or any infamous wish on my part, but out of a long and carefully nurtured affection. Or perhaps I should say a curiosity which had its roots far back, beginning with all those butterfly wings, so carefully staked, and the camera Father gave me on my fourteenth birthday.

The camera was more than Father's birthday gift. In some small way it was his revenge. I had not been to the tannery in over seven months, and though my health had improved, Mother had had me pronounced delicate by one of her tame doctors.

'I am sorry but you will never be able to return to that place,' she told me when the doctor had gone, and though at that time I believed my mother to be a good Quaker woman, whose first thought was the best interests of others, the shine in her eyes made me shiver.

Father gave me the camera because it was something I wished for beyond anything. I did not speak of it like that. Such worldly desire was not encouraged. But he knew of it anyway. So on the afternoon of my fourteenth birthday Father came early home and as I finished my tea, he instructed me to accompany him.

We went up the stairs, with Grace close behind us, to the door of a room at the far end of the corridor, a small room visited, I thought, only by the maids. Here he gave me a letter, my name and the date written in his own hand, and told me to put it away and read it later, in the privacy of my bed-room. Then he inclined his head towards the door.

'Open it,' he said, and, wondering, I did so.

There was a gas lamp already lit inside, the carpet beaters and cloths and dusters were gone and shining in the gas glow was a camera. It stood almost at my chest height on a tripod of spidery black legs, a beautiful burnished box with a glowing circle of brass which was its lens, its eye. I circled round it, not touching it, just looking.

'Pick it up, Samuel. It's not fastened to the tripod,' said my father.

So I lifted it off and held it in my hands, feeling its weight, its substance.

'It's a stand camera,' my father said. 'It needs its tripod. But you must become familiar with it. Used to handling it.'

'You could take a picture now, Sam' Grace said. 'Now. It's all ready, Father said.' She pointed to the tripod. 'And you can make the legs longer or shorter. We just did it about where we thought.' She was almost hopping with excitement, like she used to when she was smaller and needed to be excused.

I replaced the camera on the stand.

'I can't believe it,' I said.

Father cut me off and I saw, as he went on talking, that his eyes were very bright and the words were a way of keeping his feelings down.

'It's loaded with a magazine of twelve glass plates,' he said. 'And when they're all used, you can take the camera to the chemist and develop them. He has a dark room there, and by the time you're ready to do so, I expect you will have learned all you need of how to use it. You can use the dark room free of charge, as long as you purchase your next box of glass plates from him.'

He went on talking, telling me practical details, things I would need to know, but I think I took little of it in. He gave me a book too, the *Novice's Handbook to Practical Photography* by G.P. Burnshaw, and later I found all I needed to know in this.

Perhaps I should have known what Mother would think. After all Grace knew, and she was three years younger. And Father knew, and perhaps that is why he gave me one so young. But as for me, I was so captivated, it did not occur to me that anyone would gainsay my wonder. Mother detested it, my magic box, and so Father had his little victory.

It was only much later that evening, when I was preparing myself for sleep, that I remembered Father's letter. Retrieving it from the mantelpiece, I opened it and read.

My darling boy

I give thee today my fondest exhortations, so that together with the gift of science might come the gift of moral encouragement.

The age thou has come to has its own peculiar temptations. New impulses, passions and strong currents of feeling are gifts of the Lord as thou draws closer to manhood. But thou must resist the natural longing of the impure imagination and defend thyself from self-pollution just as a man might armour himself for war, if thou wilt allow the comparison. Words cannot convey to thee how fiercely thou must flee from it as from the fangs of a deadly serpent. I have known those brought to an early grave by such indulgence, and others in which it has induced insanity, enfeeblement and confusion of the brain.

When temptation arises, do not tamper with it, or it will overcome thee like a poisonous vapour. Instead strive to turn thy mind from it. Resist the devil and he

will flee from thee. Trust in the Lord who knows our
infirmities and temptations, for he will deliver thee
from evil.

This is the deepest wish of thy tenderly attached
father,

David Ransome

Had my father already guessed that in the months to come
it would be as a defence against such temptation that I would
hold my camera out? Could he see the dangers that this
instrument of science was both drawing me into and protect-
ing me from? I knew how much it had cost Father to write
such a letter of exhortation, and I prayed to God that night
that I would be able to vindicate his trust.

Maybe it was because she was so little in the company of other
children that Grace never learnt the difference between play
and other things. I never thought of it like this when we were
young. But where I had my cousin William, and then my
younger cousin Caleb for company, Grace had no one. Or
only me. Mother would not permit her to attend school as I
was doing, and disciplined her severely when she was found
once playing I-spy with a chambermaid. And our household
took no part in the boisterous gatherings and hospitalities
that surrounded the Quaker calendar. We never had visiting
Friends to stay, and never went visiting ourselves. Father
seldom attended Quarterly Meeting and though I believe he
would have enjoyed the company of other men, Mother did
not allow it. She herself had no need, it seemed, for the society of other women and her family, by extension, she deemed
to be the same.

When I showed Grace the photograph I had taken of her,
my first portrait, she said, 'But where is she?' and I, not understanding the question, responded with a laugh and some clever

remark, about mimesis or some notion of the philosophers. In the photograph, Grace was seated on a chair beneath the cedar tree, but barely seated, as if at any moment she might run away. She held a flower in one hand, and the other rested on the chair arm, palm upwards, as though someone else was about to place their own hand in hers. Her head was turned slightly and her expression was serious and expectant. I remember as though it was yesterday Grace's next words. She took hold of the photograph and walked to the window to see it better, for the day was dark with rain, and held it close up to her eyes. And then, bewildered, she put it down and looked at me.

'What have you done with her, Sam?' she asked.

'It is you,' I answered. 'And that is the cedar tree. Do you not think it a fair likeness?'

'But where is Fern?'

'Fern?'

'She was seated beside me. I had my hand in hers.' She looked at me, waiting for my agreement.

'There was no one to sit beside you,' I said.

Still Grace shook her head and would not take the picture, but got up on the sudden and walked from my room. Through my window I saw her, striding down the garden, no coat or hat against the elements and I knew then, though I hadn't the words for it, that in her distress she had trusted me with something, or someone, and that I must be careful of that.

Mother hated to have her image taken and so there exists in our house only one painted portrait of her. It was made of the two of them when they were first married. She never would allow another. She sits in plain Quaker dress, severe in the beauty of her youth, her fingers white-knuckled on her knees, her eyes angry, though I am sure the artist tried to soften them, and through our childhood this portrait hung in the darkest region of the hall.

Mother never came to see my magic box. If I took it outside into the garden and she were seeing to her flowers, she would immediately come inside, sometimes even raising a hand to keep my camera from her sight. And, as with the painting, she allowed me to take her photograph only once. She looks sternly at the camera, a finger on one page of an open Bible as though to press home some injunction. Father holds a smaller book in his hand, which I remember to have been the novel *John Halifax, Gentleman.* His book is closed but he has a finger between its pages, though he had never read a word of it, only borrowed it from my shelves for appearance sake.

For a while I tried to interest Mother in my photographs of flowers and butterflies. But even these she would not look at.

'What need hast thou to look at the image, when we have the thing itself?' she would say, her arms down by her sides. And though by now I was taller by some eight or ten inches, in her severe black dress and her hair tightly pinned so not a strand might have the chance of escape, still her voice sent my stomach to my boots. I knew then, as I do now, that her philosophy was specious, drawn only from her own fears, and yet I would not, for anything, disagree with her.

My mother was no tyrant, at least not in her intentions. She acted, I believe, more out of fear than anger and yet this fear was of the sort to scorch, and finally it was Grace who was burnt.

It is a stern thing to discover that one's own deepest preoccupation leaves the next person cold. I have never spoken to William of mine, but have known since I was fourteen that something most dear to my heart had no place in his.

I made my morning walk to school alone. Invariably I had tasks uncompleted in the morning, scriptures not learnt, lessons not done, and rushing to complete these, would still have to leave home at something of a half-run, with time only to avoid the grocers' carts, already laden, or the milkgirls, their shiny pails swinging light and empty on their broad shoulders, their strong arms hanging over the yoke, their hands free. I loved to pass these girls, and yet it was folly for me to watch them too closely, for I am not nimble. With my eyes else-where, I easily lost my step on the treacherous cobbles and I frequently stumbled, and once fell. Then their laughs followed me down the street, making my ears burn red.

But if my journey to school was a hurried affair, the return home was different. I had used to walk home with William, who lived near to me, but he had started his apprenticeship this year so I was free now to be alone. This had recently become a vital thing because I had discovered, to take the place of the butterflies in their satin colours, the wonderful array of women at large in the city. Not the women in fine dresses, against whom Father warned me at so young an age I was nonplussed, nor those like Mother who believed the world owed them no pleasures, but working women.

There was a first time and if I close my eyes I can bring it back, though still to this day I am not certain which street it was that I took. I had left the school late, being busy about some experiment with plants or insects. It was late April and though the hour must have been close to six, there was still considerable light and warmth in the day and I took my way slowly. I was walking, I cannot imagine why, in the near vicin-ity of the Minster. I say I cannot imagine, but it must be simply that my present feeling for the building began further back than I was aware. I recall one boy at school telling with pride how he had stood in the nave of the great building delib-erately keeping on his cap. This after a verger, as I think you call him, had asked the boy to remove it.

'God does not look to our caps to meet our souls,' he told us, and we all agreed, grinning and laughing. Other boys tried out the same thing in the week after and regaled us with their tales, until the story dulled. And though I had laughed with the rest on the first telling, afterwards I did not wish to, but made my own visit to the Minster and doffed my cap at the door. Who is to say that God may not be found in the beauty of those great stones, piled high to His glory, as much as in the stillness of the Quaker heart.

'Besides, so long as you look halfway covered, it's a grand place to escape the weather,' a working-class girl once told me, and I love this too about the place. No respecter of good souls, it is there for the world and its wife. But perhaps I am prone to sentimentality over other men's religions, though I have none about my own.

I found myself that day in the Bedern, a quarter of the city which, though it lies close by the Minster, I then knew nothing of. It is a poor quarter, one of the poorest, the tenements stacked high and close, narrow alleys running into dank yards where families must live heaped upon one another in squalor too horrid to imagine. That day I saw little of this, however. I had had no acquaintance with poverty, and, as I have discovered, one must know what one is looking at to recognize it.

What I did see that day was a girl. I can't be sure of her face any more, but it isn't important. She must have been about my own age, maybe a little older, and she was carrying a basket that looked to be full with cabbages, bent over to the side with the weight of it. As she went by, without so much as a glance to me, her basket brushed against my leg. She had her sleeves rolled up to the elbows and I could see, in that moment's passing, the veins in her forearm, raised, picked out with the weight of the basket, as beautiful as the pattern on a bird's wing.

I don't remember what she looked like, but I do know that her skin would have been dark with the weather and grimy with the dirt of her day's work. Her boots, probably men's boots handed down from a father or brother, patched and repaired so that the heels were uneven and the toes, misshapen earthen creatures. She wore no bonnet, only a scarf about her neck like a man's neckerchief, and a tattered shawl across her strong shoulders, a touchingly decorous gesture this – the weather being warm enough to go without.

I followed her. I kept my distance and pursued her into a maze of narrow lanes until I was quite lost. People stared at me, children shouted out in accents I knew to be taunting, though I could not make out the words. Somebody kicked some mud across my trousers and even in my pursuit the thought came that I must be sure and hide the trousers from Mother.

Dressed as I was in the distinctive broad white collar of my Quaker school, a pair of seagull's wings around my neck, and with my shiny shoes that had only ever been worn by me, and carrying my parcel of books, it was not surprising I was noticed, and I was used to that in my usual thoroughfares. But had I been dressed in something less unusual, I would have been just as conspicuous. For all our equality before God, on earth we can rank our fellow men from a hundred paces, Quaker or no.

The girl trod lightly in the lanes, her feet dancing over the loose paving stones, weaving about the children playing at their pebble games and the mothers sitting on filthy steps, babes or knitting, or some other work, in arms. I tried to follow her exactly, but I was cumbersome, catching the stones on their raised edge so that they tilted sharply down and sent up a spray of warm murky liquid from beneath, spattering my face and collar. The odour was vile and I knew that it must contain all the elements of man. But whereas the tannery's strong smells had me white-faced and retching, now I was unflinching.

It is unwise to be complacent. But I was too young to know that then, and at the very moment I was congratulating myself on having come so far, the girl leaned her basket in at a door, a door no different to the other doors in the lane, and was gone.

I stared at the house as though it was the first and only house in the world. It too was no different from those around it. The mortar had gone from between the bricks and the step was broken. The door had only the vestiges of its paint and the panes of glass that survived in the windows were all cracked, the empty squares covered with pieces of board. I peered closer at the window, hoping to see the girl within, but the dirt was too dense and all I could make out was the blurry grey of the newspapers stuffed around the corners of the frames. I stood back, suddenly out of breath, sweating, and that's when the panic began.

I was lost. A group of children, thin, barefoot, scabby creatures, gathered, watching me. It took little time for them to dare one another to acts of bravery, jeering, jabbing a finger at my legs, making a grab at my books, spitting and kicking.

'Coom on then, what are yeh? Bloody hell! Look at him and his funny shirt. Thinks he's a girl, does he? What yer doing here, fancy bugger? Looking a bit scared, a'n't you now. Got any money, posh boy?'

The girl had gone from my mind and my only thought was how to escape. But my legs were shaking and I dared not make a run for it. I had no idea where I was. The children came closer. None of them were as high as my shoulder, none of them were well fed, but still I was powerless. I stepped back, my feet uncertain on the cobbles. The children came closer again. I could feel my heart racing. A bead of sweat ran into my eye. Then the door to the house opened and the girl stood on the threshold, her hands, with their still-slender fingers, on her hips.

'Amy,' she called, 'coom on in, and bring yon baby with yer.' And for the first time she turned and looked at me, and at the children, and with a single step forward, she had them gone. Only one young child, a baby in her arms, a weepy-eyed thing, remained. With a last glance at me, the girl chivvied the child indoors and shut the door.

Without knowing in which direction I was headed, I set off walking. The sun was so low now that it had finished with these tight lanes and the air had become chill. I gathered my books into my chest like a baby and started to run, my heart pounding, my body exhilarated. I ran and ran, now somehow stepping lightly where before I had stumbled. I ran until I was gone from those lanes, and yet I knew that I was still carrying what I had found today, a connection with the girl. Her look, her last look, had caught me. It had cut through the sombre cloth of my Quaker suit like some Grecian arrow, galvanising my senses, electrifying me, and everything now was different. Earth, sky, streets, my heart, my skin, everything. This was something I could tell nobody of, something that would be regarded as unnatural, crossing the barriers of class and religion, and yet I knew that I would have to take it home with me, gather it to myself and make it my own somehow. And I knew that it was something I would have to do again.

I found myself eventually at Peaseholme Green and from there I managed to find my way to St Saviourgate, familiar ground. My uncle's grocery shop stood nearby, on Pavement, and I knew I should find William there, and a scratching of sugar to lick from around the loaf.

Looking through the great glass windows of the shop, I saw William, apron wrapped tight about his slim hips, measuring butter. I watched him drop the knife, his tongue between his teeth with concentration, and I thought better of going in. How could I explain what I had been doing? My uniform was mud-splattered and sweaty, my eyes, I could see in the window glass, were still too bright. And I knew already that however I described it, it would look different in someone else's eyes. Strange, excessive even. So I left William to his butter and walked on. Arriving home, I walked round to the area and let myself in quietly through the kitchen door and reached the safety of my room unobserved. This adventure was to set the shape of so many future ones.

In these earliest years of my watching I would have been hard-pressed to explain, even to myself, what I was doing. Though I became adroit with excuses, I was as nearly sleepwalking as anything else. Occasionally I could extract an errand from Nellie or the cook, or whisper a promise to the chambermaid to return with an apple or a twist of candy and then I would come back proudly with the commissioned turnips or stock bones, or the sweets, or the mended shoes collected from some tenement, careful always that Mother did not see. But more often than not I had no good reason to be walking those cramped streets, or sidling about on the corners. I had nothing to purchase or collect, nothing, that is, beyond what I gathered in with my senses and I became used to the taunts that followed me.

'Look at the gentleman now, will yeh? And him, what's he staring at? Hey, you've been catched a long way out of your stream, fella. What'd yoor mammy be saying, she could see you?'

Especially if they came from the girls, I would try to remember them accurately, to put down later in my diary.

My private diary. It was about this time that I started this and so for perhaps three years I was writing two. The private one, with a black cover, and the one I wrote for Father, which was red. In the first I would set down what I had seen and heard.

Third day, fifth month. Trinity Lane, no errand.
Spoke with 2 fems, one tallish, 17, one hunched, 13.
The hunched, one Ellen Goodacre, lives with
mother + 4 younger sibs. Father, drunk. Mother,

needlewoman till eyes went. Ellen, slop-worker,
making shirts. Circa 3 shillings a week. Can read, but
no opportunity. Herrings fav. food. Fingers slender.
Calluses on needle fingers. I suggested witchhazel to
ease them, but too costly. Finds hunch no difficulty
except for matter of husband, which brought tears.
Worried for brother who has cough, but no coin to pay
doctor, and behind with burial payments.

Sarah, 17, sackworker. Hands broad and fleshy. I
asked to touch – skin chapped, but leathery, smooth
on palm. Laughed at mine. 'Couldn't do owt with
'em,' she said. Proud of strength – father never touches
her now. Bareheaded, hair piled like 2 cottage loaves,
coarse, dirty skirt. Scarf and clogs.

I tried to learn the names for garments from Nellie, who
was vastly amused by my curiosity. And to recall exactly what
had been said. Sometimes girls wouldn't talk to me at all.
They'd look at me askance and walk away, or stare at the cobbles and giggle. Or they'd be too busy, and oftentimes would
regard me with what I have come to see as proper suspicion.
More than once one of them threatened me with their da. And
always I knew that should my mother, or indeed anyone from
Meeting hear of my conduct, that I'd be in great trouble, and
more so as I grew older. I knew that my diary, and later the
photographs, would likely be spoken of as something against
the natural order, though I knew them to be as natural to me
as my own skin. But I could not then do otherwise.

So, in those early days, once I'd hidden the black book
away, I would write in the red one. An entry in this might run
thus:

Thwarted expedition to water meadows beyond
Fulford due to inclement weather.

Debate upon the Corn Laws fiercely contested. As supporter of John Bright, I took side of Repeal. No conclusion reached before the dinner bell.

Dinner substantial though I do not greatly enjoy pease pudding.

Geography after dinner – map learning – and Latin. I had not memorised declensions sufficiently, and received only a poor mark in the examination. However, I am resolved to remedy this . . .

I would write of my experiments in photography, of my reading matter, of the political questions of the day, but never of the thoughts that most filled my mind. And Father would read the week's entries, initial them and hand me back the book with the injunction to keep up the good work, for the effort would repay. When, finally, after he fell ill, I stopped writing the diary for Father, I also finished making all but occasional entries in the private one.

There is a little book both Grace and I were taught out of, *The Child's Guide to Knowledge*. It is a question and answer book that was much favoured by one of our governesses, for it offered small tidbits of information on many subjects. She would instruct us to close our eyes, as though she were about to give us something special, open the book randomly and point a finger. Then we would open our eyes and see what treat the page had for us. I went and found out this volume recently, so I will offer here its opening page as a sample of its delights:

Q: What is the World?
A: The earth that we live on.
Q: Who made it?
A: The great and good God.
Q: Are there not many things in it you would like to know about?

A: Yes, very much.

Q: Pray, then, what is bread made of?

A: Flour.

Q: What is flour?

A: Wheat ground into powder by the miller.

Q: What injury is wheat liable to?

A: To three kinds of diseases, called smut, blight, mildew.

Q: What is smut?

Grace was always impatient with this book. 'Why, if they know all the answers,' she would say, 'does the person say there are many things they would like to know about?' And the governess, whose name was Margaret, would tell Grace that the situation was metaphorical and Grace would still disagree.

'So, let us see how much we know, then,' Margaret would say and we would do more of the blind opening. And always it was Grace, three years my younger, who knew more, whether it was of silkworms, or sugar, Queen Elizabeth or phosphorous.

Only with Mother did our situation change. She liked us to memorise and then recite. The Bible, our schoolroom primers, even the Meeting's Book of Suffering:

Hannah Murray had Coals seized to the value of 17 shillings. James Backhouse had a clock seized to the value of £6.7s.6d. Samuel Procter had ham, candlesticks and a fender seized to the value of 14s.8d. Hannah Brady had four spoons, a brass pan and a clock seized to the value of £4. David Priestman had leather seized to the value of £3.3s.7d.

And while I have always had a facility for this kind of pointless memory work, Grace refused to do it, regarding it as worthless.

'Good, Samuel,' Mother would say when I had recited back my portion, and my ears would glow. Then her lips would go tight as she listened to Grace.

Grace would stand before Mother and speak clearly and precisely. She did not stumble or falter, and she never blushed, but the words would be wrong. Sentences would be conflated, or invented. Names were altered or reversed. Information, whether about the Gobelin tapestry, the Acts of the Apostles or the invention of lucifer matches, was incorrect. I would watch Grace, and watch Mother, and sometimes I would think it was accidental, but more often I thought it to be deliberate.

Afterwards while Grace would receive Mother's anger like her birthright, I'd try, to no avail, to soften it.

'But hers was a harder piece than mine,' I would say, 'and she is younger.'

'No matter,' Mother would say. 'A child's brain is like a sponge. It will absorb. And if it does not, it is because the child is filling it with wrong matter and if this is so, then the wrong matter must be squeezed out, and the right absorbed,' and she would lift her hands to Grace's head, and then wring them around as though around a sponge, and I'd pray to God she did not cuff Grace.

Although Father never had us recite, he liked the clear setting down of facts as much as Mother did. Perhaps it is a good thing he never had Grace write a diary, for it would not have had the world set down as he liked to understand it. Maybe that is why he never asked her to, maybe he knew her spirit better than Mother ever did.

It is a matter of sadness to me that my street ventures were aided by what transpired to be my father's final illness. At the time, looking out through the narrow lens of youth, I merely took advantage of the shift in our household, without stopping to question what had caused it.

Grace, I am sure, knew from the first. She was never a child as other children were, and perhaps the solitude to which she was accustomed had fostered a spirit attentive, as mine was not, to the alteration in atmosphere that some particular knowledge can bring. She said later that she had simply asked Father, and he had told her that he was mortally ill and would die soon.

'And why did you not tell me then?' I asked her.

'He did not wish it. He believed it would be worse for you to know,' she said.

'But I am the elder of us,' I said.

'And perhaps you are the younger too,' said Grace. 'Besides, did it not give you some relief from Mother?'

'How do you mean?'

'From the nag and cosset which is her way with you.'

I looked at Grace hard, wondering, but she simply smiled and made no gesture that might signal some particular knowledge.

'It is true,' I said then. 'It did.'

'So perhaps that was the better thing,' she said.

'But how did I not see what was in front of my eyes?' I said. 'Father's appetite was gone. And there were his thin cheeks that I merely thought the product of some minor ailment and the time of year. And his daily rests, which grew longer and longer. And the tannery. He did not visit the tannery once in those last months.'

'It was easier for him, that you did not know, Sam,' Grace said, 'and that I did.'

HARRIET

Thomas had read things out to me before, and often from the magazine that was his favourite called *The Leisure Hour*. It was something he saved for, saying he'd rather get this than be down the pub. Reading about electric light or the pawpaw or travelling through Siberia, or maybe how to watch for the deathwatch beetle.

By now I was halfway comfortable, with my head against Mrs O'Leary's basket, which was full with our dinner. The train's jolting had me a bit lulled and I wanted to shut my eyes. But I knew he'd take it wrong, even if I was still listening, so I kept them open.

He went on with his reading. 'To an ordinary observer the limpets seem stationary, occupying the same spot on the face of the rock for weeks, months, years. Nor is this at variance with fact. Whoever saw them move?'

'Well, anyone could have said that,' I said. 'Of course they don't move.'

'No, but listen,' he said. 'It's the next bit that's the best. Now visit them at midnight. If there is a moon we may have light sufficient. If not, we strike a light and look into the fissure, and, to our surprise, the limpets are all gone! Look outside; there they all are, moving about promiscuously like sheep in a park!'

'Limpets like sheep!' I said, and he said he thought I'd find it interesting, which I said I did, I supposed, but I'd more likely be interested in something I'd not seen, like foreign places or the Crystal Palace.

We were into the country by now though it were still very flat, and I thought to myself that it were my first time on a train since I'd come to York.

'Where does it end up, this train?' I asked.

'Scarborough.'

Scarborough. Just the name had me a bit shook, it being only a shortish way up from home.

'And where do we get out?' I asked. 'You've not told me where we're going, remember?'

Thomas grinned. 'Kirkham,' he said. 'There's a ruined abbey there, meant to be, and a river. One of the lads at work said it was pretty and you could find a nice place to picnic.'

I'd not taken much notice of the man sitting across from us till now. I'd an impression he wasn't that took with Thomas reading out loud because he put his arms round his head and shut his eyes, though Thomas never noticed. But he stank of the beer and he'd not said a word till now, so he might only have had a bad head from last night.

Now he leaned forward, hands on his thighs, which were large, and tapped Thomas on the knee. He was a big man, a countryman by his dress and cap.

'You watch where you take yourselves,' he said. 'We're no more sweet than yourn towards strangers.'

'I've a liking for strangers generally,' Thomas said, but the man paid no attention. Thomas's voice was very quiet, but not having heard it like that before, I didn't know what that meant.

'I mean townsfolk getting drunk, setting up all over so as you can't come round a tree but there's some bloody courting couple canoodling. And then they're scaring the livestock and cluttering the lanes on their bicycles. And then there's all the gates left open and the messes they leave.'

Thomas stayed silent. I looked at him. I'd never seen him like this. In that short time since the man started up, his face had gone tight, the skin stretched over his cheeks and over his nose, and his eyes were still, like two pieces of glass, staring at the man.

'Thomas,' I whispered, giving him this look to say to leave the man be, because we'd our precious day before us. And maybe the man saw me do it or maybe it was his hobby horse and we'd the bad luck to be riding it, but whichever, he was off on another rant, though at first I thought he'd taken leave of his senses and it was all I could do to stop the laugh.

'And you were speaking vulgar stuff back there, young man, about them sheep, which we don't take kindly to in our parts.'

'Limpets,' Thomas said quietly.

'No, what you said of the sheep.' The man was shouting.

'And I was talking of limpets,' Thomas said again, still real quiet. Then the man got mad.

'I don't care about pets. I've nothing to do with pets. I'm speaking of sheep and the word you said about them. I know sheep and that word is an abomination on them.'

'Which word?' said Thomas, still quiet.

'You know what word,' the man said, which I didn't, but I saw that Thomas did.

'Promiscuously,' Thomas said. 'The word was promiscuously. Promiscuously like sheep in a park,' he said and he was relishing the saying of it.

'Ay.' The man was red in the cheeks by now. 'That was it. A disgusting word, and about sheep.'

If he hadn't been so big and so angry, I'd have been laughing by now. But this promiscuous sheep argument was no laughing matter with us sat in a railway carriage with a mad man. There'd been something in the papers not so long ago of a man beaten near to death in a railway carriage, and that had been first class, not third.

Thomas spoke in a whisper now, but clear as day to hear. 'And I suppose none of you country folk ever comes to the town or has a pint over what he ought, nor ever gets a leg over our women or is sick as a dog on our pavements?' Thomas waited as if to see if the man would give a reply, and then he went on. 'But anyway what I was reading out was nothing to do with that. So you've no cause for your foul mouthing.'

And that was too much and the big fellow was wiping his fists on his thighs and I was thinking he was set to give Thomas a drubbing and how this was going to spoil our day and we'd been looking forward to it so. But before I'd finished my thoughts or the man had finished tidying up his hands, quick as lightning, Thomas was out of his seat with the man's head between his hands. Thomas leaned forward so their heads were near touching, like he was to tell him a secret, and then with this quick sharp movement he dunned him. The man reeled about, like somebody playing at it, and as he fell, Thomas grabbed his shoulders and laid him back on his bench, out cold.

'Hope he wasn't getting off with us,' Thomas said, like it was a joke, ''cos he'll not come round till Scarborough, I shouldn't wonder.'

I looked at the man. You'd have thought he were just sleeping, but for the egg there was coming on his forehead. 'I hope you've not damaged him,' I said and Thomas shook his head.

'He'll take it for the beer, I wouldn't wonder. Anyway, he asked for it.'

'Where'd you learn to do that?' I said.

Thomas didn't answer straight off. He looked out of the window, and then back at the man, then he looked at me. 'Do you want to know?' he said.

'I'd not have asked else,' I said, but his voice made me nervous, and it was the first time. I could hear the edge of something.

The water was green, looking down from the bridge, and the weir made a soft rushing sound. Boys were skin-dipping further off. They'd a rope over the water and they made flashes of white as they swung and dropped. I'd have stayed longer, but Thomas was already walking on. Back home, I'd watch the birds for hours. There were cormorants and often terns, twenty or thirty at a time, but it was the gannet I loved most, flying alone and high, its eyes beading over the water, looking for something I couldn't see, some movement, some shift in the light that told of fish. Then the circling flight, the hover and the drop, just at the last tucking its wings and leaving barely a splash. Then, before you knew it was gone, it'd be up, beating off the water, beating up, back into sky.

These boys were clumsy creatures next to gannets, but they had their inch of air when they let go the rope, before the water took them in.

We found a place for our picnic in the ruined abbey, beside a mass of stone, one side smooth with leaf shapes carved from it, and the other side raw and tumbled like a piece of cliff. Though the sun was hot, the grass was still wet with the dew and full of flowers. Thomas spread a blanket and we sat down. He took off his shoes and socks and stretched out. His feet were long and white.

My mother had taught me the names of wild flowers, though not which was which. She'd sit me on her knee and make a rhyme out of them, or it was maybe more of a chant, and I'd say them with her.

'Buttercup and speedwell, horseshoe vetch to bring you luck. Orchids and dandelions, fairy flax to weave. Saxifrage and poppy, keep your pennies in a shepherd's purse. Rockrose and willowherb, but don't get caught in a lady's bedstraw.'

'What's that?' Thomas said.

'Flower names,' I said. 'My mother told me them.' I picked some of the flowers. 'One of these must be fairy flax, or speed-well.'

Thomas sat up. 'Do you really want to know?' he said.

'You don't know about flowers,' I said.

'No,' he said, 'not about the flowers.'

'I'm not sure now,' I said, thinking that the sun was shining and we were sat here together and the sound of the water and the grass and the flowers were all about. 'Do I?'

He sighed. 'Ay, I think you must,' he said. 'D'you know much of the Virgin Mary?'

'What's she got to do with your knocking a man out?'

'Do you?' he said again. I shook my head. 'Well, my mother used to say she worshipped her.'

'And did she?'

'Maybe, once a week. On a Sunday morning she'd scrub our faces and our necks till they were raw, and after that we weren't to go in the street to play for fear of the sinful mud. It was mud in the winter, and in the summer dust. Nothing green in our bit of the city and nothing growing. Then she'd button us up in these clothes we only saw then. They were always too small, and black and musty-smelling, but it wasn't our mustiness. It was the pawnbroker's. All week they were piled high, wrapped in their brown paper, rubbing up against all sorts and she'd be down and get them out of pawn on a

Saturday night and on the Monday she'd send me back with them. "You go," she'd say, heaping them on me. "They might give you a better price." I must have looked a sight, this wee lad stumbling down the street, because I was always small for my age, near on smothered. But they knew whose son I was and they never did give me a better price. So we'd be down to Mass, all stiff-legged and the trousers cutting behind the knee and the jacket pinching under the arm, and there was this big statue there with a blue cloak on and a lovely face. All golden. And she would shine with the candles lit underneath.'

'Sounds nice,' I said, and he shook his head.

'But she wasn't,' he said slowly. 'Not any bit of her.'

'What, the Virgin Mary?' I said.

'No,' Thomas said, 'my mother.'

He didn't want to tell me it at first, not the next thing nor any of it after, and I suppose he'd say I made him. But I'd say he wanted to, only he just didn't know it before.

So he told me how he'd lie awake with his brother on a night waiting for their mother to come home. There'd be the sound of the key in the lock – she always locked them in – and then her voice, drunk, and some man's. Some strange man's. They'd be reeking of drink and they'd be laughing and singing and she'd help the man over to her bed because it was dark in there. If they were lucky, the man would do his business and leave. But sometimes the men would throw their beer up over the bed and occasionally they'd start hitting his mother and she'd be whimpering. Then Thomas wanted to murder them all, whoever they were, but he couldn't do a thing.

He said him and his brother, they'd near enough hold their breath, for fear they'd be heard in the corner. And if either of them made so much as a squeak, their ma would come over, all lovey-dovey, and tuck them in, but then the next day she'd rage and hit them for it, it might be anywhere, but the worst was on the face because then they'd get those looks from the other lads in the street.

'So what happened to her?' I asked him, and he shrugged.

'I don't know.'

'What do you mean?'

'I mean, I don't know.'

'Is she alive? Dead?'

'Don't know. I don't even know if she still goes to see her bloody Virgin.'

'So what happened to you? Is that when you lived on the parish?'

'Not exactly.'

'Tell me then,' I said. And he shrugged again, and then pulled his shoulders up and nodded, to himself, not me, before starting in and telling me it.

'I became a little thief is what happened, and then I got caught, and then I got caught again and the second time they put me into prison.'

'And did your mother not . . .' I started to say. But he put out his hand.

'Let me say it now if I'm going to,' he said, and I nodded and lay down beside him and stared up at the blue sky and the swallows.

'Me and my brother, we'd nick things to eat. But one day it was raining and we were wet, so I took this umbrella. I could see it just inside this shop. It was a nice one with a carved handle, and big enough to keep the rain off the both of us. We were dry all day then and pleased, so we let the other boys have a go with it. But somebody must have told because two bobbies arrived and they made straight for the brolly. The other lads scattered like dust, and I was stood there holding the umbrella above me, it being still raining and I told my brother to get the hell out, which he did, and I was nicked. They sent me to prison for a month, and then five years in St

Sebastian's reformatory. I was eleven. It was the last I saw of my brother. I could never find him after.'

He stopped talking and I went on making a flower chain, except the stalks were too soft and kept splitting. I didn't know what to say to him losing a brother like that. After a bit I asked him what happened next, not thinking he'd say any more, but he started on again, like he was on a path and no way off.

'The other prisoners were kind. Made me into a kind of mascot, being so young. They gave me the best of the food and ruffled my hair, what there was of it after the shave. They looked out for me. But the reformatory was a different thing.

'First off, it was in the middle of the countryside, scary enough to a boy who'd never seen a sheep before except on a pub board. No houses anywhere near, no people. Only cows and sheep and rooks in the trees always making their noise. And miserable boys. But the priests were even scarier than the countryside. Father Torreno was the boss and he was fair, but there were others. Some of the boys never left. There was a lot of sickness in the winter and there wasn't a year I was there but a boy died. Some of sickness, and some of the priests.'

'Of the priests?' I said.

He nodded.

'What do you mean, the priests?'

'Wait a bit,' he said, and I saw it wasn't easy, this bit of the telling, so I put my hand on his arm, and he put his over, held it there and carried it on.

'So I was there near on three years, and doing what I could to make it safely. There was prayers twice a day in the chapel and now there was this big St Sebastian statue up where Our Lady used to be. I didn't like him as much, he didn't have the smile for me, and all those little bloody holes where the arrows

had been. We used to joke it might give some of the priests
ideas. But I liked the quiet and everybody moving so slowly,
and the dressing up and the chanting. I was next in line for
being an altar boy. It was good in the winter doing that
because you got to wear extra robes and move around a bit.

'Then they'd a band you'd have thought was holy, they were
that big on it. Drums and fifes and triangles. I was a triangle.
Band practice got you off cleaning duty, and all the band were
in the section of honour.'

'The what?' I said.

'It was for reward. You got to wear a special tunic on a
Sunday. And sometimes it meant they'd let you go early, on
licence.'

'What happened if you were bad?'

'There was a special ceremony for that if you were in the
Section of Honour. They'd line everybody up, all the boys, and
make this show of taking your name off the Tablet – it was this
big scroll really, where the Honour boys got their names.
Instead of singing "Hail Queen of Heaven", like when you
were made an Honour boy, it was some hymn full of the sins of
men. Then they'd shave your head and put you in a tunic and
trousers and cap with "St Sebastian's Reformatory" printed all
over and parade you about. Sometimes you'd be put in the
"dark cell" for a day or two. And if you were unlucky and got
Father Palance in charge, you'd not know what might go on.

'Anyway, we'd all to learn a trade, to fit you for the world
beyond where they'd tell you over and over how nice they'd be
to Roman Catholic boys with a prison record. Especially in
Yorkshire. So you could learn tailoring, shoemaking, baking,
carpentry. And that was alongside lessons, though few of us
could read or write when we left.'

'Could you not read or write then, when you left?'

'Could I hell,' he said.

'So what did you learn?'

'Precious little. They'd barely any teachers and we were a rough lot. Most of the lads ended up in the army, if they weren't back on the streets thieving again. They had me down for a baker, but all I knew to do was what I was told.

'Then there was this cold winter. Very cold. I'd be about fourteen. Father Torreno got us extra sweaters and socks, but still most of us, our fingers and toes were poached red with chilblains. Some boys had a sport to knock the birds from the trees with stones, the birds being that cold they were sitting ducks.

'One Saturday afternoon Father Torreno took us as were in the Section of Honour ice-sliding on the canal. We were in high spirits, and the Father too, but Arthur McLeary and Joseph Finn got into difficulty near the reeds where the ice was thin. Father Torreno went to help and his weight broke the ice and they were into the water. Some bargemen got them out, but the Father and the two boys had the pneumonia because of it and were all in bed for months. Brother Palance took over those months and it'd be my guess Father Torreno knew what was going on, but he couldn't do a thing.'

It took me by surprise when Thomas stopped. I'd my eyes still fixed on my flower chain, long enough now for both our necks, and so I didn't see his face before I spoke.

'Go on then. Tell me the rest,' I said, thinking he'd just stopped for breath or something, and it was only when he didn't answer that I looked up from my flowers. His face was a storm, lips and eyes tight, two circles of red in his cheeks, his brow white as ash. All of a sudden he stood up.

'Thomas?' I said.

He'd wrapped his arms around his chest, like he was trying to hold himself.

'Enough for now,' he said.

I didn't know him well then, which is how come I went on, because I'd not have done so later.

'You're not going to tell me how you got here?' I said. 'To York, to Wetherby's?'

He didn't say anything.

'You're going to leave me guessing?' I said.

'I can't say more today, except that they rescued me and I owe them more than any other man,' he said and there was that in his voice, finally I knew not to ask more. It crossed my mind he might lash out like a wounded animal, and then if it were me in the way, it'd be me got hurt. Not because he'd want to hurt me, but because I was closest. So I didn't say more, but went to put my arm around him, to comfort him, but he shrugged it off.

'I'd not have let you then,' he said.

But a moment after he reached out and took my hand and put it, awkward, on his shoulder. 'I'm not so good at this,' he said. 'You've to show me,' and I tucked my head against his chest.

We had our picnic then, not saying anything much, just leaning against that cool stone and Thomas easing his throat with the beer and me watching the birds, and after set off along the track beside the river.

We'd walked beyond the other courting couples by the time we stopped, and were stood in the shade of a tree by the edge of the river, only the sounds off the river to hear. The water was smooth, smoother than the sea, its surface only every now and then cut up by a duck. I crouched down, reached near, and dipped in my finger. It was warmer than the sea too. And even though I knew it, I was still surprised when I licked my finger and tasted no salt. Close to I could see the water wasn't smooth at all. There were tiny insects with long legs making shivers of it in a funny dance, skidding and chasing.

I stood up and turned to Thomas. He looked pale.

'So?' he said.

'So what?' I said.

'So are you still . . . are you still . . . now you know what I've told you?'

'Of course I bloody am,' I said and I took his hand, which was cold considering the heat of the day.

'I've not told that to anyone before,' he said.

'I'm not surprised,' I said. 'You've got the gift, though.'

'What gift?'

'Of the gab,' I said and that got a laugh from him at last and he chased me to the edge of the field, me with my skirts hoiked up to help the running.

'You're fast,' he said when he caught up. 'Picking up your skirts like it comes naturally.'

'It does,' I said and gave him the same show I'd given the girls in the factory and, with my skirts tucked like britches, fair leapt over the stile.

It was a sudden thing, what I did next. Not something I ought to do, nor something I'd thought to do, but it seemed like the right time and the right way. Before he was down from the stile, no warning, not even the chance to put down the picnic basket. I put my hand on his to stay him and asked the question.

'Will you marry me, Thomas Newcome?' I said.

It was a funny way for it to come out between us, on the back of his story, and of course he should have been doing the saying. But it was the same question both ways around and I knew it was right. Next thing I knew, he'd dumped the basket and we were on the ground, the grass and what have you tickling my neck, and his face above me, his nose just brushing mine, and then his lips on my lips.

Still sitting by the stile, we were dreaming later and taking turns to say the place we'd most like to have our home in. I'd shown him how to thread daisies and he'd made a chain for my wrist, quick as anything though his fingers were twice the size of mine.

'Florence, or maybe Rome, though they say it gets very hot there. Or what about Egypt and all the pyramids? Or China and the Great Wall and all the rice fields?'

'Thomas! Just because you've read about them in your magazines. It doesn't mean you'd want to live there.' I poked him in the ribs. 'Have children there. They don't speak our language, they eat strange food, they look different.'

'But that's just why I do want to go there.' He poked me back. 'All your places are made up ones, anyway. A cottage by a river, a cottage on the hill above a lake, a cottage on the cliff, as long as you didn't have to be one of them girls you used to be.' He threw a pebble high and it dropped into the river with a thunk. 'I know. It's water, isn't it. Everywhere you want to be is near water. The sea, or a river, or a lake. Have you ever seen a lake, Harriet?'

'They have one painted on those posh tins of creams at Wetherby's. And mountains with snow on the tops.'

Thomas laughed. 'Gets her education off of chocolate tins. And this is the girl I'm to marry.'

'When shall we do it?' I said. 'Next week?' meaning it as a joke.

But Thomas took me seriously and looked grave. 'I'm to go to London next week,' he said in this solemn voice. 'I've been meaning to tell you all day, but it never seemed the right time.'

'To London?'

'Yes.'

'What, for good?' I said.

'No, you daft dilly. For a week, maybe two. Not longer.'

'Why?'

'Company business.'

'Well, I know that. You'd not be going down to visit your

mother, would you. But why you? It's not as if you're even a high up clerk.'

'Because they trust me. And because I owe them.'

'What, and they don't trust the other clerks? Oh, come on, Thomas.'

'It's confidential work, and difficult,' he said.

'So they get you to do it because you owe them one. Doesn't sound very likely. Doesn't sound very like what Mr William goes on about in the assemblies.'

'No, they've never said I owed them anything. Besides, it's an honour, Harriet. To be trusted like that.'

'So what is it then? This confidential and honourable work you're to do?' He didn't answer. 'I think it smells very fishy,' I said. 'They've not sworn you to secrecy, have they?' He shook his head.

'No. They wouldn't ask you to swear, being Quakers. They just recommended I not tell anybody.'

'But I'm not anybody. I'm the girl has just asked you to marry her and you've just agreed. So I think you could tell me.'

I was furious, and so was he, our bodies rigid like planks where minutes before I'd felt soft as butter to his touch. Eventually he spoke.

'I'm sorry, you've a right to an answer. I'm just to interview some men about making cocoa.'

'Who work for Wetherby's?'

'No.' Thomas was tearing a grass stem to shreds. 'No, they don't. Look, I'll tell you, but you must promise—'

'Of course I'm not going to tell anyone,' I said.

'Not even Mary,' he said, at which I glared at him. 'All right,' he said, 'They all seem to be at it, the cocoa manufacturers. The big ones especially, but the little ones too I expect. And Wetherby's is just the same. I suppose it's a kind of spying. Trying to get the other people's secrets. Buy recipes, find out what machinery each other is using. And, if they can, get hold of the best men for the job. Sometimes that means a bit of poaching. But we pay for everything we get.'

'So Mary was right,' I said. 'It is their dirty work. And not very Quaker-like.'

'No,' Thomas said and he gave me such a dog-eared look that I couldn't help myself but laugh.

'And is it dangerous?' I said, and he answered me 'no' again, so fast I suppose I should have known.

'But they're paying me extra to do it. It means I can save some money, and that means we can get married quicker.' And he stroked my cheek like he might be stroking velvet.

'You're going to do it then?' I said. He nodded, and there didn't seem much else to say. 'Be careful, so,' I said.

It gave me such a jolt when I looked up. He must have got set up there after we'd been by, and after all it was a couple of hours we'd been along the river, but still it was the strangest thing. It was getting on in the afternoon by now, the sun was lower and under the trees there was an edge to the air which made me fish out my shawl.

Ahead of us there was a man set up with an easel and paints. He was sat in the sun facing the ruins.

'That's the picturesque he's painting,' Thomas said to me in a tone I was coming to know as his educating voice and I was about to tell him to go picturesque himself when the man held out his hand in front of him. I stopped where I was, staring.

'It's the perspective. Look, he's got his pencil lined up,' said Thomas, grinning, waiting for me to poke him quiet with all his learning. But there was something about the fellow.

'Shut up a minute,' I said.

'What is it?'

We started walking again and as we got closer, Thomas nudging me and asking what I'd seen, I saw that I'd been right.

It's how he moved his arm that told me, I thought to

myself, because it was. It was an odd way he had of lifting it, like he'd a string puppet in his fingers, his elbow high, and he'd done it the same that evening when he offered me his arm in the dark and the ground uneven.

'I know him,' I said.

'Know who?'

'The man with the paints,' I said.

'He's got a top hat,' Thomas said.

'What?' I looked at Thomas.

'I said he's got a top hat. He's a gentleman. What are you doing knowing a gentleman?'

I'd not heard Thomas talk like that before. But we were closer now, too close for me to give Thomas the story. 'I'll explain after,' I said. 'It's too long to tell. He'll notice us any minute and it'd be rude to be stood in the middle of the field talking of him.' I walked on, knowing how Thomas's face would be, but there wasn't a thing I could do about it.

He didn't look up from his painting, even when we were nearly upon him. So there was nothing for it. I had to speak.

'Good day Mr Ransome,' I said.

He nearly dropped his paints. Then he stood up and did his little bow. He was dressed in his usual black suit, all as tightly buttoned on this summer day as it had been the bitter day I first met him in November. His face had gone pale as ash.

'Harriet,' he said and I could see his eyes run over me and it went through my head that he could see Thomas's kisses on my skin, though I knew that was daft.

'This is Thomas Newcome,' I said and Mr Ransome gave his bow to Thomas and said good day to him and that he believed he had seen Thomas at Wetherby's and Thomas gave this short nod and said nothing

'We've been out for a picnic,' I said and I tapped the picnic basket as if it made it clearer. I could see Thomas out of the corner of my eye, staring at the ground.

'Indeed. It's been a fine day for one. Did you take the train?' Mr Ransome asked.

I laughed. 'Well, we didn't walk, anyhow,' I said and he smiled and nodded.

'No, of course,' he said. Then he waved his hand towards his easel. 'I've been so absorbed in my painting,' he said, which I suppose was meant to explain something.

'Let's have a look then,' I said, because he was stood in front of it so I couldn't see, but he shook his head, and then more than shook his head. He stepped forward like you would if you were to take a swing at someone, so I'd to back off for us not to be touching, and yet when he spoke he was as polite as always.

'I'd prefer you not to. I'm really no artist. And I didn't expect . . .'

Thomas was still looking at the ground and being what I thought was downright rude and I'd tell him after, what I thought. But at least he didn't see Mr Ransome come in close like that, because if he had, I'd not have been able to keep him from a blow.

'Did you come out on the train too, then?' I said, wanting to walk away, but not wanting for him to be angry like this.

'Yes,' he said, 'but not today. I've been staying a few days with my cousins. They take a house in the summer near Kirkham.'

'Mr William and Mr Caleb?' I said.

'William, yes, and his family,' he said, and I felt Thomas's arm jerk.

'What about Grace?' I said before I could stop myself. He shook his head.

'She is unwilling to leave her room. I'm returning to York tonight, and I will visit Grace soon. I trust you are keeping well?' to which I nodded, wondering all the while what he meant about Grace's room.

'Oh, very well,' I said, and maybe he heard something in

my voice, but he looked a long look at Thomas. I could feel a
blush rise from under my bodice and flood my face, and I
wished that we hadn't met Mr Ransome here, on this day and
in this place. I made to pick up the basket, but Thomas near
snatched it from me.

'We must be going on now. Good day, Mr Ransome,' I said
and he bowed to me again and to Thomas, who gave a bow
back though he'd rather not have, and we walked on, under
the ruins of the abbey and back over the bridge and to the station, and though I didn't turn to look, I know Mr Ransome
watched us all the way.

'I don't care if he's the bloody Queen of Sheba brought you
all the bloody jewels of the East. I don't like you talking to him
like that. And why's he talk like that anyway?'

'Oh, calm down, Thomas. You're acting like you own me
already. If it hadn't been for Mr Ransome, you and I would
never have met. We'd never have come out here today and
everything would never have happened.'

We were sat in the railway carriage and talking in whispers,
but even so Thomas's voice sounded coarse with anger. The
two farming types on the opposite bench were snuffling their
pipes and talking the price of cattle, but the woman next to us,
who'd been clacking away at her knitting, had stopped with
the needles and was listening in for all she was worth.

'Seems a bit too good to me. We go all the way out to the
country on the train, see almost no one and then accidentally
bump into the only man that you know, aside from me and
your father. And you're telling me it's a coincidence.'

'You're forgetting you only told me this morning where we
were going. You were keeping it all a secret, remember? So just
stop your tongue, Thomas. If you don't believe me, then I
don't think it's a good sign for the future, and I'm not a signs
and wonders girl as you know.'

It didn't get a smile. Instead Thomas put his head in his

hands. 'I'm sorry,' he said. 'I'm sorry. It's just all got too much of a sudden.' He took my hand and opened it, palm upwards. 'Can you read the lines?' he asked.

I shook my head. 'Not now,' I said.

He stared at it a while. 'Well, they look to be good and long ones, is all I can say,' he said finally.

I fell asleep the rest of the journey, my head on his shoulder and when he woke me, we were coming in to York station and I'd furrows on my face from his braces and the folds in his shirt.

We were to go our separate ways at the station, me back to Mrs O'Leary's and him to his lodgings on Leeman Road. The train slowed and lurched as it drew in to the station. Thomas stroked my cheek. I knew what was coming.

'I'm to go on Tuesday,' he said.

'Have they arranged it all properly?'

He nodded. 'The tickets are bought for the train and I've the address of a hotel in the middle of the city.'

'A hotel?'

'It's where they sometimes stay themselves, they said. A temperance hotel.'

'And is that where you'll meet all these whatever do you call them? These men with the information?'

'No. I've a room rented somewhere else and they're to come there.'

'How do they know to?'

'There was an advertisement in the right papers, the Clerkenwell Gazette, the Holborn Courier, those kinds. It doesn't say a word of Wetherby's. Just that there's advantage to be had and so on.'

'Have you seen the advertisement?'

'Yes.'

'Tell me what it says, then. You'll know it word for word, I know.'

Thomas batted at me with his hand, like I was a fly irritating him. But I was right that he knew the words, because he told me them.

To cocoa, chocolate and pastille makers.
Wanted immediately, two Foreman who thoroughly
understand the manufacture of all kinds of Cocoas,
Chocolates, Creams and Gum Pastilles. Also several
Workmen used to the trade. Good hands will be
liberally dealt with.

'But you might get all sorts.'

'They've done it before, the brothers, and they know what they're doing. Besides, I can look after myself.'

'So what are you doing marrying me then?' I said, and he muttered something about maybe he shouldn't be, that I was too good a thing for him. I started to ask him what he'd said, but he kissed me on the brow, a finger to my lips.

'So why can't they be the ones to do it again then,' I said, 'the Wetherbys, if they're so smart at it?'

'Look, I can't explain here, or now. Trust me, love. And look after yourself.'

I didn't want us to arrive, but the train stopped and the door was tugged open. The farmers climbed out, and then the woman with the knitting, giving us a smile like she understood, which gave me a pang, just a short one, of wishing for my mother. We stepped down onto the platform and there was the steam and the people and the dirt and the city, and it was just the day we'd been gone and it seemed so long and so short and now it was all around us again.

Then, like he couldn't bear for it to be for longer, Thomas wrapped his arms around me, hugged me so tight I could barely breath, and was gone.

SAMUEL

Recently, Harriet asked to see the picture I painted that day. I told her that I had lost it. Quite correctly, she did not believe me, but tucked her lovely hands behind her head, leaned back and looked down at her plate. She didn't question me further.

How interesting it is, that an object can take on attributes that have nothing to do with it. Were I to show Harriet that picture, it would provoke in her quite different emotions from those working in me. And yet there is nothing in the thing itself to engender such feelings.

That First Day, or Sunday as I would now call it had started well. Caleb woke me early and we walked through the early mist to buy eggs for breakfast. Our path took us down a cart track, the hedges high on either side and full with small nesting birds. We saw finches, tits, warblers, hedge sparrows, the sudden golden start of the yellowhammer. We heard the 'crex crex' call of corncrakes as they shuffled invisible through the pasture meadow.

We walked in silence, our track first climbing above the mist into thin sunlight before we took a path to the left which dropped back down and into a gully which was impassable in winter with snow or mud. As we walked, my thoughts ran close to the dream I had been woken from not half an hour before, a dream of some idyllic place with Grace, and other figures whose names I could not tell myself now I was awake.

'It's got high since last you were here.' Caleb's voice broke through. It was the first time he had spoken in the twenty minutes we'd been walking. Ahead of me, he bludgeoned cow parsley and high nettles with his stick. It made an incongruous sight, this gentle man with a basket in one hand and his stick raised, if only against some stinging weeds, in the other.

We bought the eggs from an old lady named Jessie Goodings. She was probably not very old, perhaps not much more than fifty, but her face was very wrinkled by the elements and her body buckled with arthritis so that her hands, as she steadied herself, would not open, but stayed as fists, which gave her the appearance of some strange, shrunken boxer.

'I'd have had them to your door for nine,' she said, but we assured her, as we did each time, that we had wanted the walk. Then she took us in to choose.

After the clear early light, the room was dark and the air close and dusty. Dogs and cats and hens made their noises in the shadows and every so often something with fur, or feathers, would brush my leg. A fire burnt in the grate, winter and summer, the ash heaped like dirty, tumbled snow, and a kettle always simmered. In the far corner was a sagging bed on which Mrs Goodings' husband lay. Caleb crossed the room and took the old man's hand and he looked up with his blind eyes and smiled.

'Mr Wetherby,' he said.

'Good morning, Mr Goodings,' Caleb said, and they had their usual chat, about the weather, and William's children, here for the summer, and William, impatient to be back at the factory after two days away. Then we picked out our eggs, laying them carefully in the basket, packing dirty straw in between at Mrs Goodings' insistence, and paid her. We stepped outside and for a moment I could not walk on, but gasped the air to clear my body of the stifle of indoors. Then we walked back in sunshine, the mist already gone.

I had announced my intention over breakfast of taking a picnic and my painting things down to Kirkham once Meeting was over. The children wailed their disappointment and tried to dissuade me. They had me top of their list for cricket later in the day. They liked me to play their games because I did not mind being beaten, and in this, too, I am unlike their father. William, Quaker or no, could no more lose a game of tiddlywinks to his six-year-old daughter than he could fly.

Meeting was held in the drawing room. The housekeeper and the cook, who were not Quakers, had the day off, so William had the children arrange seven chairs in a circle round a small table with a Bible on it. The room faced north and despite its being summer, the air was chilly. Rachel had had Caleb light a small fire in the hearth and now she took the chair closest to the heat, put her palms towards the fire and shut her eyes.

Rachel is one of those creatures whose skin is so pale, you almost think you can see the bones beneath, like looking into an icy pond and catching sight of leaves or twigs suspended there. In many ways she reminds me of my mother, plain in her dress and tastes, no reader of novels, strict with her children and stern in her morals. I knew that she disapproved of my dilettantism, and that even the children's cricket had been the subject of a debate between her and William. Unlike my mother, however, Rachel's passionate devotion to William and to her children is transparent. I had come into the drawing room the previous day and found her, characteristically, with her Bible open, and a pile of stockings to darn. But both of these had been put aside for the child who had banged its knee and now lay snuggled in its mother's lap, drifting in that lovely comforted half-sleep we dream of once we have left our childhood. My comforting had only ever come from my father, and at that moment I envied that little creature with what I can only describe as childish jealousy.

I have wondered sometimes, but I do not think William has ever spoken of Grace to Rachel. Yet though he might never have spoken to her of his first love, I am sure it was not long before Rachel knew, for she sees a great deal in her quiet way, and most especially those things which are not talked of. So different is she from Grace in this, who has never known when it was better to be silent.

It was not long once Rachel was sat down before the children were seated and quiet. And finally, when Caleb and I, too, had taken our places, William left his position at the window and took his chair. This was the signal for Meeting to begin.

The children were shuffling and fidgeting, just as I remembered doing. It is an uncomfortable thing to sit in silence and do nothing. William had drawn the curtains a little to prevent the birds, busy about their business, from becoming a distraction to the eye and it struck me suddenly as a strange thing, to be sitting in the half-light when God had given us such a beautiful day outside.

So we sat in silence, and I fixed my gaze on my shoes – as I always did – and found my thoughts drifting to Harriet, and then to Grace and the hard course of her life. After a while William spoke, as he always does. And because of what occurred later, I can still recall the gist of his words that day. He spoke of faithfulness and of trust. I felt a sigh go round our circle when he stopped, or maybe it was an easing of the body.

William's speaking, whether in the little Meeting he held at home or in the York Meeting, always marked the halfway point.

Then John, the eldest child, blushing to his collar, took the Bible from the table and read out from the book of Job, while his two siblings stifled giggles till a glance from William silenced them. And when John sat down, I noticed William gave him a little glance, and the boy blushed with pleasure. Finally, without taking out his watch, but precisely on the half hour, William stood and Meeting was over.

The children rushed from the room and Rachel left to prepare lunch. I opened the curtains and watched the children tumble into the garden, running hard, under the glare of the sun, as though to beat out all that silence. Behind me, William lifted chairs back to their places.

'God enjoins us to be good at what we do, does he not?' William said as he tugged a rug straight. Not sure whether this was spoken to me or to himself, I didn't immediately reply, especially as the answer indeed seemed self-evident.

'And I am good, am I not?' William said. Again, being unsure to whom he was speaking, I didn't reply. William stopped pacing and looked at me.

'I've been wanting to speak to you,' he said and began pacing again. Believing now that he wished me to answer him, I ventured to, but at this he started speaking again, not loudly, but in such a way as to refuse my words any air, walking to and fro between sofa and hearth, and I could see very well right then how he got his way in business meetings. Not by shouting but by a kind of quiet bullying, relentless and calm, which won't let anyone else in.

'God enjoins us to be good at what we do, and I am,' he repeated. 'Wetherby's makes the finest cocoa in the country, and it is not for nothing that I test every week's output. "Taste it personally," I tell my foremen, "and then you've nothing but your own taste buds to worry about."'

William's agitation might have been invisible to a stranger, but I had grown up with him and even now, when we were not close, when our lives had taken different paths, even now I knew the signs. His index fingers tapped at the chair backs, and now he took a coin from his pocket and squeezed it between his fingers.

'I treat my workforce justly and pay them fairly for their work, and I treat – that is Wetherby's treats – its customers fairly. We are not one of those companies that flaunts a product we do not produce.'

'It has never occurred to me that you would act but with absolute probity,' I said. 'Come out into the garden. The children would be glad of a game before I leave to paint.'

He shook his head. 'I couldn't play right now.'

'And if not now?' I said, walking to the door.

He turned from the fire. 'Please don't talk to me of playing. I want to tell you something, Samuel. It is all very exciting.'

'What is?'

'Cocoa. And not only cocoa.'

I found it hard to be excited by William's talk of business. But his tone was urgent, so I sat back down.

'Has Caleb spoken to you of this?' William asked.

I shook my head.

William stopped his pacing and looked at me. 'I believe cocoa is about to have its day,' he said, 'and I want Wetherby's to be there as the sun rises.'

It was rare for William to speak in such poetic terms, and I wondered what was to come.

'Sugar tariffs are coming down,' he went on.

'Ah,' I said.

'So cocoa need no longer be a luxury food. The day is near when each working man and his family will be able to drink it every day.'

'If they wish to,' I said.

'They will wish to, and I will help them,' he said. 'Wetherby's produces the best cocoa in the country, as you know.'

I did not know, but felt it politic to nod and William continued.

'Our biggest competitors cannot match us. Some have the Van Houten press as we do, but still they cannot equal us.'

'You are sure of this?'

'Our information is very good, and we take care to ensure that theirs is less reliable.'

'They surely do not come and tell you all their secrets, these other firms, and you simply believe what they tell you?'

'Of course not. But we have our sources.'

'Spies.'

William didn't take offence. 'We have a young man in our employ, a very reliable man with reason to do well by us, and he gathers the information.'

'But you pay for it?'

'There is nothing in this world to be had without pennies.'

'Pennies?'

William shrugged. 'We are not the only ones to be doing this. Nor the only Quakers. We think our product the best and wish to be sure of it. There is a strong consensus from the doctors now that our cocoa is beneficial to the health of young and old, and most especially in its pure and unadulterated state. This is not a claim many can make. We have doctors who are prepared to put their opinion in writing.'

'And you pay the doctors for their opinion?'

William smiled. 'Of course. As we would pay any professional for their time. And as all other companies do, Quaker or otherwise. I believe the day is coming, and it will be a great day for Temperance, when the first man, instead of heading for the pub, stops in for a cup of cocoa.'

I chuckled. 'Do you truly think men will be persuaded from their beer?'

William nodded solemnly. Clearly he was waiting for my next question, and since I found myself, admittedly, intrigued, I asked it.

'You have some plan then?'

'I do.'

'To do with the product?'

'Not quite. To do with the selling of it. You know, of course, that we have different kinds of cocoa?'

'Of course. Cocoa for the rich and poor. Let the poor eat cake too, but let it have plenty of grit.'

I shouldn't have said this, but William's complacency had irritated me. Now his face darkened.

'How much do you know of cocoa production?' he asked.

I shrugged, embarrassed, and he went on. 'Precious little, because you will never permit me to show you the factory. I'm more your father's son than you are, always too grand to mucky your hands.'

Although he had little bulk, he sat down weightily on a chair. We had been of such different proportions since early boyhood. I, tall, full-featured and already with my father's tendency to heaviness. And William still with the slender hips and sharp bones of his boyhood, with never an ounce of spare flesh. His was a nervous physique and today even his black hair, with its tight black curls, looked agitated. He rested his hands on the arms of the chair and stared blankly across the room. His fingernails, I noticed, were bitten to the quick.

'I apologise for that remark,' he said. 'There was no call for me to bring your father into this. But truly, at the factory you are always so quickly in and out, there is no chance for me to tell or show you anything of what I am doing. You have as substantial a part in it, Samuel, as I do, given your share of ownership. But it is as if my trade made you most uncomfortable, and yet it is only cocoa. Not so far, in its own mucky way, from your own family business.'

I felt abashed by his observations, but unwounded by his remarks. The truth was, I visited his factory far more often than I did the Tannery, even if, as he correctly pointed out, I had little interest in the actual processes. At the same time I had not known he noticed me so well.

'I have nothing but respect for you and Caleb,' I said. 'There are few men who would have taken the risk you two did when you borrowed money and bought the factory, even knowing how close you would run to bankruptcy and disownment from the Meeting. And fewer still who could have transformed that debt-ridden business into what you have now. You deserve your prosperity and the high regard you carry within the city, both from Quakers and from the business community.'

'I paid my debts before the money became due and we do not put grit into the cheaper cocoa,' William said slowly. 'The price is lower because we take less time and effort, fewer labour hours, less machinery, to refine out the cocoa bean husk, your grit. But it won't be long before our machinery is so good that all cocoa will be produced to the same high standard. And when this happens, how will we persuade the wealthier man to buy the more expensive box? Because if we don't, then not just us, but all our workers will suffer.'

I looked into the garden. Martha, William's youngest child, yesterday's bandage visible and forgotten on her knee, was throwing a ball up into the tree, as high as she could, and each time the ball would make a different path down, bouncing and deflected off the branches, slithering between the young leaves, till it fell to the ground. As she scooped it up to throw again, she caught sight of me at the window and called, waving her arms.

I turned back into the room. 'I must go down, or the children will have no game with me.' I was walking towards the door when William put his hand on my arm.

'Stay just another minute, Samuel. I had good reason for detaining you. Listen! This is my idea. I have been talking to Benbow and he has suggested something to me.'

'Benbow,' I said.

'Others are doing it, though none of them are cocoa companies.'

'Your plan, then?' I said, my voice impatient.

William was pacing again, his step trying to keep pace with his excitement, back and forth.

'My plan is a girl. Not an imaginary girl, but a real one. Not only a painted picture, but also a photograph. A real girl. If we put a girl on our boxes, we will sell them faster than we can imagine. She will become the Wetherby's girl and when people look at her, and she is pretty and pure and smiling, like someone they might almost know, they will think of us, and they will buy our cocoa.'

I nodded, slowly. I could see how this was going. 'So who will it be then? Martha?'

William looked at me in surprise. 'No! Of course not one of my own children. Besides, I had in mind a grown-up girl. Or nearly grown-up.'

'You have someone in mind?'

'Yes. Benbow thinks her perfectly suitable. She works in the factory and, I discovered, has been photographed before so cannot possibly have any objection.'

'What does Caleb say?'

'He is in agreement.' William paused. 'At least, he is agreed that I have a better head for these decisions.'

'And the girl?'

'What about the girl?'

'Does she know what it will mean?'

'Mean?'

'That there will be pictures of her plastered everywhere, for all the world to see.'

'It won't be for all the world to see. You talk as if we were to exhibit her all over the world. It is only to be on our boxes, on our product, and in places where our goods are sold. Such advertising is not yet so inexpensive that we can "plaster", as you term it.'

'What is her name?' I said.

'Why do you wish to know it?'

'Curiosity,' I said, though the truth was that I knew by now who the girl must be and was hard-pressed to calm my agitation.

'Her name is Harriet,' William said. 'There was not another in the factory when she came, so it is her own name.'

I would not have expected William to remember after this time that she came to the factory on my recommendation, but now I felt obscurely grieved that he appeared not to, though thinking back, I wonder now if it was that it didn't suit him to.

'If you are perfectly decided, why are you telling me all this? You don't need my approval,' I said.

William was silent a moment. 'Do you remember the trip we made to Wales one year with your father?' he said at last.

'Yes,' I said.

'Do you remember how we slept one night together, in a narrow bed? It was in some remote part and there was no other place to stay.'

I did not remember, but wanting to hear what he had to say, I did not say so. He went on.

'Your father took the floor and insisted that we have the bed because we had been travelling many hours and were very tired. And it was so narrow, there was not room even for us to lie back to back. So we slept that night like spoons, you and I, knees tucked into knees. And though we are, though we were such different shapes, if you will excuse the form of words, and we had such different knees, it was so snug I have ever after remembered it.'

'Why do you tell me this now?'

William had stopped his pacing, and now he stood in the middle of the drawing room, his arms by his sides. He seemed, momentarily, at a loss, and then angry.

'I don't know . . . I want your endorsement, your understanding, that closeness maybe, or perhaps your father's, though he's been dead all these years.'

I didn't try to answer him. I believe he wanted to leave the room, but something prevented him, and when he spoke again, in a careful, distant voice, I understood.

'Tell me Samuel, how is your mother?'

'She is growing frailer by the day, but she is as obdurate as always, and she has her wits.'

William laughed. 'She is still master of all she surveys then?'

'She is. But perhaps she surveys less than she did.'

'And Grace?' he said, after a polite pause. Both of us knew this was the question he had been wanting to ask, the reason he had not left the room.

'The same. I still have hopes of bringing her home. But not while Mother . . .' I didn't need to finish the sentence. William would have wished me to say more, and I was glad of the constraint we both laboured under in this place, the home of his wife and children.

'I must go now and play, or Martha will be a daemon to me, and John will sulk.'

The children were frustrated. They had wanted me to play a longer game, had begged and pleaded, but after my long talk with William and the day almost half-gone, I had insisted on a shorter one. This had baulked both them and me of a pleasure long anticipated, but I could not give up my chance to paint. I could only console them with my word that I would be out here again very soon.

William and I had had no quarrel, not in the end, and yet I felt as if the day, which began so well, had been stolen from me by some malignant vapour. I strode the short mile from Westow to Kirkham vigorously, my small suitcase in one hand and my watercolour bag on my shoulder, my hat jumping with my vigorous step, and gradually, as I'd hoped, the exercise of my body aided the exercise of my spirit. In the spirit of my youth I counted the butterflies, feasting on the yellows and the pinks of meadow flowers and let my thoughts rest on a subject that had been somewhat troubling me recently.

My photographic project, which I had begun only months before, was fast gaining momentum. So much so that recently Benbow had barely been able to keep pace with me. And on one occasion recently he had almost lost his temper.

I had had it in mind to try out Caleb's opinion on the subject, but in our walk for eggs had not found the right moment to speak of it, perhaps because there were things I was myself unsure of.

Benbow was certainly a very fine photographer. I had no doubts as to the quality of his work. But whether it was this new enterprise of William's in which Benbow was involved, or whether it was to do with some uncertain thing I barely knew I was seeing, as I braced myself down the steep hill into Kirkham I found a question in my mind concerning him. A small cloud that clipped into shadow now one corner, now another of the lovely meadow.

Despite his freethinking, Benbow was a Church of England man. A churchwarden, a pillar of his parish. He had told me once that he should have been an actor, for ladies often congratulated him on his fine tone when he read the lesson. And he had calculated that over ninety per cent of the front twelve pews had visited his studio to have their portrait taken.

'It is not only *your* religion that pays,' he had said, laughing, and it was a joke he often referred back to. But now I wondered whether there was another joke behind this one, and whether I might not be the butt of it.

Only a week or so ago, I had arrived at his studio as arranged, accompanied by three trotter-scrapers. I had met one of these girls near the Foss canal two days before on her way home from work, and been intrigued as to her profession. Her clothes were ragged even by the standard of that impoverished district and though she had boots, clodding things several sizes too large and held together with scraps of fabric, she wore neither bonnet nor shawl. Her arms were bare, the armholes roughly sewn, and as she lifted one arm to tuck a straying strand of hair behind her ear, I had a glimpse of her underarm and the dark curls nestled there.

But for all her poverty of dress, the girl had a lovely bearing and when I asked her what she did, she told me proudly the details of her grim and lowly work.

'It's us as cleans off the trotters and hooves and all,' she said. 'Most times it'll be bits of flesh and gristle, and hair of course, but sometimes they come with more attached and you've to clean 'em up before the lime.'

'And you have to take off the sleeves of your frock to do this work?' I asked.

She nodded. 'Else they'd soon smell horrid, for your arms get fair covered with all the mess and it's near impossible to get the smell out once it's in.' Which I could believe, for even in the open air, she had a powerful odour about her.

'And then?' I asked. 'Is it the men who steep them?'

'Oh no,' she said, looking quite put out. 'We've the whole task ourselves, first the scraping and then the lime pits.'

'And is there any place for you to sit, for your dinner, say, or when you stop a moment?' I asked. She nodded and as she spoke, mimed what she did.

'We clear a space in the lime to sit as best we can, sort of sweeping it away with our boots, but still it gives an awful fright to our frocks.' And, unconscious of the comedy of her words, she showed me the holes in her petticoats which, she told me, they called 'lime holes', to distinguish them, I presumed, from all the other tatters in her dress.

'Your master, then?' I asked, already by now hoping to procure her and others for my photographic project.

'The master,' she snorted. 'He don't come near unless he's forced, and some of the older girls say he's feared to on account of the meanness of the wage and the strength we have.'

So I made her my proposition, and soon we were agreed. She would meet me with two friends, dressed as she was now, but the clothes as clean as could be managed on account of the warmth of the studio.

It was not the first, but maybe the fortieth time I had done this, and I was amassing a considerable body of proof about the deplorable conditions of work in which many girls spent their lives.

At that time I told myself that this was, if not my sole motive, then my fundamental one. That it was the girls I wished to help. Grace, who was the only person aside from Benbow to whom I had spoken of my project, had told me the name of a journalist who was not only writing articles criticising the condition of women's labour, but also collecting material in support of his arguments. I had even written to this man, a somewhat circumspect letter, but it had drawn a very favourable response. If at any time in the future I had photographs available, he would be most interested in seeing, or better still, acquiring them.

'You will be able to send them to him one day,' Grace said, and I had agreed, believing it to be something one day that I ought to do. Though in my heart I could not imagine how or when.

I still think this was an important aspect of my picture collecting, and finally Grace was right. But it was not the most important. Now I know that there was something I wanted to possess for myself, something that these girls had, and so I collected their pictures, more and more of them, in my effort to acquire it. I could say it was their strength of body that I wanted and that would be true. I could say it was their delicacy of gesture, even despite their heavy work, and that too would be true. Or their attention, their look for as long as the camera demanded, and that too would be true. But none of these amounted to the thing itself, which I could no more name now than I could then, and after all I knew really that I could no more gain what I wanted through my pictures than I could in my forays into the byways of York, although it didn't stop me trying.

Though it was early evening, the day had been fine and clear and there was still considerable light, perfect conditions for our task. We were early, so I showed the girls into the waiting room and went upstairs to find Benbow. Unusually, the studio door was shut. But I could hear his laugh, and I knocked. There was no answer and rather than knock louder, which might have seemed too intrusive, I tried the door handle. It was locked. Another voice was audible now, a young woman's voice, I thought. I stood uncertain a moment longer and then turned and was making my way down the stairs when I met Miss Hornsgarth, Benbow's assistant. Though I do not count myself as observant in the ways of women, I was surprised to notice a blush rising from her meagre bosom.

'Mr Ransome!' she exclaimed, her expression quite shocked.

I smiled. 'Miss Hornsgarth. I am a few minutes early, and Benbow, it seems, is still occupied.'

'Did you?' she asked me, and I inclined my head and waited for her to say more, being unsure of her meaning. She looked to the ground, and then she looked to the ceiling, and finally she looked at me.

'Did you open the door?' she said at last.

I shook my head. 'It was locked,' I said, expecting her to explain this unusual state of affairs. But she did not. Instead, she pushed past me and, as far as her dress would allow, rushed up the stairs towards the locked door.

'Mr Benbow!' Miss Hornsgarth shouted, banging her hand on the door in a style I did not at all associate with this normally stern and proper lady, who seemingly had forgotten my presence only a short flight below. 'Mr Benbow!' she repeated, 'it is time for your next appointment. With Mr Ransome.'

I thought it better at this point, and before Benbow unlocked the door, to return to the waiting room. There were the girls, oblivious of the drama outside. It was the end of the working day and they were tired. So two of them had sat themselves on the floor and were more than halfway to the sweet shore of sleep, while the third, her tongue between her teeth with concentration, was entranced by the wall of photographic portraits, tracing the outline of a lady's dress, all lace and finery, with a strong, grubby finger.

Not knowing how long Benbow would be, and knowing by now how hungry such girls were, I was about to go and find some pies, by way of apology for the delay, when the door was shoved back on its hinges and Benbow marched in. He was white-faced, tight-lipped and furious at something.

'Benbow,' I said by way of greeting. He looked from me to the three girls and seemed about to say something when he checked himself.

'You were early,' he said.

'A little,' I nodded.

'You have never been early before,' he said. 'You do understand that I have other business to conduct too, and,' and here he dropped his voice, 'I cannot always be looking out for you and yours.' He spoke with such asperity that it might have been gall in his mouth.

'I have never expected you to look out for me, or my girls,' I answered quietly and evenly.

'You also understand it is most important that none of these creatures,' and he made a slight gesture towards my three lasses, 'that none of these is seen by my other clients.'

'I do not think, Benbow, that you need treat these girls in this way. They have come here only at my express invitation. Besides which' and I dropped my voice to a whisper at this point, 'I am paying you well for your work.'

At this, finally, he seemed to recollect himself and without another word, he called for Miss Hornsgarth to show the girls up to the studio, pretending to study his portraits till they had gone. Then he turned to me with what I took to be his reassuring smile on his face.

'I'm so busy at the moment,' he said, shrugging. 'And respectable people being my chief if not my most interesting clients, my stock in trade, I can't have them mixing with your girls. Better if they don't even see them. Lots of fine ladies and their children. Really I'd rather not have to, but I must give them what they want. It is my job. To give people what they want. You on the one hand, and them on the other.'

When he had finished, he stood as though awaiting my confirmation. I could bring myself to give only the briefest nod. Then I moved towards the stairs.

Usually when I took the girls up to the studio, some props would remain in place from the previous session. Tables and chairs, a parasol, potted plants, a spinning top, screens. On this occasion the studio was clean as a pin. All had been stacked away, backcloths leant with their backs to us, and nothing remained but a heavy perfume in the air, that I knew from somewhere but could not place.

Benbow conducted our photographic session with absolute propriety and promised to have the photographs ready by the following evening.

My normal practice was to pay the girls off in the studio and allow Miss Hornsgarth to conduct them out. I liked to watch Benbow at work, and I enjoyed our debates. On this occasion, however, I left the studio with the girls, who were by now in high spirits, and, having bought them some pies at last and paid and thanked them for their time, I walked home.

I am accustomed to subterfuge – deceit is often a necessary kindness – though there are many Friends would think this immoral. But something about Benbow's conduct on this day had left a bitter taste and I looked forward, for the first time, to finishing my project and spending less time with the man. My thoughts moved, as they were wont, on to Harriet, my muse, as I had come to think of her, whom I had not seen in some weeks. Though I knew by now it was as well to check thoughts before they took me too far, for they could lead me into that state of body my father had warned me against all those years ago.

To my intense pleasure, Harriet had finally become acquainted with Grace. Although I had managed my ambition badly to begin with, failing to recognize the nature of Harriet's fears, both at being seen alone with a gentleman at night and at this place of asylum, I was more than rewarded by the bond established between the two after their first meeting.

It had taken me some while to persuade Harriet to return to The Haven. Her earlier visit, with the shrieking woman and the limping dog, was still sharp in her mind, so that I was forced to appeal to that instinct she had for aiding the desperate which I knew of from some of her tales. I painted Grace as a figure most misunderstood, unable to return to her family home, unable to marry, and in mourning for the friendship she once had with another girl. This was nothing more than the truth, though Mother would have put it differently.

'So why is she kept in this place, then?' Harriet asked me. 'There are girls like that where I come from, but they're always kept at home. Why is she in amongst strangers?'

'Perhaps she will tell you her story one day,' I said, conscious of my unease about this affair. 'It would be better if she did.'

When they finally stood together in the same room, I wished I had a camera with me. As I had thought, their likeness was uncanny, though it lay in no obvious features. Harriet's hair was straight and dark, piled today above her head, while Grace's head had been crowned since childhood with fair curls. Though I was big-boned, my sister had still the elfin delicacy of her first years, and, even in the greatest heaviness of spirits, a lovely feline economy of gesture. Harriet, by contrast, was strongly-built with broad shoulders and strong hands and her movements had a forthright, downright quality to them which I had noticed on the first day we met, as though you might read the motion of her soul as simply in the reaching for a cup or the turn of her head.

Yet for all this physical difference, Grace and Harriet shared what I came to think of as some profound affinity of spirit, an affinity that from the first transcended the divides of class and history, and which I caught in something they shared, which was the way each had of holding their head and the steadiness, stillness even, with which they regarded the world.

'Do not be offended if she doesn't speak,' I told Harriet as we walked up the hill towards The Haven.

'Then what will be the point of my visiting?' she said, and I had had no reply.

I had sent word to Grace that we would be coming, and to tell me if she did not wish it. I had an answer the following day requesting that I bring with me some of Mother's compost and a new trowel. She made no mention of Harriet, and I took this to be favourable.

'She is not here?' Harriet said when we stood in the entrance hall.

'She is in her room,' I answered. 'We will go there when I have told somebody that we are visiting.'

Harriet nodded. 'It is nicer at the front,' she said, and I thought I could detect a faint smile in her voice. I felt my colour rise as I recalled that room I had given her tea in, with the red oilcloth and the map of the drains. Things had changed since then, or perhaps it was only I that had changed. I would not dream now of taking Harriet to the back door, the servants' entrance, any more than I would Grace.

'Mr Ransome,' a voice said, and then the Superintendent's wife was before us, smiling graciously at Harriet, though even in her Quaker smile I could see the question forming.

'Good evening, Mrs Pendleton. Miss Brewer is here to see Miss Ransome,' I said.

Mrs Pendleton bowed slightly to Harriet. 'I should think you might like some tea in due course?' she said, and Harriet nodded.

'Thank you, yes,' she said, every inch the lady.

'So you have brought her at last, Sam,' Grace said. We had been standing in her room for what seemed like minutes, but she had not yet turned from her plants, had not greeted us. Her hands were muddy with soil and she had hair secured from her face with a scrap of cloth tied about her head. I noticed that her blouse was untucked, and I could see the gleam of sweat on her cheek. Certainly she had made no special effort for her guest.

'I said that I would bring Harriet today,' I answered.

'Ah, but even a Quaker's word is not what it was,' she said.

'Grace,' I said, 'please. She is glad to come here, are you not, Harriet?'

'I don't know yet,' Harriet replied.

At this Grace turned, stared hard at her new guest, and laughed. 'You will like me,' she said. 'You are like.'

She crossed the room, took Harriet's hand in her own and welcomed her. Welcomed her like a long-lost friend. That was all it took.

There is something about painting, when it works, that is, for me, close to meditation. While I have the brush between my fingers, my worries scatter to the winds and I am possessed by that mental state I often long for during Meeting. I had seen an exquisite drawing of Kirkham Abbey only weeks earlier by the watercolourist John Sell Cotman, and inspired by him, whom I considered little short of a genius, I planned on this Sunday to try my hand too at painting the Abbey gateway.

Mr Cotman often stayed with friends nearby, and from stories I have heard in these parts, I know that he was anything but meditative in his frame of mind. Rather given, as many artists are, to black despair about his gift. Having no such gift, I am not troubled in this way and find in my painting nothing but pleasure.

So this day, as I set up easel and stool near the gateway and prepared myself to paint, my concern for Grace's future and for Mother's precarious health, my anxiety over the Home for Unfortunate Young Women, recently subjected to further sectarian attacks, my doubts about William's business decisions, even my feelings about Harriet: all were dissipated. And my only thought was of the buttery colour of the Abbey stone, the vertical planes in the façade and the shading of the trees behind.

It was somewhere else that boys shouted and splashed, somewhere else that birds sang as they swooped on flies and somewhere else where courting couples whispered in the long grass. Even the ratchety din of a crowd of Sunday bicyclists labouring up the steep hill out of Kirkham was far off, part of another place.

I had brought with me sandwiches and hard-boiled eggs and a flask of water, and at some point in the long afternoon hours I must have eaten and drunk. But still all I knew was the sun on my shoulders, my palette of soft colours, the thick cream paper and the piece of ancient stone with its delicate George and Dragon carved in their dance, that I wished to put there.

So when I heard her voice, when she addressed me, for a moment, no longer than a flash before the eyes, I felt only resentment, anger even, that she had robbed me of my peace of mind.

'Good day, Mr Ransome,' she said.

She had with her a young man, a strongly-built fellow whom I recognised from Wetherby's. And before she had said a word, before she had introduced him, I knew that today this young man had asked her to marry him. She might as well have held up a placard. It was written into her body, her gestures, the way she touched her hair with her fingers. It was counted into the daisy chain she wore around her wrist – 'she loves me, she loves me not, she loves me' – fastened, no doubt, by his stubby fingers. He had asked her to marry him today, I was sure of it, and I was shocked to feel the jealousy not only in my heart but also in my very limbs.

I believe I stood and bowed to her. If she introduced the young man, I don't remember it. But the next thing I knew she was trying to look at my picture, stepping forward, hand outstretched, finger reaching even, to peer round the easel, and I don't know what came over me, but I couldn't let her see it and would have forcibly prevented her if I had needed to. Afterwards I was at a bit of a loss to explain it to myself, and when next we met neither of us mentioned it.

Then they were gone, walking away towards the station. I turned to watch her, but couldn't bear it, and sat back down on the stool. I picked up my pencil and started to draw

Harriet in, Harriet and her young man, two little figures just off to one side of the lovely doorway. I sketched them in and started to paint them. But the figures went smeary and the painting became a mash of colours, no use to anyone, so I stopped. Instead I put a date on the picture, as if I might need to remind myself in years to come, as if that afternoon is not scratched deep into the flesh of my heart. Then I packed my things and walked towards the station.

I was nearly on to the platform before my wits returned enough for me to realise that they, too, would be waiting there. So I took a seat in the waiting room and sat in the gloom for the train.

At York I waited for them to walk past my carriage before I climbed down. I nearly walked into the back of them, so slowly were they going. They had to make a lovers' parting, that was why. And sure enough, I watched them embrace, oblivious, beneath that great parabola of glass and iron that usually sends my spirit soaring. Then he left her standing there, shoved about by all the people impatient, now their leisure time was closing in, to be home, impatient of a single young girl standing in the middle of the station platform, close to grief or close to joy, I didn't know which. It took all my might and main not to go to her and offer her my arm. Instead I turned away and walked home.

HARRIET

I was happy enough in the factory now. The hours were long, but when that bell rang on the dot of six, we were done. There was never a finish to the work with the fish. Even so, by Friday it seemed a long time to be sat doing one thing in one place. I was still getting used to that, after the out and about I'd grown up with.

The day before Thomas left for London, he'd arrived at Mrs O'Leary's with a whole box of raspberries and a plan. He'd divided the raspberries out into bowls and cups, with the O'Leary children shrilling around him. Then we'd taken ours up to my room and sat on my bed and he'd come out with his plan.

'We'll marry in secret,' Thomas said.

I looked at him, my mouth open in surprise.

'I've it all worked out,' he said. 'An old friend, from back in the St Sebastian days, lives in Leeds, bang in the city. We're going to use his address – he doesn't mind – and get ourselves married in a church there. Then nobody need know. Nobody. Soon as I'm back, we'll get the banns read, and one Saturday you'll put on your best bonnet, get it newly-trimmed first, and I'll shine my Sunday shoes and we'll take the train and get ourselves wed. We can get a couple of witnesses off of the street, pay 'em a shilling they'll be happy, and come back man and wife.'

He'd said it all so quick, I couldn't understand at first. And when I'd asked him some questions and got some answers, still I couldn't believe it'd be as easy as that.

'It is,' he said. 'And then there'll be no need for you to give up the job, not until you want to.'

'But we can't live together, as long as nobody knows. Isn't that the main point? They'll think we're immoral. You get married so as you can live with the person you're in love with.'

But he'd only shaken his head and told me not to worry myself with it as he had it sorted out.

'If we could live under the same roof, as man and wife, and still have it a secret, would you be happy then?' he said. 'Or do you want to give up the work at Wetherby's and all your friends and sit at home, maybe take in washing, or mind other people's children? Like other women when they're wed? Doesn't pay as well, nothing like, of course. And you don't get out, or meet other women so much. Have to stay in your home, but . . .'

'Of course I want to keep my job,' I said. 'You know that. I hate the factory law. I've seen the other girls leave the Friday before their marriage, crying over their factory dress and apron and galoshes. And Mrs Flint taking them and checking the dress for stains and the galoshes for holes, keen as mustard to find something to get them for, for going off to do what she never has. Crowing it over them, all smug in her pure body and her thin hips, and them all teary. Seems all wrong to me that they have to go. They still have to keep body and soul together, and how is it meant to be easier, just because they're married?'

'It's not that. It's because they think a woman's place is at home with her children, making a home for her husband,' Thomas said.

'I know what "they" say,' I yelled. All of a sudden I was full of fury, come up in me from somewhere, and banged my hands so hard on the bedhead, I bruised them. 'But "they" don't have to live it, do they? I bet Mrs William Wetherby doesn't have to pinch and go without just to put a bit of meat in her children's mouths on a Sunday? I bet her children can have an egg for their tea sometimes, and not have to watch their father eat the only one for his only bit of relish and then squabble over the shell for who's to lick it. I bet . . .'

Thomas had to shout to get a word in. He had his hands on my shoulders and I could feel his strength, and I saw that his eyes were grey in the streaky light that fought its way in my little window. 'I'm on your side, Harriet, remember? That's why we're going to keep it secret.'

'But I've said already, if we do it in secret, then we still can't live together. Seems like you've got the worst of it all then. Married and living like a nun, the both.'

That made us both laugh, the idea of me a nun I suppose.

'Trust me?' he said, and I gave him back a little nod. He crossed himself and made as if to pray to me with his hands and we didn't say no more on it then.

It hadn't been so long since I'd have said I'd live and die with the sea at my back. It hadn't been even a year. But my life before coming to York seemed a long way away now. It'd be a nearer thing to make the journey – just a few hours on a train after all – but a further thing in all else. I'd my friends here. I was right fond of Elsie and Mrs O'Leary. I didn't see so much of Mary as I might, not as much as I'd like to, but

I'd not leave her for all the gold in China, even if they didn't have gold in China, which was, of course, what Thomas had told me.

So too I was mistress of my own money now. And I might not be earning as much as Thomas, nor would I ever, but I was better paid than I'd be anywhere else. Better paid than I'd ever be collecting limpets off of the rocks. And till we married, and after if I'd anything to do with it, my wage was my own.

Even Mrs Flint left me alone now, which my dad never would have. He wasn't like Mary's mam, it wasn't the drink got him. It was a fury from somewhere else, from the sea maybe, and I could pity him it now I'd the miles between, but one day he'd be the death of someone, what with his knife throwing and that, and he'd be the one to be grieving most, and no storm but his own to blame it on.

I knew the factory work well now and was on to pitying the new girls when they came in and had to learn to measure the cocoa, or shape the creams, or pick out the bad berries from the good. The picture-taking was going to happen very soon. I'd been told to be ready for the week following and Mrs O'Leary had caught me practising a smile in the mirror in the kitchen.

'What are you at, girl?' she'd said. 'You don't need to worry. He'll have you as he finds you, you lucky beggar' and she'd pinched my cheeks. 'There! Roses are easy at your age,' she'd said.

Mr William hadn't really told me what I was to be doing. Only that it'd be photographs and they'd be using them to sell the cocoa. So I was guessing maybe it might be used for a tin, which would be a laugh, though Elsie told me they painted on so much colouring, you'd not be able to tell it was me anyway.

The only thing that was worrying me was Thomas. He'd promised to write each day and he said the letters should arrive the day after, or nearly. So for the first week, each day I'd run from the top of the street, expecting Mrs O'Leary to be there at the window with a letter. But there hadn't been one. No word, and I couldn't ask at work. They'd want to know what I was up to, prying. My heart was heavy as lead, weighted like a line for my precious fish, and him gone down to the deeps of London, but I said nothing to nobody.

Mrs O'Leary saw my worry well enough, and Elsie knew that I was out of sorts and tried to jolly me, which only made me cross. Even Ellen, Mrs O'Leary's eldest, took to bringing me little tokens to cheer me, but they only made me want to cry. A posy of buttercups she'd picked from the city walls, and a feather – a jay's with its flash of blue – knowing how I liked to watch them. The only one I'd have opened my heart to, but I daren't over this, was Mary. It wasn't the chalk and cheese of us that stopped me. We'd always laughed on that before. It was because she didn't like him, not in any respect. And he returned her feelings in kind. So I couldn't tell either of the other but that I got an earful, and right now I didn't need that for my pains.

Not being very quick at my letters, I'd had Ellen teaching me to write, and especially to read better, so that when I had Thomas's letters I could read them myself and not have to hear them spoken by another. Ellen had a quicker head for it than me, more like Mary, and could read next door's newspaper as fast as Thomas, though I'd never say that to him, him being proud in that way like most men.

We'd sit at it a half hour or so and then my thoughts would drift and I'd wonder, was he walking down some street in London now, or talking to men, or chatting to the girl giving him his tea in the hotel.

'Harr-ie-et,' Ellen would say, and nudge me, tread on my toes even, to get me back. 'Harr-ie-et, wake up, wake up,' and we'd go on a while longer.

It was into Thomas's second week away that a letter came,

and then it wasn't from him at all. I was late home from Wetherby's on account of the birds and Mrs O'Leary was waiting by the window.

It wasn't anything else than that I missed them. The swifts especially, but the swallows and the martins too. Back by the sea this time of year, the air would be full of swifts of an evening, their 'eee' 'eee' shrieking and their crazy flight, and I'd sit outside the house and watch them till my neck was stiff. But they didn't fly above the city, at least not like that. You'd get just a one sometimes, high, high up, but that was all and I'd like to think it had maybe lost itself chasing a fly up there. So I'd go to the river after my day at the factory and they'd be there swooping after the insects on the water and never the once even catching the wet with a wing. And after a time I'd walk home to Mrs O'Leary's.

The letter was from Mr Ransome, and I am sure he wrote it in his clearest hand so as I could make it out. Still, it took a bit of doing. 'Dear Harriet,' it said, 'I am writing to request the pleasure of your company on Saturday next on a visit to see the Belgian female acrobats perform in Leeds.' Then there was something about remaining mine faithfully and his name at the bottom.

'What does he say, love?' Mrs O'Leary said, and I pretended it was Thomas as had written and that all was well, though I couldn't stop the tears from starting, so that Mrs O'Leary gave me a cheery pat on the back.

'Tears of joy, eh? Didn't I tell you he would,' she said. 'I did, didn't I?' so I had to nod and agree she had. But soon as I could, I was out of there before I gave her a piece, and it wasn't her fault.

I didn't know where I was going when I closed Mrs O'Leary's door. I only wanted to be gone. I started to run, and there was air enough in my lungs, I could have run to the ends of the earth if I'd wanted. I could have run back home, and then tomorrow I'd be on the cliff in my kirtle and jersey, my curtainbonnet caught under my chin against the weather, a flither basket in my hand, and my hands would be soft for the work, but they'd harden and that'd be that. I'd never need to think on Thomas or Mary, the factory or Mr Ransome and his strange kindness, or the city or what I should do. I'd never need to think what I should do again, and I'd find myself well-enough in love or liking for some lad I'd known since he were in short britches and we'd be wed and get for ourselves a cottage far away enough from Dad, and my lad'd be on the boats and I'd be down to the beaches till the babies came and after.

A gentle rain had started, raising steam off the cobbles. I was glad of it, soft on my hot face. You never had rain like this back home. Not with the sea so close by, and its coldness and its bulk. There the rain was like pins so you'd want to hide your head and cover your face.

I ran out of the city and away from the people. Away from the men ducking into pubs and the women clacking their clogs, aprons pulled over their heads against the wet, and the children scootering in and out, their feet black with the wet dust. I ran past the cattle market where the stalls were empty and the animals gone. Two men were shovelling dung on to carts and I'd have liked to stop a moment just to listen to the slap and shift of the muck and watch it shiver and settle, bits of grass still caught in the brown mess of it. The men leant on their spades and called something out to me. They'd the look of my father, shoulders rounded down with the stoop of so much labour and hands red and broad from holding their tools. And they looked like kind men, but I had to keep on.

I ran down one street, all neat brick houses, and up another the same. There was a hill, at first so slight you'd swear it wasn't there. Then steeper, and still I ran, till I reached the top and my lungs were heaving and my throat burning. At last, not knowing where I had run to, nor what I had run from, I stopped. And all I could hear was the hiss of the rain and I put my head right back and let the softness cover me from the dark of the sky.

I'm not the kind of person to do something I don't know that I'm doing. When girls at work have said they kissed a boy, or drunk too much beer, or bought a bonnet and they didn't know they were doing it, I'd not say so, but I wouldn't believe them. But now I'd done the same. And without at all meaning to, I found myself standing outside the high wall of The Haven.

I was exhausted. You could have wrung a bath from my dress, my hair was cold against my neck and I was half-faint with hunger. I'd had nothing to eat since my dinner at midday and I hadn't the strength to go back. I leant my back up against the wall and shut my eyes.

It mustn't have been long I was stood there, but it might have been forever, when I felt somebody's hand on my shoulder.

'Get away!' I shouted, and I lurched towards, and then away from the figure standing before me. In the half-dark and the rain I couldn't see whether it was man or woman, couldn't see whether they meant good or ill.

'Come with me. I'll bring you inside,' the figure said, raising a stick in the air, and I could see it was a woman, as broad and strong as any I'd ever climbed the cliffs with. I'd have tried to run for it then, but I was too weak, and the next moment she had the umbrella opened and an arm round my shoulder and she near enough carried me up the drive and into the building.

It wasn't that I was frightened, so much as confused. More than anything I needed to be sat down by myself to collect my thoughts.

I had stood in this front hall before, with Mr Ransome. It was all dark wood and little tables and a hat stand and big green plants. Now my rescuer took me into a room like a

giant parlour, big settees with lace antimacassars such as Mrs
O'Leary would've given her eye teeth for, and bookshelves
and tables with chairs all around. There was a grandfather
clock in one corner and a piano in another and on the mantelpiece was another clock and some pretty bits of china. There
was a vast fern in the fireplace and more plants near the windows, which had green velvet curtains pulled across like sails.
The room was empty, but I could tell from the smell of
tobacco, and the bit of haze like a faint fog, that it wasn't long
since it had been full, and I almost fancied I could hear the
sounds still.

'Sit down. I'll fetch you some tea,' the woman said and she
pressed me down on to one of the settees and left the room.

I'd have liked to sink in there, to fall down and away and be
lost, like when I was little and we'd run up the hill behind and
jump in the bracken and it'd hold you, hidden, and only the
insects running up the stalks could see you.

But I couldn't. The settee was hard, and though the stuff
covering it was soft, it was slippery, so you'd to keep something
tense, an arm or a leg, to stay on. Still I was grateful to be
alone with only the clocks ticking, and somewhere far off the
noise of other people.

'It must be Grace Ransome I'm here for,' I said out loud to
myself, but I was too tired to think why. Too tired to think
what I can see now, that it must have seemed the oddest thing
to her, that I should come here like this, still in my work
things, so hot and bothered, though she never showed it.

'You did well to get tea! She must have liked you.' Grace
seemed to find this very funny, for her shoulders shook,
though her laugh, if it was one, was silent.

'Do you laugh often?' The words were out before I could
stop them. I clapped a hand to my mouth. 'I'm sorry. That's
very rude,' I said. 'I only meant . . .'

'You meant that you thought I did not very often,' Grace said. She smiled. Her smile seemed drawn out of the air, as if she had heard something that pleased her far beyond what I had said. 'And you're right. I don't often. Perhaps in time you will teach me sound to go with motion,' she said.

'I don't know why I've come here,' I said. 'I had a letter, I have it still somewhere, and it's not from the person I wished it to be from. It is from your brother.'

'Ah,' Grace said, as though she understood now everything that needed to be understood.

'Your brother invites me to accompany him to a spectacle of acrobats, and I don't know if I ought to go.'

I knew what Thomas would say if he knew about it, that I mustn't go, not with anybody and certainly not with Mr Ransome, who he didn't trust an inch. But now I needed to know what Grace might say, though I couldn't have told why.

Grace stood up from her chair. I hadn't noticed before how slight she was. Strong, and tall, but somehow also slight. Like a bird, almost, with her quizzy movements. And her dress was like some odd bird's too. It was of a drab colour, but had bright ribbon sewn around its cuffs, and at the neck and on to the hem. She made me feel lumbering. She walked across to a small table on which different objects were arranged. Stones, feathers, what looked to be the skull of a small animal – a mouse maybe – some shells, though not any that I recognised, some fruits, dried and shrivelled, some flowers pressed flat, a fir cone, a butterfly.

'Are they things you've found?' I said. She didn't answer, but continued to arrange them, making tiny adjustments to their positions with her finger.

I hadn't noticed this table on my first visit, and wondered whether perhaps it had been covered over. Now I noticed that, aside from the plants that filled the windowsills, the room had no bits and pieces. None of the things I'd have expected someone like her to have. No fine lace, no pictures, no china ornaments. Still with one hand on the table, she turned towards me.

'And that is what you wanted to ask me?' she said. Then she shook her head. 'No. It's not my brother's letter you're worried about. It's a letter that hasn't come that's brought you here, dripping all over my carpet.' She sat down again. 'As far as Samuel's invitation goes, I should say that it's up to you.'

'I have heard there is a girl fired from a cannon,' I said.

Again, the silent laugh. 'Then he may avert his eyes,' she said. 'Unlike me, he is squeamish over danger.'

'You would go?' I said.

'He hasn't asked me,' she said, and I knew then that I wanted to go, and so I would say yes.

Suddenly there was a scraping noise at the window. I jumped at the sound, but Grace walked over and opened the latch. A black cat walked in. It leapt over the flowers and on to the floor, then stood like it was waiting for something. Grace sat back down, and the cat, its paws muddy and its coat wet, jumped on to her lap and settled itself there.

There was a little thing I wanted to tell her, something about making up your mind and other people helping by not doing it for you, I think, but it was just out of reach, didn't come to me closely till after, and I couldn't get hold of it. Like one of those dreams that slips off the bed when you wake, and by the time you put your feet to the floor, it's gone. I shut my eyes to see if it'd come up closer, but it wasn't any good.

'You look like a fish,' Grace said. I opened my eyes. 'Your mouth,' she said, and she blew up her cheeks and pouted her lips to show me.

I knew, because Mr Ransome had told me, that his sister was here because she'd been in a bad way a few years back. Not able to take care of herself, he'd said. Too sad. But she seemed well enough to me now. Odd maybe, but nothing more. And I didn't like her doing this fish thing. She was laughing at me.

I stood up. 'I'd better go,' I said.

Grace was still stroking her cat, making these long, sweeping movements with her arm. 'Don't be cross,' she said.

'It's late. I should go home,' I said.

'I don't see many people. Don't choose to,' she said. 'So I'm not good at . . . It's only with you being what you are . . .'

'What's that?'

'A fishergirl. Isn't it? And so the fish . . . I thought it would make you laugh.'

'It'd be Mr Ransome told you, I suppose,' I said. 'Anyway, I'm not any more.'

'No,' she said, and she gave a look like I'd smacked her. 'And I'm not a girl inside a tree any more,' which I couldn't answer because I hadn't a clue what she meant.

'Besides, I can't swim,' I said. 'None of us could. Not the men either.'

'But it's not the swimming that does it,' Grace said. 'You will stay for some supper?' and before I could say a yes or a no, she'd dumped the cat on the carpet and was gone from the room. She was back a few minutes after. 'They'll bring it shortly,' she said, as if I'd already told her I'd stay. And she climbed on to the small high bed against the wall and drew her legs up under her and folded her arms around them. 'I had a friend before you,' she said. 'Deborah.' And then she put her hand to her mouth, like she'd said something she didn't want to have.

'Here?' I said.

She gave a yelping laugh. 'Oh no. Here's where they brought me because of it,' she said. 'My mother and her blame.'

'What do you mean?' I said.

She shrugged. 'She wasn't like you. Anyway, she's gone now. Long gone. Long, long gone.' She dipped her head into her arms so as I couldn't see her face. The cat was walking round the room, like it was looking for something. I watched it. Grace lifted her head up again.

'Tell me something,' she said.

'What?'

'Doesn't matter what.' She wagged a finger at me just like the schoolmistress in the village used to. 'Just one thing though.'

'I'm tired,' I said.

'That's one. Now me. I like the outside.'

I didn't know what she wanted, and I felt bone-weary.

'I don't like fish,' I said.

'It's meat,' she said. 'Your turn.'

'I need water,' I said.

'You come from the water,' she said.

'I'm thirsty,' I said. Grace pointed to the corner by the bed. There was a jug of water and a glass. I drank most of the jug and felt better.

'They smile too much here,' she said.

'But you don't,' I said.

'Tell me something about your childhood,' Grace said.

'I'd a good head for heights, on the cliffs,' I said.

'I've one too, in the trees,' she said.

'I don't like suet,' I said.

'Me neither,' she said.

'Do you climb them?' I said, but she put a finger to her lips. 'No questions. Only answers. Your turn.'

I don't know how long we played at this for, but by the time the food came, I had told her something of Thomas, and as I found later, she had guessed a whole lot more. And in her strange way, which I was not yet used to, she told me things from her childhood, and it was only afterwards that I saw that they fitted like lost pieces into a broken mirror.

The supper was brought in on a trolley by a nurse who smiled at us, which made me giggle, after what Grace had said. The nurse must have thought me very rude, or maybe she was used to such behaviour from the people living in here. The food was delicious. A stew of meat and vegetables and tiny potatoes fresh-boiled, which Grace said were out of the garden there. I was so hungry, I couldn't help myself and I'd cleared my plate where Grace had barely started.

'I won't eat more than a couple of mouthfuls,' she said. 'Do you want the rest?' and so I ate her plateful too, and then stacked the plates neatly.

'I must go back now,' I said. 'Mrs O'Leary will be worrying.'

'You must,' Grace said. 'And you will return here too,' she said, nodding her head. 'You make a great change from my other visitor.'

'That'll be Mr Ransome,' I said. 'Do you not see your mother too?' but Grace didn't answer me. She'd climbed back up onto her bed, gathered her arms around her knees and tucked her head inside her lap, like a bird wrapped up against the cold.

'Goodbye,' I said, and she made no reply. So I took my leave and walked home. It was only walking down the hill that I thought to have asked her why it was that she was living there, for though she was strange, she didn't seem sick.

The night was clear to the stars. When we were very little, my mother used to tell us the stars that shined brightest were the souls of them as we had loved. The night after my Uncle Joseph was drowned, I swore to my brother Daniel I could see a new one, a star that had not been there before, and Daniel had craned his neck back, the tears bright like snails' paths on his cheeks, and he'd said yes, he could see it too and he'd gripped my hand tight. It was only a long time after that he told me he'd only said it to comfort me, and that to him the sky looked as cold and empty that night as it had before.

My mam had kept us in that day, the day before I saw the star. There was a high sea and a storm rising, but not worse than some other days. I was glad to have a day free from flithering, and Daniel was happy to be away from the schoolroom, for Mam and Dad were set to get him some learning. But still both of us knew it to be strange, though we said nothing on it. She'd had a few words with our dad that morning and the day still dark. I don't know what she said, but I heard him telling her not to be a lass, they'd be back before dark, and he'd a fancy for some nice relish and could she find him a sweet rasher for his tea. He was trying to coddle her, but all day she was like one of those people in stories as can see ahead of the others, and she'd barely speak to us.

Come the end of the day, she wouldn't go down to the water, though Mrs Edwards came knocking for her, nor let us go and all.

'You'll stop here,' she said to us.

'But the fish,' Daniel had said.

'The fish'll wait,' she said.

So we'd to stop in and fill our hands and both knowing better than to ask questions. I'd a piece of darning and Daniel some boots to mend, but in an hour or more of waiting, I'd done barely a stitch and Daniel no more either, just sitting there listening out for the thing our mam knew, and the wind howling and the sea in a fury. And Mam, she got on with Dad's food. The rasher, like he'd asked, and the tea in his cup ready to mash.

The light was lifting from the sky and we were lighting the lamps when my dad came in. Only my dad. Mam looked at him and he nodded, like an answer to something, though she'd not spoken. He'd his head sunk low and he spoke his words to his boots.

'They have him back behind,' he said, and he was just stood there for it seemed like minutes, the water off him gathering in pools, till Mam took his hand and led him to a chair like a baby and sat him and began loosening his things.

Then he said, to Daniel and me, 'It's Joseph.'

Maybe I did know, and maybe I didn't. But anyway I needed him to say it. 'What's happened to him?' I said.

Dad looked at me and then he looked back down at the floor, all wet with water, and I wished I'd not asked. But he answered. 'He was drowned out there and the men have his body back behind.'

Then it was Daniel's turn. He was shaking his head, like it was wrong, all this.

'No,' he said. 'He can't be.'

And Dad said, 'Well he is.'

And Daniel said, 'But he said he'd finish my model with me,' and Dad looked at him.

And then I asked, 'So did you capsize?' And Dad said no, so I asked, 'Could you not hold him in then?' and at first he didn't answer me. But then he did, and in this quiet, slow voice that was scarier than any time he'd ever shouted.

'I could not,' he said. It was all he said, but I'd rather never have heard those words. Then Mam was snatching at my darning and pulling me up and pushing me towards the stair door and me letting her. And after me, Daniel, and the latch banged behind us. And we crouched in the dark for an age and listened to the silence of our parents who said no words and it was only from their breathing that we knew they were there.

I didn't believe the half of what Mr Ransome told me before we went. He was trying to speak calmly, but I'd never seen him so excited. Although he was a big man, he was hopping on his toes, or rather he was trying not to. And his cheeks, which I'd always noticed to be pale, like he might be sickening for something, had these two red spots, one in each cheek.

'You will find her appearance quite extraordinary,' he said.

'How will I?' I said.

'She is dressed quite beyond human decorum, Harriet,' he said, giving a little shake to his head. I told him I didn't know what decorum was.

'I mean by that what women ought to wear,' he said.

'But it must be on account of what she does, that she's dressed in this strange way,' I said.

'Oh indeed, it is. And when you see what it is that she does! I have read some that say she is more monkey than maiden and call for a ban on such unsightly and unsexing goings-on.'

'Have you seen her before then?' I said and he nodded and told me we were to see a young woman leap through the air at a great height, and jump through hoops way above our heads, and clasp a man around the body, and be clasped herself. And that at the end she'd get into a cannon and be fired out.

'You'd certainly be stuck doing that lot in a dress,' I said. 'A bit like me on the cliffs. I'd never have got up with my skirts all swooshing out like a tent. The wind would've had me, or they would have snagged on some bit of thorn and then where would I have been?'

Mr Ransome nodded slowly. 'Perhaps that is how it is,' he said, which I took to be a different thing from thinking such dress to be bad.

The place was very grand. Grander than any I'd ever been, with pillars carved all over with leaves, flowers and angels and painted with gold and the whole thing brightly lit. And it was very loud. Such a noise, and such a crush of people, and smoke and the strongest smell of old beer, I was glad my dinner was well-down, or it might have been dragged straight up again.

Inside the entrance, the foyer Mr Ransome called it, people were heaving and shoving, calling out to friends and cursing as their toes got trod or someone's elbow mashed their nose. The push and pull of the crowd swirled about me, and I might have gone in any direction but for Mr Ransome. He had brought a bag with him and somehow he managed to pull out this shawl from it, tugging it up bit by bit like you see a fisherman drawing in his line till you think there can't be any more and still there it comes. The shawl was a beauty, made of cream silk – he told me that, as if I couldn't guess – and embroidered with exotic birds.

With the shawl gathered in his arms, he leant down to me. 'It's Grace's,' he said, like it was a secret between us, but which I knew already from its smell. 'Let me put it round you and we'll take our seats.'

I understood. He'd bought seats downstairs, and he didn't want people staring too hard at me sat there with a gentleman, or at him with me. At least with the shawl round my shoulders, they couldn't see much of my dress. But you can't hide what you are that easily, and I still got some funny ones.

Once we were sat, Mr Ransome opened up his bag again, and took out a fruit cake and a bag of plums, and while we ate, he told me some more about the girl we were to see, having to shout a bit to make himself heard with all the racket around us.

'She won't be on first,' he said, 'because she's the main attraction. We'll have to wait through some other bits.'

'What kind of bits?'

He gave a little frown. 'The usual. Some singing, some dancing. I hope nothing too bawdy, but it is worth enduring for the girl. If my mother knew . . .' and he shook his head at the thought. 'I hope you won't be bored.'

'I won't,' I said laughing and he smiled. I thought how strange it was that a grown man like him should be so anxious at what his mother might think. And then I remembered Grace and what she'd said and I thought the woman must be some terrible creature of a thing.

When the lights dimmed, the quiet that came down was even more exciting than the noise, and then the great red curtains swept open and a man stood in the middle of the stage with a top hat like Mr Ransome's and a tail coat. He swept a bow across the floor and opened his arms out wide.

'Ladies and Gentlemen, Gentlemen and Ladies,' he shouted, 'All the way from the Cocoa Isles where the sea is so blue and the skies are so fair, where the picaninnies dance on the sand and the gents wear few clothes . . .' And here he put his hand up to his mouth like he were going to whisper and said, 'Just a loincloth, I am told,' which got some giggles, 'and the ladies fewer,' which got more, and some men shouted out things I couldn't quite get, but which must've been rude, because Mr Ransome shook his head. 'All the way from over the high seas,' the man went on, 'I'd like you to welcome the Neela Nigrina sisters . . .' and he walked off backwards, sort of bowing as he went and his hat gathering dust since he trailed it on the ground.

There was a big swoop of a trumpet and three strapping girls came mincing on. Their skin, all that you could see, which was plenty, was blacked, and they were dressed in beaded skirts and colourful shifts that left their arms bare and were cut down at the bosom so that I was sure one of them, especially the girl on the left, might come tumbling out at any moment, but she never did.

They each held a black cane and while they sang a song about being down among the coconuts, they did this daft dance, tapping their canes all the while. They weren't nimble nor very funny and I got to wondering how they'd ended up up there, and how ever long it must take them to get the boot polish off, for that's what it must have been. And it mustn't have been only me that was tired of it, for there started to be cat-calls and yells from the gallery above us, and Mr Ransome was fidgeting in his seat and they were singing faster and faster and if it wasn't that they wound up early, then they certainly made short work of the ending, and did their bows with everyone jeering, except Mr Ransome, and slid behind the side curtains. Then on came the man in the top hat again, and he asked the audience to be kind tonight, generous like true Yorkshiremen, which got a laugh, and he said that returning by popular demand and fresh from his success on the London stages with Marie Lloyd, here was Yorkshire's very own Danny Robins.

A short man came on, dressed in a soldier's uniform, and stood in the middle of the stage. The piano played some notes and when all the noise had stopped and you could have nearly heard a pin drop, he started to sing in this voice that was thin, like a bird singing, and touched you under the skin so that I was goose-fleshed all over.

> If I could choose any star from the sky or pick any shell
>   from the sea
> I'd leave off the heavens and come back from the shore
> For my dear old Annie down the alley.
>
> Annie's the girl when a fella comes home,
> And his back is weary and his light is dim.
> Annie's the girl for a fella as is tired,
> For it's she who knows how to comfort him.

After when I was telling Elsie, and singing her the song, she laughed out loud at it.

'But it was so sad,' I said, 'you couldn't believe.'

'Doesn't sound it, from what you've just sung,' she said, and I could see what she meant then, but when Danny Robins was stood there singing, it was like to break your heart:

> If I could eat any fruit from the tree or drink the sweetest
>   of wine,
> I'd run from the orchard and dash down the glass
> For my dear old Annie down the alley.

Annie's the girl when a fella comes home,
And his back is weary and his light is dim.
Annie's the girl for a fella as is tired,
For it's she who knows how to comfort him.

He didn't do anything with his hands, he didn't dance, he didn't even jig about. And he had us all in his keeping those minutes. And when the song was done, it was like somebody had hypnotised us. There wasn't a peep, not even from the topmost balcony. But soon as the clapping started there were lots around me, and blokes too, getting out handkerchiefs and wiping their eyes, even if they might be pretending to scratch their ear.

I say all were quiet and still, but it wasn't quite true. I should say all except Mr Ransome. I admit I was surprised, because of his fine manners. But not only did he move about in his seat and fish things from his pockets and root about in his bag, but he kept on muttering, so as I was tempted to give him a nudge and tell him to put a sock in it. I could see that the gentleman on his left was annoyed too, and if they'd been up in the gallery, I think he'd have booted Mr Ransome, but being as they were in the stalls, the other man had to be content just to match Mr Ransome's muttering with his own. So then I had the two of them at it and it was a hard thing to keep a proper ear to the stage. This chafed at me, more especially since it was my first time in such a place.

Danny Robins sang more songs but I couldn't fully listen on account of my companion, and I found myself wondering whether maybe Thomas mightn't have heard him in London, or just passed him in the street. And then I got to thinking of all those people that would have seen Thomas these past weeks and not cared about it, when it was all I wanted in the world, to see him.

They clapped really loud for Danny Robins and he was followed by a lady with some little dogs doing tricks calling herself Madame Cherie and her little Chee-ennes which I thought very dull though some of the ladies around me went 'ooh' and 'aah'. Then after her another lady with a great bosom stuck out ahead singing in a wobbly voice which Mr Ransome whispered to me was opera. I couldn't make head nor tail of it and was only glad when she was done. And through it all Mr Ransome was twitching about like you'd have said he had fleas. Finally it was the turn he'd been waiting for, and the man with the hat announced Mamselle Razinella.

The stage went nearly dark, there was a long pause. Mr Ransome leaned so far forward I thought he might come off his seat. Into the single light at the front came this girl, a little slip of a thing. She'd not have made my shoulder. She was dressed in a pink satin doublet with frills to the legs and cream stockings, and on her feet a pair of slippers. Her arms were bare from the shoulder. She was dark-haired and as she made her bow – not a curtsy, a bow – she looked out at us for all the world as if her thoughts were somewhere else entirely. Not at all Mr Ransome's kind of girl, I thought at first. But then more lights came on and as she did some stretching, I saw that though she was small, her arms and her legs were strong and muscled, and that her hands were large for a girl her height, and I could see why he wanted to see her so, for I had noticed long before that he loved girls' hands, asking me often about mine and other girls', and more especially if they'd been used for hard labour. This left me hard up for words since I didn't ever especially look at anybody's hands, except maybe Thomas's, and so I'd to make it up, how they looked, where they'd calluses, what they used to soften them, how their nails grew and the other strange things he'd want me to tell about. He must have known I was doing it, but he didn't seem to mind.

The swing was high above the stage, to-ing and fro-ing like it was waiting for her. When she'd finished her stretching, she stood beneath it and slowly it came lower, till she could reach up and lift herself up to it. Then I could see how strong her arms were, and how the muscles stood out on them, even as she pointed her fingers and her toes and kept her head at a coy angle.

She performed trick after trick, tossing herself about, tucking head between legs, feet over shoulders, hanging from her ankles or her wrists, twisting and turning while the swing swung and one move wrong and she'd be dropping like a bird shot from the sky, down into us all sat below.

Mr Ransome was still at last. Not a fidget, not a twitch. Sat back in his seat, his eyes and his body followed Mamselle Razinella, his mouth open slightly, his eyes wide.

When she'd come down safely, letting the swing be lowered till she could jump from it with a fine somersault, two young men, dressed very like her but in purple doublets and without the frills, came running on. And Mr Ransome shifted in his seat. The man with the top hat came on again and everybody stopped clapping and quietened. He stepped forward and gave his bow.

'Ladies and Gentlemen, Gentlemen and Ladies, Mamselle Razinella will now attempt her death-defying leap from the trapeze through the high air of this theatre, through two rings of paper which are even now being put into place above our heads, to land, safely we trust, in the waiting arms of her associate Monseeur Jones. Will you give your hands please, to Mamselle Razinella. Then he led us in some more clapping, while the young men climbed up the ladders above the stage and she jumped down off of it and came running up the centre aisle.

Mr Ransome's seat was at the aisle end of the row, and from the way he leaned out towards her, I knew he'd bought the seat just for this moment, for the second when she nearly brushed his arm as she made her neat little run to the back of the theatre.

He'd been to see her before and knew how her act went. In fact, when I turned to watch her, I noticed there wasn't a single woman with an aisle seat, and I'm nearly sure that it wasn't only Mr Ransome, but that all the men in those seats had arranged it carefully so.

I'm not mad keen on danger. Probably I grew up too close to the sea. The sea takes her pleasures when she wants them: usually it's men, but sometimes it's women too, and danger hasn't ever seemed to me a thing to be looked for. It'll come and find you out soon enough if it wants to. So watching Mamselle Razinella climb up the long ladder hanging at the back of the theatre, which I'd not noticed till now, then stand on the platform and reach out for the trapeze on these two long ropes didn't fill me with pleasure. The platform was no higher than the cliff I used to climb every day, and that with a creel full of flithers on my head, but she was doing it in front of a great crowd of people, where I had done my climbing before no one, except the gulls shrieking in and out of their nests on the cliff and sometimes a sheep grazing at the cliff top, which'd barely lift its head when a girl appeared there.

She pulled the trapeze above her head and seemed to hang on her tiptoes before launching herself out and into the air high above our heads. A long 'ahh' sound went up from the seats, as Mamselle Razinella swung her legs twice, three times. You could see the lace on her doublet shiver.

In front of her were two great hoops of paper, and behind them I could see Monseeur Jones hanging by his legs from another trapeze, though Mamselle Razinella couldn't. Even though I was seeing him upside down, I could tell he looked quite calm and as she swung, he fished in a pocket, and pulling out a handful of something, rubbed his hands together. A fine white spray caught in the lights and fell onto people's heads.

'Chalk,' Mr Ransome whispered to me, making me jump because he'd seemed so far away a minute before. 'To stop his hands slipping.'

'Why didn't he do it before getting up there?' I said.

Then without a warning, and in one long movement, Mamselle Razinella swung out high, let go her trapeze, and doing a somersault, she dived through the paper hoops to be caught and held fast by Monseeur Jones. The theatre exploded with sound. People clapped and stamped their feet and banged on anything they had that might make a noise, and the little acrobat and her man were lowered slowly down and so made their way to the centre of the stage to bow.

I was clapping as hard as the next, my body wrung out, and I saw how close in me had been the thought that she would fall. I thought that Mr Ransome might do himself an injury, so fiercely was he clapping and shouting next to me and now standing up better to see her.

Only Mamselle Razinella looked calm, her pink costume clean as a whistle and from where we were sat, which was close enough, she didn't look even to have broken a sweat.

'Just the cannon now,' Mr Ransome said, his eyes glistening, his fingers picking at some imaginary specks of dust on his sleeve.

I won't say much about the cannon. Briefly, here's what it was. A monstrous-sized gun held up with an arrangement of ropes and pointing to the roof on one side, and on the other a great net, like a fishing net, spread ten feet off the ground. First tucking a red flower into her bosom, and one in her hair, Mamselle Razinella climbed up to the mouth of the gun and lowered herself, feet first, inside till all you could see was the crown of her head. Then one of the men stood at the net, and the other came with a long taper and made a great show of lighting the cannon. There was an explosion and smoke, and before I'd even seen her fly, she was in the net, flat out. She lay there for a minute at least before moving, maybe to catch her breath, but I think more likely to catch us all in the throat with the thought that she was done for. So when she climbed to her knees and swung down, there I was again, cheering as hoarsely as the rest, and calling loud as any when she plucked the flower out of her bosom and went and gave it to a gentleman sitting not far from us.

We passed the gentleman with the flower on the way out. He was with a group of other men and crowing over his booty like a little boy. If he'd been the kind of man I knew, I'd have made a joke on it as we went by. But he was too much of a swell, so I kept my lip buttoned.

The night was still warm as we walked down to the station and there was a while before the train, so we weren't hurrying. I wasn't in the mood to talk, and neither was Mr Ransome, but I felt easy enough with him to walk along in silence. I wondered what Thomas was doing now, whether maybe he was walking along a street in London, and I was glad of the dark because my cheeks went hot at the thought of where I was now, and what he'd think of it.

I wondered, with each church we passed whether it might be this one, or that, that I'd walk out of as bride to Thomas, and the thought of his plan cooled my cheeks and set my heart to racing. So it came like a bolt from the blue when, after we'd walked silent some minutes, Mr Ransome said all of a sudden, 'So when are you going to marry him then?'

I sputtered something about not having any plans that way, and he didn't even look at me, just nodded his head and patted me on the arm.

'You can trust me,' he said. 'Your secret would be perfectly safe.'

I pulled my arm away sharply and didn't answer him. It was like he'd done some trick on me, like he might have been one of the people we'd been watching on the stage, all decked out in sequins and sparkle instead of his black suit. Because I'd heard of magicians who could do wondrous things before your very eyes, like cutting people in half and putting them together again, and making things disappear, and, without you saying a word, telling you the very thing that you were thinking.

Mr Ransome had his head down, one hand to his top hat to keep it to his head, like he was searching the paving stones for something he might have dropped, but I knew he was hurt because I'd pulled away. He made his steps longer and we walked on silently towards the station, me having to hurry to keep up, and though I was angry with him for his prying, I was glad of his company, for the streets were becoming ugly with drunken men and half-dressed women veering this way and that in beer-fuddled dances. The warm air was full of shouts and jeers that seemed to echo up around the buildings, and humping shadows blocked the alleys.

We were nearly at the station when another kind of cry brought us both to a halt. It came from an alley, unlit and rank-smelling, and from where we were stood all you could see was a knot of bodies stooped over something. Then the cry again, and suddenly, with no warning, Mr Ransome was off running towards it, and as he got closer, he let out a roar which surprised me more than anything ever had, for I wouldn't have said he had such a sound in him.

I stood watching from a distance, and saw Mr Ransome, who I would not have thought able to kill a fly, lay into two, maybe three men, hitting at them with his fists and kicking at them with his boots, in such a frenzy he seemed to have the strength of ten. And when they saw his rage, the three men took off running back towards me, and as they pushed past me, I saw one had his nose bloodied and another was clutching his ribs. 'Bloody maniac,' I heard, and 'Bloody Yid,' and then they were gone.

I walked down the alley. Mr Ransome was crouched down by a dark heap and seemed to be speaking to it. He put his arm around what proved a shoulder and half-dragged a figure towards me.

'Help me,' he said. I ran forward and found the man's other arm and together somehow we lifted the man back out on to the street.

The man was very bony and a near deadweight, with blood flowing freely from wounds to his head, though I couldn't see where or how bad in the near dark. I could only feel the stickiness on my hands and smell that metal smell.

We leant the man up against a wall and I tore some off my petticoat to wipe at his wounds with and bind the gash on his arm I could see now. He had his eyes shut behind his spectacles and I didn't know if he was conscious or not. He was an older man, perhaps older than Mr Ransome, and dressed in a shabby black suit, the cuffs frayed and the collar turned. I could see that much quite clearly in the gaslight. On his head he wore a small embroidered black cap, tight fitted to the top of his head, and his hair grew in long twirls down each side of his cheeks.

'He's a funny-looking one,' I whispered to Mr Ransome. 'What were they hitting him for? He doesn't look like he'd have two pennies to rub together.'

'He's a Jew,' Mr Ransome said, which made me look at the man again.

'A Jew?' I said.

'The curls, the cap, the spectacles. That's why they attacked him.'

The man groaned and Mr Ransome bent down to him. 'They've gone, the men,' he said. 'Is it far to your home?' The man shook his head. 'Can you stand?' The man nodded, and we helped him to his feet. He took Mr Ransome's hand in his two and muttered what I thought must have been a prayer. Then he thanked us, both of us, though I'd done barely a thing.

'Please come with me, I live very near,' he said. 'I must repay your kindness.'

But Mr Ransome had out his watch and he shook his head.

'Thank you kindly, sir, but our train leaves shortly and we must be on it.'

So we shook hands with the man again and Mr Ransome, not content to let the man walk home alone, found another fellow walking the right way and, explaining the situation briefly, asked him to accompany the Jew home.

We travelled back to York in different carriages, same as on the way. He sat in First Class and I was in Third. And when we got to York station, I was careful to walk behind him, not beside. There was no sense in making difficulties, and besides, I was growing to like this man and his strange ways, for all that we came from different places.

We walked together as far as Cliffords Tower. He'd have seen me all the way home, but there were too many might spot us as we got nearer Walmgate.

'A terrible thing was done here,' Mr Ransome said.

'When?' I said, thinking he meant last month, or at most last year.

'There was a massacre of Jews,' he said.

'That was the first time I've ever seen a Jew,' I said. 'There weren't none in my village, and I've never seen somebody like that in York.'

'And this tower's the reason why,' Mr Ransome said.

'So when was it?' I said, thinking he'd say maybe in the last forty years.

'Eight hundred years ago,' he said.

'Eight hundred?' I said.

'Jews burnt alive in the tower. They took refuge from the mob. Men, women and children, all locked in here. And rather than be torn apart by the good citizens of York, they burned themselves to death.'

I was shocked. 'Why?' I said.

'The usual,' he said. 'Scapegoats. The Jews were made scapegoats for things going badly, just the same as now. It's always easier to blame someone else.'

Something Grace had said, about her mother and the blame, was in my mind, though I didn't know what she'd meant by it.

'Is your mother well?' I said.

'Why do you ask?' he said.

I shook my head. 'I don't exactly know. There was something Grace said to me, and it's at the back of my mind.'

'She is very tired,' Samuel said.

'Grace?' I said.

'No. Our mother.' And he didn't say more, so I nodded like I understood. We stood staring a bit longer at the tower, so quiet and sturdy on its grassy hill. And then I thanked him for the time I'd had, and we went our separate ways.

There was another letter for me at Mrs O'Leary's, on a scrap of paper and looking like it had been done in a rush, though this one had also been written with great care, the writer of it knowing where I was with my letters:

My darling Harriet,
    Have found a French man. Not cocoa. Very important. Back on Sunday, all being well. About 9.00 p.m. All my love, Thomas.
    P.S. Keep it secret.

I thought I'd never sleep when I lay down in my bed that night. The night was hot and airless and a biting fly buzzed about my head, taunting. The house was restless in the heat. I could hear the children tossing about and Mrs O'Leary had set up her snore. My thoughts swung from here to there, like the little acrobat on her trapeze and I didn't know where they would end up if I let them go, nor who would catch them if they fell through the paper hoops. From Thomas to Mary, from Mr Ransome to Wetherby's, they swung, this way and that, till I was dizzy with tiredness and questions I couldn't answer, and finally I slept.

Samuel

I do not pry into the affairs of other men, though perhaps if I did, I would have been less astonished by the course of my own at that time. While I am happy to sit at a committee table with other worthy men and try to relieve distress, I am reluctant to become acquainted with the thing itself. 'He that toucheth pitch,' and so forth.

But I have made it my concern to look more closely into the lives of a certain class of woman, those whose lives are forged in the crucible of manual labour. It has been an almost altogether private task, one I have found myself powerless to prevent. I hoped then that I would be able to turn the photographs and documentary evidence I was amassing to some real social good, but as yet I cannot see how. I have not Mayhew's thoroughness nor his singularity of purpose and vision and there is more pleasure for me in this work than I suspect Mayhew truly found. Also it has happened too often that my right hand does not know what my left is doing and

I know, though I do not like to think much on it, that I have not the wish nor the will for it to be otherwise.

That summer, however, such altruism was far from my thoughts. My first worry was Mother. It was the summer of her final failing. In the space of a few months the clear-headed, severe old lady, still as exacting in her manners and precise in her ritual as she had been when I was a child, had finished with lucidity and was fast dispensing with decorum. I found it very distressing, as did Nellie, whose work, in a short space of time, had changed from housekeeper to nurse.

'Samuel! Come! Samuel! Samuel!' This was the voice that filled my hours at home. How different from my young biblical namesake, who heard the voice of the Lord in the temple calling him. The voice that called me was now a quavery, querulous, frail one, but its authority was undiminished by my mother's advanced years. She called, and in however distant a room I was, in the garden even, I could hear her. If I could not hear the words, which were anyhow unchanging, then I could hear her note. Perhaps like a magnetic field, in which all positively charged elements are drawn to the negative charge of the magnet, I was drawn to Mother's voice. Even now, in my thirty-fourth year, I could no more resist it than I could when I was eight, or eighteen, though I knew that it was a wizened and cantankerous ancient child that would greet me with some demand, some task that must be performed on the instant.

Mother had not left her bedroom since early May. May had always been the time in her year she most loved, the time in which, like her cherished garden, she most unbent. Just as the trees were pushing out their soft, new leaves and the plants their sappy stems, just when Nature seemed at its most pliable, so this was when Mother unbent a little. More likely in May or June that she might send her daughter some small gift of cuttings rooted, or plants nurtured into the bright hope of their first summer than at any other time in the year. More likely at this time that she might enquire with a mote of tenderness after her daughter and I might safely tell her a little of Grace's well-being.

But this year she had turned her face from such things. She kept her curtains drawn and refused all my or Nellie's efforts to have them opened. If either of us threatened to do so, suggesting all the while that it would be good for her spirits, she would start to wail.

'You are hurting me! Stop it! Cruel Samuel. Cruel to thy mother. Where is Anne?'

And should I persist, drag back one heavy drape and allow a branch of light to spread across the room, catching in it such a rich dance of dust, then she would hide her face beneath the covers. And short of dragging her from them and forcing her hands from her eyes, nothing I or Nellie could do would draw her out.

The strange thing in those months was that she seemed no more ill then than she had since my childhood. Frailer, certainly, but still with an appetite for food. Only where before she had relished the delicate sweet sharpness of summer fruits, raspberries, strawberries, gooseberries, blackcurrants picked fresh from the garden, now she refused these and favoured instead bland nursery food, custards and blancmanges, jam roly-poly, minced chicken in white sauce, scrambled eggs. Afterwards it was this returning to childhood, as though her gaze was retreating backwards through her life, that I saw marked out her coming death.

Frailty had been Mother's dominion, and she had ruled it well, and with it commanded her household. But this was something different, something that was taking her beyond frailty. And as it dawned on me, through those hot months, that she would never now leave her room except to be buried in her plot next to Father, I found in myself a furtive euphoria that was perhaps quite unseemly, but also solitary. At times I would skip around the house, even try out a quiet whistle, only to clamp my lips shut and sedate my step the minute after, whether out of guilt, or apprehension I am not sure.

As if I were making appeasement, I would go to look at Mother at odd times, opening her bedroom door with a light touch, slipping round and into the room on stockinged feet. She would be lying in bed, a cloth invariably over her eyes, the covers pulled to her chin though the thermometer showed the temperature to be well into the seventies. On the table beside the bed, her Bible and a glass of water.

Always, until this year, she would have the garden full of sweet peas, wigwams of colour at each end of the vegetable beds. They would be cut and placed in every room, their perfumes crowding out the musty silence of our dark house. But not this year. So I took her a posy of sweet peas I had bought in the market and placed it near the Bible.

'Mother, I think they are the colours you like,' I said, feeling pleased with myself, my solicitude. And she had reached out one arm and dashed the vase to the ground.

'Bought flowers!' she said, her voice little more than a whisper, but tight with anger. 'Anne would not have brought in bought flowers.'

There was little point in reminding her that her daughter Anne had been dead the past thirty years, or that she had died before she could have an opinion on bought flowers. I merely picked them up in silence and took them instead to Grace that evening and she laughed when I told her the tale. But what had shocked me more than Mother's fury was to see her naked arm as the nightgown fell back. The wizened skin had hung like a sleeve, reminding me, despite myself, of the corrugated white ribbons that lay in their naked glory in the windows of the tripe butchers on the Shambles.

Those last days with Mother, the force of her dying had pushed Harriet and my thoughts of her far from me, at least until I achieved the quiet of my own room. But when I had climbed beneath the covers of my bed exhausted and my head had found the pillow, then all the thoughts I might have had in the day crowded into the short hours of my sleep. She was there before me, and in my dreams I was free to gaze, my mother's strident voice banished.

My certainty that Harriet would marry Thomas, and I was surer of this than of my own name, only made my dreams the more urgent, and I would wake from them exhausted, my sheets tumbled as though I had been waging battle. And yet, despite Father's warning words on my birthday all those years before, it was not the fear of sin that haunted me when I woke, but the pain of separation. I would wash and dress, barely able to face Mother's harangue, and nurturing my tiredness for the connection it kept with the girl I knew by now would haunt my dreams whatever.

There was much sympathy for me at Meeting during Mother's illness. Each week for a month of Sundays, or First Days I should say, somebody had stood to say a prayer for Mother or to read a small portion from the Bible that they felt to be appropriate. I know it was thought, for I had thought it myself before, that these words would be of succour to me, as well as being heard by God. But I discovered that they were not. What is more, I became determined that once Mother's death was done with, I would attend Meeting only in so far as I wished to. I would no longer be obliged to perform another person's faith, but would be true to myself, despite the inevitable consequences.

Ever since I was a boy I had found Meeting hard to endure. To go into a room every First Day with fifty or so others and sit in silence for an hour, unless the spirit called on you to speak.

'Let your thoughts rise to God,' my father would tell me, 'meditate and listen for His voice. But do not struggle. Be at peace.'

But the silence made me fidget. Despite my best intentions, I could not bear it. So while my neighbours would sit in pacific meditation, my skin would crawl with imagined rashes, my legs cramp with pins and needles. Though not a natural sportsman, during that hour I would long to leap and bound and throw my body hither and thither. A giggle or a cry would rise in my throat like gorge and I would have to swallow again and again to keep it down. I would long to chortle, or whisper, sing hymns, God forbid, or even to laugh. But I did not. I did none of this, and kept the silence and willed the hour to end.

It seemed to come naturally to Father, this state of mind and body that so eluded me, and not only to Father, but also, and even more enviably, to William. Both would come in to the room at the start, take their seat, perhaps adjust their cuffs or coat tails and then sit still and upright through Meeting from the first minute to the last, hands on their laps, eyes closed. They always looked at ease. I never saw them stir, except as it might be to blow their nose or to scratch their lip, or stand to speak and I knew that their minds were not frantic as mine was, but that they, unlike me, were thinking on God. Even when Meeting was ended and people stood and stretched and greeted one another, Father, and William after him, might sit on a minute or more before standing and joining everyone else.

Only once did I try to explain to my father how it was, and he looked at me with such concern and incomprehension that I muttered something about it being nothing really, and left the matter there.

Now, with Mother on her deathbed, I sat, as ill at ease as ever, staring at my shoes, while different voices raised their prayers and thoughts for a woman they had no knowledge of. 'Gentle Master, be watchful over our humble sister Ransome, who is frail abed and cannot be here with us;' 'Hear our testimony, dear Lord, that Hannah Ransome is a worthy and exemplary Friend whom we entrust, in this hour of her sickness, to your tender care and mercy.'

Petra Flint, the hard-faced woman who was one of William's trusties at the factory, put in her penn'orth: 'Knowing that you look upon the heart, our sister Hannah Ransome is one who has made her spirit bow meekly to your will, be it stern or mild, and now in her bodily weakness and time of need we ask you to give her succour.'

And William, who was the only other member of Meeting to know my mother truly, inside her own house, made his offering, standing and declaring in his calm, authoritative voice, 'Hannah Ransome, the Lord lift up his countenance upon thee, and give thee peace. For as it is written, "to live is Christ, and to die is gain."'

'She will die before the summer is gone,' Grace said. She had made no comment on William's prayer when I reported it to her, but had laid Mother's rejected flowers out on her bed-spread and was picking them, stem by stem, congratulating them on being chosen, before arranging them in a glass vase.

'But you haven't seen her,' I said. 'It is not even clear what is wrong.'

'She has no wish to live. Besides, it's time,' Grace said.

'What do you mean?' I said.

Grace shrugged. 'She's given up at last. It's my time,' she said. 'I've been in here long enough, don't you think, Sam?'

'Will you come and visit her? Before she . . . now that she seems so ill?'

Grace shook her head. 'She would only curse me. I have a life to live, and she has a death to die.' She put the vase on the table beside her bed, and they seemed translucent in the gas light, their petals glowing.

I knew better than to dispute with Grace over what she said, or to try to change her mind.

'I'll tell you then, if she makes any request?'

'You may, but she won't,' she said.

She was right. Mother died on a hot night early in September, and she never did ask to see Grace. I stood beside her bed and watched the last hour. It was hard, nearly impossible, to think that this woman had borne me into the world, this tiny, furious dying woman. And I struggled to find in me some fraction that had anything more than pity for her. Every part of her was clenched, as though to keep a grasp on this final possession that was slipping from her. But just as her husband and her daughter had slipped from her tight grasp, so too her life was shivering its way out from between her fingers. And when the doctor checked her pulse, and then her heart, for the last time, and took her fists and laid them by her sides and smoothed a stray lock of hair from her cheek – actions that should have been mine but I didn't think to make them – and when he shook his head and took my hands in his, all I felt was joy.

When they started praising my mother's piety at Meeting, the first Meeting after her death, I still held my tongue. For all the Quaker claims to plain-talking and speaking the truth, it was better on this occasion that I dissimulate by remaining silent. Whether this was construed as grief, or as another mark of the peculiarity for which I had already been noted, I do not know. It was kinder, anyway, and I left the Meeting house alone and relieved that this was done.

I always liked the walk home on a First Day, the city so quiet, the market swept and empty. I would take a drink from the water fountain in the centre and stand and watch the dogs and sparrows for whom this day was as hard as any other, though perhaps even they enjoyed the freedom from the usual kicks and shooings that this day brought. Today, more even than usually, I relished the quiet. There were few people about. I drank deeply from the iron drinking cup, and as I raised my head, saw that another man was standing, waiting I presumed, for his turn. But the man was John Benbow, and he didn't want to drink.

'Haven't seen you in a while,' he said.

'I've been very busy with family matters,' I said. 'My mother's death.'

'I am sorry for your loss,' he said.

I shrugged. 'She was old and ill, impatient with dying and glad for an end,' I said. 'It will be a good thing for me to return my attention to those who are yet fully alive.'

Benbow nodded and when I resumed my walk home, he accompanied me. We walked for a few minutes in silence up Petergate towards the stony mass of the Minster. When we reached the Minster's vast West doors, there was a creaking and a groan, the doors swung open and people began to throng around us, released back into their day. Beyond them, distant, I could hear the sharp thrill of boys' voices lifted in sacred song and something passed through my breast and I was sorry, not for the first time, that we Quakers had no song in our worship in this country.

'Girls sing just as sweetly,' Benbow said.

'Only they cannot go as high,' I said.

'But they can,' he said. 'It is only that it would not suit.'

'Would not suit who?' I said.

'It would not suit the clerics. Just as it does not suit the employers to pay females equally to males.'

'All employers are not the same,' I said. 'My tannery employs no women, to my knowledge. But William has many at the Cocoa Works and has taken great pains with their working conditions. Better than any other employer in the city. Better than many of his Quaker peers.'

Benbow nodded. 'That is true. But still he grants them no rights. He does not regard them as equals to the men. I know they are paid on a vastly lower rate though their piecework is often faster than the men's. And then the day they marry,' he drew a finger across his neck, 'it's goodbye.'

'And is he so different in that from other employers?' I said.

Benbow tossed his head impatiently. 'No. Though there are many now who will let married women work.'

'And what do you think to be the solution to this?' I said.

'Female suffrage is the first and crucial step,' he said.

'And you know that I concur with you in this,' I said. 'And that William is publicly opposed to such a thing.'

Benbow nodded. 'More than that,' he said. 'He'll dismiss any worker he finds involved in such a campaign. We argued over it the last time I was at the Cocoa Works. He quoted St Paul's letter to the Corinthians to me in his support.'

'That the head of every man is Christ; and the head of the woman is the man . . . For the man is not of the woman; but the woman of the man . . .' I said.

'Yes,' he said. 'And "neither was the man created for the woman; but the woman for the man," and so forth.' He gave a short laugh again. 'But you'll have heard him on this,' he said.

I nodded. 'Yes.'

Benbow took his leave after this, retracing his steps, while I walked on past St Mary's down Bootham. Across the road, set back in its own parkland, was the forbidding edifice of the Lunatic Asylum. Its practices had greatly improved in recent years, but still I was glad that Grace was not there. A hunched figure approached from the inside, walking towards the gates, a cloak gathered about her shoulders despite the heat of the day. An old crone, I thought. But as the figure drew nearer, a couple of boys, shoeless tykes who must have been playing in the trees, joshed at her and one threw a stick. They didn't throw more, for straightening her back, the woman stared at them. She was a young woman, barely in her twenties, and beautiful. She held nothing in her arms, but her hands cradled an imaginary baby. She made no sound, only stared, but the boys fled.

I visited Wetherby's the following day, hoping more than anything for a glimpse of Harriet. My mother's death and the arrangements arising from it furnished me with sufficient alibi, though in the event I had no need of it. I was directed to find William in the clerks' office. The room was crowded, there being more young men employed than when I had been here last, but I could not see William. Thomas was seated at his high stool at the far end of the room, his shoulders stooped over a pile of receipts and a large red ledger. I walked down the room and stood behind him, watching his pen, which seemed to produce its precise and elegant figures of its own volition.

'Good day, Thomas' I said to him quietly, and he jumped round so suddenly, I was afraid he might have spilt ink on the ledger.

'Mr Ransome,' he said, his face suspicious.

I nodded towards his work. 'You have a fine hand.'

'Thank you,' he said. 'If you will excuse me,' and he nodded towards the desk. 'Mr William wishes these to be done.'

'Of course,' I said. 'Excuse me.'

I was walking back towards the door when William came rushing in, his eyes wide with excitement, his breath coming in short bursts, his hair dishevelled.

'Samuel,' he said. 'What fine timing. You must come with me. You must come and see what I have upstairs.' Even in his excitement, William kept his voice low, and I wasn't sure, but I fancied some of the clerks sitting straighter on their stools as if trying to listen in. He had me by the arm and was pulling me away and up the stairs, tripping in his impatience. 'He's just done his first sample and . . .'

'Who?' I said.

'Come on. His rooms are through the top.'

'Whose?' I said and at last William heard me and looked at me as though I were an idiot before replying.

'Our new man, of course. Our Frenchman, with the recipe we've been waiting for. Searching for, I should say. Better than cocoa.'

'Where did you get him from?' I said.

'Where?' William repeated. 'It was Thomas. Faithful Thomas found him. Paid him a pretty penny too. I confess that when I first heard the amount he'd given over I took him to task. It was too late to stop him then, he'd paid up already.'

William's voice was so low now that I was reduced to leaning in towards him to hear, like some stooge.

'Twelve pounds for the recipe,' he said. 'When we've never ever offered more than six. And the man's come up here, and wife and child, on a salary the like of which . . .'

'Why?' I said, intrigued, for though William was a fair employer, he was not given to throwing money away like this.

'Because we had to get him, any way we could.'

'So Thomas went to France? Paris?' I said.

'No, no.' William was impatient, as though somehow I should know the story he had not yet told me. 'He's been working in London, for Richards, you know, the French confectioners. I don't really approve of such things, but it's all had to be a bit cloak and dagger.'

'Cloak and dagger?' I said and he nodded.

'We've contracted him to secrecy,' he said.

'Why?' Other firms had started to do this, and I had heard William speak forcefully against such things in the past. As far as I knew, this was the first time he had taken such action.

'Thomas did nothing illegal. Nothing at all. The man came of his own free will.'

'So why the contract?'

'As I understand it, and I have to trust the Frenchman on this, there is some question of a verbal agreement in the

Richards company, to do with not divulging information. It's not legally binding. We've asked our lawyer. But it would be somewhat embarrassing if it came out. If the other chocolate companies here in York found out, for example. The territory is too close.'

'And his salary is high.'

'Higher than any other employee's. So keep it under your hat or we'll have trouble in that quarter. We don't want him setting an example.'

The suggestion that I keep this under my hat seemed somewhat unnecessary, but I assumed that the surreptitious nature of recent events had briefly gone to William's head. We had reached the top of the stairs by this time, and I was out of breath.

'Should have had that game of cricket with the children,' William said, and, unexpectedly, he ruffled my hair. 'They're still holding you to it.'

I had never been this high up in the factory before. We were standing on a small half-landing, the light coming through a dim skylight above. Above us was a short stretch of stairway leading to two garret doors. William produced a large key and, without explanation, he proceeded to unlock a small door on the landing I took for some kind of cupboard. It creaked open on rusty hinges, and William led the way through.

'Where are we?' I said.

'We're going next door.'

'The church?' I said, confused.

He nodded. 'Mind your head here, we've had to rush on the alterations, what with the Frenchman progressing so quickly.'

'You've bought it?'

'We're very short of space anyway. And for now it gives us somewhere private for the fellow to do his work. It's in a bad state. Not been used for some time. Now, careful over here. You can stand up straight. It's perfectly safe, but don't go leaping about.'

William had brought me out on to a small platform, room only for the two of us, on the outside of the factory wall. It looked as if it might once have been a loading platform, for there was a rusty winch above our heads, the hook swinging slightly with our weight. I am not fearful at great heights, but we were more than five storeys up, with only a flimsy rail between us and the alley below that separated factory and church tower, and I could not help my arm shaking as I held on to the rail. I had not been conscious of a wind, walking to the factory that morning, but now it whipped and caught at my coattails and I had need to keep a hand to my hat.

Attached to the platform was a form of bridge, so crudely built that even a man like myself, untrained in the rudiments of construction, could see the makeshift quality of the work. It crossed the space, perhaps eight yards wide, between factory and church. William pointed to the small door in the tower to which the bridge led.

'In there,' he said, and without further ado, he stepped out onto the bridge. It shifted under his weight and gave out small creaks, but seemed otherwise perfectly sturdy and safe. He crossed in a few steps, and taking out a key, unlocked the small door, then beckoned to me.

To my surprise, the sweetest smell of fruits assailed me, so intense it was as though their very essence had been extracted and held in pure suspension.

'Come on,' William called. So, ignoring the creaks and the roughly hammered nails, I stepped onto the bridge and across.

I had known the virtue of concealment since I was a young boy. What good did it do if somebody discovered something that they had not the power to understand? Better by far if that thing remained hidden.

By contrast, Grace is constitutionally unable to conceal anything, even when in her own and others' best interests. This compulsion towards transparency, which is a weakness of the Quaker faith, had caused her to live out nine years of her life in The Haven. Even now with Mother's death, no reconciliation between the two of them had been possible, and only because Grace could not hide an intimacy which Mother could not understand.

William had another way. He testified to transparency but he practised concealment. He would never tell his wife Rachel that his heart had been given over irreversibly, years before they met, to his half-wild cousin Grace. And about the factory he spoke to me more and more of the need for the left hand not to know what the right was doing. For inasmuch as Thomas was working to discover the secrets in other men's factories, and William had finally admitted that this was Thomas's task, so he must assume they were doing the same in his. Better for all, then, if few within its walls knew the whole story.

So, as he led me down the tower, both of us stepping gingerly by the light of his lantern, the fruit smell growing stronger, penetrating not only my nostrils, but somehow my skin, even my sight, I assumed that it was the secrecy of this affair that fuelled my cousin's excitement. And I was right, though I didn't know the half of it.

William pushed open the great door, studded with iron from another age. And, with an uncharacteristic flourish, he gestured me to enter.

The room was obscured by steam, so that at first, like a landscape in fog, I was unsure of any outline. But my eyes quickly adjusted and objects began to resolve themselves. In an earlier incarnation the room must have functioned as an ecclesiastical storeroom. This I guessed at from the old coat hooks and a row of deal cupboards along one wall. However, William had clearly already put himself to considerable expense for his Frenchman, for the broad pipes that fed the pans, the oven and the boilers had been newly cut through the walls and the coat hooks were now hung with magnificent iron and brass sieves.

A boy was stirring a great riveted copper pan from which steam was issuing forth in such volumes that I wondered he was not scorched. Instruments were laid out on one table, some I recognised, like stirrers and a vast thermometer, some that were mysterious. And, on the other side of the room, a small man stood at a metal-covered table, poring over some notebooks and frequently wiping the steam from his spectacles, which he wore on a fine gold chain around his neck. At the far end of the table was a machine resembling a small mangle that appeared to have small diamond shapes cut into the rollers and from which extended a metal plate.

The man was plump, clean-shaven, nearly bald and dressed in a suit of elegant cut, though he had a white apron stretched across his stomach, and on his feet he wore clogs, like ordinary factory workers.

As I watched, he put his hands to his head, as though to shut out the world, and taking a pencil from behind his ear, he scribbled some emendations to the figures written down. He appeared not to notice our entrance, but continued over his books, so that William and I were left standing uncertain in the centre of the room. If it had not been for a cry from the boy stirring, I do not know how long we might have stood there.

The small man, paying us no attention, hurried to the sink, picked up a pot which seemed to hold nothing more elaborate than cold water and crossed over to the boy and his pan, from which the steam was now issuing in greatly reduced volume. First dipping his finger into the water, the man plunged it into the pan, and after no more than a second drew it out and returned it again to the pot of water. He waited only a few seconds, fixing his spectacles in place, before holding the finger up close for observation, rather as if he had an important point to make in some philosophical debate.

'Soon,' he said to the boy with an unmistakably French accent, while wiping his finger on a cloth, and the boy nodded and resumed his stirring with what I now saw to be a spade-like implement, scattered with small holes across its broad blade, and which I discovered later to be called a skimmer.

Before the man could return to his figures, William took the opportunity to make his introductions.

'Samuel, this is Mr Philip Mazange. Mr Mazange, my cousin Samuel Ransome.'

We shook hands, Mr Mazange's finger sticky in my palm.

'Mr Mazange, where is the sample? I want to show Samuel what all this is for,' and William swept his arm around in an expansive gesture I did not associate with him.

'But it is not at all perfect,' said the Frenchman.

'No matter,' said William, and he looked expectantly at Mr Mazange who, despite an exaggerated shrug, was thus obliged to open one of the cupboards, and instead of taking from it priestly robes, as I am sure it held in earlier years, he brought from it a tray on which were laid out small sweets of pale pink and yellow.

'Taste one,' William ordered me. I looked at Mr Mazange, but he had turned away and was supervising the progress of the bubbling mixture, first directing the boy to stir more strongly here and there, then seizing the skimmer and sweeping the pan with it himself.

'Lemon or raspberry?' William said, lifting the tray towards me. The sweets resembled small diamond shaped lozenges and looked unexceptional, but William's excitement was not to be refused, so I took a yellow one and ate. I had never tasted anything like it. The flavour spread across my palate like a wave breaking across dry sand. I could not hide my pleasure from William, who set the tray down and shook me by the shoulders, all the while laughing, indeed nearly skipping in his excitement.

'Of course the colours need to be strengthened,' he said. 'But that is a small thing. It is the taste that matters, and the texture! We shall be the first in the kingdom with these. A good, honest pleasure for a good, honest people!'

I was somewhat taken aback by such absurd hyperbole from my austere and reserved cousin, though I was relieved to see that Mr Mazange seemed not to be listening. I hastened to quieten William with a couple of observations. I did not intend to dismay, merely to give pause.

'You cannot argue that these jujubes, or whatever you intend calling them, will pull the men out of the public houses, or persuade women off the gin bottle.'

William laughed at me. 'I know what you are trying to do, cousin,' he said, 'but you cannot deny the taste of that sweet. Perhaps men will throw away their pipes and you will find chewing tobacco a habit of the past once these are for sale. We will have them in every grocer's shop in the land, you will see.'

'I can't keep up with you, William,' I said. 'You are determined to turn the fortunes of the company and the morals of the country with a mouthful of sugar.'

I had not intended speaking like this, but William's presumption goaded me to it. If I had hoped to subdue him, I was mistaken. He took me by the shoulders and spoke now in an undertone.

'But what you see is not all,' he said. 'For the greatest venture in taste is still ahead of us, a venture Mr Mazange has only hinted at, a venture that is still, like the unconceived child, only a dream in the parent's eye. And for this we must truly keep our nerve.'

'Oh,' I said, still struggling to accustom myself to my cousin's language, so different from the sombre and careful words with which he conducted the rest of his life.

'Thomas is the man,' William said. 'He is the one who will find it out, if it can be found out.' He drew me even closer and dropped his voice even lower. 'Imagine, Samuel, an amalgam, a fusion between the two halves. Between chocolate on the one side, and pastilles on the other. It is something they have been working on at Richards, Mr Mazange has told us. Now we must find out how, and then beat them to it.

'And you intend asking your clerk to do this for you?'

'He is already at work on it,' William said.

All this while Mr Mazange and his boy had been busily engaged with their pot, stirring, testing, scraping and so forth. Now Mr Mazange came bustling towards us, with an 'Excuse me, genteelmen.' He opened one of the deal cupboards, and taking advantage of my presence, asked me to help him carry over a large galvanised iron vessel which was full of a dark gelatinous substance.

'What is it?' I asked.

'Gum,' he said as we hefted it up onto the stove edge.

Mr Mazange had to stand on a chair for the next process. First he removed a layer of tough scum from the surface of the gum, dumping it into a bowl. Then, with a deep-bellied ladle taken from one of the coat hooks, he spooned the gum mixture into the bubbling sugar, letting it pour into the centre in a smooth, viscous stream, counting all the while the number of ladles, 'Huit, neuf, dix, onze . . .' while the boy stirred.

'Doucement! Doucement!' Mr Mazange cried so that the boy, his shirt soaked with perspiration, his face the colour of a raspberry, looked up and asked: 'Faster or slower, sir?'

William took no interest in any of this, but stood staring at the tray of sweets, absorbed, I supposed, in grander questions. I was right in this, for when I had finished watching and returned to his side, he took up our conversation as though there had been no interruption.

'I have made a grave decision, Samuel,' he said, so that for a fraction of time I thought he was going to tell me that he was to stand for Parliament, or to emigrate to America. But then he went on. 'I have decided the sweets should be sold in our name. Wetherby's Fruited Gums and Pastilles,' he said.

'And this will be something new?' I said.

'Samuel, how is it you know so little of my business, when I know so much of yours?' he said, exasperation overcoming the calm he prided himself upon. But I was not going to be browbeaten like this.

'It is because we hang our interests on the world so differently,' I said, and he was on the point of answering, with a rebuff I am sure, when he remembered where we were, and that there were others present who were neither members of the family nor Quakers, but only workers. So instead he put his hands together as a child does in prayer, and nodded his head.

'Well, so I will explain. Sweets are sold by grocers,' and he looked at me questioningly.

'I do know that,' I said crossly, but he gave me such a teasing grin I was disarmed, and so quite unprepared for what he was to say only minutes later. I looked across at Mr Mazange. He appeared to be tapping the base of the pan with a clean skimmer and listening intently to the sound it made. I thought it unlikely that he was listening in to our conversation.

'Good,' William said. 'So the grocers keep the sweets in large boxes and sell them by weight, simply measuring them into a bag on which, perhaps, they will have printed the name of their own establishment. Or if they are providing for a lower class of clientele, then the bag will have nothing at all upon it. This is what I am going to change. Because we will supply our sweets, these sweets that Mr Mazange is creating for us, already wrapped, in our wrappers with our name. And we will do the same with our cocoa. So when the woman makes a drink for her husband, she will look at the tin and think, "Ah, that was Wetherby's Cocoa. I must be sure and get that again." And when the boy fishes in his pocket and gives a pastille to his friend, and when he does it again for another friend, it is our name that will be branded on his mind. The grocer will no longer measure out any of our goods. They will all, as the more expensive already are, of course, be packaged here, in this factory.'

William paused to take breath, for he was not used to such long speeches. I had been watching Mr Mazange and the boy while he talked. The boy had been rubbing a large marble slab with oil. Then lifting the pan off the stove, they had suspended it with the aid of a rope and hook over the slab, and poured the sugar and gum mixture in a glutinous stream onto the marble. At which point Mr Mazange, standing again on a stool, had proceeded to knead it in the same way I had seen Nellie knead our week's bread. Now they were spreading the mixture into two large tins and the room was quiet except for the slip-slap noise of their spatulas.

'But that's not all, Samuel,' William said, his excitement unabated.

I put a finger to my lips. 'Show me the rest of this building,' I said, and at last William paused and took stock and nodded.

'Yes, of course,' he said. 'You're a busy man, after all,' and nodding a goodbye to the Frenchman, who made no response, he led me out, locking the door behind us.

It was a shock to come out of the fragrant, steamy warmth into the empty and disregarded church tower. I followed William in the near dark down a last flight of stairs, then he took the bunch of keys from his pocket and unlocked another heavy door and all at once we were in the church itself.

Sunlight came through the windows in shafts, lighting up the stained glass with its knights and virgins, and watering the dusty floor with faded colours. Making his way around the pews, William busied himself down in one corner with something. And thinking our conversation was, thankfully, at an end, I stood in the centre aisle, shut my eyes and enjoyed the quiet. I was relieved that William had stopped his tale for now, as I could only listen for so long before my attention lagged and my heart sank at all his busy money-getting.

But then the thought came that it was easy for me, with my wealth already earned and not by my labour, and I felt guilty at my impatience.

A sudden clattering noise and the slight rush of air above my head made me open my eyes in time to see a swallow swoop to its nest on a beam high above. I watched it thrust some food into several gaping beaks and then it was away and out through a small hole in a pane of green glass where St George pushed his lance through the dragon's gullet.

'That'll have to go.' William's voice took me by surprise. He had finished whatever he'd been doing and had followed my glance to the window.

'It won't be here much longer,' I said. 'Once the fledglings are raised, they'll all be gone.'

'Not the bird,' he said, 'the coloured glass.'

'It's beautiful,' I said.

'It makes the room too dark,' he said and he gestured with his hand. 'This'll be the gum room. It has to be sorted, ground into small pieces and melted before it can be used. And then this,' and he gestured in the other direction, 'will be the packing room. Just for the pastilles and gums.'

'Did you ever visit a church before?' I asked.

William shook his head. 'No. This is the first,' he said.

'Not even the Minster?' I said, and he must have seen the surprise on my face.

'Why? Should I have done?' he said. 'The more beautiful they are, the more they interfere. People end up praying to the pictures in the glass or the statue, and not to God.'

'Still, I find them beautiful. They're all to be broken up?'

William nodded. 'Soon as we can finalise the plans. What I showed you up there, all in one room? That'll be a whole province one day, a whole department: Gum-grinding room, colour-mixing room, fruit-sorting room, starch room, boiler room, sweet-boiling room, caramel room, moulding room, refrigeration room, packing room.'

I could no more have stopped William in this flow than Canute could keep back the waves. But I could not swim in it, and as he told me his plans, all that went through my head was the wish that I could bring Harriet here while the place was still empty, still as it was now, still with the swallow and her nest. And we would just sit in the pews a while, she with her hand resting in mine. Her hand, its nails short for her work, the faint hairs along the first joint of her fingers bleached almost to transparency.

It seemed like necromancy, that William should speak of her just then, into the middle of my dream.

'Now this is the most exciting part, Samuel, the part nobody else has ever done. Listen,' he said. 'If you were to meet a beautiful young woman and on the same day somebody was to give you a delicious sweet, or a cup of cocoa? Which of those things would you remember most vividly?'

'The young woman of course,' I said, 'but this doesn't sound like your kind of dealing, William.'

'Just bear with me a moment, and you will see where I am tending. Now, we are agreed that cocoa powder, or even my Frenchman's delicious pastilles, while tasting very good, are of little interest to gaze upon. But what if the pastille, or the cup of cocoa were to be given to you by a lovely girl? What then?'

William paused, but not for my response, only for breath.

'Of course I do not mean to employ girls to serve our products. But if we were to use a pretty face to sell our products? Even the sweetest things benefit from a pretty face. So that when you saw her, you thought of raspberry pastilles? Or when you drank a glass of smooth cocoa, its froth catching in your beard, if you had one, its sweet warmth caressing your throat, you thought of the girl? Would that not be a clever thing?'

Twice I had tried to interrupt, and William had put his hand on my arm to prevent me. Now I was determined to ask my question.

'And this girl. You talked to me earlier in the summer of putting a picture onto your tins and boxes, but there is something very different in what you say today. What do you intend doing, William?'

So caught up was he in his own thoughts that he didn't hear the worry in my voice. Instead he turned to me, his face bright with what seemed to me a terrible vision, for I could see it before he even spoke.

'She'll be on boxes and on tins, certainly. But it'll be far more than that. This face will become the face of Wetherby's, the length and breadth of the country. On posters, in newspaper advertisements, anywhere else we think people might usefully be reminded of our products. It may not happen all at once, it may have to wait till there is the technology to support it, but it will happen sooner than you think.'

William left off here for a moment, his eye caught by something in the roof. I sat down in one of the pews, my limbs all at once unbearably heavy. I was shocked by the gross insinuation in his words and could barely credit it, that the cousin I had known since boyhood, who had always been a fierce moralist, an old-fashioned Quaker to his fingertips, the man I had known enter a public house and haul out by the collar any of his own employees and see them home to bed, a man who would never read a novel, or visit a theatre, was now telling me his plans to make a graven image and plaster it up and down the length of the country. A graven image of Harriet.

Somebody had carved their love into the wood of the pew in front: AH loves MB. And the thought came that perhaps I must do some carving of my own. But William's voice again broke into my thoughts.

'You know who gave me the idea?'

I shook my head.

'It was Grace,' he said. 'Years ago. She was reading something out from a play. You remember how she used to? I wasn't listening, I've never liked such things, you know that, but she must have read it three, maybe four times and I suppose it stuck. "Was this the face that launch'd a thousand ships." That was the line, or near enough.' He gave a thin laugh. 'She'd be horrified if she knew what I'd remembered it for.'

'She would,' I said.

'She brought the book to Meeting for several weeks. Read it under cover of her Bible. I took her to task over that and she just laughed. It was before that time, you know,' and as his face crumpled, I hastened to tell him that yes, I knew.

Anxious to distract him from such memories, I returned reluctantly to his grand scheme. If he was truly to go through with this, then better that I know as much of it as possible. I didn't see then how I could do anything about it, but still better the devil you know.

'So, when are you going to start with Harriet?' I said. 'I gather Benbow is on the premises today?'

As far as diverting William from past griefs, I couldn't have done better than that. His mouth fell open.

'How did you know who I had in mind?' he said.

I shrugged. He had not the same reason as I for remembering our earlier conversation that weekend in the country. But he was too excited with his plans to wonder for more than a few seconds.

'You're right,' he said. 'She is the one I plan to use. Benbow is making photographs of the factory today. For our records. So I intend to put the proposition to him at once. And when I have Caleb's approval – which will be a simple matter – we can start planning. I am not one for delay, once a scheme has been approved of. We might have some preliminary shots done in a week or two, I would say.'

'Have you consulted with –' I said, and would have spoken her name again, but he interrupted me.

'I never take any difficult decision without spending time in prayer. I spent much time over this at the weekend, and I am convinced in my spirit that this is the right course.'

'What of the cost?' I said.

'It is a risk, of course,' William said, 'but we will not over-extend ourselves. I think it will pay.' And I was sure he was right, for he had a nose for such things. Finally, he turned to me.

'What do you think?'

And I did not know how to answer him. For how could I say that this plan of his, to have the girl's face always before people, was a thing I had already carried out for myself? That her photograph was tucked into the rear cover of my Bible, and beneath my mattress, and in half a dozen other places by now, so that she was always before me? How could I tell him that his graven images were wrong before God, when hidden in my room I had the photographs of over a hundred girls. And though it was true that I had in mind some social good, that I intended finally to use my archive for the well-being of working girls, I could not deny that my first, and most pressing reason, was that I wished to have the photographs for myself, and who was to say that his way was corrupt, when mine, to many, might seem so?

So I answered my cousin by saying that I was sure the plan would prosper and only to beware of rivals, by which, of course, I meant principally myself.

William invited me to return to the factory and see Benbow at work, but I hadn't the heart for it, and we left the church by its great oaken doors. When he had locked the last and largest of the doors with a great key, holding it in both his hands to turn the bolt, we made our goodbyes.

HARRIET

Mary shook her head. 'I shouldn't be here,' she said.

We were standing close by the river, closer than I'd have thought she could bear, its sleek surface shiny and solid in this city darkness.

'I make sure never to come here, not in the dark and not in the day, but I was too busy thinking about you. Sometimes they want to bring me and I refuse, though there's been a couple don't like me stopping them.'

'You don't need to tell me,' I said. 'I know already. Don't tell me.' But she didn't hear me, or she didn't heed me.

'Shoved up against the dirty bricks and pigeon shit, skirts hoiked and in they poke. I don't need to see it to know how it goes. Mr Benbow says it's often the posh ones as want to slum it a bit. But I've always said no, found some excuse, and Mr Benbow's given me the wink and muttered something about "perks of the job" or some such as I haven't wanted to hear too much. And then they think I'm being uppity and go on about me giving myself airs. "Benbow's special piece are yeh?" they say, and "Better than the other girls, then?" "Just cos you've got your picture up, you're better'n the rest, are you?" And I tell 'em they can go find theirselves another girl if they want that. And they say, "Well, what about the pictures, then" and I tell 'em that's all they are, pictures, and it's not the same as doing it. The girls die of it, the ones you see down here, Harriet. D'you know how quick they die?'

'It's their choice,' I said, and Mary shook her head.

'It's bloody not,' she said. 'They've to live, haven't they. And some bloody life since it kills 'em all. You find me a one turning tricks as is over twenty-five.'

'And you're different, are you?' I said, which was down-right nasty, but I didn't know how else to stop her. 'Mary, come on, we're like sisters, you and me. Doesn't matter what happens. I've slept with your feet, for God's sake.'

She didn't laugh.

'You're so tucked up now in your comfy job and all its perks, and your snug little room in the attic. And Mr Ransome, wouldn't you like to know what other girls he's got under his big black wings? And your nice little lover-boy, though he's not half as nice as you think, and you'll be hitched soon, or perhaps you are already. Tell me, Hal, why was it you left Mrs O'Leary's? And I'll bet she was weeping and crying, wasn't she now? And the children? That nice girl Ellen, and the lad? So why did you leave? There must have been a good reason, mustn't there.'

I thought she'd finished, but it was only a pause for breath, and then she was off again.

'I don't know what yer bloody see in him! You're a bloody tart is all you are! We should've stayed by that grey sea, damn it, and let ourselves get like our mothers.'

By now Mary was yelling fit to burst and waving her hands about, though you could barely see to pick your own nose in that dark. I might've thought she'd gone and got a screw loose, she was shaking that hard, and spitting, and if I could have seen the colour of her face, I'd have reckoned it for bright red. But I knew this fit hadn't just come upon her, and she knew it too. Because she'd taken good care not to start up till we were underneath the arch of the bridge and there was no one to give us a stare except a couple of tramps and some sleepy pigeons. And the tramps just muttered something from their bit of shadow and the pigeons put out their soft mew-call, which was a gentle sound, as if Mary and her yelling was a piece of a lullaby to shush them to sleep. So I knew she'd thought to do it here, this yelling, and that it hadn't come over her like a flood.

'If you don't stop, I'm off,' I said at last and I started to walk away, thinking that I'd had enough of this and I'd cut across the bridge and back home. There was this cold rain coming down, making the cobbles shine even in the dark, and it wasn't strong rain, but fine so as you didn't for a bit know if you were getting wet. I heard Mary running behind to catch me up, her shoes' clitter-clatter a different sound from the solid crunk that mine made. She put her hand on my shoulder, the glitter off of her rings catching the bit of glow of the lamp above us, and so I stopped walking and waited to hear what else she'd to say.

'Hal,' she said, 'listen.'

'I've been listening and I don't much like it,' I said. 'Waiting till I couldn't see you, speaking in the dark like that when you could've said it before. We've been sitting in a chop house this past hour and you didn't say a word on it.'

'I wanted us to have a nice meal,' Mary said, 'like in old times.'

'Give over, Mary, it doesn't suit you, wheedling,' I said, nearly laughing at the sound of her, despite myself. 'Besides, in the "old times" we never had money for the chop house. Never dreamed of such a place. A rasher of bacon and a jug of beer and we thought we were princesses. It's just because you don't like him, isn't it? That you're saying all this? It's because you've never liked him.'

'He's in deeper than he knows,' Mary said.

'In what deeper?'

But Mary didn't answer me. She was looking about her as if she hadn't noticed till now where we were and then she banged her head with her hand like she'd been an idiot, making her bracelets jangle.

'In what deeper?' I asked her again. 'What is Thomas in?' And that was enough for something and she came right up close to me and suddenly her fingers were round my neck, pushing my head back, and for a moment I thought she was out to strangle me and I was too surprised even to let out a cry, but she was searching for something, tugging on the buttons at my neck, ripping them away. Her perfume, something lovely, filled my head and my body felt heavy, I'd no power to move. I saw the buttons drop, the one and then two more, catching splinters of light as they met the cobbles, bouncing jittery and disappearing in the dark.

'Where is it?' Mary was nearly shrieking. 'I know you've gone and done it. I know you have. But you should have it round your neck, girl. That's what you all do. Where is it?' and I knew what she was looking for, and made up a little prayer of thanks that I hadn't it on a string, like some girls I knew, but instead safe in my lodgings.

'Mary!' I said. 'Mary! Stop, please!' and I pulled at her hands which had a grip like iron, and quick as it had risen, her fury dropped, and she was smoothing where she'd been ripping, and making these almost stroking movements.

'God, Harriet, your bloody buttons,' she said and she was near to sobbing and down on her hands and knees on the ground, the skirts of her fine dress clinging to the wet like the membranes ripped out of a huge fish.

I took a hold of her under the arms and lifted her up. She was cold, shivering in the warm rain. Her jewellery was heavy on her arms and her hair had come loose from its pins and trailed like seaweed across her face.

'It doesn't matter about the buttons,' I said. 'It doesn't matter,' and I wiped the hair from her cheeks and her eyes. But maybe she didn't hear me, because she kept saying to me not to do it, and then telling me I shouldn't have, because she knew him, she knew what he was like and I didn't.

I pulled Mary back to the arch under the bridge. She wasn't yelling now and her skin was clammy under my fingers.

'Are you all right?' I said. 'You're not . . .'

'I've not got a disease,' she said. 'But it's very cold here.'

'Perhaps if I hold you hard, it'll help the shaking,' I said, and I held her even tighter round the shoulders. We stood like that some minutes it seemed, not saying nothing, and she stopped shaking and I was sure her skin felt warmer. I waited long as I could, till she was calmer, but then I couldn't wait any longer.

'What you were saying you knew about him,' I said. 'Please tell me. About Thomas.'

'What's to tell?' Mary said, but not sounding foxy now. Just downright miserable. 'I just know, because I heard what I oughtn't to have done, that he's been up to things this last time down in London that aren't properly what he ought to be doing. And that it's more'n a bit dangerous for him.'

'But it's for Mr William, isn't it?'

'Oh yes, it's for your Mr William. His dirty business. He's having your Thomas do his dirty stuff, Hal.'

'Thomas owes them his life.'

'So?'

'So what are they having him do, Mary?'

We'd been speaking in low tones, the tramps snoring and the pigeons still cooing, and me with my arm still around Mary's shoulder. Neither of us noticed the men till they were right up close and their beery, sharp breath in our faces.

'Bit close for comfort, you two,' said one, so near that his jacket tickled my cheek, a thick, damp smell coming off it and making my stomach turn over.

'Wouldn't mind a bit of that, would you, Tom?' said the other.

'Ay, we could learn a thing or two, I'd say.' He had his hand deep in his pocket, coins jangling. 'What about it, girls?' and the way he said 'girls' had the hair on my neck standing.

Neither of us said a word. I was scared stiff. They were big men and more than halfways over with the drink. But Mary wasn't scared. Mary was angry, I could feel it.

'What are you after, gentlemen?' she said in this wheedling voice.

'Oh, we're just enjoying the show.'

'Like to take part?' she said then and the men started to laugh. 'It'll cost yeh,' she said, and they laughed louder.

'We've a good big bundle to pay with, haven't we,' the one nearest me said and he jiggled his hand in his pocket even more, and leaned even further in on me so I leant back so hard I could feel the sharp edge of a brick dig into my back.

'Well, good,' said Mary, and she'd gone rigid, her shoulders like whips under my arm. She put her hand on my elbow and gave it a squeeze, and I knew she was about to do something. I think she must have kneed them in the groin, though I couldn't see how she'd managed it. But suddenly they were both of them grovelling and roaring on the ground, and behind their roars I could hear the clatter of the pigeons as they took flight, and Mary had me by the hand.

'Come on,' she said and she was pulling and we were running and up the steps and on to the bridge and the rain coming down steady now and not a soul abroad to see us.

It was strange, ending up in that hall again, and the coffee urns steaming and the ladies in their black dresses and bonnets, as if it were only yesterday we'd arrived in the city, Mary and me. I knew what these ladies were now, these Quaker ladies, who smiled at us. And they thought they knew what we were, only they didn't. They smiled so hard, I reckoned at first they must've seen me up on the walls, but then another girl came in, and they did the same at her, which I was glad about. Though Mary'd not believe it, it wasn't a thing I'd liked in any way, being looked at in the street, and people doing it like they owned some bit of you.

There were maybe a dozen other girls, sipping coffee at tables and talking in low, tired voices. They gave me the once up and down and that was it. But Mary. She was something of a different order. They'd their eyes all over her as we fished coins from our purses: her dress, her hair, her shoes, the flash of stocking when she walked, her jewellery, her make-up. It was such fierce curiosity, I thought they might have nearly pulled her apart, given half a chance.

'Nice of them, to give us coffee and a bit of pie,' Mary said, a bit too loud and giving me a look, as we sat down at one of the deal tables. 'After all, they can't know what we might have been up to, this time of an evening.'

'Hush up,' I said, not wanting anyone's attention. My clothes were wet, though I didn't know if it was the rain or the fear made them so, and I wondered whether others could smell me too, even in the fug of cheap cologne that filled the room.

'No, but it is kind. Keeping girls like us off the streets. And then tomorrow we can all go and work in their nice factories, can't we?'

'Stop it, or I'll go,' I said.

'Oh, I forgot, you work in one already.'

There were crumbs on the table, and Mary was pushing them this way and that, her finger down flat on the cloth, making shapes. A circle with a dot of crumbs lifted in, something like a triangle, a square, and then another square outside. She often did it, and I'd got well-used to it, but tonight the crumbs got under my skin.

'Stop it,' I said.

'D'you know how much money I've got put away?' Mary said.

I shook my head.

'Well, how much have you saved, then?'

I shrugged. 'Can't save a lot on my wages, but Thomas is hoping to have enough soon to set us up together,' which wasn't exactly a lie.

'They pay you for those pictures, though.'

'Not exactly. They give me cocoa, the best sort, sometimes. Or creams, depending. Anyway, we haven't done that many yet.'

'Depending on what?'

'Sometimes there are some as don't come out right, and Mr William, he's got very high standards and so they can't be sold. I get those ones. Anyway, the picture-taking, it's in my working hours. It means I get away from the sorting rooms.'

Mary shook her head like she was amazed. 'Jesus, Harriet. I don't believe it,' she said. 'Your picture up there for all to see, and they're paying you in sweets!'

One of the Quaker bonnets turned towards us. 'Sssh.'

'D'you think they know your Mr William in here?' Mary said, keeping her voice low this time.

'Course they will. And Mr Ransome, I've no doubt. There a'n't that many of them. But Mary, please . . .'

'You want to know about Thomas.'

I nodded. Mary's voice was flat, all the anger gone. I looked across at her. She looked bone-tired. I smoothed a damp wisp of hair from her cheek and touched one of her hands which she had laid on the table. The skin was smooth, and cold as one of my chocolate boxes, and her painted nails as bright and shiny as the paint I'd seen them dab – ten in the minute some could do – on the most expensive tins. It wasn't like when I first held her hand and it was wet and hard and rough as a piece of bark and she was so scared on that cliff she couldn't move.

'Tell me, Mary,' I said, and as she started to talk it crossed my mind that she was scared now too, just as scared as she'd been on that cliff. It was just she covered it over a bit more, so you'd to look a little harder.

'I'd been doing some pictures with Mr Benbow and I was getting dressed behind the screen, you know, in the corner.'

'Getting dressed,' I said.

'Yes.' Mary looked at me over the mug of coffee. 'I was getting dressed. You know what I do, so don't start on like one of them bloody women,' and she jerked her head towards the ladies in their bonnets, and one of them caught the movement and smiled at me, and I smiled back.

'Yes, I know,' I said.

'So, let me tell what I heard. As I said, I was behind the screen, changing, and taking my time over it, being as I was tired to the bones.'

'Tired, after sitting around?' I said before I could stop myself.

'You say one more thing, Harriet Brewer, and I'll leave.'

I put up my hands by way of apology, and Mary started her tale again, and this time I held my tongue.

'So I'm standing there in barely a corset, and Mr Benbow's packing away the equipment. Very careful with it all. I've watched him that many times I can tell what he's doing just by the sounds. There's a knock on the door and William Wetherby marches in before Mr Benbow can stop him.'

'Mr William?'

'Ay. Mr Wetherby, and shut yer mouth. You look like a fish out of water.'

'Mr William. Not Mr Caleb?'

'I've never seen Caleb. The other one's the only one I know. Now let me tell the bloody story. Well, he's talking nineteen to the dozen even before he's into the room, and Mr Benbow must be beside himself, what with me behind the screen, and what if I come out, and what'll Mr Wetherby think then? I can picture them, the light fading from the sky now, the lamp lit on the desk, the one seated, the other upright and pacing. It'd make a good picture.

Anyway, he's had a lot of business from the man, as you should know. And lose one Quaker and you've lost the lot. They move in a pack. But I know better than to shift about. I sit tight and keep my ears open. I'm still not dressed. My stockings are hanging over the chair like a couple of snake skins and my dress is on the hook and I daren't move any of it for fear of the noise.'

'I've only ever seen Mr William calm,' I said.

'Calm's never to be trusted, Hal, you should know that. Like the sea. Never trust the sea, not even when it's calm, not even when you can see down to the crabs, we was taught. Don't trust it further than you can spit. And you can't spit no distance, Hal, everyone knows that.

'So I'm sitting there almost in my altogether, breathing so little I'm likely to faint any minute and give the game away, when Mr Wetherby starts to talk, and can you guess what his talk is of?'

I shook my head, glancing round me, for I felt sure that everyone in the room must be listening in to our talk.'

'Thomas. His talk is all of Thomas,' Mary said.

One of the black bonnets came over then, and asked were we all right? Mary was about to give her a blast, but I kicked her under the table and she held her tongue.

'We're very well, thank you,' I said, 'and so grateful to have somewhere like this to come to,' and the bonnet nearly gagged she was so pleased and went prancing away. That's how Mary told it afterwards. And it was that funny, Mary near on cried, and said she'd have wet her knickers if we'd not been sitting down. Then she told me what she'd heard.

That Thomas was gone to London, I knew of course. He'd been there twice again since that first time. That he was gone to do Mr Wetherby's dirty business, that I knew as well. He'd told me a bit about it the day of the picnic and I knew there was more and that it frightened him, though he'd have said it didn't and though we'd never talked of it again. But what Mary overheard was worse than anything I'd imagined.

'Mr Benbow tries to get Mr Wetherby to sit down,' she said, 'but the man won't. He's blurting out his story, quick as he can, like he's trying to get it out of his mouth as fast as possible. "The clerk was given a clear brief," he says. "He was to gather information, place an advertisement in the local press and recruit staff."

"And?" Mr Benbow says. "Did he do it all?"

"Oh yes," Mr Wetherby says. "He did it all, and . . ."

"And what?" Mr Benbow says. Mr Wetherby doesn't answer immediately. "Of course I can keep confidences," Mr Benbow tells him, "much of my work is confidential."

'There's a pause, neither of them saying anything and my reckoning is that Mr Wetherby's weighing it up, pros and cons of telling Mr Benbow. Then he starts talking again.

' "The difficulty is that our man has been very eager."

' "Doesn't sound like a problem," Mr Benbow says, and I can hear the laugh in his voice, though Mr Wetherby can't.

' "Perhaps not," Mr Wetherby says, "but if the press got hold of it all, the wrong press, I mean, it could be rather awkward for us."

' "Aha?"

' "Well, it could look as if we were maligning our competitors, and without sufficient cause."

' "And you're not?" Mr Benbow says. Mr Wetherby doesn't answer. "Because it sounds to me like you've got involved, whether you wanted to or not, in a touch of sabotage," Mr Benbow says. "Or am I wrong?"

'Mr Wetherby still doesn't answer him. He starts pacing up and down. I know it's him doing the pacing, and after what seems like an age, but is more likely only seconds, he starts speaking again, but very quietly and very quickly. There's something about recipes and factories, I couldn't understand it quite. "Spanners in the works being taken too far," and "adulter-something or other," which nearly makes me giggle.

'Mr Benbow asks then why Mr Wetherby's come to tell him all this.

' "Because of our overlapping business interests," Mr Wetherby says, "and, please don't take offence, but I'd heard you got involved in things that went too far. I thought that perhaps you'd understand my predicament more than most. That you might have some useful advice, as far as the newspapers and the journalists go."

' "This man, your man. Can you trust him?" Mr Benbow said.

' "He's like a son to me," Mr Wetherby says.'

'A son!' I couldn't help bursting out, bonnets or not. 'He's no more son to Mr Wetherby than I'm daughter to the Queen!'

'Well, anyway,' Mary went on, 'that's what I heard him say, and after that he goes on about how the clerk, because that's what he is, Harriet, about how the clerk had a dicey past and they took him in and all. So Mr Benbow says, "Well, there you are then. Your scapegoat, just in case you need one," and Mr Wetherby doesn't reply. But even sat behind my screen I can feel how angry Mr Wetherby is at that, though he doesn't say a word, just keeps up his pacing. Mr Benbow says he'll make some suggestions, things Mr Wetherby could do, things he's found useful in the past, and Mr Wetherby says, "Are they legal? Are they moral?" And Mr Benbow says, "Is the Pope a Christian? You get involved in sabotage, you do what you can," and Mr Wetherby gives a gasp, at Mr Benbow saying it so clear this time I suppose, sabotage, that is, but he doesn't say anything. I hear Mr Benbow go to the desk and take out a piece of paper and whatever it is he suggests, he writes it all down.

'Then Mr Benbow asks Mr Wetherby something like whether it's had any effect on the business so far? And Mr Wetherby says it's had a marked effect on sales, and that taken together with the picture campaign, it's put the company up there at the top in pastilles and on the way there with cocoa. So Mr Benbow says, "Then what's done is done and the important thing is to ensure it doesn't happen again. Or at least not so as to put you at risk."

'And Mr Wetherby says that isn't quite the issue, and Mr Benbow says isn't it? And he starts to laugh, and says, "Christ, William, you're no better than I am," and I almost feel sorry for Mr Wetherby then, except I know he's only come tonight to save his own skin. Then he says he must be home soon because of the wife, and all my pity goes up the spout.

'By this time my legs have gone to sleep, the day's gone into darkness and it's all I can do to pull on my stockings and hitch the hooks and eyes on my dress. Mr Benbow's sitting at his desk, writing, when I come out. He doesn't say a word, doesn't even look up. But I can read the toss of a man from his face better than most, and he knows I've heard it all. So then

I send you the message, because I've got to speak to you. Because the thing Mr Benbow doesn't know and I do is who that clerk is. And here I am, telling you.'

I had finished my coffee a while back, but I stirred the grounds round and round with the spoon for something to do.

'Makes you happy, does it, telling me all that?' It was out before I could stop myself. Mary didn't answer. Just sat back in her chair and looked at me, till I wished there was somewhere I could hide in that bare room and the other girls talking low and the bonnets behind their counter, counting out their money so I knew they'd be turfing us out soon.

'You have your wish and I have mine,' she said. 'Thomas and me, we're . . . I don't know, maybe I think I can see what he's up to,' she said, 'for all that I know he loves you. And no, I don't like telling you all this, but I'm worried for you.'

'You worried for me, Mary. That's a rich thing after what you've got your fingers into,' I said.

'Ay, but I know what I'm up against. Or enough of it, anyhow, and that's more than you do. Besides, I've got a plan.'

'A plan?'

'Yes. And once I make my money, I'm out. Off and away,' she said.

'Off and away?' I said.

She nodded.

'To where?'

'It'll depend,' she said. 'On all sorts. But mostly on Jamie. I promised him,' she said.

'How promised?' I said.

'I a'n't told him it, but I promised all the same.'

'And what if you get, you know, what makes 'em all so ill and to die so quick?' I said, though I could hardly think on it, Mary at it like that with men who'd just paid over their money for it.

'I'm to go to London this autumn. Did you know? Not for long. As a companion for this gentleman as likes me mightily. He's to be there for some business to do with the government, just for a week and then home to wife and children. And he knows the score with me, I've been on his arm before. But down there he'll be able to take me out, to the theatre, and these restaurants he's been telling me of. It's showing me off he's after. If he wanted the other, he'd have to find a different girl, he knows that. And he's to pay me well enough, and Mr Benbow's got it all drawn up, for his little penny mind, so as it might not be much longer before I leave. And especially not if he takes me more'n this one time.'

'But surely he'll want you to do it with him, won't he?' I said.

Mary spoke like she'd a mouthful of pins. 'Doesn't matter if he wants it or not. I told you that before. Not like the girls under the bridge. I'm careful. He'll have to get a girl in if he wants that down there. There's plenty for the asking. It's the pictures I get the money from. Just like you at the factory. We're both at it, letting them take pictures of us. And then that makes them want something. Only I'm paid for it and you're not.'

I didn't see it at the time, because it came in the middle of her fury. But afterwards I saw that what she told me next, it was a message. Not for now, but for later. Something to make plain what was to come, though she didn't know how it would. She sat back in her seat and looked at me and I thought she was angry for what I'd said, but it wasn't that in her face. It was more like that she wanted me to know something and couldn't see how to tell me.

'But do you know what I'd really like to do?' she said. 'I'd like to be the one taking the picture, or the one making up the rules. And I could do it too, the pictures. I've learnt it.'

'How?' I said.

'That first day in the studio, you and me, I could see the shape of what he was taking. See it as clearly as if it was me with my head tucked under the cloth and not him. How it'd all piece in, the odds and sods and you look at them and say, that doesn't look like the sea, and that doesn't look like a beach, and you can see it's only pretend. But I could see how it'd come together and with the light of the day that's in it, why you'd to be round that way and how the shadows would fall. I understood the light.'

'But how have you learnt it?' I said.

'Mr Benbow,' she said. 'What I couldn't see for myself. He's a good teacher, for all else he is. "No reason why a girl can't," is what he likes to say, and so I can.

'But I don't tell him the half of my mind. Like how it feels for them to go without their relish on a Friday because some Quaker prig has docked their wages for something they don't even want, and won't pay them properly for what they give him,' she said, and she was leaning forward now, like she wanted to pin me with her eyes. 'And I'll tell you something, it's only Mr Benbow has said different. It's only him. He's teaching more than I could have dreamed of, if he'll only let me go in the end.'

I didn't say any more to her about her brother Jamie then, but it seemed to me she knew it were just a pipe dream. Just a story she was telling herself, because, even if he were still this side of heaven, she'd never be able to take that frail little fellow off and away from his home, and I thought that somewhere in her head she must know that.

The bonnets were rounding us all up to go home. They had their hands clasped together and Mary whispered to watch out or they might come and pray on us. Outside, the rain had gone and the sky was clear.

'So what will we do then? Either of us?' I said.

'Nothing but what we're doing already. Just don't have your eyes shut. Keep them halfway open at least, however much you think you love him.'

Then we kissed each other like as if we were going on long journeys and I walked back home, wishing, that night, I had Mary's feet beside my cheek, and I dreamed dreams of fish and salt that slipped away from me in the morning.

I couldn't tell how Mary knew it, that I'd married Thomas, and I never did tell her afterwards. It would've only rubbed salt in.

We'd done it like Thomas said we should. He'd used his friend's room in Leeds to give us an address, and taken the train over one Saturday and gone to the parish-clerk so as the banns'd be read on the Sunday and two after. I tried to imagine how it'd sound, the vicar standing there and saying out our names, Thomas Newcome and Harriet Brewer, before his congregation, and them hearing, and not knowing who we were and maybe wondering for a moment.

And exactly the four weeks later we were on a train, me with new gloves and my bonnet freshly-trimmed and him in his Sunday suit, and off to be wed.

Instead of meeting at the station, I had Thomas come to Mrs O'Leary's for me that morning, though I didn't tell the why, but let him think it was a female touch on account of it being our wedding day. The truth was that I was upset for Mrs O'Leary and strangely feared of Mr Ransome.

Thomas had fixed our new lodgings and I'd all my stuff, which wasn't much, ready to leave when I came back later that day. But I'd made up false truths to Mrs O'Leary over my leaving and the both of us knew it, which left her tearful and made me stern, chiefly so as I'd keep my lip buttoned and not blurt all out. Thomas coming for me made this first parting of the day easier, though when she saw Thomas in his freshly sponged get-up, Mrs O'Leary knew well enough what we were about.

And then there was Mr Ransome. It wasn't that he'd wish to hurt me, which I couldn't think of him ever doing, but that I was sure he'd somehow know the day that it was and that there'd be a horrid awkwardness between us. So I wanted Thomas with me to protect against such a thing. But Mr Ransome wasn't there.

Thomas didn't read me out things on this train journey, and there was no drunk fellow, thank God, or anything to disturb us. So we sat, the both of us silent for most of it, which was rare enough.

'You've the money all right?' was all I said. And he only nodded, and took my hand in its new glove and held it firm.

There were those back home who could tell the future in the innards of a fish. They could see things in the weather too, and shake about the grounds of tea to read off lives in.

Oftentimes if a girl was to be married, then the day before she'd stand and wait on the quay and they'd bring a tray of fish before her for her to pick out a single one. When the girl had chosen, they'd lay the fish on the harbour wall and the girl'd be pale and the women would gather round, all ready for it.

By the time Mary and I left for York, I didn't have a lot of time for this. But when I was smaller I'd stand around the edges with the other children and I'd wonder whether the girl was worried choosing, for what if she got the wrong fish, and then she'd get the wrong future?

The one that knew how to do the telling, she'd be handed a knife and then with a flourish like she'd never use normally, she'd slit the fish along its belly, and there'd be something like a sigh around her, which, not understanding how these things went, I thought strange, because these women had their hands in fishes' bellies from dawn to dusk. They knew the feel of the fish better than they knew their husbands, better than they knew their children's bodies, so what were they sighing over?

With her eyes on the fish, quickly then the woman would start to speak the girl's future, easing the bloody shapes this way and that a little only to see better, and each sentence, you could see the girl storing up the words, eating them almost. Then all of a sudden it'd be over, and the fish'd be flung into the tray along with the rest, for there's no sense in waste. And the women would be at their work again and the girl, like as if she'd been forgotten, left standing on the quay and only a stain on the stone to tell where her future had been.

So then it might be that same girl, when her time was near, she'd be sat down to drink a cup of tea most fearfully, and when it was drunk it'd be taken from her and out of the shapes in the leaves would come more tales of the future, to be spoken over her full belly.

Sitting on the train on the way to my own marriage, it wasn't that I believed in those mucky entrails, or in the tea leaves. But I'd have so liked somebody to speak important words over me. For all that we differed and for all that she'd never have let me go in the first off if I'd asked her, I missed my mam and wished, so suddenly that it took me by surprise and I found my eyes full of tears, that she was here and sitting right across from me and giving me a bit of a squeeze on the arm, like she might have, to keep my spirits up.

But there could be none to do that on this wedding day, which we'd pledged to keep secret. And so we sat on that early train all alone in our carriage, each in our own thoughts, though I wonder now whether Thomas's that day had to do with me, or whether his thoughts had already taken him far off.

In the end, Thomas's friend had agreed to give me away. I'd not met him before, and Thomas had told me nothing except that he'd been with him in St Sebastian's.

'Harriet, this is Sean Boland. Sean, this is Harriet.'

He was a queer-looking fellow with a head that seemed too big for his body. He looked me up and down, right solemn, and then he looked back at Thomas and then he looked at me again, and then his face broke open into this smile which made me feel like the best girl in the world and I forgot about the something strange there was to him.

'Pleased to meet you, Harriet,' he said, with something very proper about the words, and he made a little bow.

'It's kind of you,' I said, and didn't know how to put it, but he nodded in such a way as to make me think he understood it all.

'Anybody loved by Thomas is loved by me,' he said, and though they were strong words and not the kind you'd ever usually speak to a stranger you'd met just a half minute earlier, you couldn't take it wrong from him, nor doubt him. And I thought right then that since I couldn't have my arm tucked into my own father's on this day, and anyway wouldn't have wanted it, then Thomas had somehow found the best man in the world to take me to my wedding.

I'd never had much dealing with churches, I'd not been brung up to it. Some of the folk back by the sea were goers, and there'd always be more in the pews after a big storm. But mostly I only went for deaths – my uncle's was the last, and I'd not been in a church since.

At the last minute, Thomas looked as nervous as me, and it was Sean who stepped up to the door and turned the handle. I don't know why, but I'd imagined it'd be all lit up inside, but it wasn't. It seemed next to dark at first, till our eyes got used to it, and after the warmth of the new day outside, it felt cold and damp.

The place was enormous, and so gloomy, I couldn't make out a single one of the statues or even the pictures in the glass. I looked up towards the rafters and all that air above seemed to weigh heavy, so I fixed my eyes on the little light at the front. We all of us stopped at the top of the aisle, and I wondered if they felt like I did, Thomas and Sean, like it'd be easier to run out than stay in, even after their years of church-going in St. Sebastian's. Our second witness was a cheery woman with a bosom like a plank who was happy, at the promise of a shilling, to wait a little before buying her vegetables. And only she seemed easy in the place, so holding her basket before her, it was she that led the way to the altar rail.

The wedding was a quick affair. The vicar was waiting for us and we'd barely time to get ourselves lined up before he was off, telling us at the start that he had an important wedding to get to after ours, the daughter of a Mr so-and-so, a gentleman out towards Ilkley, and then going through the words like a dose of salts. He barely gave us time to give our answers before he was on to the next bit. Did Thomas take me and did I promise to honour and obey, then we were pronounced upon and so it was done. We were finished and out on the pavement so fast that if it wasn't for the ring on my finger, I'd not have believed it.

'Doesn't take up a lot of time, does it, getting married?' I said. 'We'll be home before dinner.'

The buxom lady wished us well and was on to the market, her pocket fuller by the shilling, and we watched the vicar speed away in a carriage. Thomas looked as surprised as I did that it was all over so quickly, this time we'd been waiting for all these months past, and surprise wasn't something you'd catch him out in often.

We were both stood there on the pavement like a couple of Lot's wives, so that Sean, to help us along in that moment, and all the world and its wife bustling about its business, clapped his hands together. He shook Thomas's hand, and kissed me on the cheek before I knew it.

'It isn't any wedding or gentleman in Ilkley,' he said. 'I'll bet he's got some trouble there with his stomach. Did you not notice the way he was clutching under his belly? I'd say he couldn't wait,' and his joke got us laughing.

'Or maybe it's his woman as had warned him not to ruin the eggs again by his delay,' Thomas said and with the mention of eggs I found I'd got a punishing hunger and so we headed in to a nearby inn that Sean knew and got ourselves a wedding breakfast: Chops, eggs, bacon, black pudding and beer. Sean wanted some tripe, but I warned I'd have to leave if he did, that I'd had a bad time over some when I was small. And he said, seeing as it was my wedding day, he'd put it off.

By the time Thomas and I took a train back to York, we were in high spirits, even though we'd only the hour or so on the train left to us to be man and wife for all to see. Never mind that they were using me for all their photographs, never mind how good I was at the job, if I wanted to stay working at Wetherby's, then, so far as they knew, I must be an unmarried girl, else they'd shake my hand and wave me goodbye. So before we got in to York station, I'd have to take off the ring and hide it, though everything in me wanted to show it to the world.

Thomas had made me a tiny box for my ring. On the outside it was plain deal, to act as disguise for its contents. But on the inside it was the prettiest wood – walnut he told me – and carved with a curvy line which put me in mind of a wave, and with a base of velvet for the ring to sit on. We'd both agreed some time ago that even to wear it about my neck was too risky, for I knew girls who'd been found out in this. And so until things came to a different pass, my ring would live in the little box and the little box would be tucked away somewhere safe.

'Let me take it off this first time, since I only got to put it on a few hours ago,' Thomas said, and he tugged it gently free and placed it in the box. 'Now, remember what I told you about your new lodgings? You're to go there – the landlady's expecting you – and wait for me.'

'You've become a regular man of mystery these days,' I said. 'Will you not tell me any more?'

But he only winked and put a finger to his lips. So all I could do was trust him and make my way across the city, my bits all collected in Mrs O'Leary's carpet bag, to my new lodgings on The Mount.

This house looked too grand for me. It had a gate to be pushed open, railings, a front garden and two steps before you even reached the front door. Then there was a bell to pull, which I could hear clanging way away. The house seemed to go up forever, tall as a small cliff. Thomas had said my room was at the very top.

A little maid let me in and took me to my room. The landlady was out, she said, and she'd been left instructions. So as we climbed the stairs, she gave me out the rules. Only a few minutes later I was in my new room, my things were unpacked and I was sat on my bed. This new room was much smarter than the one I'd had at Mrs O'Leary's, with its flowery jug and bowl, and rag rugs on the floor, but I felt homesick for what I knew, and I hoped that whatever Thomas had up his sleeve, it'd happen soon.

I thought it to be a mouse at first, the scratching behind the wall. Except that it didn't go, not even when I made some noise clacking my boots together. And when I tapped the wall, it tapped back. I'm not a believer in ghosts, but for a few minutes I wondered if I must become one. Then, crossing my arms in front of me, like I'd take no nonsense, I demanded of the scratching noise: 'What are you, behind there?'

And the answer came back: 'Your husband!'

Set into the end wall of the room was a small door I'd taken no notice of till now. Thomas's voice was coming from just behind this. So I opened the latch and tugged. The door mustn't have been used for years, because it was fixed stiff with whitewash, and it took my tugging and some hefty blows from

Thomas's boot before the paint cracked and the door opened. Thomas stepped into my room, cocky as I imagined he must have been as a little lad, till I remembered the miserable tale he'd told of his childhood. He took hold of my hand and pulled me through the little doorway.

'Come in to my abode,' he said, which set me laughing, him using the word abode, and he led me, crouching, under the roof laths. I could see the roof slates and above them, here and there, scratches of blue sky. Looking along, I could see roofs stretching beyond, and behind, and I wondered how many other lives I could creep alongside of up here. Only a few steps, and we were through another little door and into another room and this was Thomas's.

'Aren't I a clever husband?' he said. 'My bed's bigger than yours, and your room's not big enough to swing a cat, so I'd reckon we'd better sleep in here,' and my heart started beating faster, because of course it was my wedding day and I'd heard dark tales from girls at the factory about what happened then.

'What if somebody hears us?' I said.

'She's deaf, my landlady. She's got an ear trumpet the size of a saucepan which she says makes no difference anyway, so she doesn't carry it with her,' he said and he looked so pleased with himself, I couldn't help but swipe him one. He caught my arm and drew me to him and kissed my forehead, a fierce kiss that led to others and then he caught me up in his arms and carried me the two steps to his bed and lay me there, and him beside me.

'You'll not mind me carrying you this time,' he said, a bit of worry in his forehead, 'because I know you're not the girl for it. It's what I love. One thing I love.'

'Did other girls let you, then?' I said. He didn't answer me straight off, but set himself leaning up on one arm and stroking clear the fret of hair that'd got loose and tangled over my brow.

'I didn't have a lot to do with others,' he said. 'Which isn't to say I never kissed one or two. They look queer at you in the office if you don't,' he said after.

'Mr William?' I said.

'The other clerks,' he said, smiling.

'So were they like me, the others?' I said. 'A bit like me?'

He shook his head. 'They'd lips and dimples and there was one was as pretty. But they weren't fierce like you. And I love you for it.'

'You'd walk across me, else,' I said, and he nodded.

'I'm not proud of it,' he said. 'But you'll not let me.'

'No,' I said. 'I've seen it enough.'

'Where?'

'It isn't that he doesn't love her, but my dad's got a rage deep in him, and when it's up, he's that hard on my mam, we couldn't bear it, me and Daniel. We ran from it all through when we were children, and I a'n't doing any more running now.'

'So I'm like your dad, then?' Thomas said.

I shook my head. 'I'd not have married you if you had been. But you've got it in you, somewhere it's in you,' and I ran my hand over his chest like I might be able to find it out if I tried. He took my hand and moved it over his head, slowly, over the smoothness of his hair and down over his face.

'What have you promised to them, Thomas?' I said.

'Who?'

'To Mr William and Mr Caleb? How much?'

He shook his head. 'I'd a room in his house, Mr Caleb's, for three years. I ate my meals at his table. Same food.'

'And?'

'So I owe him.'

'That's it?'

'That's it today. Now, Mrs Newcome, ease up. The time is ours at last,' he said. His fingers on my bodice put the rest out of my head, and slowly, like we had all the time in the world, we undressed each other, till our clothes made two piles at the foot of the bed.

But though he was gentle, he seemed frightened too, and his movements as he unhooked me those of one in some kind of trance. And once we were both naked, Thomas pulled away and stared so long, looking me up and down, from the crown of my head to the rough skin on my heels, not saying anything, not touching, that at last I pulled the covers over, embarrassed.

'What is it?' I said, and then at last he seemed to come out from his trance. But he buried his face in my neck and it was an age before he spoke.

'I don't know how to touch you. I've never seen a girl before,' he said.

And so I took his fingers and guided them over each part of my body, letting them rest where they wished to, and showing him what I already knew, which was how to make my skin sing and my spirit rise up high, most like some seabird, I thought, which climbs above the waves and soars.

I had grown up with my brother and shared a bed with him till I left home, so Thomas's body was not so strange to me, and as he touched me, I longed to kiss each uncovered part of him. Then he acted guide for my fingers, and so we went on, slowly, quietly at first, finding in our bodies different places and something stranger and newer to me, which was a shared heaven and by the end we thanked God for the lady and her ear trumpet below, for nothing could have quietened our tune by then.

So it was our honeymoon, that room, and on Monday when I was back in the factory and the other girls talking of jaunts and such, I'd not a clue what the day had been like on Sunday. There might have been snowstorms and thunder and lightening for all I knew, and there could have been battles fought below our window and we'd not have known a thing about it.

Thomas left his house a few minutes before I left mine. We'd agreed that it'd be safer that way. And we'd fixed to meet further in towards the city, just beyond the tram stop. Of course I'd no ring on my finger, it being put away safe in its little box, and hidden in the roof, but still I was sure people could tell from my face what had happened and was only glad it was Monday and so most had their heads down facing the week.

We'd been in the habit of walking arm in arm to the factory of a morning, only separating when we came in sight of the church tower next door, and so this morning Thomas took my arm like usual, but we hadn't gone more than a few steps before I shook free.

'They can tell,' I said.

'What?' said Thomas, and he sounded a bit cross.

'People know. They're looking at me,' I said.

'Oh, come on. You think all the world's looking at you, just because you've been and done what most of 'em do anyway?' Thomas's voice was scornful. I turned and looked behind me. A man had just passed us, a farm labourer from his clothes, and he had his head turned back and I couldn't doubt it now, he was staring at me.

'Stop a minute. Look at me carefully. Just check I've not got a smear of something on my cheek.'

Thomas gave this groan, like a 'look what I've married' kind of a groan, but he did look at my face and, before I could stop him, gave me this smacker of a kiss, which even though it was a Monday and I'd the whole week of work ahead, made my stomach turn over. There wasn't any mark on me, he promised. But still I was sure I was getting these looks and I wouldn't take his arm. So we walked through the bar and down Micklegate with air between us, and something else, which was our first married quarrel.

I kept my eyes to the ground to avoid people's faces, still being certain they were looking at me. So Thomas saw it before I did.

'Harriet!' he said, and he stopped dead in his tracks.

'What?' I said. I didn't look up. I was counting the paving stones, like I used to sometimes count cobbles when I was younger, and then it was often after I'd had a fight with someone.

'Harriet!' he said again.

'What is it?' I said, and he didn't say, so I had to look up.

We'd got to the bottom of Micklegate and were nearly up to Ouse Bridge. Thomas was still stood stock-still, and he wasn't looking at me. He was staring at this bit of wall high up on the corner of North Street, and he wasn't the only one. There was almost a crowd stood there, men and women in their work clothes carrying their dinner pails, their tools. There was a whole lot of faces I recognised from the factory. And all of them, they were staring at the wall.

It was a bit of wall that was always covered with bills and posters. Electioneering, circuses, travelling doctors, pills with powerful properties, toothpullers and liquid female remedies. Even respectable firms sometimes stuck a bill up there, to sell their ironmongery or their animal feeds.

The poster everyone was looking at today was high up, clear of the muddle. Somebody must've used a ladder to paste it. It was bigger too, and in colour, and at the top it had across it in these large letters: 'Pure and sweet' and at the bottom it had 'Drink Wetherby's Cocoa', and in the middle, larger than life, it had a picture of me.

I'd no idea it would look like that. I'd no idea it *could*. It was the first time I'd ever seen a real photograph used like that. That big. And they'd never told me they were to go on posters and be stuck up on walls like this where everybody could gawp.

All pretty and smiley I looked, all coloured-in, and like the thing I loved best was to stand there, pink-cheeked, with a cup of cocoa in my hand. The picture showed me at a kitchen table piled with fresh bread, and a song-bird's cage at one end, and looking for all the world like the thing that I truly was now, if any but knew it, which was a wife. But it hadn't really been like that. The photograph was fooling.

It'd got to be a weekly thing, Mr Benbow coming, and me being summoned and taking off my pinafore and making my way to the top of the factory. So much of an ordinary thing that the other girls had grown used to it and tired of asking me about it, specially as I couldn't tell. I'd sworn them that, Mr William and Mr Caleb.

It was a dusty, cobwebby room he used, with old flour sacks and packing crates down one end and cobwebs dancing round the walls, swaying in the draughts from the windows. Or sky-lights rather, which was why Mr Benbow used it, because even on a cloudy day there was lots of light, especially once he'd had me up there, cleaning the cobwebs off the glass.

He brought up all he needed by himself, props and that, with me helping him, and only getting another man in for the bigger things as were too heavy for him and me. And best of all this huge camera, more than twice the size of the one in the studio and a stand more like a small tree trunk to carry it.

'Did you already have that?' I said when I saw it the first time.

'It's been made specially, to get a bigger picture' he said. 'The cabinet-maker had never built one so large. And all for you, darling.' He said this last to annoy me, but I didn't mind these ways so much any more and only ignored him.

One day he brought up some pieces of old wood and I couldn't see what they were for, and I wasn't going to ask, until he had some grass turf added and the wood became a fence and stile.

'But why can't we go outside and do this?' I said, when he had me sitting on the pretend stile on the square of wilting grass with a box of pastilles and a parasol over my head. 'And it'd be easier with the light.'

'Money. And secrecy,' he said, and that was that.

It was on account of the secrecy that I had to work as Mr Benbow's assistant, putting the props on the table how he wanted them, helping him get the stile in place, even adding a touch of paint here and there. Because nobody was allowed in here while he was working, nobody but the Wetherbys, and me. I asked him after a bit, was I as good at it as Mary, but he didn't answer, only smiled.

Over the weeks I got quite used to pretending, because that's what it was really about. Mr Benbow would say 'Now, dear,' and I'd make my mouth smile. Sometimes I'd be dressed like a country girl, with a rake in my hand and there'd be stooks of corn behind me, and I'd be holding a packet of fruit pastilles. Or I'd be a maid, all in white frills and holding a silver tray, and on the tray there'd be a cup of cocoa and the packet saying 'Wetherby's Purest Cocoa Powder', to prove it. Mr Benbow had a little stuffed dog brought in for that one. It'd been one of those fluffy little dogs once, that aren't much good for anything. It was sat up on its back legs like it was sniffing, and I'd to do a face like 'Isn't it sweet, it wants my mistress's cocoa.' I'm not one for dogs, but this was good and dead, so I couldn't be too bothered.

Once even he had me dress in a bathing suit, a strange thing it was and I felt like I was near to naked with it clinging to me and next to nothing beneath and only to my knees and elbows, but they never used the picture. Mr William wouldn't have allowed it, I don't think. But I never got to be the things I'd really been. I never got to be a flither-lass nor a factory girl.

Now, standing on the corner and everybody staring at the picture, and me in it smiling down, all I could think was how odd it looked, and surely everyone else could see that? Because it wasn't the cosy kitchen it looked like, it was just a few things put together in the middle of a big, dirty room. And I didn't bake bread really, I worked in a factory. They didn't know that the range was cold, propped up in place with a couple of crates, or that the bread had been stale, hard as rock, Mr Benbow having got it cheap off the baker's on his way that morning. Or that the bird in the cage was dead and stuffed, for all it looked like it was singing, or that I don't do smiles like that, not normally, and my cheeks are never that red, it was only the engraver's ink. Nothing was right.

I started to run, on down Micklegate away from the picture and the people looking at it, over Ouse Bridge and into the market on Parliament Street. It being a Monday, there was no fish, which I was glad of somehow, but there were stalls piled with vegetables. Potatoes and carrots dark with soil, and apples and pears and blackberries catching the bits of light that got under the awnings. I stopped my running and walked slow amongst it all, the traders jangling the big pouches they wore round their middles for the money and calling out their goods, the women with square baskets piled around them on the ground and a fierce set to their shoulders ready to sell for a price, until my heart had stopped its fierce beating a bit.

I'd like to have stayed there, just dawdling, not thinking. But Thomas found me after maybe a quarter of an hour. He came up from behind and made me jump with his hand on my shoulder. His face was so pale and worried, and his breath was coming in such gasps, that for the time it took for him to speak, I felt bad that I'd run away.

'You shouldn't have gone off like that,' he said, and he tried to draw me to him.

'Oh, for God's sake!' The words were out of me before I could stop them, and I pulled away from him, anger blazing

up in me, and it was all I could do, not to pull over one of
them stalls on him. Or so it felt anyway, because in truth I
knew I wasn't much good at the doing of things. They mostly
stayed as thoughts.

'Leave off, Thomas,' I said. 'You're no better than they are,
Mr William and Mr Benbow. So long as it makes more of 'em
buy your cocoa or your pastilles, you don't give a blind man's
toss how it's done.'

'You should be proud, girl. They chose you. Out of all
them, they chose you. And now you'll be famous.'

'Well I'm not bloody proud,' I said, my voice louder by far
than his, which he was keeping hushed. 'You might be, but
I'm not.'

'I don't know what I am,' Thomas said. 'All those men staring at you and not a thing I can say about it. Makes me feel
bloody strange.'

There was something in his voice that wasn't pleased at all,
but he didn't say any more, only put his hand back on my shoulder and was pulling at me, his fingers fair digging into my skin.

'Please?' he said. I was stood stock-still. 'We'll be very late
for work. They'll have docked the quarter day already.' But I
couldn't move. 'Come on,' he said, pleading. 'They're looking
at us.' Which was true enough, and we must have looked a bit
odd, a girl stood like a rock by the drinking fountain with a
young man tugging at her, and it being the morning, not the
night, and both of them stone cold sober.

I took a drink from the fountain, and the touch of the
metal cup and the water cold in my throat calmed me down.

'It's a funny one, you being embarrassed that they're looking at us here, when you're telling me I should be proud with
them staring at the poster,' I said, and it set us both to laughing which was what we needed.

They must have had someone posted for us, because the
factory doors were usually locked till the quarter day had gone,

so as if you were late you couldn't sneak in and pretend you'd been there earlier. But soon as we were stood there, the only ones waiting, the door was opened by this wee lad who was hopping a bit from foot to foot like he needed to go, but I think it was that he was nervous, getting ready to tell us something.

When it came out at last, his voice was this high little noise and I saw he must've been even younger than my brother, and his voice not settled yet.

'Mr William says he'll not dock the girl's wages if she gives him proper account,' he said, and Thomas nodded at the boy as if he were a boss not a clerk and ordered the lad back to his job, and the boy went.

'I don't want to see Mr William and I don't like being talked of as "the girl". I don't know as I'll be able to keep my tongue,' I said. Thomas held my head in his hands and kissed my hair but didn't say a word in answer, for which I was glad because he'd only have made me more angry in the mood that had me, whatever he said.

'Come on,' Thomas said.

I shook my head. 'I'm going to my work.'

'You have to come up,' Thomas said.

'I don't.'

Thomas pleaded with me. 'Come on love. Just bite your tongue and do it. It's not worth standing on your high horse,' and he'd have dragged me up those stairs kicking and screaming if he thought it'd work. But I wasn't budging, so in the end he strode off and away up to his clerks' office at the top, and it was just in the nick of time that he did. Because he was barely out of sight when Mr William came into the hall. He must've been making his rounds, checking on all the production rooms, else he'd have been tucked away in his office. He stood there, nearly motionless except for a finger he had tap-tapping against his leg, looking at me with this expression like he couldn't imagine what I was doing stood there by the stairs at that time of day, but he didn't seem angry. It was my jaw that was tight with it, but I kept as calm as I could.

'Shouldn't you be in the Creams Room, Harriet?' he said.

I nodded.

'So is anything the matter?' he said, the blue of his eyes the dark colour of the sea before a storm. A colour to get a distance from.

'It's my face.' I was stumbling, not knowing the words to say and him standing there all proper in his funny black suit and waiting. 'My face. It's all over town. I was on my way to work and there was this poster.' He smiled. 'It was me, plastered across the wall,' I said. 'Even coloured up there was no mistaking it.'

'Well, Mr Benbow has been working with us for some months now,' he said, as if I didn't know it. And besides, I couldn't see what that had to do with it.

'People were staring at me,' I said. 'I didn't know it'd be for posters, all the stuff with Mr Benbow. I thought it'd be packets, tins at the most.'

'We are doing what we think is best for the company, and most of all what is best for those who buy our product. Did you see the pastilles or the cocoa?'

'There are two up?' I said.

'Which did you see?' he said again.

'The cocoa,' I said.

'The other shows a girl on a stile, holding a pastille to her lips. And the caption: "Pure and wholesome, Full of Natural Juices."'

'But it's not just a girl,' I said. 'It's me.'

'Listen, Harriet,' he said. 'Our cocoa is pure, and it is important that people know that. Especially in these days of adulteration.'

He must have seen I didn't understand, because he explained to me then about how lots of cocoa makers added things in, like flour and sago and worse, and how as we were one of the only companies that didn't and this was a way of telling people something important they needed to know when they bought their cocoa.

'Does that help?' he said.

'But I didn't think they'd know who I was,' I said.

'Well, they won't, outside York,' he said, like it was meant to reassure, which it didn't. 'And we won't be using all the designs outside this city. We're using York as a testing ground. Now, is anything else bothering you?' he said, and I couldn't tell him the half of it, I couldn't tell him how angry I was, so I just shook my head.

'Good,' he said. His finger had stopped twitching and I saw he had a spot of colour in each cheek, like my mother used to get when she was cross at my father and keeping it down in front of us children. But his face was the same as always. 'If you go straight to your room, I'll have your quarter-day pay restored this time, in view of the circumstances,' he said.

Then I was sitting in the Cream Packing Room with a hundred other girls around me, all of us in our pinafores and caps, and it didn't matter what my face looked like, or whether I was smiling. The only thing that mattered was filling the boxes, the right creams in the right places.

'Raspberry, strawberry, lemon, then mint. Violet, blackcurrant, coffee, don't stint,' I whispered under my breath, till, like the others, I was into the swing and all that mattered was to fill my number of boxes each hour and to take home my money each week.

SAMUEL

If it hadn't been for Harriet, I believe Grace might never have come home, but lived out the rest of her life within the walls of The Haven. I'd be lying if I pretended I was not jealous of the alliance that had developed between the two girls, which I had observed though they had told me little of it, but thank God my gratitude outweighed my envy.

I still do not understand Grace's fear.

Ten years before she had met Harriet, Grace became fearful of the outside. I don't know how better to put it. In the space of a single day she became unable to go out of doors, unable to stand or run beneath the sky. She would not, or could not venture out, even into the garden. And yet ever since she was a tiny creature, to be deprived of such freedom was the greatest punishment anybody else, by which I mean our mother, could inflict upon her.

I can mark the day when I first saw this in her. I had returned home from a morning's business in York. I was at that time even more concerned than usual about Grace, for only the week before she and Mother had had their terrible battle over Grace's friend, Deborah Harnford. Nellie came to me almost before I was through the front door, her eyes wide with alarm, but her voice hushed, so I knew that whatever she was about to communicate was something she had so far kept from Mother's knowledge.

'It's Grace' she said, and for a moment my heart stopped for I thought she was going to tell me the worst.

'Is she ill?' I said, and Nellie shook her head, but her eyes told me something different.

'She's in the garden,' Nellie said. 'I've set Francie to watching her.'

As I approached the French windows, through the glass I could see the maid standing on one side of the lawn. And in the middle, motionless, a hunched figure. Grace made no move at the sound of my approach, but continued in the same position, squatted down, arms cradling her head.

'Grace,' I called to her softly when I had come close. 'Grace. Are you unwell?'

She made no move, no reply. A light rain had started to fall and the wind had begun to whip around the bushes.

'Grace, it's lunchtime. Come inside with me,' I said.

Still no reply. I came closer and put my hand out to her shoulder. It was like touching a piece of stone. Rigid, unyielding, cold. I continued to talk to her for a while, but she made no move, no sound, and if it hadn't been for the slight rise of her chest as she breathed, I'd have thought her dead.

The rain was coming down harder now and the wind blowing more fiercely. There was a sharp edge to the air and I was concerned she would catch a chill. Mother would be eating her lunch, for she was a stern abider by the rule that if one did not sit down for a meal at the correct time, then one would go without. She would not have waited for either of us to take our seats. And it seemed to me better if possible that I should get Grace to her room without Mother seeing us.

'Grace, you must help me. I'm going to take you indoors and then we will call Doctor Pendleton.'

I circled my sister with my arms and somehow lifted her, she with her arms still tucked around her head, knees still tucked under her chin. That short distance, from the middle of the lawn to the French windows, where Nellie waited to help me, was the hardest journey I ever had to make. And I felt, as I stumbled my way, as I imagine the man they call St Christopher did when he bore the Christ child across the raging torrent and the child grew heavier and heavier. As if I carried not just Grace in my arms, but the whole of her potential life, and if I dropped her, it was far more than just her young body that would fall to the ground.

As soon as we were indoors Grace began to shake. It was with considerable difficulty that Nellie and I managed to take her up to her bedroom. That was the first attack.

It was not until days later that Grace tried to tell me what had happened, but all she could say was that the sky was too large and that she felt it would crush her if she moved. She refused to speak to Mother and it was only a matter of weeks after this, during which time Grace took not a single step outside, but kept to her room, that Mother, with Dr Pendleton's support, had her admission to The Haven arranged.

I do not see how Grace's sudden horror of the outside, which as good as chained her indoors for ten years, could have had anything to do with her quarrel with Mother over Deborah Harnford. And yet it is strange that the two events came so close together, so perhaps I should speak a little of this ill-fated friendship.

Deborah Harnford was the daughter of a prosperous Devonshire Quaker family which had made its business out of leather fancy goods. With the growth of the railways, we had been able to sell our tanned hides further afield, and for some years now we had had an arrangement in place with Harnford's Best Leather Manufacturers. It was only natural, then, when they sent their daughter to school in York, that we should take especial notice of her, and Mother, though not naturally sociable, took pains to have the girl back for the day after Meeting on occasion, and sometimes, by arrangement, for tea in the week.

The girl had been brought up to a delicate existence and I found little to interest me about her. There was no evident strength in her form, none of the grace I found in the young labouring women, nothing to hold one's eye. Perhaps this is why I failed to notice the strong friendship that developed between Deborah and Grace. To use one of Harriet's expressions, given the 'chalk and cheese' of them, it never occurred to me that the two girls would have any especial common ground.

There was one evening in particular I remember, when Grace came to my room. I was perhaps twenty-two, and so she about eighteen. I had engaged myself in a strenuous reading programme at this time – Huxley and Darwin, the eighteenth-century philosophers, also the treatises of John Stuart Mill and such like. Grace knew that these late hours were precious to me, my days being busy with business and charitable affairs, so consequently, when she knocked on my door, I knew her reason must be serious.

'Sam, will you talk with me?' she said. As had been her habit since she was small, she took possession of my old arm-chair, pulling the rug that covered it up and under her arms. In this position she waited for me to settle myself down again, which I did, though as ever too slowly for her quick person.

'You are like an old dog, Sam. I am surprised you do not turn and turn about before you sit to be sure of the wolves.'

I laughed. 'Grace, you are too pert. Since you have seen fit to interrupt me, something must be bothering you.'

She nodded, her face instantly grave. 'I have no wish to marry,' she said, straight out. The use of indirection, or indeed prevarication, is something she has never understood.

Not knowing where this observation had come from, I asked her whether she had reason for concern over the attentions of any young man, and she told me she did not. Certainly I had never noticed her exchanging more than the barest greeting with any of the young men at Meeting, aside of course from her cousins, Caleb and William. And at that time I had no idea of William's powerful feelings for Grace.

'So why are you worried about this now?' I asked.

'It is on account of Deborah,' she said and despite the narrow light of my table lamp I was sure that she was blushing.

'Deborah Harnford?' I said. She nodded. 'Does she have strong views on this subject, then, that she has persuaded you of?' I said, perhaps finding the exchange slightly less confounding after my reading of Mr Mill this same evening.

'No,' Grace said. 'But she and I intend to live in a house together. We believe it will suit us better, our temperaments, than having husbands.'

If she wished to surprise me, she had succeeded. But though she has often surprised, even shocked people, I don't believe Grace has ever set out to do so, and she had not intended to this evening in my bedroom. What did surprise me was that I had no strong sense of this other girl and so was at a loss as to what it was that took Grace's fancy so strongly.

I didn't answer, but picked up a pencil and began to scribble, paying no attention to what I was setting down, in the effort to order my thoughts. It was only much later, long after Grace had left the room, that I saw I had covered the paper with sketches of hands. Women's hands, fingers stretched out, for I have not the skill to give the fingers any other position.

However I must have been silent too long, because finally she broke into my thoughts.

'What do you think of our notion?' she said.

'I don't know,' I said, a poor reply, but a truthful one. 'I cannot speak about the girl herself, as I know little more than her name and we have exchanged no more than the passing courtesies of the tea table. But you are both very young. It seems likely that with the passing of time you might discover in yourselves the desire for a husband, for children. I am not sure that it is a wise thing for two girls, barely women yet, to wish to exempt themselves from the natural order.'

Grace's face was impassive.

'Why not?' she said. 'There are more than enough children being born. Even the Quaker community will not suffer greatly from my or Deborah's abstention.'

This made me laugh, and I could not but agree. 'No, you are right. But what of your impulses?'

'Why should I not wish to spend my days with another girl, as much as with a man? It is what I want, and I can imagine no better companion,' she said.

'And what of Mother?'

Unusually, Grace had no answer to this. Or only in the hunching of her shoulders and the action of her fingers, which now began to pluck at the fibres of the blanket tucked about her. She sat like this for some minutes, her face closed over, so that I knew better than to ask her any more. Then suddenly, violently, she tugged the blanket from her and stood.

'Good night, Sam,' she said, and she kissed me on both cheeks, as was our habit, before leaving the room quickly and silently.

I am certain that Grace never spoke to Mother as she had to me, and I cannot imagine what improprieties Mother could possibly have judged the two girls as having committed that she should have forbidden Grace any further communication with Deborah. However, this is what happened. Grace would tell me no more of it but that Mother had come upon them in a secluded part of the garden while she and Deborah were reading poetry together. Christine Rossetti. The afternoon being cool, Grace had begged a rug of Nellie and they had this over them. And to this, for some reason, Mother had taken powerful exception.

As I have indicated, it was only a few weeks later that Grace was struck with her fear, and once it was apparent to Dr Pendleton that it was going to be of long duration, though how he established this I never knew, Mother had her mind made up quickly and a room at The Haven was secured.

Mother had never asked my opinion, and I felt I could not in fairness dispute her decision if I had no better suggestion to put in its place. Had I been older, I believe I would have tried to keep her from this course, and yet I suspect it would have been to no avail, for it is in her that Grace's fierce intransigence originates. And she was used always to having her way. I was sure, if Father had been alive, that he would have searched for and found another way, but I could not stand in his place now, however much I might wish it, not against Mother.

I would rather have been away from the house that day, for I thought my heart would break.

Grace was removed at teatime. Even now to think of it puts a chill across me. Not wanting Nellie or Francie to do so, Mother had packed her things, while Grace sat, like a living wraith, on her bed. I pretended to read in my room, listening to the unfamiliar step and creak of Mother's steps next door. When she had finished the packing, Mother knocked on my door.

She came in uncertainly.

'Samuel?' Her voice was strangely hesitant. I don't believe she had been inside my room since I was a child and thick with fever. 'She is nearly gone,' Mother said. 'The carriage will be here directly.' She turned to leave, not waiting for my reply, but then stumbled and would have fallen, had I not just managed to catch her in my arms. I sat her in a chair, the same chair that Grace had climbed into, and saw now what I had somehow failed to see before, that her face was wet with tears.

'Go to Grace,' she said, and, as I left the room I heard her say, 'I have to do this,' though whether she spoke this to herself or to me, I have never known.

Dr Pendleton and another from The Haven came for my sister. They talked to her as if to a child, and she let them escort her to the carriage. As the front door opened and Grace walked out a few steps beneath the sky, she shuddered so violently that they were compelled to carry her the last yard to the carriage. And I could do nothing. Only stand by, my throat dry with grief, my eyes fixed upon her blank face through the carriage window until I could no longer see her.

Ever since Grace was very small, Mother had found her hard to bear. A changeling child, too separate and too strange. So she made a virtue of being stern, of finding fault, for it was a way of setting the bounds between them. Now that Grace was gone into The Haven, Mother need no longer fear her. And yet the day of Grace's departure seemed also to mark the death of something in Mother, as though, unwitting, she had cut something out of herself. She seemed visibly to shrink so that her clothes hung about her, despite the maid's efforts to tuck and alter, and she would not buy any new, for the old were of good cloth and so must be still used. She had always worn at her neck a circular golden brooch I loved. Father's gift on the occasion of my birth. But now her neck was so thin, and become so shrivelled, that the brooch had the appearance more of some punitive weight that might be attached to a prisoner than a piece of ornamentation. Her appetite, which had always been small, disappeared and she appeared to take nothing but the sweet, weak tea to which she had always been partial. Once, when I had seen no food pass her lips for above a week, I asked Nellie whether she was not more ill than usual.

'She doesn't take much,' Nellie said. 'But also she doesn't like you to see her eating,' and she explained that Mother would often have a maid deliver her a thin broth or some sweet porridge late in the evening when I was safely retired.

And although she did not, like Grace, refuse to leave the house, she too retreated increasingly, making out of her plants a kind of shield. The garden, the glasshouse and the few rooms she inhabited: these marked the limits of her world. Within these places she tended with gentleness and wisdom, giving to her plants the care that should have been for Grace. Whereas for her daughter she had only the ruthless husbandry which orders the blighted plant to be removed from all the others, and if not destroyed, then kept separate.

Mother didn't visit Grace. She made no excuses for this, believing, I think, that her action was proper in the eyes of God. I went to see Grace every week, once or twice, sometimes more often, and this too Mother thought right. That I should visit, but not her. Had Father been alive, I think she would have thought his visits proper too. Sometimes she would give me some money for Grace, or something she had had the cook prepare. Biscuits or a fruit cake. A few years on she would send me with cuttings or bulbs. Or if nothing else, advice. How much water to give a particular orchids, or how to divide tubers. But she never saw her daughter again before she died, and Grace would not come to the funeral.

Although Grace said at that time that Mother had a death to die, and she a life to live, I wondered what kind of a life it was, when she would barely leave the confines of her room.

Perhaps it was habit more than terror that kept Grace indoors after ten years, though I suggest this only with the benefit of hindsight. In the first years when I still asked her to come out, she would only and always say, 'I cannot.'

'What about a walk, just down to the rose garden,' I would say. Or 'Come and see the sweet peas, they're topping their poles,' and she would answer only, 'I cannot.' In the later years I no longer asked her.

And yet when Harriet had coaxed her to leave the shelter of a roof and venture out again beneath the sky, once Harriet had achieved this, for which I shall ever be in her debt, Grace re-entered the outdoor world as a man desperate with thirst rushes into a river.

When I asked Harriet what she had done to achieve this, this thing that neither I, nor doctor, nurse or any other person had managed in all these years, she looked embarrassed and said that she had only sung Grace a song, a silly song really that her mother used to sing to her.

'Will you sing it to me?' I asked and she gave me a pained look, and began it in a sweet, uncertain voice.

'Buttercup and speedwell, horseshoe vetch to bring you luck,' she began, and then broke off.

'The rest was like it,' she said.

'There was nothing else?' I said and Harriet shook her head.

'It was my mam taught me the rhyme when I was small enough to be sat on her knee. But she'd no idea how to tell one flower from the next, and so nor had I. Grace said she must show me them, those that flowered at this time in the year, and she took my hand and we went out.'

'Without further ado?' I said.

Harriet nodded.

'And was she quite steady, once you were out of doors?' I said and Harriet had nodded again.

'Only she didn't know which way to go, to find the flowers. But I took her to the stray, just behind, and we spent an hour nearly. We made a posy. She'd have stayed out longer, but I insisted. Said if she didn't come back with me, I'd have to go for the matron.'

I had invited Harriet to my house for tea so that we might talk of Grace. Mother had been in her grave for only a couple of months and I still felt her shadow on my skin when I penned my invitation. I could not have done this when she was alive, though it was not she who was peculiar in her convictions, but me. Those other Quakers I know well believe as Mother did, that the classes must respect one another and work to the common good, while being sure not to transgress what they regard as natural, even God-given boundaries between the different states. I wrote,

> Dear Harriet, May I have the pleasure of your
> company for tea at 4.00 p.m. on the fourteenth day of
> this month? I would be glad of the opportunity to
> discuss the well-being of my sister, to whom you have
> of late become such an important friend.
> Respectfully yours, Samuel Ransome

Most unusually, I forgot to let Nellie know of this invitation. So that when Harriet had come to the front door, Nellie had been perfectly polite, but perfectly firm too.

'Are you one of his Quakers?' she'd asked, and when Harriet had said she was not, Nellie had taken her round and in through the kitchen door. She'd sat her down at the kitchen table and had the cook pour her a large cup of tea from the brown teapot that always sat upon the range, then come to find me.

Of the three of us, I was the only one embarrassed. Harriet and Nellie seemed already the best of friends and were laughing over it, Nellie promising to have the cook bake a fresh cake the next time.

'Besides, you'll find the rest of the house far less comfortable than the kitchen, when you see the state the master has it in right now,' Nellie said with an impudence lent her by the novelty of the situation.

Although this was a moment I had dreamed of a hundred times in the past year, still my heart was racing and I could feel a bead of sweat breaking on my brow when I took Harriet in to the drawing room. If anybody of my acquaintance had seen me entertaining a young working girl, unchaperoned, in the drawing room of my family home, they would have thought me a gentleman in name only who demonstrated no proper respect for the conduct and propriety expected from one of his class. They might even have questioned my morals, for no one but the debauched entertained girls of Harriet's class anywhere, let alone in their home.

Harriet seemed remarkably at her ease, and I wondered again whether this was because she had had so little previous acquaintance through the years of her childhood with people from the higher classes.

It was a strange setting. The furniture was shrouded in white dustsheets so that it was as though we were surrounded by an unwieldy arrangement of lumpen ghosts. And on the floor, stacked one behind the next, were a dozen or more family portraits, the earlier ones done in oils, and the most recent done in the photographer's studio. Harriet knelt down and began to pull the portraits forward, almost flipping through the generations. She stopped at one in a heavy gilt frame that had hung all my life just inside the dining room door.

'She's Grace's relative,' she said. 'The eyes, and the hair, the little bits coming out from under the bonnet. And she's got a gleam in her eye too. But it's funny clothes they're wearing.'

I looked over her shoulder. The portrait showed a young woman seated, and her husband, an older man, behind her. She wore a plain white starched bonnet and a drab grey dress, while he was dressed in a dark suit, the jacket cut away as Quaker custom had so long demanded

'Plain dress,' I said. 'There was a rule about it until about twenty or thirty years ago. Till then you could be put out of the Society of Friends if you dressed too much with an eye to worldly styles.'

'Even if you'd the money for it?' Harriet said.

I nodded. 'Come and sit down now,' I said, for her looking at my family like this made me uneasy. 'I'll have the dustsheets removed.'

'Don't,' Harriet said. 'I like it. It's like being a child again, playing at things.'

So I left it all as it was and we sipped tea and ate cake in a white landscape, broken up only by a little vase of flowers on the mantelpiece, whose frail petals in red and pink, purple and yellow, reminded me, as I had intended them to, of what my project was for this house now.

'Grace picked those,' I said. 'She has come to the garden several times.'

Harriet smiled. 'She told me,' she said.

'Do you know how I persuaded her?' I said and Harriet shook her head. 'I told her it was growing wild since Mother's death. That I would have to arrange for someone else, some stranger, to take care of it as I had neither the time nor the knowledge.'

'And she couldn't bear that,' Harriet said.

'No. She couldn't. She was out the next day, and standing at the back door asking Nellie, who hadn't seen her in all the ten years, to bring out her gardening shoes, quite as though she'd never been gone. Nellie came running in to me amazed. It was little after eight in the morning and I was still at my coffee. "It's Miss Grace," was all she could say, and she had tears in her eyes.'

Grace worked in the garden all that day, had Nellie bring her lunch on a tray, which she ate beneath the cedar tree. But she wouldn't come into the house. She still won't.'

'Is that why you're doing all this?' Harriet said and she gestured to the dustsheets.

I nodded. 'I'm going to have the house painted throughout. I've asked Grace how she'd like it done, if she were here.'

'Did she tell you?' Harriet asked.

'Not exactly,' I said. 'She quoted me some verse, about birdsong and kitchens and forests, but I took it for a good sign. I'm going to be rid of much of the furniture too. It needn't be sold. There are those in Meeting who would be glad of the loan of such good quality stuff. But I want to make this a new house, a place that maybe Grace could bear to have as her own home.'

'Perhaps it will be like the garden,' Harriet said. 'If she thinks the house needs her.'

'It is quite a walk each day she has from The Haven. But she will not hear of me sending a carriage,' I said, 'and insists on walking home.'

'I'd say she was stronger than you think,' Harriet said, and I knew she was right. If she'd been strong enough to survive the last ten years, then the walk from one side of the city to the other wasn't going to do her any harm, and I must let her be, to find her own way back into her life.

'I trust Thomas is well,' I said.

'Yes, thank you,' she said, but no more.

Although she wore no ring, I knew they were married. I had argued with William in the past about his rule only to employ single girls. He was adamant that a married woman's place was in her home rearing children and keeping the house, and when I pointed out the privations this might bring, it was like speaking to a deaf man. Or else he said that for a wife to work was only to encourage a husband's idleness and no good could come of it. So Harriet could tell nobody of her wedding, or she would risk losing her job. But I had woken one Saturday morning and known in my bones that this was the day and upon visiting the factory on some pretext, discovered that, uniquely since he started working there, Thomas had made arrangements to take that morning off work and make up the time later. In the same way, I found that Harriet had moved lodgings and now lived in a house adjoining Thomas's. And though I didn't know how, I could only assume they had found some way to conduct their marital life.

'And the photographs?' I said to Harriet. 'You are still working with Mr Benbow?'

'He's finished for now,' she said. 'But there'll probably be more to do after Christmas.'

Like everybody else, I had seen the posters around York. And I knew from William that they were up now in every city in the country. I knew too, for William had insisted on telling me in detail, how much the sales of cocoa and pastilles had increased. But I could hardly bear it. To see that precious face paraded across wall after wall for all to look at, to leer at if they wished. To see her pretending to such gaiety, in those costumes that had nothing to do with her! Costumes unlike anything she would ever wear. Unlike anything any Quaker would ever wear.

At first, each time I came upon one, it was like a body blow. But now, at least in York, I knew where each one was and I would avert my eyes when walking past.

'And are you happy with them?' I asked her.

Harriet looked at me. 'What do you think?' she said, and I was both shocked and hugely relieved at her words.

'But they have made you famous in a way,' I said.

She gave a small laugh. 'And where's the use in that?' she said.

I knew the conversation pained her, and yet I had to continue.

'And Thomas?' I said. 'How does he find it?'

'He doesn't like them any more than me,' she said, 'but he'd sell his soul for Wetherby's,' and she started, quietly, to cry. I tried to reassure her.

'There is not a soul I will tell of our meeting,' I said.

'No, it's not that,' she said. 'I know you won't tell. It's saying it out loud. It'll make it happen. Oh God!' and suddenly she was sobbing, her head bowed, her hand scrabbling in her sleeve for a handkerchief.

For the first time in all the months since we had met that day on the bridge, I was unsure of what to do. I wanted to comfort her, to put my arm round her shoulders, have her cry her tears into my waistcoat. But I could not, and so I sat and waited and watched the crown of her head, the straight line of her parting, the sleek brown hair smoothed tight each side.

She wouldn't tell me what it was she was afraid of, and I didn't press her, not wishing to distress her further. Soon she rose to leave.

'Please believe that I would do anything within my power to ensure your well-being,' I said.

Harriet managed a grin at my portentous words. 'It'll be nothing,' she said. 'Maybe it'll be nothing.'

And then she walked off down the drive and was gone.

I had often reflected on the liberty that Mother's death would bring, and formed for myself an itinerary to be pursued immediately afterwards. But now that she was dead and the time was come, I felt no freer to take my imagined routes than I had felt in the years before.

In the last months of Mother's illness I had been forced to suspend my photographic scheme, and I had looked forward to resuming it. But I did not do so, not because of Mother's death but because of William's advertising campaign, which sucked the impetus from my project as a spider sucks the blood from its prey, and leaves only a lifeless husk.

The sight of Harriet up there so publicly on the walls of the city made a travesty of what I had believed photography could do. I had thought it could capture a truth about somebody.

But now I saw that it could just as easily hide one, and so who was to say which was which? Which was truth, and which falsehood? I still believed I had tucked into my Bible a true image of Harriet, and that the pictures of a hundred or more other girls locked into the cupboard in my room truly showed what they were and what they did. But I could no longer look at them with a clear eye and so my self-appointed task was undone.

I had thought that with Mother's death I might travel, to the Continent or beyond. My role in Ransome's Tannery was barely more than nominal now, and though he would be angry about it, I knew that if I went, then William would undertake my responsibilities there, such as they were. Economic prosperity walked so closely together with piety for him that he would regard it as a religious duty to ensure that my business was sound.

Friends making adventurous journeys abroad often circulated their diaries around the Meeting and I had read a number of these – voyages to Egypt and America, Switzerland and Greece, to Africa and India – and dreamed of my own journey. But, liberated by Mother's death, Grace had started on a journey more exciting to me even than crossing deserts or climbing snow-capped peaks, and for her sake I stayed in York.

Mother had often said she wished I would marry, but I knew this to be only a form of words, for she wanted no rivals for my affection, and resented even the time I spent with Grace. In earlier years I should have liked to have found myself a wife. But now it was too late. I had met Harriet and knew her to be the only girl I would ever wish to make my own. This was impossible, and not only because I knew her to be already married. How could a man in my position marry a woman from her station in life? It could only make misery for both of us.

But thank God I had not gone anywhere far away, and thank God I was not married, so that when Mary Bourne came to me that winter, I could help her. And in the spring, when Caleb came running down the drive, against the wind, out of breath and his hair white with blossom, I was there to hear him and free to act.

HARRIET

After me I'd say it was facts Thomas was wedded to. Or what he took for facts, which was anything put out by *The Leisure Hour*. It surprised me at first, him being such a shrewd fellow, that he'd believe anything written in there, because he wasn't one for being gulled. Not like me. It surprised me that I'd not noticed it so much before. But then over the months we lived together as man and wife, I saw it was on account of it being printed, in the same little black letters, all spaced out and put into blocks and with headings, and photographs for proof sometimes, and then bound up properly. And it didn't do a mite of good for me to say that anyone could get something done out properly if they'd only the money.

Summer lasted long into September that year and as long as we could, we'd walk down the hill to the Knavesmire when we got home from the factory. There were blackberries in a patch of wild and I'd eat and eat at them, my tongue turning to purple, while Thomas watched. And then we'd walk way beyond the trees and the cattle and the horses, out into the middle where the grass was rough and thick and there was nobody else near. And lie down, till it was dark sometimes, and read and talk and dream.

'I saw a blackberry fox when I was younger,' I told him one of those end of summer days.

'What's a blackberry fox?' he asked, so I told him the tale of it. How I'd truanted off from school and how it must have been this same time of year because it was the blackberries the fox was after too.

'We must have had the same bush in our heads that morning,' I said, 'only the fox got there ahead.'

'How old were you?'

'I don't remember. Nine maybe,' I said. 'The teacher used to tell us, "You'll get nowhere, knowing nothing," which I knew for a lie, because once we were done at the school, we'd none of us go further than the beach or the boat, so there wasn't any use in it.'

'But you did, didn't you,' Thomas said, 'and Mary too.'

'Well I'd never have dreamed it even, then. And anyway, I wasn't the only one not to be making letters on my slate. There were always others.'

'A group of you,' Thomas said, and I shook my head.

'No. I liked it better, being on my own, so I'd duck away quick till any of the rest were far gone.'

'Didn't Mary go with you?' Thomas asked, but I told him we weren't friends till later. That Mary liked school, being the one whose slate got held up for the rest of us to look at. How everybody knew her for a sharp tongue out, but in school butter never melted on her.'

'So what about the fox?' Thomas said, and I told him about the valley, back behind the last house on our street, and how once you were through the couple of fields and into the woods, then it was like another world altogether.

'It was earth-smelling there, not salt,' I said, 'and the trees so much over, you'd to strain to see the sky. It was always where I went, if I could, the days I didn't go to school. And that morning the air was still cold when I got to where the black-berries were and I thought to leave my picking till the sun was higher, till it had warmed the fruit, else they'd be too sharp on the tongue for my taste. So I sat down and waited.

'I don't know whether I was maybe daydreaming, but I didn't see it till it was there. Not an "it", a "he", a big dog fox with a great bush of tail. I sat still as stone and watched and hoped he'd not smell me. The wind was blowing my way, which was maybe why he'd not done so already. I thought first there must be a bird or a rabbit or something caught in the brambles, but then I saw it was my blackberries he was after, reaching in and plucking, and not waiting for the sun to warm them sweeter. When he stood on his back legs for the high up ones, he was taller than me. He ate all the best ones and when he dropped back down and turned, I saw how his muzzle was purple with the juice, and then he was gone.'

When autumn came, written over the leaves and into the air, we stayed in Thomas's room. He liked to read sprawled out on the bed.

I told him once: 'If someone said they could fly you'd believe them, just as long as they said it in a book. Or better still, one of the journals you're so keen on.' But he only rolled over onto the other shoulder and pretended to ignore me and then wouldn't read me out anything the rest of the evening. So I didn't bother saying it again.

Perhaps if we'd had longer we'd have grown tired of it. His favourite thing was for me to be sat up on the bed and for him to lay with his head resting on my lap. Then he'd open up *The Leisure Hour* and I'd do a bit of sewing, if the light wasn't too dim, or doze.

It was hot that September, and some of those evenings we'd get back to our lodgings and it'd feel like all the heat from the houses was rising and resting in our rooms. You'd feel it as you climbed the stairs, and I'd be sweating more even by now than in the factory, which always had a certain temperature on account of the boiling pans and such.

Soon as Thomas got to be alone in his room, except for me, soon as the door was shut, he'd want to get shot of his proper dress. So he'd be unbuttoning his collar as he walked in the door, and then his necktie would come off. His waistcoat would go on the end of the bed, his socks stashed inside of his shoes and his braces slipped off the shoulders, the curve of them swinging and like to catch, sometimes, on an elbow or a knee.

Finally, once he had his head resting and he was started on his reading, his fingers would start their wanderings. They'd go across his stomach, like some little animal they looked, till they came to a shirt button. Then stop and feel around it, touching it almost like it were alive before easing it through the button hole and tugging it free. They'd do this with each one till his shirt was open from top to toe, and all the while I'd be watching and not touching.

I loved that. To look and not to touch. I'd get to feeling nearly jealous of his fingers, except I knew at the back that it'd be my turn later which gave me a sharp pleasure, one I'd feel in the pit of my belly.

So I'd let him lie, and not touch, though it was a hard task when I could see the curve of his collar bone and the few dark hairs on his breast and everything in me wanting to stroke him.

I'd given up asking if he'd read me out the story – they always had one going, a romance, done in parts so you'd to keep on buying each month to get the whole. But Thomas didn't like them. They weren't real, he said, and after the first time, when he obliged me, he wouldn't read it again.

'No, but listen, Harriet.' That was his phrase which I still have in my head, can still hear him saying now. 'You'll like this bit, love,' and he'd stop me in my sewing or wake me from my doze and tell me something about sea-shells with a thousand eyes, or how in Finland the girls went out in the boats just like the boys, and I'd hear his words and let myself stroke his hair. Sometimes he'd even want me to look at complicated drawings with labels on them that I couldn't read, and they never looked much like anything to me, but I'd nod to keep him happy.

He'd read me things about the sea, because it was what I knew and he didn't. Of course I didn't know the most of what he told me, but that didn't matter.

It was an evening a good couple of months after we'd been married that was the start of the end. It had been only the past couple of weeks I'd begun to settle in properly, not as fearful each day that we'd be found out, which Thomas had teased me over. He'd never seemed to be worried about it, but then it was my job, not his, that'd go if they knew.

We'd fixed a way for most things, even for getting our tea at the same time, and neither his landlady nor mine having a clue what we were up to in the attic. What's more, Thomas thought his landlady had a bit of a glad eye for him, which gave us a giggle. My work at the factory was back to normal – I'd not seen Mr Benbow in months and I barely noticed the posters now – and Mary's warnings about Thomas had gone dim in my ears. Perhaps she'd been exaggerating what she'd overheard. So far as I could see, he was doing his job, no more and no less, and he hadn't said a word about London.

That evening I was doing some mending – I'd a fair hand at darning which was something you'd to learn early where I came from. I was getting to know a bit about Thomas's moods and I could tell from the hunch in his shoulders that he'd something pressing on him, but there was no point in asking.

I knew that by now too. He'd only deny it and get cross. I'd learnt how he kept down the thing that was really bothering him and would talk on all sorts but that, and that it was up to me in the end to guess, but I mustn't do it too quickly or he seemed to feel cheated somehow.

'It's written here that "Photographs are often Deceptive,"' Thomas said.

'Mmm,' I said. I didn't know which way this was going.

'No, listen up,' he said. '"In regard to beauty," it says, "in regard to beauty, a photograph tells nothing beyond form of face."'

'So? We all know that,' I said. He pulled his head off of my lap.

'Well, it's a doctor saying it, so maybe he knows a thing or two more'n you do.'

'Oh,' I said.

'He says how his wife looks horrid in pictures even though she's pretty. And then he says he know a lady and she's dead plain, but in pictures she looks pretty.'

'Oh,' I said again.

Thomas cricked his head round and gave me this hard look. 'Can you not say anything but "Oh"?'

'Depends on what you're telling me,' I said.

'So I'll read in my head, then,' he said, and for what seemed like an age, but it probably wasn't, he did that, and I counted the holes I'd filled.

I'd got up to six when I noticed Thomas inching his head back towards my lap. I didn't stop my darning, nor him his reading. And when he had his head back fully on my lap, he read out in his most solemn tone:

'It says here that pretty girls have pretty tempers, minds, and dispositions,' which I took as cause to tickle him and which he took as an invitation to kiss me and our quarrel was gone, so I thought.

'Natural History Notes' was one of Thomas's favourite bits of the magazine. They didn't have it in every week, but they had it this one. There was something about how they ate seaweed in other countries and swore it did a power of good.

I couldn't imagine eating seaweed. Seaweed was something you caught crabs out of and it stank when it dried. When we were little, we'd have fights with it on the beaches. Sometimes sword fights, because there was this one kind that grew like a small tree only softer, and we'd find it thrown up after the tide, its roots all twisted about and gritty with sand, and I used to wonder if there were maybe forests in the bottom of the sea. We'd swing our trees, crash and slap them round each other's legs till they broke.

Then there was the bladderwrack that hung off the quay, murky green on the outside and soft like jelly inside its pods. When you stamped on it, they popped and squirted.

And there was another sort you'd to find in the pools, scrambling over the rocks to the deep places, the barnacles scratching at your feet. Lean over and plunge your arm in. There'd be the jerk of little animals, fish and shrimps, against your fingers and they'd be off in a panic to the other side, jittering away too quick to follow. And there was the soft suck of the annies on your fingers. They had tentacles that moved with the swish of the water, and if your fingers brushed them, they'd draw them in to their jelly house, red as blood and shiny. Sometimes we'd see a big crab go in there under the rock at the bottom and we'd do a dare to stick a finger down. It was a hard nip you got if they caught you. Then I used to hang my nipped finger in the water and watch the blood, a thin line of red disappearing and disappearing.

The seaweed in the rock pools was the greenest green, green as the fresh grass in May. It was like an angel's hair there in the water, or like a mermaid's maybe. You'd grab it in your fingers and tug it out, then wonder where it had gone to because all you'd have in your hands was this mess of slime, the bright May green gone from it, the life gone.

We'd collect a fair bit to make it worth our while and then it'd be back on to the sand and there'd be us and them. Sometimes us would be the French and them the English, or the other way about. We'd ball up the weed and hurl it at the other side. It didn't hurt to be hit by, but it was as bad as something harder, to get this cold wet stuff that streaked across your face and got twisted in your hair.

'Ucch,' I said, laughing. Thomas was looking at me like I'd caught it in the head.

'You didn't hear a word I said, did you,' he said.

'About the seaweed?'

'Harriet!' and he pinched me, but gentle. 'I don't know why I bother.'

I said I was sorry, and when I'd been humble a bit, he said he'd tell me whatever it was again.

'I only read it out to amuse you,' he said. I stroked a curl of hair that was falling across his eyes and at last felt his shoulders relax.

He read this time in a special voice. I knew it from somewhere, and it was only when he was well on that I remembered where. It was how Mr William spoke when he was giving us his talking to of a morning.

'Friends have exercised a wholesome social influence on the nation. They have encouraged philanthropy and an enthusiasm for humanity. And yet the Society of Friends may almost calculate the time when the last survivor will be seen in England, though the leavening influence they have exercised during their long and honourable history is a thing of which they have a right to be proud.' Thomas looked up at me again. 'What do you think of that, love?'

'Seems a long way round to say that there aren't many of them left,' I said. 'Makes them sound a bit like them birds you was telling me about. It's Darwin's rules for Quakers just the same as for the birds. Though we seem to have more'n our fair share in York.'

'It's not only them as are in danger of extinction either,' said Thomas and I looked up from the magazine at his words, because his voice sounded different, a bit caught up in his throat, and now I saw he was very pale, but couldn't think whether he'd been so earlier.

'What is it?' I said.

'I've to go down again.'

'To London?' He nodded. 'When?'

'Saturday,' he said.

'So we'll not have our weekend together?'

He shook his head.

'How long for?'

'They say a week.'

'Is it important? Does it have to be you?' I said. He nodded again. 'Well, if it is only the week, it'll not be so bad,' I said, wondering why he'd gone so white. A thought came to me. 'Have I made things worse? With the pictures and that?'

Thomas shook his head. 'They'd only have used someone else,' he said. 'But it's certainly worked, your face up there. It's made people buy more pastilles, more cocoa. Anyway, it's not the time away that I mind, though I would rather be here.' Then his rush of words stopped and he took my hand real fierce and held it tight between his two and then kissed it so hard, it was like he wanted to eat it.

'Thomas?' I said.

'I can't tell you,' he said, and then not a word for minutes, only my hand in his and it was getting to be numb at the side with him clutching. Finally he muttered something so low, it was like he wanted to tell me something, and didn't.

'You'll have to let go my hand, I can't hear what you're saying,' I said.

'There's a letter,' he said

'A letter?'

'It's in the roof,' he said.

'Who from?'

'From me.'

'What's it doing in the roof?' I said.

'It's for you,' he said.

I pushed myself up on my arm and looked at him. 'What are you on about?' I said.

'There's a letter to you in the roof from me, tucked behind a beam, and if I don't get back when I should from London then you're to open it.'

I started to ask something else, but he put his hand over my mouth.

'Please, don't ask. I hope you never have to read it and you never have to ask. But it's there. You need to know it's there.'

'Mr William and Mr Caleb. They'd not have you doing anything you oughtn't?' I said.

'They'd not have me doing anything they have to know about,' he said. 'So long as they can pretend they don't,' and he wouldn't explain any more, wouldn't say another word, only clutched at me like a drowning man is said to clutch at straws, though any as knew the sea could tell you, there weren't any straws there.

Thomas was a man with a rock on his shoulders till he went, but he was home inside the week and then he was restored. So I didn't ever see the letter, didn't even look to see where it was.

When he got back he was funny and so affectionate with me, I was sure we'd be heard down below. He found out new bits in *The Leisure Hour* to read to me. Greek stories about

these madcap heroes, Achilles and Heracles and the like, who'd
get up to all sorts, and be brave as brass, and get away with it,
in the main.

He kept whispering me things, whispering them in my
ears, my hair, my tummy, my toes even, how I was his this
and his that and the saving of him and so forth. He was like
a nuzzling dog that's forgotten its job of ever being fierce.
Except for every now and then, maybe once every day or so,
when a shudder would go through him, like something crossing his skin a moment, and his face would shut off. But
seconds later it was gone and that was that, so after a bit I
barely noticed it.

The leaves were off the trees by now, pools of them swept
up the hill from the Knavesmire by that sharp wind that seems
to like the flatness of the York plain so much. The wind would
stir them up against us as we walked to work. Sometimes I
wanted to kick and fling them, throw them about like I used
to when I was little, but others, I'd be cross at them, not wanting them to smudge my clothes, and I thought this must be on
account of growing up, because I was a proper age now being
nearly eighteen.

Maybe it was on account of growing up that I wanted to
take Thomas back home. I wanted him to meet my mam, and
said it to him, but he wasn't keen.

'She'd like you,' I said. 'She's not like my dad, she's not
why I'd to be gone from the place.'

But Thomas shook his head. 'Not families. We said we
were fine without, Harriet.'

'We are fine. But I'd like her to see me,' I said. 'To see me
and what I've caught for myself,' which got a laugh, but still he
said no.

'Go by yourself,' he said, but I think maybe he knew I
didn't dare do that. I don't know why, perhaps in case it was
hard to leave again. In case I could see that she needed me. It

had only been this last time with Thomas away and me missing him that I thought how much she must miss me, because
I hadn't thought it before.

It was an odd thing at the time, though after I saw how it must
have come about, to hear about what had gone on with Mary
from Grace. I'd be pretending if I said I wasn't hurt that she
hadn't told me first off, but things were too bad by then for it
to be worth holding to.

It was winter and things had gone along fairly smooth. Still
nobody knew Thomas and me were husband and wife, and
the being careful of it and keeping it secret had got near
enough second nature to me, though we'd talk often enough
about me leaving the factory and having a regular home, children even. It was Thomas now who was the keenest of us, ever
since getting back from the last trip to London. The fear I'd
had ever since Mary telling what she'd overheard was gone.
Nothing had come of it all, nothing bad that is. The trips
seemed to have finished, and Thomas was only relieved to be
home.

'I want to march you about in front of everybody, ring on
your finger, proud as punch. I want to show Mr William what
I've got,' he said.

'You make me sound like some kind of special toy,' I said.
'One of those bicycles, or a new football.'

'No, it's not like that,' Thomas said.

'Thank God, or it'd be a short marriage,' I said, but
Thomas was still being earnest.

'No, but it's not. It's just with him being pleased with himself, and always speaking as if his bloody factory's the only
thing that matters.'

'But he's at work, Thomas. And so are you. It'd be a bit
funny if he suddenly started on about his children, or his wife
and how pretty she was or something,' I said.

It was Sunday morning and I'd been brushing out my hair. Thomas took the length of it in his hands and drew it to his face, so tightly to him that the tug on my neck made my eyes water.

'Well, anyway,' he said, his voice muffled in my hair, 'I've nearly had it with this, and when we've got our money, you're out of there.'

It wasn't his decision, when I left, or no less than mine anyway. But I let it go then. There was time enough to find our way, so I thought.

I'd not seen much of Mary those last months, though not for want of trying. The last time had been in November. We'd met in the chop house like before and I'd such an appetite on me, it was a while before I noticed she was barely eating.

'Mary?' I said, and she'd looked up from the table where she'd been up to her usual fiddling, making shapes with the cutlery and the salt and mustard and pepper pots.

'You sick?' I asked.

She shook her head. 'Just not hungry,' she said, so I had the rest of her plate too, and she went on with her shape-making, putting one thing inside and the others around it, then the other way about, till there were little pools of spilt sugar and salt and grains of pepper for her to run her finger through and add in to it all.

While she went about it, she talked. She told me she'd been to London with her rich gentleman, about the same time Thomas had been down last, and there was talk of another trip in the New Year. Once that was done, she was out of it, she said, out of York altogether.

'Tell me about it,' I said. 'Not about you and the man, but about the theatres and the food.'

'I'd rather not,' she said, and thinking she was being modest, though that had never been her way in the past, I pressed her.

'Come on, Mary. Did you see lots of beautiful dresses? And go in a smart carriage and eat meat for breakfast?'

But she gave me this look like she were a dog I'd just kicked, and though I couldn't think how I'd kicked her, I left off asking.

I noticed she was pale, but it was that time of year, and besides it was the fashion. And when we left the chop house, our footsteps silent in the snow, she seemed odd on her feet, hunched forward.

'Send me a message,' I said as we parted. 'Come over to my room next week. We'll have a meat pie and cold tea like we used to,' because it was something she'd always liked to do, to remember how it was with us. But she barely nodded before turning and walking away, all of her old pertness gone so as I was worried for her.

Although they'd never got on, I asked Thomas to help me write a note to Mary the next week.

'I'm worried about her,' I said. 'She didn't seem well.'

'She'll get over it,' Thomas said. 'Leave her be, Harriet. She's no good for you.'

That had me furious and I yelled at Thomas as how Mary was my oldest friend and my closest, how he couldn't know what she meant to me, all this stuff, and he didn't say a thing back, which surprised me because he always gave as good as he got, right or wrong. But when I stopped and asked him again to please help me with a note, still he shook his head.

'No,' he said. So I'd to write it myself, which I did and posted it in through the letterbox at Mr Benbow's studio, and I never heard another thing from her, not till months after.

The ground was deep in snow, the day Grace spoke to me of Mary. The snow had taken us all by surprise, though we ought to have known, because after all the weather often got up to this kind of lark in the spring. But we'd had a week just before and it had been so warm and the earth smelling sweet and flowers here and there daring to come up, that even those as were always down in the mouth were tricked out of it.

Since the days had got short, I'd taken to going straight to their house from work on a Saturday. Thomas didn't like me going there on account of Mr Ransome, but I told him it was Grace I went to see, that she needed me, and if he couldn't trust me for that, then things'd be at a pretty pass between us very soon. He worked late most Saturdays, so it wasn't our time together I was robbing him of, only his ease of mind. And since he'd given me so much in the way of worry, I didn't see why he shouldn't have a taste of his own. He'd leave off arguing then, only still muttering things about Mr Ransome and what he'd do if the rich bugger touched his wife, which it was easiest for me to ignore than anything else.

Grace would be in her garden whether it was rain or snow or what. Mr Ransome was having all the house painted and done out, but so far she'd only been persuaded into the kitchen, which Mr Ransome pointed out was a room their mother never went into.

That day I had on my galoshes, and I borrowed an extra shawl and mittens from Grace and we stamped about and she told me her plans for the garden, how there was much to clear after her years away, and much to plant. And how some of the plants had been badly neglected, and she'd vowed to each to care for them. I didn't say anything. It was fine just listening.

She'd a great pair of shears and as we walked, she'd cut a branch here, a branch there and we'd drag them to the pile she was making on the snow.

'Poor garden,' she said.

'But it's got you back,' I said, my first words for a half hour.

Grace turned to me and her face was murderous. She swung her branch down off of her shoulder and crashed it into the snow, which was that light, dry kind, and it flurried up like a bag of flour. Then she made to swing it at me and I'd to block it with my own, and she tried to swing it again, and again I had to put my branch in the way. I'd thought I was stronger, but she'd a furious strength in her arms and her shoulders.

'Grace, stop! Stop it!' I yelled, but she didn't stop. I wasn't sure she'd even heard me. Still she was swinging and the snow was in our faces and our ears. She was gone mad and I didn't dare leave her for fear of what she might do in this bad weather. So with her still swinging and swiping, I dropped my branch and ran at her, grabbing her by the middle and toppling her to the ground and we fell, the both of us, in a tumble of snow.

Everything was quiet. Neither of us moved. Then Grace stood up, slowly.

Apart from Mary and the carry up the cliff, I didn't go in for rescuing things. Not many of us did. But my brother Daniel, he was a funny one like that. He'd rescue all sorts of small creatures that had fallen from a nest or been got by a cat or kicked by a man and he'd make a place for them, in a shed or a corner of the yard.

There was only this one time, and seeing Grace like that in the snow put me in mind of it, when I was all with Daniel on his saving lark.

We're down at the water one early evening while the men are bringing in the boats, him and me, dawdling, maybe eight and nine years old or so. I don't know what he's up to, but me, I'm stood on the beach watching the birds above the rocks. It must have been summer, because the swifts and the martins are in a frenzy for flies and what have you to take back to their young ones in the cliffs. I'd say it must have been a warm day and there's always a pile of flies in the seaweed in the summer.

The tide is coming in over the rocks and the birds are swooping very low. I'm watching them and thinking, "One of them's going to get it," because the tide is doing its own swooping, pretending it's going nowhere, then reaching its wet arms out and smothering another bit of rock and any minute it's going to catch one of them not looking. And I know, without being told, that these birds can't swim. They're not like the gulls and the terns and all the others. They're not meant for the water. So I'm watching, and they keep getting away, but they don't even know that they're getting away.

And then the sea does get one of them. This little darting thing, a few feathers is all, on a bit of bone, and wingtips that cross behind its back and that great shriek when they're shearing about which sounds only like a whoop of joy. It must've shut its eyes, or had its eyes on something else a second, I don't know, but that's all I can think has happened, because one moment I'm watching it nip and tuck, and the next it's a dark smudge, no more, in the tide, which is drawing out again before the next wave pulls it back and throws the bird hard onto the rocks.

I yell out. 'Daniel,' I yell, 'Daniel, in the water, a bird,' and he looks and sees and we both of us race across as fast as we can over the rocks. The bird's already sunk under in the swell, but Daniel, he's in there after it, up to his waist nearly, bracing against the suck of the water, because he can no more swim than fly. But somehow he finds and somehow he gets a hold of the bird and holds it high above the sea.

'I have it, I have it,' he shouts over, this little heap of feathers in his hands. I help him back to the beach, and I haven't saved the bird, it's my brother, but I've done something by yelling and my heart's pounding with excitement.

We climb to the top of the beach where the water can't reach and there's a scuff of wiry grass and Daniel bends right down and uncups his hands.

The bird is so small, I can't credit it for the same creature I saw screeching so cocksure above the water. It doesn't move.

Not its beak, not its eyelids, which are closed, not a wing twitch. Daniel lays it on a bit of rock and we watch it, not saying anything, for ages. Then he makes a place for it, a bird's grave open to the sky, tugging the grass out and into a heap with a dip in the centre where the little body must lie. He lets me place the bird there and we get up and go.

Daniel is turning over stones again, crouched right down staring, like the whole world might be under that stone, and I'm watching him, watching the sea, not doing anything much. I turn and look back to where the bird is and I see that it's not dead at all and it's not lying down any longer. It's stood and tugging at its feathers, I don't know what for. As I watch, it spreads its wings out, very shaky, the feathers all scrawny still with the water, and it moves them a bit, just trying them out, not trying to fly yet. I watch it. Daniel sees me, and he watches it too. It's way past the time we should be back and our mam's going to be angry, but by the time we leave the beach, the bird is close to flying again, and Daniel and me, we might as well be flying, and it's the one time I know why he does it, all his rescuing.

Grace had lost her hat and her curly hair was matted against her head. Her skirts, being soaked now with snow, clung against her legs and her shawl was halfway down her back. She looked a wet-through bird of a girl.

She held out a hand to me.

'Harriet,' she said and I knew it for an apology. With that odd strength of hers, she pulled me up and we stood in the white garden, brushing what we could of the snow off of our skirts and our hair, and being so cold now that our teeth were chattering, we dropped the last of the branches and went back to the house.

Nellie had had the cook get up cocoa for us, and some biscuits, and she bustled about the kitchen, pleased that we were cold and wet, because it gave her something she could do. Something for Grace, I mean.

I was still eating when Grace started the poem, or maybe it was a song, since she didn't quite say it and she didn't quite sing it, but somewhere between.

> And they had fix'd the wedding-day,
> The morning that must wed them both;
> But Stephen to another maid
> Had sworn another oath;

It sent a chill up my spine and I thought it must be doing the same for Nellie for I saw her fingers go very white around the kettle and she turned away from us, her head bowed down. Grace went on with her saying of it, and no book to be getting it from, saying it just as if neither Nellie nor me was there.

> They say, full six months after this,
> While yet the summer-leaves were green
> She to the mountain-top would go,
> And there was often seen.

'Miss Grace,' Nellie said, 'Miss Grace, please. Don't go singing that now, not now,' but Grace paid her no attention and went on.

> 'Tis said, a child was in her womb,
> As now to any eye was plain;
> She was with child, and she was mad,
> Yet often she was sober sad
> From her exceeding pain.

Then she stopped. 'The cocoa was very nice, and the biscuits. But please leave us now, Nellie,' she said in a quiet, clear voice and though she didn't want to, though she wanted to say something, Nellie went.

'Samuel wanted this,' Grace said.

'What?' I said.

'This,' Grace said, opening her arms as if she meant the kitchen and the table and us two sat there.

'I'm to bring the cat if I come,' she said.

'Is the house finished?'

She nodded. 'Every room painted over,' she said. 'He promises me it is.'

'You haven't been in to see it yet?'

She shook her head. 'The garden needs me more than the house. The house will bide its time.'

'Is it your song?' I asked.

She shook her head. 'Oh no,' she said. 'I sang it because I have a message for you.'

'Who from?' I said.

'I think it is from my brother, but I'm not entirely certain,' she said.

I looked at her face to see if I could tell anything from it, but I couldn't. 'What is it?' I said.

'The message is that Mary is to have a baby,' Grace said, right straight out like there was nothing more to be done and nothing more to be said than that.

'My Mary?'

She nodded.

'And the father?'

She shrugged.

'Is it Mr Ransome told you?' I said.

'Yes.'

'Why?'

'It's the best of names if there's no father. Good company,' Grace said. She wasn't laughing or even smiling.

'She's my friend,' I said.

Grace nodded.

'But she didn't tell me,' I said, 'and she doesn't like Mr Ransome. He doesn't like her. Why's she told him?'

'I didn't say she had,' Grace said.

'Where is she?' Grace shrugged. 'At Mr Benbow's?' I said, but then I thought, how could she be if she's pregnant? 'Have you seen her?' I asked.

She nodded.

'Where?'

'Here.'

'Here? How did you see her here?'

'Through the window. I'd expect to see her through the window. Most things can be seen that way,' Grace said.

'And is she here still?' I said.

Grace shook her head. 'She's gone now.'

It was snowing when I set off back home. I'd Grace's shawl and mittens on again, still warm and stiff with being laid to dry near the stove. I can remember feeling how they ought to be comforting. It's like you're being looked after, like your mother's looking after you again, to have your things warmed before you go out. But I didn't feel it and I'd no one to tell it to, because Thomas'd not understand. Or if he did, he'd not want to and I could hear him already saying, 'I could've told you this would come of it. She's no good, that one.'

It must've been me, not Grace, as looked the mad one that night walking home, for I had in my head a nursery rhyme I can't have sung for ten, twelve years or more. At least I thought it was in my head till a policeman stopped me. I was stood on Lendal Bridge, watching where the water was, when there was a tap on my shoulder and a policeman was stood there. He held his lantern up towards my face.

'You're singing on the street,' he said.

'I am?' I said.

'You're not the worse for anything, are you?' he said, and I wanted to tell him that yes I was and would he help me because nobody else would. But I shook my head.

'Sing it for me again,' he said.

'But it was only in my head,' I said.

'No, because I heard it. Something about Mary, and the garden. I've heard it on my children.'

So I knew I must have been saying it out loud, and I sang it for him quietly.

> Mary, Mary, quite contrary,
> How does your garden grow?
> With silver bells and cockle shells
> And pretty maids all in a row.

Then I'd to breathe in his face.

'Cocoa,' he said, and he let me go after that. The snow was falling so hard, in thick shapeless flakes, no grace to them, it was all I could do to see my way round past the station and on to The Mount. But I paid no heed to the weather, and it paid none to me.

Thomas was gone to the pub with some other clerks and I was in our bed by the time he returned. I kept my eyes shut and curled myself around so he didn't know I wasn't sleeping. And before the night was over, I knew that I must see Mary and not ask her any question, only maybe hold her a bit, like I did that day I'd to lift her up the cliff.

SAMUEL

The studio was very cold that night, no fire lit, though the sea of papers on Benbow's desk indicated he had been at work there before my arrival. I kept my overcoat on. I had arrived at the hour he had demanded, and yet he appeared agitated, almost as if my appearance were a surprise to him. Miss Hornsgarth, I assumed, had been dismissed for the evening and he seemed to be in some difficulties finding candles.

We'll have to manage like this,' he said, holding a few stubs. These he lit and stood on a plate, which he placed on the box beside the two chairs lifted out from amongst the props stacked to one side.

In the candlelight, his camera looked like a huge insect, bulbous body on tall stick-like legs, and the photographs on the walls showed no more than the faintest shapes, seeming more like shadowy maps of unknown islands than like family portraits or children solemn in their best sailor suits. If I had had an imagination of that somewhat over-reaching kind, I should have thought myself on the brink of some dark secret. As it was, I had no idea what was coming.

'Please,' Benbow said, indicating one of the chairs, an elaborate affair with heavily carved arms. I sat. It was not comfortable. He took the other, a flimsy garden chair, and busied himself lighting his pipe, to steady his hands, I guessed, or to hide their shaking.

Benbow hadn't told me why I was to come. He'd sent a note urgently requesting my attendance this evening, but said nothing more. We hadn't seen each other for some months. There'd been no disagreement voiced, no conscious rift. But our differences had become too great for us to tread upon our previous common ground together. Benbow believed any sort of battle was justified, if the end sought was justice, education and freedom for the poor. I did not. Nor did I believe there were any grounds for exhibiting women as I knew he did. Even when he said it kept them off the streets. It was immoral and degrading. And the knowledge that I had led at least one girl, Harriet's friend Mary, to his door, albeit inadvertently, caused me some considerable pain. It made no difference that I did not like her. I had helped her into a life of what I knew to be sin.

I did not know, I had no wish to know, what he thought of me. And my thoughts on him were simple. That he was one of those men who acted in the world as if his left hand need not know what his right was doing. It had taken me long enough to see this, for I am not quick to look behind people's actions. Though perhaps I knew more than I realised, for I was not shocked, as many of my conviction would have been. Only disappointed. Greatly disappointed.

He pulled on his pipe, the bowl glowing and fading, glowing and fading in the poor light. Then he seemed to turn to the props, as though seeking some kind of support, or endorsement. Finally he spoke.

'I will never have talked to you of my father,' he said. I
shook my head. 'He has been dead these past couple of years.
He found my politics hard to tolerate, being an old Tory. A
farmer. But that isn't what I want to tell you. If you'll have a
few minutes' patience, I want to tell you a story.' I was moving
about somewhat in my chair and he paused, perhaps thinking
me unwilling to stay. But I told him my restlessness was due to
the chair, not his circumlocution, making him laugh, a short
bark of a sound. So he fetched me another, dragging into the
thin circle of light an armchair, which I sank into and waited
to hear him out.

He spoke in a low, clear voice, with little by way of inflec-
tion, and with not a single hesitation, so that afterwards I saw
that this was a story he had decided upon ahead of our meeting and even perhaps rehearsed to himself.

'My father brought me up strictly but fairly,' he said. 'At
least fairly by his own lights. There were grades of disobedi-
ence, clearly stated, and corresponding grades of punishment.
His discipline did not stem from religious conviction, as it
might for one of your persuasion, but from some other innate
but powerful sense of proper conduct.

'But we knew where we were, the six of us children, and
while we didn't tell tales, equally we knew there was little point
in trying to evade our father's justice. We experienced his punishment very like the weather. If you were caught in the rain,
you got wet. If you didn't wear a hat during the harvest, you
would likely get sunstroke. So if you failed to feed the hens one
day, you went without your bread and milk, and if you broke
a window in a game, you replaced it yourself, with money
earned from extra duties. He was a hard father, showing us little
in the way of affection, though our mother tried to make up
for it, and I was afraid of him. But at least I knew what it was
I had to fear, I knew its proportions. And for that, now I am an
adult and have seen how other childhoods go, I am grateful.

'Father punished us for our misdemeanours, whether they were deliberate or not. However, I remember as if it were yesterday the one occasion when I did a terrible thing, and he broke with his rule. I was perhaps ten years old and I'd got to an age, that short-lived period in one's childhood, when I thought I knew what there was to be known. Anyway, this particular afternoon, I was ten years old and on a simple errand for my father. I was to deliver over his rifle to our neighbour, whose house was perhaps three miles from our own. The neighbour had a troublesome fox, and wished to borrow an extra rifle for his eldest son. They were to stake out the creature that same night.

'I was in a good frame of mind, carrying the rifle as my father had taught me, broken and hooked over my arm, for I had a friend, Danny, living on the neighbour's farm and if I was quick now, we might have a half hour's play together before I had to return. I knew how to fire a rifle, because my father had shown me some years before, not so I could use it, but so I could clean it.

'You'll be the right age when I say so,' was what he said about anything he judged you to be too young for. And though Danny's father let him use a rifle, I knew I was several years off the same, because my elder brother Robert had only been allowed to look down its sights for the first time the previous year, and he'd been twelve which was all the difference.

'I cut my way across the fields and into a spinney of oak trees where the sun came through the leaves, turning the light into shade, and then the shade into light. My excuse has always been this sunlight, because it made things seem not as they were, but I never told my father this. He would not have seen it as cause for anything. Anyway, I stopped here a moment, the rifle being heavy on my arm and because I liked the place. The air was sweet-smelling, warm, full of small sounds – birds and insects. I leaned my back up against an oak and shut my eyes.

'Then I heard another sound, of a larger animal breaking through the cover. I opened my eyes and looked towards it. I saw, I still swear I saw, a dog fox, bold as brass, standing just inside a pile of brambles.

'I gave my father's injunction barely a moment's thought. "Danny's allowed to," I said to myself instead, and as quietly as possible I clicked the barrel back in place and raised it till I had the animal in my sights. How pleased all the men would be if I got the bugger, excuse the language, Samuel, right now. How they'd praise me to my father. Just the thought was enough to raise the hair on my spine.

'The fox was still there. I could just make out its colours through the dappled leaves, the browns and reds. So I took aim as best I could, pulled the rifle tight into my shoulder, remembering what my elder brother had said about the kick, and squeezed the trigger.

'If I hadn't had the tree behind me, I'd have been on the ground. The rifle crunched back into my shoulder, but I didn't even notice the bruising till much later. I was sure I'd got the fox. I ran over, tearing away at the brambles, oblivious to cuts and scratches, to see my quarry.

'Imagine my horror. It wasn't a fox, and I'd by no means killed it. It was a young deer, a pregnant hind, her belly so full that even in my first shock I could see that she must be close to her time. She tried to get up, her eyes wide, terrified, but she couldn't. There was a dark stain on her back where my bullet had struck.

'I knew I should put another bullet through her head, but I couldn't do it. I couldn't bear to see her face, her fear, those eyes staring. Dropping the rifle, I ran.

'I ran all the way home, hoping against hope that I might find my brother Robert first and persuade him to come and finish what I could not. But it was my father I saw, and what with the shame of what I'd done and the awful sternness of his gaze, I couldn't pretend.

'I followed my father back to the spinney. She was still alive, her breath coming in short bursts, belly heaving, eyes still wide and full of panic. My father picked up the rifle, loaded the breech, took aim carefully and pulled the trigger.

'My stomach heaved and before I could even turn away, I vomited, all over my boots, all over the leaves lit up with the sun.

'The hind was dead, but for a minute or more her belly still kicked out. Then everything was still.

'I was so full of disgust. Even telling you the tale now, thirty years later, I am horrified. I stood, my feet like stone, my mind blank.

'My father had watched the deer through her death, standing calmly, the rifle already broken on his arm. It was something he despised above almost any other, causing animals unnecessary pain, and that I had shot a pregnant deer only made it so much the worse. Now he turned to me, and I knew that this time the penalty would have to be very great.

'He didn't raise his voice, didn't lay a finger on me. He spoke just two sentences.

"Go home, John," he said. "You know what you have done."

And that was it. Nothing more.'

Benbow stopped. He had been leaning forward, talking towards the floor. Now he leaned back in his chair, seemingly exhausted by his narrative.

I nodded slowly. 'It is quite a story,' I said, but I knew that the point of my summons would be in what he said next.

If he had thought that the telling of this tale would make his task in speaking to me easier, then it seemed he had misjudged. I had never before seen the man so ill at ease. He couldn't get comfortable on his chair and so he stood.

'Mary Bourne,' he said.

'Mary Bourne? Harriet's friend?'

He nodded.

'She is . . . she has got herself . . .' and here he stopped, appearing unable to go on. I waited. I had had the best possible training, being a Quaker, in how to sit through silence. He said the next bit in a rush, pacing, turning and turning about with each phrase.

'I'm sure there is talk already,' he said, 'looking at my receipts. I can't be seen to be harbouring, and people have such rigid proprieties. Even Miss Hornsgarth. Because she thinks I am responsible, I'm sure she does, but . . .'

Then he checked himself, stood still.

'She's pregnant,' he said.

'Oh,' I said, and not knowing what else to say, added, 'And the father?'

He shrugged. 'She won't say. But I'd hazard a guess at her time in London. The dates fit, more or less. Anyway, she's on her own.'

'And is she very?' I said

He shook his head.

'But still it's too late for anything now. Neither gin nor jumping's going to dislodge that little creature, not that she'd have allowed it.'

'I'm glad of that,' I said, chilled at his words, which he must have heard in my voice, because he apologised.

'But it is like the story I told you of me and the deer. I think Mary has suffered enough in the knowledge of what she has done. Indeed, so much so that I fear her morbidity may endanger the life of her unborn child. Her guilt is more like that of one who has killed something, as I had done all those years ago, not one who is bringing a life into the world that has come somehow before its proper time.'

'Others might feel there to be more at stake than a question of timing,' I said, and in the uneasy laugh we shared there was some piece of ice broken between us.

'Still you have not told me why you have called me here,' I said.

Benbow sat in his chair and looked me in the eye.

'Could you take her in? To your Home? I'll pay. Only it'd have to be quite soon. Very soon. Within the next week.'

'You mean the Home for Unfortunate Young Women?' I said. He nodded.

'I have had little to do with it in these past months, what with Mother's death and so on. But I will do what I can.'

'Thank you,' he said. 'I will call her and let her know,' and before I could say a word, he walked to a door I had never noticed.

'Mary,' he called gently.

She had never looked beautiful to me before, but now when she came in, her hands resting on the gentle curve of her stomach, I thought I would weep at the sight of her, her black hair coiled around her head, her slender fingers. I had a memory of a painting I had seen in a book belonging to a friend, of a girl, a Madonna perhaps, painted over two hundred years before, and it might have been this figure, haunted, alone, filled with anticipation, who was walking over to me now. It was difficult to find in her the girl fresh from the sea, hands still raw and salty, still chafed with the barnacles' edges, the palms strong with the heavy handling of all those fish.

It was in this moment, too, looking from Mary to Benbow and back to Mary again, that though I believed him when he said that the child was not his, I saw that in some important measure he loved her.

'Mr Ransome has said he will do what he can,' Benbow said.

Mary nodded. 'Thank you.'

'I'll find out tomorrow and return to let you know,' I said. 'It will depend simply on whether they have a bed free.'

Mary nodded again.

'You do know they are a Catholic order?' I said. 'You would be expected to . . .'

'I know,' Mary said. 'I can turn my hand to most things.' Her words reassured me, showing something of her former spirit.

'I saw Harriet only a few days ago,' I said, in the effort to be friendly. 'She seems well.'

To my surprise, Mary gave no reply, only a small curtsy, which I found disturbing too, not thinking of her as a girl who curtsied, and walked back through the corner door.

We sat quietly a minute or two after she had gone.

'It's quite a thing,' I said at last.

Benbow stood. 'Not what you were expecting,' he said.

'No. I expect it might cause you to reflect on your trade a little? The more delicate side?' I said, smiling despite myself at the thought of how my fellow Quakers would have reacted if they'd heard me shilly-shallying like this over something known to be a vile practice.

'Not at all,' Benbow said. 'I am committed to all the parts of my trade, though I confess I would shed no tears if obliged no longer to photograph babies,' and he laughed.

I still don't know quite how it happened, and of course it never would have if Mother had been alive. In this respect, Mother's death was a boon.

Had my action been discovered and drawn to the attention of the Elders at Meeting, one of these being William, of course, I should probably have been disowned, especially since I would have stood by them. Such actions were thought to belong only to the province of the dissolute, and though I did not count myself a part of any such community, I saw now how close to all that I had drawn through my photographic interest and my acquaintance with Mr Benbow.

For someone accustomed to reflecting at his leisure over any important question, I made my decision with surprising rapidity. It was important I do so, of course, but I would not have thought I had the kind of forthright vision needed for such a thing.

I had visited the Home the following day. It was a while since I had last been there and I'd forgotten the smell of the place, as distinctive in its way as the tannery, or William's factory. It was an odd smell, a mixture I imagined to be made up of milk, bleach and the incense I had once watched being swung in their small chapel. The Sister in charge had been neither shocked nor surprised at my request. After telling me the girl must be free of illness, she said they should have a bed available in a week. So I had only to find somewhere for her in the meantime.

I spoke to Nellie that same day. I found her in the kitchen, sleeves rolled up, standing over the stove.

'Nellie,' I said, and she looked at me as if I had caught her in a guilty act.

'Tea cakes,' she said. 'I asked the cook to make them for Miss Grace.'

I nodded and sat down. She looked at me uncertainly. I had never sat at this table before.

'Please,' I said, 'sit down. I have to talk to you.'

She pulled out a chair, her face worried, her strong arms, her hands, red with work, squarely on the table. I started at once to speak of what I had to.

'I have a request to make of you,' I said. 'It is one I am sure the Lord would honour. Something he himself might have done. But I know there are many God-fearing people who would differ from me on this, and I will respect your decision.

Nellie sat motionless. I could only imagine how this must appear to her, the master of her house sitting at the kitchen table and talking in this way, and I told her my request.

'Harriet has a friend who is in trouble,' I said. 'A girl called Mary. She needs somewhere to stay for one week, or possibly two. Somewhere private.'

'A girl,' Nellie said.

'Yes. I have met her twice, perhaps three times. Not more.'

'Met her,' Nellie said, and after a moment I understood her meaning.

'I met her first in Harriet's company, at Mr Benbow's photographic studio. As I said, she is a friend of Harriet's. They came to York together, from the same fishing village.'

Nellie walked across to the range. I hoped she might open the oven for the smell was tantalising. She lifted the kettle from the heat, the ridges of muscle in her forearm shifting like so many slender hawsers as she set it down on the grate. She picked up the tea caddy and spooned three teaspoons of tea into the kitchen pot. Her fingers, though broad, were precise, almost delicate in their movements, and it struck me that I had been so busy about my business finding women in their labour, that I had not looked carefully within my own house. I had never thought very much about the work our own servants did, about the demands my household made upon their bodies, and now this realisation embarrassed me.

Nellie returned to her seat and we resumed our awkward conversation.

'So what's this girl got to do with us?' Nellie said. She knew what I was asking, but she wasn't going to make it easy for me.

'I want to assist her,' I said.

'You want to offer her a bed here,' Nellie said flatly. Her tone now was unmistakably hostile. I pressed on.

'As I said, she is a friend of Harriet's. She requires somewhere to stay for a short time. About a week, till she finds a more appropriate place. Nobody need see her. She need see nobody.'

'She's not married then?' Nellie said, and I shook my head.

'And she's not diseased?' she said, which took me aback, for I hadn't thought she would know about such things, nor speak of them so frankly. 'Because if she is,' she went on, 'she's coming nowhere near. It can do things to the water and all sorts, can Disease. And I've time for so much, but the girls as gets like that, they've got it coming to them.' Then she looked at me as if she dared me to say yes.

'No,' I said. 'She is not. She is . . .' and I was unsure how to express it, so I used the word I recalled my mother using. 'She is expecting. But I know no more about the affair than that.'

Nellie gave her bark of a laugh again. 'So that's it. You should have said so first off. Oh, I can tell you how it happened easily enough,' she said. 'I expect I've a better idea than you have, though for a moment I was wondering, but I won't go muddying your ears with that kind of talk.'

I had never heard Nellie speak like this, but then I had probably never had as long a conversation as this with her in all the years she'd worked in our house. And I knew she would never have spoken like that to Mother. Mother would have given her notice to leave immediately. But then Mother would never have found herself in this situation, nor would she ever have made Nellie such a request.

'Some would say pregnant comes to much the same as diseased', Nellie said.

'And do you?' I said.

She shook her head. 'No, I don't. But the one person you've not mentioned in all this is Miss Grace. Have you thought of her? She comes into the kitchen now, as you know. She sat where you're sitting just two days ago and ate bread and jam, for all the world as though she were the child she once was. And she's near to going further in the house. It's Harriet has done it. She's got Miss Grace's curiosity touched – how this room looks and that room. If this Mary girl you're talking about was to make a muck of that . . .'

'Grace needn't see her,' I said. 'We can make sure Mary's out of the way when she comes, and it's only for a week.'

Nellie shook her head, hard enough that a single strand of hair found its way out from under her cap and snaked down behind her ear. She caught it up with a finger and tucked it out of sight again.

'I know why you said Harriet's name back a bit, and you're right that I'll do it for that girl, if for nothing else, after all she's done for this house.' She gave me an odd look, then stood up and went to the stove. Opening the oven door with a heavy cloth, she pulled out a tray of golden teacakes. The smell that filled the room, of cinnamon and sweet dough, was so fragrant, so delicious, that I forgot for a minute where I was.

'She can have the room behind the kitchen,' Nellie said and the harshness in her voice brought me back. 'She can have it so long as she keeps my rules while she's here.'

'Thank you Nellie,' I said, but she had her back turned, busy over her stove again, as if my audience with her was over.

A day later Mary was installed. She brought only a single carpet bag with her, which was just as well, for the room had space in it for little more than the trestle bed, chest of drawers and single chair it contained. Nellie had seen fit to place a large Bible on the chair, which amused me for I was sure she rarely dipped into one herself, though she had always made the necessary motions at family prayers until Mother's death. But the room was otherwise undecorated, unadorned.

I thought it must be a shock, this bare little place with not even a scrap of mirror, not even a jug and bowl to wash in, after the life I guessed that Mary had become accustomed to. But if it was, she gave no sign of it. Indeed Nellie told me how

she made a great act – I assumed it to be an act having never
seen her behave in such a way previously – of thanking Nellie
graciously, and offering her services in whatever way Nellie
thought appropriate. To my chagrin Nellie was charmed by
her, which she had never been by me.

'She'd do whatever I asked of her,' Nellie told me later.
'That's what she said, and I believed her. She's only so many
months gone, after all, what, five or so? So I said, "What
could she do?" And that flummoxed us a while, because there
didn't seem to be a thing of much use she knew how to do in
this house. But we got to a bit of chat, and she told me such
stories of living by the ocean. Though I'd think her kind were
given to a bit of enlargement and I'm not sure some of what
she said wasn't stretching things.'

'What did she say?' I asked.

'Oh, about going up the cliff, and down again, on a rope.
And wearing trousers for it, all the women did. That was the
one thing I knew to be an enlargement.'

'And I know that one thing to be true,' I said.

'Well, then I may as well believe the lot,' Nellie said.

'And there was nothing she wanted?' I said.

Nellie shook her head. 'Only not to be seen by anyone. She
was insistent about that. Rude nearly. Not a single person, she
said. And especially not Harriet, who I knew to be her friend.
"Why ever not?" I asked her, and she said it was on account of
letting her down so, and she patted her stomach here, just in
case I didn't know what she was speaking about. Anyway, I
didn't think Harriet'd be like that about it, but there's no sense
in others' rhyme or reason, I know that much, and it wouldn't
be hard to hide it from her, her only coming at the weekend. So
I didn't press it. "It might be hard with Miss Grace, though," I
said, "because she often comes unexpected," and Mary nodded
and said she'd just have to do what she could. We decided it
were best if she slipped out of the kitchen, into some other bit

of the house, the dining room maybe, when Miss Grace arrived. Then I'd come and tell her when Miss Grace was gone. And I was right to warn her,' Nellie said, 'because it was Miss Grace, not anyone else, not even Harriet, who saw her. That was Mary's own fault.'

I decided it would be best if I were away on business for the week or so of Mary's stay. William was travelling to London for a meeting to agree cocoa prices with other Quaker manufacturers. As he also had some other business to transact, he would be away the best part of the week. I arranged to travel with him and do something in the way of tannery business that I had long overlooked and I would join with him and his family in their visit to their country house near Kirkham at the weekend. If William suspected something peculiar, which I am sure he must have, he made no attempt to extract the information from me. Indeed he seemed almost absurdly his childish self, pleased to have his elder cousin for company.

By the time I returned to York, relieved first of all to leave the metropolis behind, and then equally relieved to be delivered out of the bosom of my family, Mary should have been taken in behind the heavy doors of the Home for Unfortunate Women. But her entry had been delayed a day, though of course I didn't know it.

The scene I witnessed I remember almost like a dream. It has both the clarity of mood and the imprecision of detail that I associate with dreams. The day was warm, one of those early spring days that takes the world by surprise, luring the flowers out of the earth, only for them to be scorched by the frost and smothered by late snow. The house was quiet, no sound anywhere. I walked through and into the kitchen, anxious to hear from Nellie that all had been well with Mary's departure. Nellie was not there – she had gone on some errands I found later – but I saw Grace's shawl in the kitchen, slung over a chair, and so I went into the garden to see her.

Not finding her anywhere, I was just on the point of worry when a small movement right up by the house caught my eye. Apart from the kitchen, Grace still rarely went near the house, and the drawing room especially she had an aversion to, perhaps because it had been one of Mother's favourite rooms. But now I saw her, and with her face right up close to the glass, peering in.

I walked closer and was about to call out, but Grace's gesture made me hesitate. She was tracing something with her finger on the glass, one finger making pattern upon pattern, and so intent was she that I feared to break the spell. So I stood and watched her, and as I looked, I saw that Mary was on the inside of the window, the long French window that opened on to the garden, and that she too had her finger on the glass. And as hard as I stared, I couldn't decide whether it was Grace making the pattern or Mary. Whether it was Mary following, or Grace.

After a few minutes – I say minutes though it might have been a far shorter or a far longer time – I crept off and in to the kitchen. I didn't think either of the girls had noticed me, so intent were they in their game. I made my way quietly through the house to the drawing room and there I stood at the door and watched what I had already seen from the outside looking in. Mary inside, her hair sleek and black, piled loosely on her head, standing with one hand on her stomach, its swell fuller than when she'd arrived not even a week earlier, and the other on the glass. Grace outside, her expression intent, absorbed, just a small smile haunting her lips, her fair curly hair tousled and unkempt. It was like a strange, silent dance.

But just as I was about to leave, somewhere else in the house a door was caught by a draught and slammed shut.

Mary started, dropped her hand from the window like a child caught with their hand in a jar of sweets and ran past me and back into her little room behind the kitchen.

Grace said nothing to me of her encounter with Mary. She spent another hour, maybe more, in the garden, by which time Nellie had returned. When I joined them in the kitchen for some tea, though I did not take the step of sitting at the table this time, we talked of what would be planted that spring. Then Grace wrapped her shawl around her and left. Mary, shut in her tiny room, not a yard away from Grace's chair, had made no sound. So that it was almost as if I had imagined them together at the window, and that were I to mention it, either girl might have laughed in disbelief.

It is difficult, with all that has happened since, not to see this meeting between Grace and Mary as in some way a pre-figuring of what was to come. Perhaps it was.

HARRIET

I found it out, where Mary was, from Mr Benbow. I went to see him in his studio, though I didn't go all the way up, but waited in that little room where me and Mary had waited what seemed all that time ago, though it must only have been about a year and a half.

I'd made out to Thomas I'd to see Elsie after work. He'd got to hating Mary even more these last months.

Some of the pictures were the same, of old ladies, dogs and little boys stood with books or trains. But there were pictures of me, I noticed now, ones Mr Benbow had taken at the factory, and a couple of lovely ones of Mary. One especially, I don't know how she'd done it with her bosom, because she never did have a lot, but in the photograph she looked like she'd never wanted for a thing. And the dress, it was that elegant, she was like one of the ladies in *The Leisure Hour* stories, one of them that's born grand and then loses everything because of a wicked uncle or something, and then spends the story getting it back again. Mary, who'd never had no more than the feet and legs she was born in till last year, and she's looking like she's never done a day's work in her life.

So I couldn't help myself but I was admiring her even when I had a feeling in my belly like somebody had kicked me there and I was glad when Mr Benbow came in after only so many minutes, because I couldn't have stood to feel like it for long.

He walked in the door and he didn't barely even look at me, so I thought, 'It's him, he's the one.' We didn't, either of us, say a thing about the pictures, or the hours we'd spent doing them in the room in Wetherby's.

'She's in a home,' he said straight off, before I'd even asked him the question.

'What do you mean, a home?' I said, because I could tell he didn't mean anything belonging to a person, or a family.

'It's a place where they look after girls like her,' he said, and he looked like he couldn't bear the saying of it.

'I a'n't going till you've told me where,' I said, and I was ready for a fight if I needed to. But he told me where it was and no delay, and I wasn't so sure then it was him.

We said goodbye all politely, and neither of us speaking what was in our heads, him no more than me, and I set off for the place he'd named.

'The Home for Unfortunate Young Women' it was called, and no wonder I'd not seen nor heard of it, because it didn't make itself very plain. It was a big brick building, but set right back from the road and with a wall all round and the gates fastened. Mr Benbow had told me about the blue door in the corner, that this would be open, and it was, so I stepped in.

Afterwards, when I knew from Mary about those girls inside, some waiting for their time and some with their babies, and some, which were the saddest of all, without their babies and doing duties around the Home till they were free to go, then I felt like each window was full with eyes, watching me in and then watching me out again. But this first time I didn't know any of that, and what I saw, what I couldn't stop from seeing and it seemed like something back in a fairy tale when I was knee-high, was the empty cradle on the porch. I wasn't sure that was what it was at first, the small square thing, but there was no mistaking it when I was nearly at the front door. It had blankets and a quilt and something which reminded me of what the men put over the boats back home, like a tiny tarpaulin, as if the baby might be going out to sea after.

I pushed the front door open and walked into the hall. It was dim in there, just a couple of sputtering gas lamps to see by, but even so I couldn't miss the statues. There was one by the stairs I took to be the Virgin Mary and she'd the baby Jesus dandled on her knee, though she didn't much look like she'd held a baby before; and the other which was bigger and up on the wall to one side, which was Jesus on the cross, his skin more yellow than anything and the blood on him very like the real thing. It gave me a shiver and I didn't at all like the thought that it was what Mary must've seen when she arrived. It seemed strange to have Jesus there as a happy baby below the stairs, and then up on the Cross, all jaundiced and bleeding, on the wall above, and I was stood wondering when a nun came out and asked me my business.

'There's hours for seeing the girls,' she said when I told her, in a voice that reminded me of Mrs O'Leary's, but very stern. But maybe I show more of my heart in my face than I ought, because when I was nearly out of the door she spoke again, very quiet, perhaps in case any of the others heard.

'Go on then, this one time. I'll bring her down if you wait here.'

I'd never seen Mary look like when I saw her come down those stairs that first time. She might've had a collar round her neck and a leash. Hang-dog. They had her in this shapeless dress like nothing I'd ever seen on her before. It was grey and coarse and hung like a sack. I wondered why it'd to be so big and then I thought of course it was so as to have enough room for her belly as it grew. I could see her belly, a rounded swelling there.

She walked down those stairs like the dress didn't have a thing to do with her. Like it was an accident she'd ended up inside it. Not even when we were flither-lasses, not even when she'd to hitch her skirts up into britches and climb the cliff in the rain and the wind, not even then did she look like she did now.

'You can have seven minutes,' the nun said. 'I'll sit over here,' and she sat on a chair on the far side and took out some beads which she fiddled with.

'Why've you come?' Mary said. She wouldn't look me in the eye.

'What do you mean, why have I come? You're my friend,' I said.

'You shouldn't have.'

I hadn't known it before, that I was angry with her, but I knew it now.

'It was Grace told me,' I said. 'You never told me, but you told her?'

'I didn't tell her,' Mary said. 'She saw.'

'And Mr Ransome? And Mr Benbow? They didn't only see. I'll be hearing it from Thomas next. Or Elsie. Why didn't you tell me?'

But Mary didn't answer, just shrugged, and if it hadn't been for that belly, I'd have shook her.

'I don't care that you've got knocked up,' I said, my voice fierce for all that I kept it low as I could on account of the nun, 'and I don't care who put it there, but I'll not have you bloody going off on me.' I looked up and there was that Jesus still on his Cross, still looking agonised and no wonder, but it can't have done any of their spirits any good, having him like that all the time.

'Come out with me Saturday,' I said. 'We could go for some chops like before and sit by ourselves and bloody talk, which you won't in here,' but still Mary shook her head, and even my language, which'd always been her patch before, not mine, didn't get the rise I was trying for.

'It's not allowed,' she said.

'Oh, come on,' I said. 'That's the workhouse, where they'll not let you out,' and she didn't reply, just shrugged again, till it was all I could do not to slap her.

'If you shrug again, Mary Bourne, baby or nothing, I'll knock you one,' I said, because there was a storm rising in me at whatever it was had done this to her.

She lifted her shoulders then a bit, and looked me properly in the eye. 'Listen, Hal,' she said. 'You'd do best to give me up now. I'll get through being here and then I'm going to leave and go to some other city.'

'No, Mary. That's not what we agreed,' I said.

'That was before,' she said, as if 'before' was some foreign place, and she shook her head at me like I was some child who didn't know their elbow from their ass.

'Another minute only,' the nun said from across the hall.

'I'm coming back,' I said, 'I don't know what's got into you, but I'm not giving you up like that,' and for a moment, like when the sun sends a line of light through a cloud and then it's gone, she smiled.

'You've been reading too many of them novels,' she said.

'Not me,' I said, my heart jumping with her smile, grinning back at her, 'my letters is no better than what they were back home. It's Thomas reads them for me, except not often because he doesn't much like the romances.'

But somewhere in my speaking she left me, her face gone tight, shut up, like when she'd come down the stairs, so that when the nun came over, she were more like some stiff-armed doll to hug than the girl I'd carried up the cliff.

'When can I visit again?' I said.

'Saturdays, between five and five thirty,' the nun said.

'So I'll be back on Saturday then,' I said to Mary, and got in answer a shrug as she walked back up the stairs.

I'd felt her pregnant belly when I'd hugged her, hard and tight like a wall, and it was only when I was going out through the blue gate, shutting it behind me, that I wondered how it would be to have a baby growing inside. It was that stuck in my thoughts more than where it had come from.

The last time he'd had to go on a trip, Thomas hadn't wanted to, though he didn't say that to Mr William, only to me. He'd been scared of something, though he wouldn't tell me what. "The less you know, the less you'll worry," he'd said, which I told him was nonsense, and he'd said about a letter in the roof I was to open if he'd not come back when he should. But there was none of that this time.

This time he was that excited I'd to tell him to hush up a bit with all his stomping about or he'd have his landlady up here and then there'd be a bit of explaining to do.

'Sit down,' I said, patting the bed beside me, and I'd to pull both his hands to get him to.

'Go on then, do my shoulders,' he said. 'I'm so knotted, I can barely lift my arms, and he had me pressing my thumbs in as he liked, and he was right, they were tight so I'd to put my full weight in to ease them out.

'Now tell me about it slowly,' I said.

'I will,' he said. 'But first there's some other business to finish telling.' And he took my hands off of his shoulders and lay me down for the once, so that my head was on his lap.

'Our day at Kirkham,' he said. 'Do you remember?'

I laughed. 'I'm not likely to forget,' I said. 'Me asking you to marry me.'

'I meant before that,' he said. 'When I told you all that . . .'

'All that when you were a lad,' I said.

'Yes,' he said. 'I stopped, before I'd done with the story, but I can finish it now, seeing as I reckon I'm a whisker from repaying my debt.'

'Debt to who?'

'To the brothers. The Wetherbys.'

'So tell me then,' I said, laying hold of his hand. Then I put it on my chest, so as I could feel the thump of my own heart, and kept it there. He didn't start at once, and when I opened my eyes and looked up to see what he was up to, I could tell, even with my head on his lap and upside down, that he was deep in somewhere and I knew better than to speak.

His voice, when he did start, was flat. Like he was telling about something that happened to somebody else, somebody he didn't care about. And aside from things I didn't understand, I didn't interrupt but let him tell it out.

'Brother Palance,' Thomas said. 'He was the mean sod at the orphanage, the one as liked to hurt boys. He liked the belt. Which always seemed odd, being a priest. To prefer it to the cane, or even the hand.'

'What?' I didn't like to ask so soon after he'd begun, but I didn't understand.

'Well, they've no need for belts, have priests, not wearing any trousers. They use rope girdles round their middles. So he must have ordered the belts specially for the job. Special belts for beating boys.

'Do you remember, I told you how Father Torreno fell through the ice?'

'He was the boss priest, you said.'

'Yes. And he was a fair man. But while he was ill, Brother Palance would always take the morning prayers. Brother

Palance had a liking for sermons. For giving them. The right-eousness of God; the goodness of God; the sanctity of God; the holiness of God. And any morning he preached about the justice of God, we knew the itch was on him, and all of us, the other priests too, would keep a distance.

'A boy could be caught by God's justice for all sorts. For having their hair combed wrong or for not looking holy enough in chapel, or for eating in a slovenly manner. And if God's justice had it in for you that day, it didn't matter how hard you tried, you'd be caught by it.

'He was scary as hell. Couldn't have been that old, maybe thirty, maybe more, it's hard to tell when you're a lad. Anyway a lot younger than Father Torreno, and I'd guess, thinking back, ambitious. I think maybe he was bitter at being walled up miles from anywhere with all these wicked boys.

'He was like a cat, was Father Palance. He walked on velvet feet, so you'd not hear him coming. Then suddenly there'd be this finger on your neck, just light and soft. No claws. Or he'd pinch your ear, but so gently. You'd look up and he'd be smiling down with his yellowed teeth and you'd catch a whiff of his breath, and the other boys backing off in case what you'd got was infectious. He never raised his voice. He'd have you follow him, keeping a few paces off, to his cell. It was a room but he liked to call it a cell. He'd beckon you in and close the door, putting his weight against it to make sure it clicked shut. Then he'd cover the white of the sheet with this old blanket, and still very softly, push you towards the bed.

"Hands above," he'd say and when your hands were in the air, he'd unbutton your trousers and pull them down below your knees. Then pull down your underthings. A hand on your stomach and one on your back, he'd bend you forward till your nose met the bed and your arse was in the air. The blanket smelt and the hairs tickled.

'When he'd got this far, he'd slow down. You couldn't see a thing with your face into the blanket, but he'd tell you what he was doing. I'll never forget that voice. Saying how he was reaching deep into the cupboard, and rummaging, and feeling that lovely piece of leather, so smooth, so firm. And then he'd say how it felt to hold it, and to wave it about. Christ, you'd be wondering what he was on about sometimes.

'But you knew sure enough when he stuck the socks between your teeth that it was coming. And when he brought it down on your buttocks, there'd be a flash across your eyes.'

Thomas stopped. He didn't groan, or get up. Didn't even change his expression. Just stopped. But I couldn't bear him to. I had to know what happened after.

'Thomas?' I said.

Something like a sigh went through him and he stroked my hair with a finger and started on again, but saying it like it was nothing to do with him. Like all this happened to somebody he only knew a bit.

'The worst of it was afterwards. He'd say how it hurt him to do it and how it'd make you a better boy. He'd start on about Saint this and Saint that and the stories, all about how they were hurt, and St Sebastian and his arrow holes, though he only mentioned him because it was the name of the place, and Jesus Christ and them whipping him on his way to Calvary. He'd talk and talk and with you still laid there, buttocks to the sky and red and welted. Then walk you back and leave you by your bed, and just before he left, he'd put his hand on your head and bless you.

'There were other boys as well he took to his room, but none of us talked about it. And that winter, when Father Torreno was ill, it got worse and worse.'

'But the other priests?' I said.

Thomas shook his head. 'It wasn't the hitting. They all did that. Believed in it. It was the way he did it. Taking you to his private place. You felt he might be licking you if he wasn't hitting you. And he was very careful. Kept his claws in, except in his room. But this one day he made a mistake and that's how I ended up here. There was a boy, a runty little fellow. He shouldn't have been in the place, he was still a baby. Sean Boland.'

'Sean at our wedding?' I said.

'Yes, him,' said Thomas. 'He was in for nicking food. A shilling's worth he said, and they gave him five years not four because the food wasn't returned.'

'What do you mean, not returned?' I said.

'He got longer because he'd eaten the bloody food before they caught him. Some pies, he said it was. Off a pie seller.

'Anyway it was still cold. Father Torreno was still ill. We'd none of us seen him for weeks. There was snow on the ground, fresh stuff, and we were doing drill. Brother Palance was doing it. Left about, march, right about. That kind of thing. And all of us miserable, freezing, and there's Brother Palance in this thick cloak and gloves with a big umbrella.

'Sean Boland, like I said he was only a wee lad. Maybe he was too tired to wait, or maybe . . . I don't know. But he peed on the ground. We were stood all stiff-backed and him at the front being the littlest and Brother Palance stood in front of him and all of a sudden there's this little yellow puddle and a bit of steam from it.

'Sean didn't move. He didn't try to hide it, kick snow over it or anything. Just stood, eyes forward like he was told and you could see Brother Palance look down and look up and walk across to him, his face still smiling.

'Boland?' Brother Palance said, and Sean didn't move a muscle. 'Boland, what is that?' But Sean didn't answer him. Didn't look scared, didn't apologise, didn't speak. Brother Palance asked him again, twice more, and we were all stood watching, waiting. Such a hush. Not even the rooks. Maybe it was too cold for them.

'Brother Palance stood as still as the rest of us. And then he went right up to Sean, whispered something and walked off. There were plenty of us knew what that meant and we waited for Sean to follow. But he didn't. Just swayed a bit where he was stood, and the little patch of yellow at his feet. So Brother Palance walked back to Sean and he took off a glove and he struck him across the face. Cut the boy's cheek open with his big ring. It was the first time I'd ever seen him touch another boy.

'Sean still didn't move and nor did Brother Palance. There was a red line down to Sean's chin and, slowly these drops dripping on the snow, next to the yellow, these red drops.

'That was when I went berserk. Berserk was what Father Torreno called it later, though he was on his sick bed when it happened, he wasn't there.

'I walked out from my place and round to the front and bunched my fist and hit Brother Palance, hard as I could.

'They told me afterwards that they had to pull me off him. That I punched him and punched him, that I was screaming at him. But all I remember is the first punch. The pleasure of it. The rightness.

'They told me after, that boys went on a rampage. Burnt and broke up the place. And they had me down for ring-leader. But all I remember is hitting his face. Nothing else.

'It was after that the Wetherbys took me.

'I was in the punishment cell for four days or so after, my head shaved it felt like to the bone and in punishment uniform which had no warmth. I'd only a thin blanket to start and the weather was still bitter, so Father Torreno had another one given me. They were long hours in there, nothing to do and only the thought of a place worse than this one to go to.

'There was no question but that they'd to send me to the prison for what I'd done. They made that clear. Father Torreno came to see me and he was so thin and pale and disappointed,

I started to wish I hadn't done it. But when he told me Brother Palance would be laid up sick for some time, and that he'd needed stitches to his chin, then I'd no regrets and I kept my eyes open when the Father said his prayer over me.

'There'd been a riot after, after I'd been taken and put in the cell, and the boys had set fire to some rooms. The schoolroom, where Brother Palance taught, and a storeroom. Nobody had been hurt, but the newspapers had heard of it somehow and made a song and dance.

'Brother Palance came to my cell once. I thought he'd be out for giving me a hiding, but he never touched me and it was worse. He sat on the mattress and patted it to make me sit beside him. There was a bandage over his chin. He spoke in this soft voice. He said he'd withdrawn his testimony against me, though it'd make no difference over the prison. He said I'd helped him greatly. I'd made him a hero, and so he could afford to seem generous, and soon he'd be away from this hole and into a city and a life with good food and clean sheets and warmth, and no foul boys. And where would I be? I'd be breaking stones in some nasty place where they'd be a lot rougher than he'd ever been.

'Another day men in dark suits, not priests, came to my cell door and peered, but didn't step in. They spoke in strange voices, hard to understand, asking questions. How long was I here, what was I fed, what had I learnt, how often was I up in the night for chapel. Joseph Finn told me, when he brought my meal, that they were inspectors come up from London, come up because of the riot. So when another man dressed in a black suit came to the cell, I thought he was another inspector. But he wasn't. He was Caleb Wetherby.'

'Not Mr William?'

'No. Mr Caleb. He'd taken off his hat to come in the cell and his hair was all matted into tight curls. He was wearing this black suit, like I said, but he'd the waistcoat buttoned up wrong and his tie was crooked. Also one of his jacket pockets bulged, until he pulled out of it two apples, shrivelled and red with yellow blotches. I'll never forget the conversation we had.

' "Nearly the last out of the cellar," he said and he gave me both of them. I ate one there and then. It was sweet. The other I kept, but I never ate it. I still have it.

' "Thomas Newcome," he said, nodding at me. "I am Caleb Wetherby. My brother and I have a cocoa factory in York and I've come here today on behalf of both of us to offer you a job."

'I shook my head. He couldn't have seen Father Torreno, he obviously didn't know what I'd done. "I'm going to prison," I said.

'Mr Caleb gave that smile of his I know now. "You can go to prison if you wish," he said. "But if you prefer, you can come, on licence, and work in my factory. You will be apprenticed like other boys of your age and your wage will be three and a half shillings a week. We'll undertake your supervision which will include the practising of your Catholic faith. I've spoken to Father Torreno and he is in agreement. If you wish to, you can come with me today."

' "Are you not Catholics then?" I asked.

' "We're Quakers," he said.

' "Is that a religion?" I said and he laughed. "You're Christians, though, or Father Torreno wouldn't have let you go," I said and he nodded.

'So I went with him that day, and here I am now.'

Thomas bent towards me and, all upside-down, kissed me long and soft.

'I've wanted to tell you all this for so long,' he said. 'Finish it off, like it were something to be got from between us.'

'So you've done it now,' I said.

'And you're not . . .'

'No,' I said. 'I love you, Thomas Newcome. And I know you,' which must have been what he needed, because it set him off again explaining.

'Once I've done this trip, I'll not need to go again,' he said. 'It's the last of it. I'll be free after. Our man down there, the one I've been to see before, he's employed by Richards, the company where Monseer Mazange has come up from, and he sent a letter to Mr William and Mr Caleb, very secret with "Private" all over it and it arrived today. They showed it me after dinner. He says that he's got it worked out, what we need to be putting in.'

'In to what?' I said, for I'd only the vaguest idea what he was on about.

'In to the pastilles,' Thomas said, speaking the words slow like he were talking to a child, though in truth he'd never told me any of this before.

'But Wetherby's is already making pastilles,' I said.

Thomas stood up, like he couldn't be still any longer, and began his pacing again.

'Not like the ones we've got planned. Nobody's making anything like those, nor anybody will except us.'

'That's what you said about the cocoa.'

'And it was true then, but there are others getting close with the cocoa now. Some are close to bettering us even with the chocolates and creams. But not the pastilles, if that's what to call them. We're going to bring out a sweet that's chocolate and pastille together, a perfect fusion. And the rest, they'll be left standing. They'll be sweets like nobody's seen before.

'Richards' man is keeping the secret for us. He's in our pay, but working it out down there. And they don't know the first thing. So now I've to go and see the fellow this last time and do what I've done before, which is remember the mixings and that, memorise them, and then back up to York, and spit them out, like you see a bird do for its young. Bring the worm back up for my masters. And I'll be sure to get a pay rise this time. Else I might just go and tell somebody else about it. Then we can find our own place to live. Babies even.'

'But you never would tell about it, would you? I mean to another company?'

Thomas shook his head. 'Course not. But they can't be sure of it. Not completely sure. I don't think they'd ever trust anyone completely who wasn't one of their lot. Though I bet Quakers are as big a load of gossips as any.'

And now Thomas was so excited again, that even though I'd Mary and her belly heavy on my mind, he had me excited too, and landlady or not I couldn't help myself, but laughed when he put his hands about my waist and swung me round, in that little room where you couldn't barely swing a cat. And I never told him of my visit to Mary, not wanting to put him out of sorts.

'I've to go tomorrow, love' he said, 'but it shouldn't be for more than three, maybe four days.'

And it was such a short time, and him so keen, so happy for the two of us, I wasn't cross, but only made him promise to write me a note when he was there, that I could be sure he'd not been attacked in the train or anything.

He went out for some cooked pie and a jug of beer to celebrate and we made more noise that night than we ever had, which was at the thought of our own place soon, where we could stamp on the floor and run about in our underthings and kiss in each and every room we chose, which wouldn't take long since there'd more than likely be just the two.

Then it was 'Goodbye, love,' into my ear the next morning, and he stroked my cheek, me still half-asleep, and he was gone to catch the early train.

SAMUEL

John Benbow's tale of shooting the deer ran through my thoughts in the days that followed. And seeing Mary that night, I knew why he had told me it. He believed it was punishment enough for her, bearing the consequences of her actions.

I had received a note from the Mother Superior at the Home informing me that Mary had settled in and was behaving appropriately. That she was quiet and seemed chastened, fulfilling her duties without delay, though speaking little with the other girls. But this account, which should have made me glad, did not, for though I confess I had had little time for the girl, nor she for me, I found that I could not wish upon her this loss of spirits, and indeed I was surprised at the extent of it.

However it was not this Home, but another, The Haven, that was chiefly occupying me at this time. There had been some unseemly politicking amongst Quakers recently over alterations being made to the establishment, and I felt it my responsibility, given my position on the Board of Trustees, to make my own opinion known.

Once completed, the alterations would materially increase the comfort of all the inhabitants, and the chief among them took the following form. Four bathrooms were being added, several bedrooms, a steam room, which the Medical Superintendent had long wished for, it being of proven efficacy in the raising of the spirits, and a range of recreational facilities. The first steps had been taken towards the levelling of ground for two tennis courts and there was serious thought of building an open-air swimming pool, as long as it could be made secure against suicidal tendencies.

But voices, including my cousin William's, had been raised against these changes on several grounds. It was asserted that such luxury was not helpful for those in the grip of an illness that might, in part, be a suspension, or a warping, of the moral faculties. Where this was the case, it was argued, a firm hand was needed to bring the person back to a proper estimation of their own state, and steam facilities, tennis courts and swimming pools would not make this task easier.

I had detected, of late, a slight hardening in William's attitude towards Grace, and though I was reluctant to ascribe personal reasons to his public position over the alterations to The Haven, I could not but think it likely. Just recently he had approached me after a First Day meeting and asked after Grace, as had often been his wont. When I had replied that she was well, he had shaken his head slightly.

'Do you not think, cousin Samuel, that it is time she took some responsibility upon herself, then? If she is as well as you say?' he had said.

'I believe that in her own way she is doing just that,' I had replied, but William had frowned.

'There is too much of this finding of one's own way, he had said. 'God has a right way, and it is our responsibility to walk in it,' and before I could reply, he had turned his back.

I did not know how, but I was sure he must have heard about the recent changes in Grace's life. If he had known at all of Harriet's part in it, then she would have been sacked from the factory, photographs or no photographs, for he brooked no incursions by middle or working classes upon the other's territory. Unless, of course, they took the form of First Day Bible Schools, or soup kitchens. But even without Harriet's part, it seemed that Grace's visits to the garden had angered him, though surely he remembered the way she had been as a child. Perhaps it was because of his strength of feeling towards her. If he could no longer pity, then he must scorn her.

They allowed Grace considerable freedom to come and go at The Haven. She visited our garden almost daily now, after all her years of self-imposed seclusion. And I was conscious that this probably owed a considerable amount to my position on the Board, and William's. And though as a principle I deplored nepotism, I also knew I would put my sister's well-being above anything.

So, in penning my letter to the Board, I was aware of the dense tangle of sympathies which influencing our dispassionate judgements. And it was while I was seated at my father's desk, paper out before me, pen in hand, that my concentration was broken by the sound of raised voices.

I set down my pen and opened the drawing room door to find Caleb running towards me, his dark hair stippled with the white blossom which the wind was dragging from the trees in flurries on the drive. He stopped some yards from me, his hands resting on his thighs, his chest heaving, as though he had run a considerable distance with some pressure of purpose.

'Caleb,' I said.

He stood up straight. 'I must speak with you,' he said.

I gestured towards the drawing room. Once I had shut the door behind us, he sat down heavily on a sofa, the same sofa that Harriet favoured on the rare occasions I had persuaded her to sit in this room. He leaned forward, his eyes towards the carpet, still catching his breath. He still wore his laboratory coat, so must have come directly from Wetherby's. Taking out a handkerchief, he wiped his brow before twisting the hand-kerchief into a knot for upwards of half a minute. I cleared my throat gently.

'Caleb. What has brought you here?'

He looked up and his expression told me, before his words, that he did not wish to be the carrier of such news.

'There is a terrible thing happened,' he said. 'A man is dead.' Although the rest of him was still now, Caleb's finger was tapping an urgent message upon his thigh.

'At the factory?' I said.

He shook his head. 'In London,' he said.

I replaced the lid on my pen and shuffled my papers into a tidy pile. 'A friend?' I asked, and again he shook his head.

'Not exactly. He was on business for Wetherby's. A talented young man, a clerk by the name of Thomas Newcome.'

It was my turn now to be winded and it took me several moments to regain my breath.

'Thomas Newcome?' I said.

'I was in William's office when he took the telegraph. 'It said "T. Newcome dead from fall stop. Advise on action urgently stop. Await directions."'

'Dead from a fall,' I said, which words I found somehow to prevent myself speaking the others that came into my head, to prevent myself speaking the thing that I knew even then in those first minutes, the thing I could see too in Caleb's look. That William had killed him, that this was a murder somehow.

'I do not know how she will bear this,' I said then, and finding my legs heavy beneath me, I sat down.

'William won't talk to me,' Caleb said, 'and I didn't know what else to do.'

'Have you spoken to anyone else?' I said.

'No. I came here directly.'

'Still it will be in the air by tomorrow, and she will hear whispers of it,' I said. I only wondered afterwards what Caleb can have made of this mysterious 'she' I had mentioned, though I am sure if I had taken him into my confidence, that his heart would have gone out to Harriet as William's never could.

Although I could not yet think about what had happened, and though the fact of Thomas's death was barely real to me, I knew what I must do.

It was not quite dusk when I arrived at Harriet's lodgings, that time in the late afternoon of spring when the light is dropping out of the day. The city was falling into the shadow territory that comes before the darkness of night.

Harriet's landlady said that Miss Brewer had indeed come in from her work, and though suspicion was creased into every line around her eyes, she agreed to call her down, if my news was as serious as I said. I thanked her for the offer of her drawing room in which to conduct my 'interview', as she termed it, but said it was not necessary.

When Harriet appeared, her hair still tightly pinned from work, her shoulders weary, I wished I did not have to tell her this thing.

'Mr Ransome,' she said, with surprise and, I thought, a note of apprehension in her voice, for I had never called on her before in this way.

'Good afternoon, Harriet,' I said, and keeping my voice low, because the landlady, though staying further back down the hall, was still visible behind her, I suggested she accompany me on a short walk.

'Are we to go anywhere particular?' Harriet said, her voice more animated. Thomas, after all, was away and she perhaps thought my arrival offered her an unexpected, even pleasing, diversion.

'I thought the Knavesmire,' I said.

She nodded and we walked down the hill in silence. As we approached the edge of the racecourse, Harriet smiled.

'It's where I first met Thomas,' she said. 'Properly, I mean. On the racecourse. In a circus tent.'

'I don't think I knew that,' I said and there must have been something odd about my voice, because she looked up at me as I spoke, a question in her eyes, but I didn't answer it then.

The daffodils were in flower beneath the trees. Their yellow heads shone out into the dusk, the only colour beneath the greys of the encroaching night.

'Perhaps we should sit,' I said, gesturing to a bench. Harriet sat, surprised I knew, for I had always taken pains not to be seen with her in this kind of compromising position. She placed her hands flat on the seat on either side of her and looked out at the grassy expanse.

I would have liked to hold those hands at this moment, to hold onto her. But I could not, so I sat apart a little, my hands on my lap.

'I have some very hard news,' I said. 'Something has happened that I would not wish upon anyone, and least of all in the world would I wish it upon you.'

She looked at me, her face blanched even in the failing light.

'Not Mary? Not her baby?' she said, her voice small, apprehensive.

'No,' I said, and now she held my eyes so steadily that I had no choice but to return her gaze.

'Say it then,' she said.

So I told her what Caleb had told me, sitting apart on that bench in the fallen dusk. She said nothing in response and she was so still afterwards that I was concerned she might be falling into what they were calling hysteria, though from what I had read this was more likely to occur in women of a higher class. But she did not. She only sat as though she were turned to stone.

Expressions went through my mind, formal expressions of condolence and sympathy that people had murmured to me last summer on Mother's death, which I myself had said to others. And other things, angry ones to lash my cousin with, but I held them in, and so for a time I was lost for words. At last I felt I must speak.

'I will do anything within my power for you, anything to help you, Harriet,' I said. She made no movement to show that she'd heard me. And perhaps it was this, that I thought her beyond hearing in the first shock of grief, that brought me to whisper the very thing I thought I never would. The thing I had barely allowed myself to know. That I loved her and would care for her always. I whispered it so softly into her hair that perhaps she never heard me. If she did, she never afterwards made mention of it, and no more did I.

Though the day had been mild, the sky was clear that evening and it was now cold. The moon, only a slender crescent, gave out little light, but I could see Harriet's shoulders shivering. I took off my coat and put it over them. She looked at me as if surprised, and murmured something I couldn't make out, but she neither accepted nor rejected my gesture. For what seemed an age she neither spoke nor wept, though my own eyes stung with tears. But finally she gave a sigh.

'I thought to have done with this, being away now from the sea,' she said.

'With what?' I said, not understanding, but she went on as if she had not heard me.

'Because the sea takes men. You know that it will and so you hope, pray, that it is not your father, or your uncle, or your brother, though the praying makes no difference because when the sea is hungry, it must be fed. But I left there, I left the sea and so I thought . . .' She seemed to struggle for the words and then she went on, asking a question more to the air than to me. 'What was it that was hungry this time, that it must take Thomas?'

She said nothing further, and after a while longer, I coaxed her to her feet and we walked back up the hill to her lodgings.

The tall thin house behind its black railings looked bleak and unyielding. Harriet's landlady watched our return from the first floor window, unperturbed by my fierce glance.

'May I call on you tomorrow?' I asked. 'Perhaps we will know more by then.'

She nodded, and turned to go in. 'Is there not anyone I can call upon, to come here?' I said, for it was terrible to think of her going alone to her room.

'I cannot risk losing my job,' she said.

'But he is dead,' I said. 'Surely they would not sack you if you no longer have your husband?'

The words were uttered before I had a chance to check them and it was as if I had struck her with my fist.

'I am sorry,' I said, angry at my inadvertent callousness. 'I did not mean to speak so harshly.'

But still her look answered my question and then there was nothing more I could do than leave her with this first chill of her grief, the grief I had been courier for.

I was beyond the gate when the door opened again and Harriet stood in the threshold.

'Mr Ransome, please would you tell Grace,' she said. Nothing more.

My unfinished letter concerning the alterations to The Haven still lay upon the desk at home. It needed little more than a signature, but I could not bear to write it. I put it from me and, after writing to tell Grace I would visit her the following morning, which I instructed Nellie to have delivered, I went to bed, to spend the night tossing in uneasy sleep.

HARRIET

They'd a proper coffin for my Uncle Joseph, because we had the body back. When they got him into the house, they laid him out on the kitchen table, my mam and his other sisters, and they washed him all over, though God knew the sea had done its fair share of washing before. Then they dressed him all up in his best things and lifted him into his coffin, putting his hands just so across his chest and making sure his shoes had a good bit of polish and his hair was combed.

So we'd all to come through and pay respects, which wasn't to do a lot but kneel down a bit and be quiet at it. Some might have prayed something, I suppose, but I didn't have a thing to say to God, so I set my eyes on this mark there was, on the cuff of Joseph's jacket, just a bit of stain where the cloth was darker. But I knew it because I'd put it there not so long before. It were a spat of bacon grease I'd dripped by accident that I couldn't no ways get out after, and my Uncle Joseph had clapped me round the ears for it even with me being near enough a grown girl. Now I was glad it was going into the ground with him, my bacon spat, my mark.

But it was often enough a man'd be lost and no body to be brought back with the life washed out. Sometimes it'd turn up weeks later on a beach and then it didn't look much like anything it had done, after all that time in the water and the fishes' teeth. But often there was nothing. Only the heavy stones in the eyes of the men returning. And that was hard, because you need to have a body first if you've to let it go. Only I didn't know how hard it was until it was Thomas's body that I didn't have.

We used to play this game when I was a child and what you'd to do was press your hands hard as you could against a wall and count to fifty. Then you stretched your arms out to either side of you, like a bird's wings, and for a few seconds they'd feel like they were lifting, floating, before the feeling went.

Next day in the factory, after Mr Ransome had told me about Thomas, my whole body felt like it had been pushed against a wall and then brought off of it, only the floaty feeling didn't go. I did everything like normal, even ate and drank, but it was as if I wasn't really there, but somewhere else.

There was Assembly like always, and Mr William up on his stage. Elsie said something to me about him looking like her aunt had before she got took with the cholera, a funny colour under the eyes.

Mr William read out from the Bible about life being dust to dust and ashes to ashes, and when he'd finished, nobody except me had the least idea why he'd chosen that bit. Not until he went on.

'Sometimes it pleases God to take a person to himself when it is least expected,' he said. 'A young, hale and hearty person, seemingly in the prime of their life, and it is hard for us to understand why.'

'Something's happened,' Elsie whispered to me and I nodded. I knew what it was, but still Mr William's words didn't have anything to do with my Thomas. They were for a different person, not for the man who was my husband, the man that loved me, because I had my Thomas protected in a secret place. A place he'd stay put in, no matter what.

'Yesterday I received word that a diligent and worthy employee of this factory had died in the course of discharging his duty to the firm,' Mr William told us. 'Although his death might seem a tragedy, for he was a young man, only twenty-six years of age, God in his ineffable justice will have had good cause to take him from us, and it is our duty to trust the Lord in this. We can only be grateful, under the circumstances, that Thomas Newcome had no family known to him to be afflicted with this loss.'

There was a hush and murmur at the name and Elsie nudged me. Then he went on.

'Let us bow our heads in a minute's silence, in memory of Thomas Newcome,' he said. 'And lift our hearts to God in gratitude for His divine mercies.'

Mr William looked over all of us sat there, and he bowed his head, and the hundreds of heads about me bowed too.

I don't remember running to the doors, but Elsie tells me that's what I did. She says I didn't make a sound. The doors were locked, like they always were during Assembly, and I banged on them, again and again, nothing else about me moving, only my arm, she said, until the minute was up and the overseer with the key came over quick as he could and opened them. She says I ran out and when she got to the packing room I was already there at my bench working and that nobody liked to say anything to me, not even Mrs Flint, but that at the end of the morning and the bell rung for dinner, Elsie'd to stop me packing any more and coax me up. Then she fed me from her dinner pail, because I'd not brought my own, and sat beside me till it was time to go back in to work. She said I never spoke a word. Which is strange, because I thought I never stopped talking that day, I couldn't, and that it was only a wonder Mrs Flint didn't dock my pay for it.

At the factory, everybody knew what I was to Thomas, though they none of them knew we were married. Everybody except Mr William, that is. And so they steered wide about me like I'd some kind of acid on my skin that'd burn if they touched it.

It was Mr Ransome who had told me what happened. He had told me Thomas was dead, dead from a fall. I don't remember the words he said, but I do remember him putting his coat over my shoulders and it smelling of him, as why shouldn't it, but still it had taken me by surprise. And me thinking, How does he know I'm cold? and saying this to him and him not hearing it.

When he came the next day, like he said he would, we walked down by the racecourse again.

'Did Thomas tell you what he had gone to do?' he said, and I said no, he hadn't properly, though it came back to me about the bird bringing up the worm for its babies. But I couldn't tell it to Mr Ransome. Not then.

'What about the funeral?' I said.

He didn't answer at first, but spent a minute or longer looking out across the grass.

'What about it?' I said again.

'It's to be in London,' he said.

'London!' I said.

'Yes. William has taken the train down today.'

'But how will I be there?' I said, and he shook his head.

'But I must,' I said, my voice loud inside my head, booming.

'You cannot,' he said. 'It will be done by tomorrow, and even if you were able to, it would lose you your job.'

'I don't care about my job,' I said. 'I'll go still,' and he cursed his cousin then. But it wasn't the words he used that shocked me, which I'd heard worse of from the urchins up the alleys, it was his voice, which cut through me like the coldest wind.

I don't remember now what words Mr Ransome said or how he persuaded me not to go to London, but he did, and I didn't see Thomas into the earth, nor the shovels piling it over him.

'So he is a drowned man,' I said. 'No body for me.' And it was an age, weeks or months, before I knew for sure he was gone.

The day after the funeral, I went through the little door, which had been the door to my love till yesterday, into the roof, and into Thomas's room next door, and I took out his things. Scuffled them across to my room like some mouse with its squirrelings under the roof. There wasn't much. He'd taken the best part of his clothes, the suit he wore to marry me, to London and they never came back. But there were his books and his writing things and his stack of *The Leisure Hour*. Once I'd got them set down in my room, I didn't do anything with them, didn't look at the pictures. But when I came back from the factory, I'd sit on my bed and stare at the pile.

Mr Ransome was on at me to move my lodgings, but I couldn't at first. I knew Thomas was dead, I'd been told, I'd heard Mr William, I'd seen them duck their heads to me at the factory in pity. But it was the closest I could get to him, being up there in the attic with his things, and sometimes if I looked at them hard enough, I was sure I could hear his voice. I don't know what it was put me in mind of the letter, the one he wrote before in case anything happened to him. But nothing had happened that time, so I'd never gone after it, and maybe he'd taken it out, torn it up after.

On a beam in the roof, that's where he said he'd put it. So I'd to reach into the dark spaces where I'd never before even looked, through the spiders' webs like soft nets in my face, and search for it, my fingers making trails along the wood in the thick, dark dust. When I found it, laying flat along a broad beam, it was covered too, so covered I couldn't even make out my name. But I didn't blow it clean up there for fear of rousing the dirt of years and having it settle on my head and arms and hands. I carried the letter down all the stairs, the turn and the turn of the banister making me dizzy, along the hall and through the front door and out of sight of the landlady, till I was outside, and the world and its wife going about its evening business, and then I blew the soot and dirt off of it.

'Harriet Newcome'. The envelope had my name written on it, in Thomas's writing. My name, my married name, and me and him the only ones ever to see it written like that. I broke the seal.

The letter was written on Wetherby's paper. 'My darling girl,' it said, and then the next bit, which took me longer. 'If you're reading this, then it will not have gone well for me.' I must have been stood there some time in the making out and maybe I looked a bit odd, because there was a woman, a lady rather, staring at me from out of her window across the road. There was pages more and I couldn't be stood there forever, so I folded it up again and went back up to my room.

But sat in there, all I could do was think how he'd been alive when he wrote down these words, heart beating, warm arms, eyes so keen. I could see him sitting at his desk in the clerks' office in the factory, writing it secretly, his tongue at the front of his mouth, so as you could just see it, like he did when he was concentrating very hard, and maybe as he closes the letter up, he puts a kiss on the seal. Just a small one so as no one would've seen him do it. And then he slips it inside his shirt to bring home.

I opened the letter again. After the first couple of pages, which was what I'd read so far and which had broke me up with his tender words for me, there was words underlined at the top of the third: *Memo of Works Carried out for Wetherby's*, they read. The pages from then on were thick with Thomas's writing. Mr William's name was there, and Wetherby's, and there were lots of other names I didn't know. Richards was one I could see and Mazange, who was the Frenchman with the pastilles. But there must have been near enough a dozen sheets, it was going to take me hours to make it all out, and I felt weary with the thought of it. What was the point now, with him dead and gone? And anyway, I couldn't bear it.

I turned the pages over till I got to the last one. 'Goodbye my darling,' was all that was written on it, and 'I will always love you. Thomas.'

There was something odd about the beginning and the ending I couldn't quite put my finger on for a moment. Something about the way they looked. It wasn't Thomas's writing, which I'd know anywhere, and it wasn't what he'd said. I spread the pages out on the bed and then I saw it. All the other pages were filled tight with writing, the words packed so close, it put me right off reading. But the first three and the last two, they only had his greeting on, and his farewell. He'd kept his words to me separate from the rest.

Thomas never normally left gaps, not when paper was the price it was, and he'd done it for a reason here.

'Canny bugger,' I said and it made me smile, how he'd thought it out. It was so as I could give it to someone, show them what'd gone on, and there not be any mention of me.

I must have slept after, and the pages all scrumpled under me. When I woke, I flattened them out carefully. I'd made a decision sleeping, like sometimes happens. When you wake and know what you've to do with a thing. I'd give the letter to Mr Ransome. Not so as anything'd be done, but so as somebody else would know. He'd understand better than I could what Thomas was on about too, since Thomas had kept me in the dark so much before. And I'd put away the first and the last two pages, fold them up small and tuck them with my ring into my little box.

It was maybe three weeks after Thomas was gone, maybe more, when my time of the month came. I was never very regular, not like Mary who'd know the day ahead of time and get rags and whatnot ready. Sometimes it'd be a month, sometimes nearly two, and it'd nearly always catch me out.

I'd not have let on to myself then, though I can now, that I'd a little hope hidden away, a barnacle of it stuck on tight to the back of my mind somewhere. And sometimes when I'd been staring at Thomas's *Leisure Hours* for a time, it'd creep forward, the hope would, till it was in my sight, and it'd stop there, like one of them spots before the eyes you get if you've been looking near the sun for too long. Once even, I let myself cradle it and stroke its downy hair and feel the clutch of its chubby fist. So when I saw that it was my time and I'd to get the rags, when the cramps started up in my belly, it was only a tiny hope that died, just a shred of shell really, but still it hurt like something much bigger.

They'd let Thomas's room within the week, so I'd lie on my bed and hear a strange man's noises through the wall. More than once I'd drop to sleep and then start awake in the night hearing Thomas. His pouring of water into the bowl, his slipping off of his boots, his hum even. I'd be halfway to the little door, my eyes barely opened but my heart jumping in my chest before I'd remember and so I'd listen some more. Only then I'd hear how it wasn't him but a stranger and I'd be that angry I'd be close to banging on the wall and shouting at the man, as how he'd got it wrong, because the shuffle of his stockings was different from Thomas's and the creak of the bed took another note with his weight. But then I'd lie back down and cover my head with all I could to keep the sounds away and there'd be no more sleep.

My first visits to Mary after Thomas's death, we barely said a word, either of us. Just sat on the bed and I cried and she stroked my hair. But this third time I'd such a need to talk, because there was nobody but Mr Ransome I could talk to, and because now even my bit of hope was gone, that I started in on it as soon as I was with her. And when I told her about it all – about the rags, and how full my room was with Thomas's underthings and his *Leisure Hours*, and hearing the stranger – first off she didn't say a thing, then she laughed.

'You mustn't stop there, Hal,' she said. 'Not in that house. Because you'll not be able to breathe if you stay.'

'I can't leave him,' I said.

'He's not there any more.'

'He nearly is,' I said.

'That's his shadow.'

'It's better than nothing,' I said.

Mary went and looked out of the little window. A great tree made the whole of her view. It wasn't in leaf yet, but Mary told me that when they came they'd be red, though she'd be out of the place long before then, her baby being due so soon. Now it was bare branches criss-crossing their way about themselves and little birds quizzing the bark for things.

'He'd have said you should leave, wouldn't he?' she said. 'If he'd known this was to happen?'

'But we didn't speak about it. What we'd do, either of us, if the other one was gone,' I said. 'It was what we'd do together, soon, that we talked about. Not what we'd do if we were apart. Anyway, what made you laugh?'

Mary turned back towards me. Her belly looked so huge I was sure it must be near her time, but I didn't like to ask.

And it looked to me like she tried for a smile but it wouldn't stay.

'It was on account of you being so cross at the stranger's sounds. I'll bet he'd have liked that. Have laughed at it. That and you keeping all his precious *Leisure Hours*.'

'It's why I'm keeping them,' I said.

Mary looked through the window again, giving me the back of her head, her lovely hair sheeny and bright even when it was so tightly bound, not a single hair escaping, in the thicket of pins the nuns insisted on.

'I didn't barely know him, and he always made me mad,' she said.

'And you made him,' I said.

'Yes.'

There wasn't much in Mary's room. A bed, a chair, a nightstand, a picture of the virgin and baby Jesus on one wall and two small shelves with Mary's clothes and hairbrush. And a Bible.

'I've been thinking I might change my way of life, once this is done,' Mary said, picking up the Bible.

I couldn't hide my surprise, and she smiled.

'How do you mean, done?' I said.

'Out,' she said.

'But you'll have the baby then,' I said, and she didn't answer me that, which I noticed at the time, though I didn't guess for a second what I know now was in her head already.

'Change your life to what?' I said.

'What do you think?' she said, having a game with me.

'If it was that way you were going,' I said, pointing at the Bible, 'you'd not be joking on it.'

'They're not as solemn as you'd think,' Mary said. 'I've been surprised. There's some are stern, and you'd never catch them in a smile or owt. But there's a couple have quite a bit of humour in them. They've to keep it under wraps, of course, if the others are about. But if it's just us girls . . .' She grinned at me again.

'Still I can't believe you'd do that,' I said. 'It's too much of other people telling you. And then there's God laying down the law left, right and centre.'

'No worse than them Quakers,' Mary said. 'Making you feel like you're never good enough. I know a bit about it since being in here, and they're onto something with confession. Getting it all off your chest. It's not a bad one, that.'

'But you're not really thinking of joining up?' I said.

Mary didn't answer me that. Instead she opened the Bible and took a wafery piece of paper from between its pages. On one side it had printed words, and on the other she'd written something on it with a pencil.

'They won't let me have any paper,' she said. 'But I figured they wouldn't miss a page. It's only from the front, anyway.'

She held it out to me. 'Will you give it to Mr Benbow? Him and not anybody else. Not the old cow especially.'

'Is it about . . .?' I said, pointing at her stomach.

'It is and it isn't,' she said.

'Not photographs though?' I said, and I couldn't keep the pleading out of my voice.

'No,' she said.

'So will you tell me?' I said, and she shook her head.

'Not yet.'

I took the piece of paper, folded it and tucked it into my boot.

'They won't make you give the baby up?' I said, jutting my head at the door, towards the nuns.

She nodded. 'They'll try.'

'But . . .'

'I won't let them. Whatever happens, it'll not be them that has this one' and she put a hand to her stomach and then a finger to my lips.

I don't exactly know what went on then, but I can only figure I must've gone on faint, because next thing I was sat on her bed and the blood rushing in my head and my fingers feeling all odd. Mary was sat beside me and she'd her arm about my shoulder.

'That day when you took me up the cliff,' she said. 'You remember it?'

'Course.'

'And it was mizzle and mist and everyone gone but me?' she said.

I nodded.

'We never spoke about it after,' she said. 'Never said a word on it, but it was there, your doing of it and if you hadn't, I'd have drowned. We both knew that and it didn't need the saying.'

She took hold of my hand, which was like a dead thing on my lap, put it on her great hard belly and she went on talking. And as she went on, every now and then under my hand there'd be the flip or nudge of something, pressing up, like it was doing a dance in there, in the dark.

'But what I never said, because we never talked on it and that was what I wanted, what I never said was how I'd got not to mind it, about drowning, about dying. Not till I heard you calling. When I was there on my own and I couldn't climb the rope, no matter what I couldn't, and when the tide was getting close and the back of the cliff just behind me and nowhere left to go, I started not to mind it. Started to look forward, the water covering my feet, and my legs, my hips, and on up till it was over my head. Told myself about it over and over, got myself into a state, I suppose. That's what my mother would have said, and clocked me round the side of the head to prove it.

'But then you. Your voice first off, and then your legs with your skirts all trussed and your face sharp with the danger.

Then I wanted to leave the sea, and after I couldn't bear to be near it, or any water, because I was afraid I'd want to go back in. Didn't matter my mother beating me, or the others name-calling and pushing me. Didn't matter, because I wanted to live and you'd been the only one to see it.'

'But where will you live? You're not thinking of going back?' Mary's fingers dug into my shoulder, gripping like a crab.

'No. Not there,' she said.

'But with the baby?' I said. 'Where'll you go with the baby?'

Mary lost her temper then and pushed me out of the door.

'Just give Mr Benbow the note, Hal,' she said, and I didn't see her again until after.

SAMUEL

Harriet had asked me to speak to Grace of Thomas's death, and I had done so. I had stood in her room at The Haven and told her of it. Grace sat upon her bed and listened. She made no remark on my unusual morning visit, nor upon my news. She barely raised her head when I came in to the room, and seemed engrossed entirely by her beloved cat. Calling me to her side, she requested that I observe a small bald patch on the creature's underbelly.

'D'you think it to be mange?' she said.

Had William heard our conversation, I have no doubt he would have taken this as yet further evidence of Grace's dubious moral path. But I knew it to be no more than her own way of managing distress.

'Having no knowledge of cats, or of mange in animals,' I said, 'I can hazard only a guess, that it seems possible.'

'Then I shall have to wait and ask Harriet,' she said. 'She

is knowledgeable in such things. Will you tell her that I am anxious for my cat, for I doubt I will see her for a while.'

'Shall I also tell her that you are very sorry for her loss?' I asked gently, and to my relief she nodded my question away impatiently.

It wasn't until I questioned William about Thomas's death that I realised finally how firmly the collar of capital was tightened about his neck. That he had done something Quakers foreswore above all, and set up an idol in his heart, whose saccharine taste made it no less a graven image.

When I first read Thomas's 'Memorandum', entrusted to me wordlessly by Harriet, I read it with a certain scepticism. Which is not a turn of mind that comes naturally to me, but Thomas's allegations, though framed as a progress report, were very serious. And I did not believe that William had knowingly gone so far.

Thomas did not speak in generalities, but in specifics. He gave the dates of five separate trips to London in the last two years, the longest being for fifteen days and the shortest for just two. On all but one of these trips, he had rented a room in the city and there conducted interviews with a view to poaching skilled labour, recipes and any industrial information he could from other men's factories.

He gave the address of the hotel in Bloomsbury he had stayed in – The Greenwood Temperance Institute – which I knew well, having stayed there myself more than once. The rooms he had rented on different occasions were scattered across the city, though he didn't explain why: Hanbury Street, Spitalfields; Hartham Road., Holloway; Saffron Hill in Farringdon; Lexington Street. in Soho. Each of these addresses was given as a title, and beneath it the names of the men he had seen there, their current job and mention of what they had offered, and what he had paid them for it:

Henry French (28 yrs), a roaster at Taylors, on 20/- a week. Recipe obtained for Taylors cocoa at cost of 10/-.

James Garnett (34 yrs), 'grinder' & 'mixer' at Unsworth & Mercers. Previously at Taylors for 14 yrs. Understands making of Rock Cocoa but not other confection. Agreed to engage him for 23/- a week, also present of £5 for all recipes and £1 for fare to York.

Frederick Mead (32 yrs). Clever, but no energy for looking after things. Recently moved to Richards from Unsworth & Mercer's. Was head of fancy department at Unsworths. Now making all fancy & 'sweet' chocolate. Paid 10 shillings for Nibbling Mill information:
Eggs: Unsworths do not grind shell with any of goods, fine or common, but nibs for fine work are more thoroughly blown than for common.
They do not use gum or fat of any kind.
Roasting cylinders have not got wire ends, only holes for steam to escape through.
Chicory from continent is *double* kiln dried. A roast (84 lbs) can be turned out in 15 mins.

Jean Mazange (41 yrs), a Frenchman. Was given to drink, but has now a 'delicacy of the stomach' which prevents him. Has thorough knowledge of Creams and of Pastille manufacture. Claims special knowledge of Richards' recipes, in particular of new technique for Blending. Would be willing to move to York for £1.8.11 a week plus some percentage sales. Named 2nd man, James Ford, also employed by Richards. See Memo, p.4. [Note: Mazange later hired at £1.5.2 a week and no percentage sales.]

There were perhaps twenty such names, most appearing only once. But when he had finished his list, it was to Jean Mazange and James Ford that Thomas returned.

Mazange was a figure with enough expertise and 'inspiration', as Thomas described it, to carry out the grand plan William had devised. And so with financial inducement, and the promise of proper recognition, the Frenchman left Richards Confectionery and Cocoa House in London and came to York. William quickly milked him dry of all Richards' recipes and technical information before drawing up a legally binding confidentiality document to safeguard his own factory.

Mazange promised William that within the year he would produce a pastille second to none. What is more, it would be a pastille coated with the finest chocolate, something never before achieved. Only Richards might come near to equalling it. He also mentioned that Richards' chief confectioner, James Ford, was a good friend. A good friend with a money problem. William agreed to clear Ford's gambling debts, and he did so several times, in exchange for what Thomas dryly described as 'Ford's observations on the daily workings of the Confectionery Department.'

'Mr William was clear from the start,' Thomas wrote, 'that he wanted to be first in the country with the new pastille, and he would go to some lengths to prevent a competitor putting one out before him.' At first this meant keeping abreast of Richards with regular intelligence-gathering by Thomas in London, and elaborately coded written descriptions from Ford, in which not only ingredients but even procedures were given letters of the alphabet. 'However,' Thomas wrote, 'it quickly became clear that in order to head the market, more substantial steps would have to be taken.'

So Thomas became involved in acts of sabotage. Doctors were paid not only to write positive testimonials about

Wetherby's, but also to throw doubts over other men's products. Advertisements were placed decrying the dangerous additions made to other companies' cocoa, and throwing into doubt the safety of their goods. And Thomas's trips to London took a different turn.

James Ford would liaise with Thomas at the Turk's Head, a public house, some hours after the factory gates had closed. He would follow Ford at a distance, Ford unlocking gates and doors and Thomas slipping in to the factory unnoticed. Ford habitually entered the factory after hours, so his presence was not suspicious. Inside, Ford would keep watch while Thomas went about his business.

Ford had shown Thomas an escape route out through a window and over a roof with a twelve foot drop into an alley, should the occasion arise. The occasion had not so far, but on the second visit Thomas had had to take cover, listening from the inside of a boiling pan to Ford explaining his presence in the building at midnight to Mr Richards's nephew.

Thomas's aim was simple. He was buying time. Wetherby's were to bring out their new pastille in the autumn, ready for the Christmas push. With a few months' grace and no rival near, they could establish their name. Fuse the name 'Wetherby's' to 'Chocolate-Coated Pastille' for ever and the market would be theirs. So Thomas must prevent Richards getting there before them.

To this end he doctored Richards's Private Experiment Books and the Recipe Books, kept in duplicate as in Wetherby's. Ford unlocked them from their cupboard and Thomas, with his clerk's hand, altered the figures. Nobody could have known by looking at them, and his adjustments were not steep enough to be noticed, but were grave enough to render the outcome unsatisfactory.

Then having locked the Books back into their cupboard, Ford let Thomas into the Gum Rooms. 'My task in here was much harder,' he wrote, 'for any failure in the equipment or the stove would be immediately apparent and thus immediately remedied.' He explained how on his first visit he merely observed the rooms' layout and considered what he might do next time, and it was only at this one point that he gave expression to his fears, writing how 'At night the machinery, the cauldrons and melangeurs, sit like dark monsters and I must be wily, like the Greek heroes I have read about, to creep past them and find out their secrets.'

On his second visit, he brought the necessary tools &c. to make good his decisions, having received a verbal assurance from William that he had his unwritten but firm endorsement. The tools were little more than a spanner, wrench and, most inconveniently, a weight of firebricks, 'which,' he writes, 'I had to shoulder in to the factory, but not out.' What Thomas did precisely, either to the Books or to the machinery he did not specify. He ended the paragraph, and the letter, by remarking only that he hoped and thought that he did not need to pay a third visit, and with the cryptic remark that 'we have made a bargain with another god,' which I assumed referred to himself and William.

If it were not for the objective and calm tone, I should have suspected there was some 'cloak and dagger' fantasy at work, perhaps out of an exaggerated sense of his own importance. But exaggeration or no, the Memo did confirm my impression that my cousin was indeed sailing very close to the wind in his business affairs, and should the Elders hear of any of this, then his cherished status amongst York Friends would be blasted from the rock.

But all that was nothing beside the agitation of my dismay. That my cousin, whom I had known since our innocent days with the butterfly nets, should have made such a bitter thing from his talent; that a man should have died of William's ambition left a rank odour that turned my stomach just as fiercely as the tanning pits had all those years earlier. And I found myself doubled again now, a full-grown man, over these sheets of paper that smelled as foul as anything found in my tannery.

I understood that Thomas had written this Memorandum not for his own well-being, but for Harriet's. So that should anything happen to him, she would have this account. And I guessed that he knew she would give it to someone else to read. Mary perhaps, if not me. However for now I did nothing with it. Harriet made no allusion to it, so neither did I, since I could see nothing in what it had said that might make her pained mind easier. Nor did I yet say anything to William, but held my tongue, though it was never far from my mind.

I visited Harriet perhaps twice each week during the next month or so and grew increasingly anxious for her well-being. She continued to work at the factory, but I could not see her managing to do so for much longer. She was growing thin and drawn and her expression was that of someone who had gone very far away. I still passed almost daily an advertisement for Wetherby's Pastilles, pasted to the gable wall of a grocer's shop, and though in the past I had turned my eyes away from it, and then become almost indifferent to it, now I stopped and gazed at the smiling girl perched on a stile, holding a red pastille to her mouth, reminding myself of the girl Harriet had been only months before.

When I asked her what she was doing to occupy herself in the hours between sleep and work, she would shrug and say she was doing enough. But I thought it likely that she saw no one and spent the time only in sad dreams, and it was clear to anybody that she was not properly sustaining herself.

'And Mary? Have you visited her?' I said, knowing already that she had done so. This was perhaps indelicate of me, given the unfortunate nature of the affair, but I was eager somehow to rouse Harriet from what seemed to me her apathy. But she only nodded.

'She is very close?' I said, and again the nod.

'Grace asks after you,' I said, which Grace had not, though I knew Harriet to be much in my sister's thoughts. 'She wonders if you will visit her again in her garden?'

But my efforts were to no avail for she did not visit, and I was at my wits' end when, nearly a month after Thomas's death, Grace did at last speak of Harriet. The day was bright, the sky clear blue, and the wind light, allowing some slight warmth into the air. I followed Grace around her garden, me with a basket in either hand, she stalking its bounds, her secateurs ready, like a young cat. Every so often she would stop and cut away an offending twig, or else snip the stalks of a dozen crocuses and lay them carefully in one of my baskets, or prune back some new growth, startling in its early green, and tuck it beneath my arm. I was relieved to see her thus, for I had become concerned about her since Harriet had ceased to visit, that she was once again retreating to a silent place. I had noticed, and Nellie also had remarked, that she might go for days without speaking.

This gathering up was an old habit of ours. As far back as I could remember we had walked the garden in this way. When she was still only small and able to snip little more than daisies and dandelions, even then she would have me follow, basket in hand, as she skipped about the garden and gathered up her trophies. She would take them in proudly to Nellie and set them in jam jars and old pots.

There was one occasion, when Grace must have been perhaps eleven years old. It was late spring, like now. I was in my room when I heard a cry, like the cry of a wounded creature. Rushing from my room and down the stairs, I came upon Grace running like a wild thing from the kitchen and through the hall, her face a blaze of fury and pain. She didn't stop for me, but ran up the stairs and into her room, banging the door shut. In the kitchen I found both Nellie and Mother. Nellie shocked, Mother perfectly calm. The table was covered with branches of sticky buds, horse chestnut I think, that Grace must have rescued from the gardener's pile. Her room was always full of such things, their leaves bursting open, their earth and air smells. Mother had a branch in her hands and she did not stop upon my arrival in the room, but carried on bending and twisting it, tearing at it with a strength she did not normally possess. The branch was hard to break, its sappy greenness refusing to snap, so that the table was becoming a sticky mess of white fibres.

'I do not like such coarse prunings,' she said. 'I will not have them inside.'

She did not relent until every last branch was torn and twisted, though neither Nellie nor I assisted her, but only stood and stared. Then she had Nellie gather up the bits and take them back into the yard till the gardener could add them to his burning pile.

I wondered now whether Grace remembered this, and knew of course that she must. It was so strange, I thought, as Grace piled the baskets full with flowers and green stems, that such a passion could run in both mother and daughter, and yet run in such opposing currents.

'It is scorched.' Grace's voice shook me from my thoughts.

'What is scorched?'

'The magnolia. Look.'

At first I could see nothing wrong. Then I saw that the tree's swollen white buds were edged with brown.

'They won't open now,' Grace said. 'They won't flower. It was last night's frost.'

'Does it take only one frost to kill them?'

She didn't answer. Only picked one of the buds and laid it, tenderly in a basket. Her spirit had altered. I would have liked to console her, but I knew better than to speak.

We were returning to the kitchen when she spoke next.

'She should live in our house,' she said.

'Who should live in our house?'

'Well, I'm not speaking of the Queen,' Grace said crossly.

Her face, when she turned to look at me, was perfectly serious.

'Or else who will look after her?'

'Are you talking of Harriet?' I said. I could think of no one else, and yet we had not spoken of Harriet for several weeks. 'But you do not know how she does. You haven't seen her.'

'You've told me,' she said.

'I have spoken barely a word of her.'

'There's no need for you to speak,' she said, making my heart turn over, for I had no idea that my concern was written out so clearly. We walked on towards the house. 'I'll bring her here,' she said.

'How?' I said.

'I would have to move in, too' she said. 'I would have to leave The Haven. Because you'd have to tell them she was my companion.'

She took the baskets from me, heaved off her galoshes at the kitchen door and went in.

I don't know how long I stood there, Grace's branches clasped so tight to my chest that many hours later when I looked at myself in a glass I saw that my shirt and cuffs were smudged green. I knew that what Grace had said was true, though I did not know how to achieve it. But again I had reckoned without my sister's strange percipience and her frightening habit of making her own ends, regardless.

It was only a day later that I received a message from The Haven that Grace could not be found. She had not told them she was coming to our house, she had not told them she was going anywhere. Their concern was the greater because she had left her cat unfed, a thing she had never previously done.

The messenger found me not in my house, but at William's. William had asked me there that Saturday to discuss 'important business matters'. Although I found his use of me as a sparring partner incongruous, given that I had never shown any interest or talent in either my own tannery business or in his factory, and knew that it had more to do with our childhood intimacy than our present positions, I had met with him because to refuse would be to precipitate the argument I was not yet sure how to have. William mentioned, too, that after several days watching the girls arrive through the gates, he believed he had spotted a new poster girl, to replace the other.

Having no stomach now for William's business ventures, nor for his advertising, I was only relieved to be interrupted, even by such grave news. It was now after midday, and Grace had been missing since the early morning.

William and I set off at once, each of us saddling a horse. I rode only occasionally, preferring, when I could, to walk, and so I knew that I would be painfully stiff in the morning. We rode first to my house and searched both house and garden, William's voice as urgent as mine. It pained me to see his fear, only because it held a mirror up to my own.

On hearing my news, Nellie had broken down in tears at the kitchen table, tossing her apron over her head, and it was all I could do to gain from her an assurance that she would send message if she saw any sign of Grace. A jug of branches, those Grace had gathered only the day before, their greens bright in the kitchen's dim light, stood taut and tall like taunts on the dresser.

'No good will come of this,' William said. 'They will have to take more rigorous steps at The Haven.'

'We don't yet know what has happened,' I said, though my heart was already beating fast with apprehension.

'There is the railway line and the river,' he said. 'We should search them next. I think it best if we stay together.'

It did not occur to me to countermand my cousin, for all that Grace was my sister and that I was the elder of the two of us. The superiority I had had when we were children had long gone. William, by contrast, could no longer think except by command.

The sky had darkened by now and it was clear there would be rain. I hoped Grace was not out beneath it, for she had neither coat nor shawl. Both hung still in their places in her room at The Haven. We found no signs by rail or river, for which I gave silent thanks to God, though as William reminded me, if the river had her, it might not give up its treasure swiftly.

We had finished up on Queen's Staithe near Ouse Bridge, where the bargemen were going about their business as though all was well with the world. Dismounting, we walked the horses along the cobbles. My cousin checked his watch. It was gone four. He seemed suddenly nervous, unable to stand still on his feet.

'What is it William?' I said.

He checked his watch again.

'I cannot bear to, but I must go to the factory,' he said. 'I have made an appointment with Monseer Mazange.'

'The Frenchman? Is it very important?'

He nodded. 'It's a final lip test. For his new pastilles.'

'A lip test?' I said, and I think he can't have seen my expression, because he continued to explain as though I truly wished to know. But as I think back to that day, I can see how different are the diversions our minds find to save us from thinking on the thought we dread. William's mind, perhaps, retreated to the safety of his factory. And my mind – I do not know.

'We carry out a series of tests, such as the lip test,' William was saying, 'to be sure of no abrasions to the lips. These pastilles are to be sugar-coated, and there has been much debate between myself, Caleb and Monseer Mazange as to the coarseness of the crystals. As to whether finer would be better, or coarse.'

'I am sure coarseness is to be avoided,' I said, and still my tone of voice did not deter him. It was not that I believed him to be only uncaring, for I knew better than any his feelings for Grace, but I did not wish to join him in his distraction, especially since it had only to do with sweets.

'Certainly smoothness is preferable in most ways. But there is a certain pleasure in the abrasiveness of the crystals when they are followed by the smoothness of the pastille. There is also a question of cost.'

'Coarser is cheaper,' I said.

'Considerably,' he said. 'Caleb has made the calculations.'

'Well, you must go to your sugar crystals, cousin,' I said. Irony is not a condition for which I had ever before had much use, so perhaps William could not hear it in my voice.

'You will send word, Samuel?' he said, and I nodded. He embraced me. 'My prayer is with you,' he said, dropping his head in a moment of silent importuning, and then he was gone.

I stood undecided as to what to do. The thought that Grace might be somewhere out here, alone and in distress, I could not bear, but I could think of no good way of searching further for her. I worked at a loose cobble with the toe of my boot, angry with myself for my indecision, pushing away as best I could the shadows of foreboding.

A few yards away a man was loading a cart with pallets from a barge. His exclamation shook me from my reverie.

'Damn!'

I looked across. He had tripped on a rope in his haste with the last pallet, wrenching his ankle, and even as I watched, fish seemed to fly from the pallet onto the dirty wharf, their silver bellies catching the light. I walked closer. The man was hurrying now to pick up the fish, their flat, still bodies sliding from his fingers. Gathering the main of them, throwing their lifeless bodies back into the pallet, he hefted it onto the cart, climbed up himself and was gone, the wheels rattling over the cobbles.

I looked at those that remained. Their shiny skin was coated with black coal dust, scraps of straw and dirt. I kicked one and then another into the water. They floated only for seconds before the gulls were at them. I picked up a third, smoothing off the dirt and feeling the cold slippery scales, before I tossed this too into the river.

'Where have you gone, Grace?' I said, pleading with her to tell me somehow.

I do not know, but perhaps it was the smell of the fish on my fingers that made me think of Harriet. She was the only other person I knew of whom Grace might wish to see. I remounted my horse and set off for The Mount immediately, cutting an awkward figure, for in my urgency I rode with no thought to style.

Harriet's landlady opened the door to me with ill-disguised suspicion. My hair was unkempt and my brow shining not with rain, for it still held off, but with sweat. I made little attempt at politeness, but requested immediately to speak with her lodger on a matter of some urgency. While I waited, I gripped the railing that ran beside the house, so hard that when I let go, my fingers were white with the effort, and I endeavoured to compose myself, but I could see from Harriet's expression when she came to the door that I had not succeeded.

'What's happened?' she said, and at the simple sound of her voice, my anxiety overwhelmed me. Tears filled my eyes and my throat began to ache, so that not wishing to cry before her, I stayed silent until I could command myself better.

'It is Grace,' she said then, and I nodded.

'She's disappeared. We can find no sign of her,' I said, 'and I am afraid . . .'

'I'll come with you,' Harriet said, and I was glad that she had prevented me from finishing the sentence. Gathering a shawl, which was poor protection against the rain now falling, she insisted on joining me in my search.

My heart had sunk again when Harriet said she had heard nothing of Grace, and I questioned to myself whether she, a young woman of working stock with no money to spare and few resources, could really help me in this search. But I knew that aside from myself, William, who had his own family to look after, and Nellie, who was too old to be of much practical assistance, there was no one else who cared for her as profoundly.

Harriet's face looked so pale that I wondered, not for the first time, whether she wasn't sickening for something. Her eyes, dark in the late afternoon light, were very bright.

'You are well? Not sick?' I said.

'Well?' she said absently, as though the word was not one she understood. 'You've searched the garden?' she said then.

'Yes.'

'I'm not being rude, but where did you look?'

I knew what she meant and was not offended, so I told her of the places in the bushes and the long grass, the corner behind the glass house, and the dip in the ground beyond the fruit bushes.

'And the trees?' she said.

'We looked,' I said.

'But you didn't climb,' she said, and I shook my head.

'That's where we must go then,' she said.

As we made our way across the city, I should have loved to tell her of my last conversation with Grace, but knew right now that that would be foolish, so I held my tongue.

There was an old cedar tree at the end of the lawn beneath which Grace used often to play as a child, incurring Mother's wrath if she sighted her, for her frock and pinny would invariably be covered in dust and so forth. Harriet walked straight to this tree and stood below its canopy, staring up. I joined her, but I could see nothing except the spread of dark leaves.

'There's no sign of her,' I said.

Harriet made no answer, except to hitch up her skirts, as though she were about to climb down the cliff. Without even a look to me she pulled herself up into the branches. Soundlessly she climbed upwards. I could tell where she had reached from the slight shake her movements gave to the branches. Otherwise, she was silent, and invisible.

When I heard the murmuring, I thought at first Harriet must be talking to herself. She was gone so high I could not now see even the movements of leaves or the bending of branches. All I could do was stand beneath and listen. After a minute or so, I knew there to be two voices, and strange as it may seem, my first feeling was one of jealousy. I can admit to it now, though I should have denied it then, even to myself. When the voices grew no louder, and there was no sign of any descent being made, I stepped out from beneath the tree and stood in the rain and waited.

It was the longest hour of my life, that hour beside the cedar tree. Nellie brought me an umbrella, but otherwise I don't believe I moved. All thoughts left me, all hopes, all fears. Or perhaps it was that they gathered far up in the leaves above my head. I could hear only the sound of the rain on the umbrella as the light thickened towards darkness. It was not like any time before or since, though it was close to what I had heard other Quakers speak of when they felt they had come into the presence of God. There was no God there that I knew of then, but I did feel myself to be at the end of something.

When eventually the two girls came down, Harriet first and then Grace, I heard them before I saw them and I called their names up into the canopy, for what reason I could not say. Their movements were stiff from sitting so long in the tree. Fearing that they might fall if they jumped the last few feet, I insisted on lifting them down from the lowest branch. First Harriet, her waist firm and strong between my hands, her fingers cold when I took them to steady her. Then Grace, her body just as slight in my arms now as it had been when she was a little girl, and just as she had been then, so now, though she was a woman of twenty-eight years and wet through with the rain, she seemed the brilliant delicate jewel of a creature that she had always been.

I took them both in to the kitchen, where Nellie wrapped them in blankets and fed them with warm drinks. I cannot tell what it was I felt then, except to say that I knew I had found the thing I had been searching for for many years. Looking at the two young women, I was supremely happy.

'So now she must stay here with us, mustn't she, brother?' Grace said, a smile in her eyes, and I thought then, as I still do now, that maybe Grace had done all this only to bring about such an end.

I had Harriet conducted safely home later that evening, and sent word to William that Grace was safe. The next morning before First Day Meeting, William wished to hear all that had happened, and so I told him, more or less, though omitting Harriet's part in the tale entirely. He listened gravely and said he would speak more of this with me afterwards. I asked him how he had got on with his sugar granules, and he told me, with equal seriousness, that they had made their final decision, and this too he would let me know more of.

During Meeting William stood and spoke a prayer for a female friend, requesting that God defend her mind from the disturbance and imbalance to which it was prone. He asked God to help those that cared for her to find her a safe place in which she would prove no danger to herself, in which she could be looked after and given the help she needed. As I listened, I felt the hairs on the back of my neck bristle. I knew that William was speaking as he thought best, and I knew that such treatment would be the death of Grace.

'She must be prevented from such actions again,' William said afterwards. 'For her own sake, she must be detained until she is in a sounder state of mind, against her will if need be. Next time she will come to some real harm.'

'There is a reason for her behaviour,' I said, but he didn't listen.

'Are you certain she did not intend some harm to herself?' he said. 'Why else did she climb such a tall tree?'

'It's a tree she's always loved,' I said, at which William raised his eyes to the ceiling. 'I believe she had her own reason for her actions,' I said again.

We were speaking in a huddle, while around us others from the Meeting talked and gossiped with the relief there always was after the hour's silence. William had one hand on the wall, and his finger had started its tapping.

'If there is a reason for what she did yesterday, it is the reason of a person who is not in her sound mind,' William answered. 'The climbing of that tree and telling nobody of her whereabouts.'

'She does not see things as you or I,' I said. 'You remember how she was when we were children?'

'But she is no longer a child,' he said. 'And when we grow up, we must put away childish things.'

Thus we continued for some minutes more, though it was quickly apparent to me, and I believe also to him, that we would find no agreement.

'So you will decide what must be done,' William said at last.

I shook my head. 'It is for her to decide.'

'But you will make sure she is safe,' he said.

'Of course I will do everything within my power to ensure her safety, but I will not have her forcibly restrained, either in The Haven or anywhere else. I have suggested to her that if she wishes to leave The Haven, which she does, and move back home, then a companion will be a good idea.'

'And how on earth will you find such a person? No easy matter with her.'

'I believe we already have,' I said.

William shrugged, his expression anxious.

'Somebody suitable,' he said.

I nodded. 'She is already known to Grace.'

A young man approached William. 'It is time,' he said. 'The committee is gathered.'

William's finger stopped its tapping. 'I'm coming,' he said to the young man. 'You should join us,' he said to me. 'We are meeting to discuss the poor schools. Your experience with Benbow and his classes would be extremely useful, and I am sure you would not object to young men learning their letters from the Bible.' I made no reply. 'God help you if she should come to any harm,' he said then, which was a prayer that, for once, we shared. Then he was gone to his meeting and I stood in the midst of the bustle of Quaker men and women, as much alone here as if I were a single traveller in the heart of the desert.

HARRIET

Grace wanted to jump. She climbed up that tree to jump out of it. I've always known that, but I've never told anybody. I've never even told Grace, but then I don't think she knew it herself. She wanted to jump and so she climbed high as she could, and when she got up there, she couldn't do it. It's hard out of a big tree. The branches get in the way. You've not got a clear drop. And she hadn't the time to get down and find a better place, not without them finding her first. So she just stopped up there and waited to see what would happen.

I didn't think about it much, climbing up and in, the branches like steps. But I was out of breath by the time I reached her. She was hunkered right down, back against the trunk, one arm hooked over a branch, and talking. I could see her talking but I couldn't hear it, what with the noise in my ears of my climbing.

When I reached her she stopped, and just looked at me like it was no surprise to see me here.

'You're not as good at it as I thought you would be,' she said, as if her climbing up and me climbing after her was a game we were playing, hide and seek maybe.

'I'm short on practice,' I said.

'Don't you miss it?' she said. 'That cliff of yours?'

I shrugged. 'It's dry in here,' I said.

'Listen,' Grace said and we listened to the rain falling, and us dry as a bone under all the leaves.

It was Mary I thought on up that tree. Mary and her baby, which must be about born, and the scrap of paper I'd given Mr Benbow like she'd asked. She knew I wouldn't try to read it. I can guess what was in that note, and maybe Mary was right not telling me, because I might never have delivered it. I might have stood on Ouse bridge, scrumpled it in to a ball and dropped it into the river. I might very well have done that, though I'm glad now that I didn't.

I'd gone to the studio on Coney Street and rung the bell. The street was busy with women shopping, with ladies making purchases, and one or two still caught their eye on me, knowing they'd seen me somewhere, but it wasn't more than one or two now. I'd stood at the door and waited. Eventually Miss Hornsgarth had come. I'd told her I'd a message for Mr Benbow and she was sour, her mouth like vinegar when I wouldn't give it her. But in the end she had to call him down.

'It's from Mary,' I'd said when he came, his forehead knitted. I'd pulled the scrap from my boot and put it in his hand. He'd read it quickly and started to say something, about being sorry, but I'd stopped him.

'I promised her I'd give it you' I'd said.

'Do you know what it says?' he'd asked me and I shook my head. 'Will you take a message back?' he'd said.

'I don't know when I'll next see her,' I'd said.

'Well if you do,' he'd said, 'will you tell her . . .'

'One word then,' I'd said.

'Tell her "yes".'

I'd turned to walk away, and so he spoke to my back, and people watching us.

'She's right about you,' he'd said.

It might have been five minutes, or fifty, I couldn't tell. But it was getting dark and I'd a twig sticking me in the back and pins and needles in one foot, to say nothing of the cold of sitting there.

'It's cold,' I said. Grace didn't answer me. 'Will you come down?'

She gave a sudden laugh. 'You'll come in and have some tea,' she said. 'Nellie'd be cross if you didn't,' and she made a face to show Nellie cross which I couldn't help but laugh at, though I don't know where the laugh came from.

'Did you know I'm leaving?' she said. 'That room? I'm coming back here now. Just me and my cat. Today would be a good day I think.'

'Grace,' I said.

'You're too thin,' she said. 'You're not eating like you ought. That's why you feel cold,' and before I could answer her, she scrambled past me, and started down the branches at such a pace, it was all I could do to keep up.

She was talking all the way down, and if it was to me, I couldn't make out the words. But it was an odd thing that just when she stopped speaking, and we were still high enough that you couldn't see the ground, she nearly fell. I say she fell, but I saw her step out on to the air quite carefully, watching her feet, clear as day.

'Grace!'

The shout came out of me, forced itself out of my mouth, out and into the tree air.

Something had made me see it just before, like she was moving different, or maybe it was that she'd gone quiet. She stepped, and just in time, catching my elbow a blow that left it swollen the next day, I caught her by the collar and yanked her back. We stood, both of us shaking more than the leaves.

'It was Fern,' Grace said. 'I couldn't see her, but I could hear her.'

'Fern?' I said.

'She was here before you,' she said. 'A long while back. I expect she'll be glad to meet you.'

Underneath I could hear Mr Ransome's voice calling, anxious. 'Grace? Harriet? Grace?', doing turn and turn about with our names.

'It's torn,' she said, her fingers feeling at her neck. 'Will you tell Nellie I couldn't help it? That I slipped? She'll be cross at me tearing it otherwise.'

You know how it is when you get cold, so cold you can't feel your feet or your fingers, and it's all right except you know you've to get warm again and it'll hurt? I remember it when I was little and my mother telling me off for staying out so long, being cross and gentle at the same time. So as I'd not know whether I hated being so cold for the pain of it, or liked it, so as I could put my hands between her warm ones, and then my feet, and have her rub them, finger by finger, toe by toe, taking them in turn like she used to tell the rhyme about the piggy after a bath. I'd have to sit in close to her those times and if I thought I'd get away with it, I'd bury my face in her apron for the smell of her which wasn't like any other.

That's how I was in the first months after Thomas had gone. So cold it didn't hurt almost and I didn't much care what happened to me, and not daring to get warm again. I didn't want anyone to rub my fingers or toes because I didn't want to feel it hurt, and it was going to hurt so badly, and not even my mother'd be able to help, besides which I couldn't go home. Not now.

When Mr Ransome asked me would I be companion to Grace, it wasn't like a question, though I could have said no, I suppose.

'But I'm not the right kind of girl,' I said. 'You want to find another Quaker lady. An educated lady. I don't know things.'

'She won't accept anyone else,' he said.

'What about my job? At Wetherbys?'

'You'd have to leave it,' he said.

'How could I?' I said.

'I'd pay you a salary, and you'd need to move in to the house, of course.'

I wasn't used to Mr Ransome being like this. It seemed like he'd made up his mind before he even asked me.

'And then there's Mr William? He'd find out soon enough. A Wetherby's girl living in his cousin's house. There'd be talk. From my lot and yours.'

'I don't believe there would be any trouble from William. And we would say you were a maid.'

'Grace wouldn't though, would she?'

'No. She wouldn't. And it is true it will likely bring censure upon me,' he said, 'but I believe it to be in her best interests and I stand before God acting as I do. Let men find me as they will.'

'But if the vicars of your church think you're doing something very wrong? You and Grace? They could put you out of it, couldn't they?'

'I don't believe they would disown me,' he said, and he'd a smile at the corners of his mouth, though I couldn't think why, 'though certainly they could make my life difficult. But I've made my decision. My sister's well-being comes before the good opinion of the Meeting,' and his face was stern.

'What if I say no?' I said.

'Then Grace will stay in The Haven. Though she no longer wishes to.'

Girls had left Wetherby's, to be married mainly, while I'd been there, but I'd never paid a lot of notice to how they did it. I didn't know what you'd to do, or what you'd to say, or who you'd to say it to, so I asked Elsie. We were sat by the river after work, our legs dangling over the edge of the jetty. The sun made the water sparkle so bright I couldn't look at it straight.

'I don't have to say it to Mr William, do I?' I asked Elsie.

She laughed.

'No. Don't you think he's got better things to do? You tell Mrs Flint and then she goes and tells one of the clerks. You're sure you want to go?'

'Yes.'

'And it's not because of Thomas?'

'No. I told you.'

'Because it's not bad money here, nor work, as work goes.'

'I know.'

'And even the assemblies, you can just sit there and think on something else when you're bored. Me, I don't mind a few minutes sitting. It's the only chance I get otherwise.'

'No, I know. It's not the assemblies, or the work,' I said, which was true, because the work was just work. You'd to get through it, which you did, and it was boring as sin, but then gutting fish isn't a bundle of laughs. 'I've just got a better offer. I'll be able to save a bit even.'

Usually when Elsie talked, her eyes were going all over, watching the other comings and goings, just in case. But now she looked at my face, which made me feel uncomfortable, and not being used to it, I couldn't tell what she thought she was seeing, because I wasn't used to her looking.

'You're not telling me, are you?' she said at last. 'There's something up and you're not telling me,' and it wasn't her that did it, not really, only she was the one that was there when it happened, but I got blazing with anger then.

Across the river from us, dirty water spewed out of a hole in a barge, a brown froth of it hitting the water in gulps while a man pumped.

'It's funny, isn't it? That Thomas gave his life for Wetherby's,' I said. 'Gave his actual life, and gave my life too. Because now he's gone and I couldn't care if I live or die. They've had that off me. The factory has. But there's Mr William and Mr Caleb and they just go on like before.' I started to laugh, felt it building in my chest, tightening in my throat.

'Making cocoa and pastilles and buckets of money. And we do our jobs day and day out, and then we're just chewed up and spat out.'

I was laughing hard now, loud enough to make people turn.

'And so long as they think they've spat us out the right side of heaven, they don't care. Isn't it funny, Elsie?' I said.

'You shouldn't talk like that,' she said. 'You should have married him.'

I looked at her, my laugh gone cold in my throat, and she put a hand to her mouth, because she saw what was in my eyes.

'You did,' she whispered. 'You married him, didn't you?' and I nodded, I told her yes, because there was no reason not to now.

I went at the end of week. Gave my notice to Wetherby's and to my landlady and that was that. Come Saturday, which was my last day there, when the bell rang at two, I made a pile of my Holland pinafore and galoshes, got a quick hug from the other girls and it was finished.

Even Mrs Flint didn't mind my going or give me a hard time like she did with other girls, because after all I wasn't getting married. I'd already done that, if she only knew it. It was only Elsie who minded and I told her she'd be used to it before another week was out, find herself another friend. That was

how it went. Just like Mr William would find another girl for
the pictures. There'd be nothing to say I was ever there. But I
didn't care very much. I didn't care about anything very much
then.

It was like a tide of girls leaving at the end of the day, and
Saturday more than most, it being a half-day. Everybody
wanted to be outside, in the light, away from the smell, which
I'd never have believed when I started because it seemed so
sweet after the fish. That smell of roasting cocoa nibs and of
sugar syrup and the smell of the fruit. But it clagged about
your nose and went into your head, that sweetness. It made
the air thick to breathe so that though I didn't want to go
home, I longed for the salt and wind of the sea which made
the air thin and sharp.

So that last day, when I wanted to go the other way, I felt
like some tiny wave turning against the ocean. I'd to fight
every inch against the drift. But I forced my way to the side
and went back up the corridor again.

You weren't meant to go into the factory rooms once the
last bell had rung. You were meant to go straight to the cloak-
room and then out. It was written in the Rules which were
stuck to the wall, though there weren't a lot of girls could read
them. But I'd nothing to lose now, so I pushed open the roasting room door and walked in. It wasn't anything special I
wanted, and it was more because of Thomas than because of
me. Just to stand a last time in here.

The heat hit me in the face like a wind. The room was
empty, which I was glad of, except for the one man, a big
fellow with sideburns and a great beard. He didn't see me at
first, being busy with some shovelling from out of the roasters.
His cap, which he had pulled full down over his brow, and the
back of his waistcoat were dark with sweat so that he looked
near as wet as a fisherman coming back from a day's work. He
was whistling, not so much a tune, it didn't sound like, as just

a noise. I stood in the room and imagined Thomas coming in just then with some message, maybe, or a number to check in his books. How he'd push open the door, like it were something put in his way on purpose, and then come in to the middle of the room with his quick steps and stand looking about, impatient, eager to be on with it, whatever it was. I imagined him finding his man and standing close to him while the fellow might be tipping hot cocoa beans, or shovelling coke into the furnace, or up a ladder adjusting some great cog or wheel. Thomas never was much of a respecter of other people's tasks, and he never gave a body peace till he had his answer. I knew that as well as any, even if it was me who did the asking on the question of our marriage. I smiled, imagining him halfway up another man's ladder, and then a voice from outside my head shook away my daydream and I was back standing in the middle of the roasting room and my last day at Wetherby's finished.

'Harriet Brewer.'

I looked round. Mr William had come in the room and he stood there, calm like always, waiting for me to answer. I didn't say anything.

'What are you doing in here?'

I still didn't answer him, though I'd a thousand words on my tongue I'd have liked to say. The man on the ladder had turned and was glaring at me.

'Please explain yourself,' Mr William said, still in his oh-so-calm voice.

'I'm gone, Mr William. I a'n't here any more,' I said.

'That may be so, but you know the rules,' he said.

'The Rules!' My voice wasn't loud, but it made him flinch. I was speaking to him in a way I'd never have dared even an hour before. 'What's the Rules for, Mr William?' I was trying not to say much, because I didn't trust myself. Didn't trust what I might say, whoever he was stood before me.

'I don't think your tone is necessary, Harriet Brewer. You know that they are for the safety of the staff and for the good of the firm. We can't have girls wandering about the roasting rooms. It's not safe.'

The man in the cap was still up the ladder, listening in. Even as I was standing there, I could guess what he was thinking. 'What the hell is that fidget of a girl doing talking to the Master like that?' Mr William must have noticed him the same time as I did, because he gave him a look and told him to get on with his job, before speaking to me again, in a lower voice.

'As I said, it is not safe for you to wander about in here, and as your Master till you leave these premises, I must ask you to leave.'

'You're very good to us, a'n't you, Mr William? Looking after us? Making sure we never get hurt. Girls and men. Clerks too, I don't doubt. Making sure we never fall badly, like that fellow might do if he gawps at us any longer,' and I pointed at the man in the cap, who was still staring, and left the room, making sure to slam the door after me.

I hadn't a lot to take when I left my lodgings. More than when I'd first arrived in the city, more than I could carry, but still not very much. Thomas's *Leisure Hours* weighed the most. I sat them on the seat beside me in the carriage, but I didn't think on him, on how he'd sprawl out on the bed to read, or how he'd wiggle his toes when he got to a bit he liked. I just sat there with my cold fingers and my cold toes and thought that I'd never be warm again.

Thomas used to read me out about explorers and scientists like they were people he knew.

'Listen to what Mr Huxley's been up to,' he'd say, or 'Look, Mr Common's got a smashing photograph of Orion,' and he'd be excited by it all and telling me how they did it. But that was gone now and it was like they'd shut up shop when

Thomas died, those men discovering things, and I was left
with all the useless lumber of their work.

Nellie showed me my room, which was near hers, told me
what was what, that Grace would be coming in a couple of
days, that Mr Ransome was gone to his cousin's country house
for the weekend.

'That'd be Mr William, would it?' I said.

'That's right,' she said. 'He's a house near Kirkham Abbey,
if you've heard of it,' and I nodded.

So it was just the two of us in the house since she'd given
the other servants two days' leave. Then she left me to unpack
my things.

I was done in minutes and sat down on the bed, wondering
what to do after. The mattress was the softest I'd ever sat on. I
laid my head on the pillow, just to feel it, and it must've just
come over me, the sleep, because I didn't even remember
falling into it.

It was dark when I woke and Nellie was sat by the bed.
There was a rug tucked over me she must have put there.

'Harriet. Wake up now and have some tea,' she was saying
gently, one hand on my shoulder. The touch of her hand. I
didn't know how long it was since anybody had put their hand
on my shoulder, much less a hug, or a kiss. It felt like an age,
but it mustn't have been much more than a few weeks.

Down in the kitchen, while Nellie was busy about pouring
the tea, I sat silent at the table, my head flooded with thoughts.
Nellie had shown me round the house. Grace's room, the
Master's, the old Mistress's, what she called the Dark Room,
which was full of photographic machinery, the Nursery. I knew
Mr Ransome had had the house painted to lure Grace back,
and that's what it still smelled of. It didn't smell of a family any
more, only of the paint that fairly gleamed.

I'd passed the paintings that hung in the hall and up the
stairs before, when Mr Ransome had me to tea, and after with

Grace, but I'd never really looked at them. They stopped me in my tracks today.

'The family,' Nellie said, following my look, and she pointed out the old faces, Grace's parents and grandparents and back before even, all wearing what I knew now were their Quaker caps and collars, funny-looking and solemn, their hands holding a Bible, or clutched on their lap. To keep them out of mischief, I thought.

'Not exactly a cheery lot,' I said.

'Harriet!' Nellie said, but her face was smiling.

'But can you see Grace anywhere?' I said. I pointed to the one nearest the top of the stairs. 'Mr Ransome, I can see him just a bit in that one.'

'That's his father,' Nellie said. 'He was a good Master. A tanner,' and she took me in to the kitchen for tea.

Nellie was glad to have me there, I could see that. Maybe because she'd a funny place in things as well, being a bit of everything to Mr Ransome and Grace. Housekeeper mainly, but something closer too, which the other servants weren't. So while she fetched our tea, and again the next morning over some breakfast, she gossiped about how things went on here, and what Mr Ransome liked, and what Grace. And her words swirled about me and touched on my skin like pins because it wasn't my family she was talking of, no more than it was hers. And I wondered most of all why I didn't go home now, even though I knew it was my dad kept me away. But there was nothing I'd have loved so much as my mam's arms holding me tight and the smell and the sight of that kitchen. The smell of wet wool there always was with my mam drying off the socks and the sweaters from the boat, and the marks on the wall and the dark boards of the ceiling. I was so homesick, and I'd never been so alone.

But I couldn't go. It'd only take one night. Or one day or one hour and I'd never have left again. Never have wanted to leave my mam, never have been brave enough to fight my dad. Not without Mary's skirts to ride on. 'One day, when you've somebody to go and come away with,' I told myself. And until then, it'd be a note sent to tell them I was doing fine and that'd be the sum of it.

It had been more than two weeks since I'd last seen Mary, and I couldn't wait through till the next Saturday, which was the day for visiting. Nellie had shown me everything there could be in a house to show now, and fed me up at dinner like a pig for Christmas, so I was glad of the walk across the city.

The big house behind the wall looked just the same. Maybe I thought there'd be a sign that'd tell me Mary had had her baby, I don't know. I stood in the hall again, with Jesus hung up on one side, and dandled on the other, and told myself I wasn't going till they let me see her.

It was a new nun that came down the stairs.

'I'm here to see Mary Bourne,' I said quick.

'I'm sorry, but—' she said, before I interrupted.

'I'm here to see her and I a'n't going till I do,' and I folded my arms like my own mother used to when she was set on something.

The nun was stood at the bottom of the stairs. 'You can't see her—' she said, but I didn't wait for her to finish, pushing past her and up the stairs, along to the room Mary was put in.

'Mary,' I said, and I knocked at the door. There was no answer, but I could hear somebody moving inside. 'Mary,' I said again, louder. 'It's me, Hal,' and before the nun could stop me, I turned the handle.

The room was just the same as before, and the tree outside the window, except it wasn't Mary sat on the bed. It was another girl, a red-headed creature closer to being a child than to being an adult, in another ugly sack dress with another swollen belly, and she was looking up at me, scared.

'Where's Mary?' I said. 'Why're you here, in her room, on her bed? Where is she?'

The girl didn't speak, just put her hands over her belly, like you might put your hands over the ears of a child to stop it hearing bad words. But a voice behind me, which was the nun's, answered.

'She's gone.'

I turned round. The nun was stood there, her face as much of a mask as her dress and hat were.

'She's gone,' she said again.

'You've sent her away?' I said, too shocked to be angry yet.

The nun shook her head. 'She left. It was her decision,' she said. 'We tried to persuade her to stay. She hadn't a proper sense of her duty.'

'But the baby?'

'She took the baby with her,' she said.

'It's been born,' I said, something tight twisting itself round my stomach.

The nun nodded.

'But why did she go? I said. I was dazed, like somebody had belted me one across the head.

The nun shrugged, which didn't seem like a thing nuns should do, put an arm across my shoulders and took me out of the room again, shutting the door on the strange girl. When we were down in the hall, she sat me in a chair.

'A gentleman came for her,' she said. 'Three days ago. She left us no address.'

'And the baby,' I said.

'As I've said, she took him with her.'

'A boy then,' I said. 'So you didn't get him,' which got the mask off of her face. And I left and walked back towards the city.

I could have gone straight to Mr Benbow's studio, but I

didn't. Something stopped me. I was sure Mary'd be there, but she must know how much I'd want to see her and the baby, help any way I could. So if she hadn't found me yet, there'd be a good reason. I knew she was up to some plan, what with the note she'd had me deliver to Mr Benbow and what she'd told me last time I'd seen her. Maybe, whatever it was, it'd all gone by the board now the baby was out, but I didn't think it likely. She's stick to a thing like one of Thomas's limpets, Mary would, once she'd got it in her head.

I'd nothing to gain but a slice of her tongue by jumping her. So I walked back to the Ransome's house, sat down at the kitchen table and told Nellie about the baby boy, and tears streamed down my face, which was strange because I didn't think I was crying.

SAMUEL

My father wasn't a religious man, but he was a good one. He supported those Quakers who battled for years to change what – by the middle of the nineteenth century – seemed obstructively exclusive and odd about our faith. Such as disownment of any who married out, and plainness of dress. Because banishing any who married a non-Quaker and the wearing of strange collars and waistcoats, bonnets and black, the unusual stigmata imposed upon us, didn't so much keep Quakers from the world as keep the world from the Quakers. Quaker numbers were falling rapidly.

Although he could no more imagine himself an Anglican, a Methodist or a Muslim than he could imagine flying to the moon, Father believed strongly that people must be allowed to find different ways of living their lives.

'It's like an algebraic problem,' he said. 'There are different routes to the same solution,' and despite my incompetence with figures, I understood the analogy.

'Catholics and Quakers, Roundheads and Cavaliers, we're all the same before God. And we all have similar fears,' he would say. 'That if you take away the forms, then nothing will be left of the substance. Quakers are no different. Our peculiar dress and speech, they're just a different form of fetishism.'

We had these conversations on the walk to the tannery, or at the end of a meal when Mother had retired. I knew not to raise such questions when she was there, for this was something over which they disagreed. Even Grace, who is so rarely subject to other people's fears, understood that to voice such views would be to jeopardise her parents' fragile calm. Anyway, it was only herself she ever acted against. She always went to great lengths to protect those she loved.

When we were children, Mother used to have us read out the testimonies of deceased ministers. We would sit in the drawing room before dinner on First Day, and each of us but her would have to take a turn. It was painfully dull and, despite my efforts, Mother's frowns and Father's silent appeals, I would fidget as fearsomely as Grace.

Once it happened that the testimony was of someone we knew, and on this occasion it was Grace who was reading:

Martha Tidcup understood the purity of the Lord's ways and from adulthood she desired that others would know of them too. She was born in Pickering to parents whose lives were given up to corruption, to the fashions and pleasures of the world, including the pernicious habit of novel reading. Knowing no better, she, too, spent her early years in pursuit of such things. But in her quest for a better way, she attended every kind of religious gathering, including those that would be best avoided, until in her sixteenth year she was taken by a friend to a Quaker Meeting. Here she found what she had been searching for.

Soon after she came to a knowledge of the Lord, and
from this time on was fearless in her proclaiming of his
truth.

Driven from home by her corrupt parents, whom
she was unable to convince of their error, she dedicated
her long and fruitful life, the most part of it in York, to
convincing others of the true path of righteousness . . .

It was Mother who interrupted.

'Thank you Grace. We will leave it there.'

And we all knew why. This woman had dedicated her life to
making others miserable. The testimony, which had already
been read out to Quaker leaders, was little short of a tissue of
lies.

'I read the rest of it,' Grace said to me later. 'It gets worse.
You'd think she was Napoleon, she had so many victorious
battles. Then at the end, going out in such a blaze of glory.'

And standing on a chair, she declaimed a version of Martha
Tidcup's life that ran so close to the fact as to provoke in me an
uncontrollable wave of laughter.

I remember well what Grace said next, for it was quite a
speech for her, and I wrote the words down in a notebook.

'Lives are not so rounded,' she said. 'You can't see the end in
the beginning.'

'But they say that Napoleon's future glory could be read
even in his earliest steps,' I said

Grace shook her head.

'No. Lives rear up like startled horses. They change direction, and not when expected. And at the end they often seem
not something shapely, but a tangle.'

Then she climbed down from her chair and I glimpsed her
from my bedroom window, running down the garden, her
bootstrings trailing, hair flying behind her.

It has taken me longer than it took Grace to see that horses rear. Or, to use a different analogy for myself, there are times when one's life is swung round, head and feet both, like a child turning a clockwork mouse, and made to face in a different direction. And unlike the testimony for Martha Tidcup and unlike the great generals, it doesn't all come neatly to a proper end, but is a ragged business from which one makes the best shape one can.

Harriet's arrival fulfilled two of my greatest wishes. That Grace would return home, and that I would at last have living with me the girl I knew I loved.

Yet this business was not the simple thing I had thought it would be. I had forgotten, for instance, Grace's habit of absenting herself when she so chose. Not in the way she had done when she had climbed the tree, because in general she made no secret of where she had gone to, but simply in her refusal to respond, or participate in the daily round. I saw for the first time how in certain ways she resembled Mother, quite happy, if need be, to have the household revolve about her daily whims.

Then, too, I had thought that Harriet's arrival with us would lift her spirits, and indeed it did. But she was still mourning for her dead husband and there was something in her that did not care much what happened, to herself at least. Even more than Grace, she seemed likely to go out unprotected in a rainstorm, and, as Nellie told me, what she was eating wouldn't keep a butterfly alive.

Harriet would not eat with us in the dining room but insisted on eating in the kitchen with Nellie and the other servants, and nothing I could say would persuade her. And she demanded that I issue her with instructions on her daily tasks.

'You need have none,' I said. 'You're here as companion to Grace.'

But she shook her head and said that if I did not issue them, she would not stay.

I supposed that her tone was impertinent, but I could see the justice of her demand. She could not be all things to all men, nor all things to me, but must know where it was that she stood. So I had Nellie draw up a list of light duties.

And in the privacy of my own room, even more than in the house at large, I discovered how Harriet's arrival had left all changed.

With all that had gone on in the previous year, Mother's death, William's advertising and so on, I had done little for some time in pursuit of my private photography project. It was many years since I had taken my own. But it was months, too, since I had accompanied a girl to Benbow's studio. I could still have bought photographs from him, as I had done in the past, of all sorts of girls from all sorts of places, such as the pit brow girls, the chain workers, the Welsh tip girls, or even the French fishergirls in their distinctive coloured petticoats and white frilled caps who smiled so prettily for the camera. But now I had discovered three things, the first two over a period of months, the third only since Harriet's arrival.

Firstly that not to meet the girls, fresh from the fruits of their labours, their foreheads and their forearms still sheeny with the sweat of dignified labour, was to lose much of my purpose. Secondly, that although I believed my pictures to show something true, the Wetherby's advertising campaign had proved that photographs could as easily lie as tell a truth, and this had drawn the fire from my project. Thirdly, and most importantly, I need gather no more girls because the one I wanted beyond any other was here, living in my house.

When I began my collection of photographs, I had organised them by date. The first girls I photographed were at the front of the first album, and so on. This went on until I found that if I were looking for the photograph of a particular girl, I was more likely to remember her appearance than I was the date on which I had had her photograph taken. And anyway there were all those I had never met, but whose photographs I had only bought, and I did not necessarily keep a record of the date of purchase. So I tried a different scheme. Working on broadly similar principles to those within which I had mounted my butterflies, I grouped the girls according to distinguishing characteristics. As I had grouped my butterflies by wing shape and size, veins, markings and colour, so my girls were grouped by features such as stature, hand size, length of forehead, size of skull etcetera. It was a crudely phrenological arrangement that would have pleased William, who was much taken with models of physiological determination, but it quickly dissatisfied me, proving no easier a method for locating particular girls than the previous one.

It was a formidable labour to unmount and remount what had, by now, become a sizeable collection. But it was a labour of love. And finally on my third attempt I discovered the most effective system. I simply grouped the girls by occupation, or trade, including as a last section a miscellaneous category, where I could no longer remember what the girl's work had been and where she held no props in the photograph to indicate it.

Since Mother's death I had shelved the albums openly, in a small set of oak shelves from Father's study, which I stood to the left of the fireplace in my room. They looked handsome in their red morocco bindings, each volume numbered and indexed. I would take one out at random, place it on the table and let it fall open where it would. I would open the volume in this way and there would be a girl facing me with her strong young face, a spade or a hoe, a sack or a basket in her hand or over her shoulder. I would stare in at her, imagining her hands at work, her expression intent, her shoulders braced with the effort of the task, and sometimes I would be caught unawares and find myself a half hour later exhausted with the intensity of my regard. Other times I would be content simply to have put such an image into my mind's eye, a figure held at the back of my mind even when engaged in such tedious but necessary duties as reviewing the accounts for the tannery, or writing letters in support of the Home for Unfortunate Young Women or some such.

However, with Harriet in my house, I no longer bought photographs. I might open an album as before and let my eyes fall upon a picture at random, but I did not focus. And when I lay in my bed at night, my thought was that now at last, I had with me the girl I had been looking for.

I do not know that the stoppering of anger is a good thing. But it is what I was brought up to and I am too much in the habit to change now. But as far as Grace is concerned, I believe I have only ever been angry with her the once.

It was a few weeks after Harriet's arrival, the evening Grace came to see me. Though the sun had dropped from the sky, the air was still close. Being given somewhat to perspiration, in the privacy of my room I have always undone my collar, removed my waistcoat and rolled up my shirtsleeves when the weather is warm. But my sister is different, and aside from this one occasion, I have never seen even the slightest shimmer of heat upon her.

If she knocked, I didn't hear it. I didn't hear her open the door, nor did I hear her enter. I don't know how long she stood behind me while I pulled albums from the shelves, in a somewhat desultory fashion, turning the pages over so fast that the girls flicked before my eyes, heads and arms and legs shifting, like the dancer in a zoetrope or some child's book of magic pictures. And it was no movement of hers that made me turn finally, but some sound elsewhere in the house.

She stood silent before me, which was no more than she'd done all her life, being someone who had never spoken to fill space, and her brow was shiny with sweat and her cheeks so flushed that I thought first she must be carrying a fever. And it may be that the pitch she had brought herself to had indeed raised the temperature of her blood.

'Is there something you need?' I said. 'Or want to talk to me of?' I still had a volume of photographs in my hands, and I moved now to set it down on the table.

It was the suddenness of her gesture that caught me out, her arm reaching for the book that took me aback, so that it was without thinking that I pushed her away, anger rising unbidden in me like bile, the book falling to the floor where it lay spread-eagled between us.

'What do you want?' I said, and I think we were both shaken by the fury in my voice, I no less than her, for I stood still then and let the sound of it die in the room, making no move, saying no word till I could be sure of myself again.

'Grace?' I said finally. I hoped she might sit down, curl herself up in my armchair as had always been her habit, tug with her fingers at the loose threads in the rug. But she stayed standing.

'I have no photograph,' she said.

'Photograph?' I said.

'Mother allowed me nothing that she could take from me,' she said.

'Nothing of what?' I said.

'Your girls have been a comfort to you,' she said. 'She made me go with nothing, not even a photograph,' and I realised at last that she was speaking of the time of her leaving. The time after her friendship with Deborah, when she had first gone in to The Haven. Then she shook her head. 'But that is not what I came about.'

She walked over to the albums and ran her fingers along their spines, pausing over some as though she might pull them out and open them. And watching her, I knew suddenly that she had been in here before, that she had looked at the pictures not just occasionally with me, but also by herself.

'You can give them up now, Samuel. It's that time,' she said, and she left the room.

The cadence of Harriet's footfall haunted me. The timbre of her voice, which oftentimes I could hear about the house or garden, laughing with Grace, or gossiping with Nellie, or humming some vague tune as she worked, found a correspondence in my senses. When, occasionally, we passed one another in a corridor or on the stairs, she with her head ducked, me with my eyes slightly averted, not wishing to embarrass her, I was content simply to feel the instant of proximity as our bodies drew close for a short moment before she was gone. The photographs now seemed pale imitations beside the living, breathing creature I had so close.

I soon learned to guard, not my mouth, but my eyes, though perhaps not soon enough, for I know that Grace and I suspect that Nellie knew something of the measure of my regard for Harriet. That her presence in our house had as much to do with my wish as with anything else. Still I was grieved that this change of society and of occupation had not pulled Harriet from her slough of despond.

So when I received the note from Benbow, I hoped it related to Harriet's friend Mary and her baby, who must surely be born by now. Because at the very least this would offer my beloved girl some diversion.

'I request the pleasure of your company at your earliest convenience,' the note read. 'The boy who brings it will await your answer. Sincerely yours, John Benbow.'

The scrap of a lad standing before me regarded me with an apprehensive expression, and when I told him to go that way, to the kitchen, and ask the cook for some bread and milk while I replied, he did not go, but stood his ground and told me that Benbow had instructed him not to let me out of his sight till he had his answer.

I had no idea what Benbow could wish to speak to me of with such urgency, but directly dinner was over, I went.

The evening was balmy. A slight breeze caught at the trees and the air was sweet with the fragrances of early summer. Snatches of late sun still flashed through the leaves. A bevy of fledglings lurched with still-primitive wings in the air above my head, their parents singing out warnings. I had taken one of my father's walking sticks, one I had loved as a child for its head carved into the shape of a fish, and I strode out with an unusual sense of freedom. It felt, for the duration of the walk, as though all my burdens and responsibilities, which I did not resent but whose weight, nevertheless, I always felt on my shoulders, as if all those had been lifted away. And, but for the lack of wings, I was as free as the wood larks and the wood-peckers I heard about me.

Only when I drew near to the studio did a proper sense of my duties descend once again upon my shoulders, pushing off my wishful wings, though I could still hear the lark's song in my head.

Benbow must have been watching for me, because he was there before I could even ring the doorbell.

'Thank you for coming so swiftly,' he said. He led me up the stairs to the studio at the top, and as I entered, Harriet's image crossed my sight, as she had been on that first occasion when she met me here, so near still to the sea, timid and raw.

As I had speculated, Mary Bourne sat in the room. She rose to greet me and I was struck for the first time by what I now saw was her uncommon beauty. So struck that I believe I forgot for a moment what it was she had just become, and noted the crib behind her only as one of Benbow's props, so that I remember the question crossing my mind as to what such a thing was doing there, and why it had not been tidied away into the shadows with the other studio paraphernalia.

Her face met mine with an expression that has stayed with me always. Something between hope and defiance, her eyes wide with hope, her mouth taut, as though she were waiting for a refusal, though of what I had no idea.

The expression lasted no more than a second, for then a noise came from the crib, and she bent to it, one hand to her bosom, the other already pulling back the crib covers.

The noise, of course, was the thin wail of a new baby, and before my eyes Mary lifted out a bundle and cradled it in her bosom, so that as quickly as the cry had risen, just as quickly it dropped. She seated herself again, and looked up at me, for without realising, I had stood when the baby wailed. I sat down, my body heavy with embarrassment, both that I could have forgotten, even for a minute, that she had only just given birth, and at the prospect before me, of mother and suckling child.

'We've asked you here on a matter of grave importance,' Benbow said.

'We?' I said.

He nodded, and before I could say anything further, Mary spoke, her voice surprising me with its firmness.

'Mr Benbow has agreed to wait outside while I speak to you,' and even as she said this, he was walking to the door.

'Is this something he knows about?' I said when he had gone.

'Yes,' she said. 'He knows everything. He has been a very good friend in these last weeks. But before I speak, please tell me how Harriet does?'

'She wonders why she has not heard from you,' I said, which was a cruel thrust and one I instantly regretted as Mary dropped her head.

'She grieves,' I said. 'She is stronger than she was, I believe, and eating a little more, and her companionship of Grace . . .' I stopped. 'You knew, did you, that she had left the factory?'

'I had heard,' Mary said. 'I cannot bear it, not seeing her.'

'Harriet is fond of Grace. But still, there is nothing that fills the hollow place Thomas left.'

'Did you know Thomas?' Mary asked.

I shook my head. 'I met him but I did not know him.'

She lifted the bundle to her shoulder, her hand making small circles on its back, her head inclined slightly giving her a gentler demeanour.

'You didn't like him either, then,' she said, and I could not gainsay her.

'I must come to the point,' she said. 'It's not kind to leave Mr Benbow waiting in his own waiting room,' and she gave an uneasy chuckle. I sat quite still, not wishing to distract or impede this speech, which, for one as forthright as she, she appeared to be having some difficulty with. When minutes had passed and still she had not spoken, and finding this silence harder than any Quaker Meeting to endure, I could no longer keep quiet.

'I can go home again, if you prefer,' I said.

With a kiss to its head, Mary tucked the bundle back into its cot, rebuttoned her corset and put a hand to her hair. Then she beckoned to me.

'You haven't seen my baby properly,' she said. 'Come.'

Although I had seen her replace the little creature, I approached the crib feeling as though it might contain something explosive, something that might scald me if I drew too near.

I bent down over the crib. There was the tiny dark crown of his head and his fists bunched up beside his face. It took me a moment to adjust to the light, which was fading rapidly, and Mary fidgeted above me. Then I could see the baby's face. It had the lovely repose of the sleeping infant, its mouth puckering every now and then, as though dreaming of its mother's breast, I thought, looking away, a blush on my neck.

'So?' Mary said above me.

'I am only just seeing him,' I said, and I looked once again.

'Do you see now who the father is,' she said, and this time I saw it, the thing she had wanted me to. All at once there was no mistaking it, none, though I think if she had not suggested it to me, I would never have noticed.

I went back to my chair and Mary sat again in hers. She looked at me intently.

'You have seen it,' she said.

I nodded, and although I did not wish to know what had happened, I knew that I must ask her, and that she must tell me.

She told the tale in a flattened voice and though I could not bear it, I listened to her.

'I was gone to London to act companion to a wealthy man,' she said. 'You need not know his name, though it is one you would know, for he lives in this city. It wasn't the first time I had done this, and he was paying me very well for the honour. I wouldn't have done it otherwise. We were not to travel together, because of the risk of being recognised. I would travel down the day before and then we would meet at his London hotel. I was already booked into a separate room in there, and I looked forward to my one evening alone.

'He had given me the money to travel in the first class, but I bought a third-class ticket and kept the change. I had only seconds to spare in catching the train and had no time, as I would usually, to look over the occupants before taking my seat. Had I seen Thomas in time, I would have chosen a different carriage.

'My heart sank when I saw him there. The train was gathering speed by now. There was nothing I could do. Apart from a gentleman already asleep beneath his newspaper, we were the only two occupants, and despite our dislike of one another, we could not very well maintain a silence indefinitely. So we

began to talk. Polite things at first, things that could not
offend, such as the weather, or the state of manufacturing,
about which I surprised him for my knowledge was considerable, which I had, of course, straight from the horse's mouth,
though it wouldn't have done to tell Thomas which horse.

'It is a hard thing to explain, what happened. The man
asleep beneath his newspaper, the train carrying us away from
the people we knew, away from the girl we both loved,
London ahead, where we were two strangers, knowing
nobody. It was as if we both had the thought at the same
time. That just for this one night, this one free night, we
could be strangers to ourselves. Pretend we had just met, that
we liked one another. It was to be a joke between us, a joke
between us and Harriet.

' "Think how she'll laugh when she hears of it," I said, and
so in some important way we were doing it for her when we
arranged to meet for dinner that evening. And when the train
pulled in at Grantham, I changed carriages, because I knew it
would not do to test our fresh acquaintance too far.

'I will come to the point quickly, for it will not do to make
my excuse further, since in truth there is none I can make. We
met that evening and, in our nervousness, drank too much
wine, which neither of us was used to. He was a handsome
man, Thomas, and when he saw me back to my hotel, I asked
him up to my room for a cup of tea.

' "Cup of tea," he said. He laughed at me for it, but he
came to my room. And when we had drunk our tea, there
seemed nothing left but to . . .'

Mary paused here and made her hands into a steeple
beneath her chin. She looked across, not at me but at some
place that only she could see. For a moment she was unable to
say the words which even I, who was nearly as innocent as the
baby in the cradle as to such things, knew to be coming. Then
she looked down at her lap again and continued.

'We made love, Mr Ransome. If you can call it love. But still I think perhaps it was, though not for one another. It began as taunts, name-calling, and I don't know how it altered, except that it did. We made love as if each of us was telling the other how much they loved Harriet and the fiercer we were with each other, the more it proved it . . . I know this must sound corrupt and wrong. Evil even. And it was. But it was true also. We were two poles of the magnet. Two like poles. That's how Thomas put it.

'When we had finished, Thomas left the room without a word. The tea was still warm in the pot. I was too shocked to think on what had happened.'

Mary gave a fierce laugh. 'Can you believe it. I poured myself another cup of tea and drank it and went to bed. I think I knew at that moment that I was pregnant, just as I knew that this would never happen again and that neither of us would ever tell Harriet.'

Mary paused. I felt myself to be perfectly calm listening to her. It would not be until much later, in the privacy of my room, that I would give free rein to my feelings, ranting and yelling as a drunk man at the cruelties in our lives.

'I'm not asking for sympathy,' Mary said. 'I've told you this only after much consideration and only because I need to. If Thomas hadn't died—'

'Why do you need to tell me?' I said, interrupting her. 'Why can you not bear it as your secret? Or go home with it. Take it back to the village by the sea.'

'It'd only be my brother I'd go back there for,' she said. 'and I'm too late for him. I met someone from our village in York a little while back and they told me what I didn't want to hear. I made the money, but I took too long. Harriet was right. So there's nothing for me to return to there.' She stared at me a moment. Then she rose. 'I'll call in Mr Benbow,' she said, and when we were all seated, she spoke again.

'We asked you to come here because Harriet must have my baby,' she said. 'For her sake, and for mine. But she must never be told who the father is.'

I could not disguise my astonishment. 'You wish to visit the fruits of your sin, of your shame, upon Harriet?' I said, my language, despite myself, lapsing into a form of melodramatic utterance I powerfully disliked.

'She needs him,' Mary said. 'You have told me already how she is. And he is the baby she should have had with Thomas.'

'And you,' I said. 'Do you want to be rid of him?'

'No,' she said. 'Or rather yes, but only to Harriet. I would not part with him for any other living soul.'

'Then why do you wish for it?' I said.

Since returning to the room, Benbow had remained silent, staring into his lap. Finally he spoke, leaning forward, his elbows on his knees.

'We have often talked of the rights of women,' he said. 'Of the day that must surely come when women may have as much of an education as men, when they are able to vote, when they are able to work equally and for equal wages.'

'We may have,' I said, 'but we're not on any hustings now. And surely you would not advocate that a woman leave her baby. What are you telling me?'

'Mary has a talent and much ambition. If she were a man then this would be a simple thing.'

'What is her talent?' I said.

'She is to become a photographer. And I will help her all I can.'

'A photographer?' I said.

'There is a course that will teach me what I still have to learn.'

'In York?' I said.

'No,' Mary said. 'I'll have to go to London. But I can't do it with a baby.'

'And you would give up your baby for such a thing?'

'I don't know if I can. I couldn't to anyone else but . . . I can't give it the home that Harriet could. With your support.'

I sat back, still stunned. Benbow and Mary might be debating some point in a coffee house, they were so calm. I looked at them, at the room, at myself. There was something unreal about discussing these things in a photographic studio. As though any moment one of us would stand up, stretch our legs and call it a day.

'We would make a fine tableau,' I said. 'What should it be called? "A Pressing Question" perhaps. Or "Asking for Her hand".'

But this was no studio photograph, nor was it a hypothesis. It was real, and as if to remind us of this, the baby gave a small sleep cry and then was silent again.

'It's too much,' I said. I looked at the ground to avoid the steady gaze of those two sets of determined eyes. 'How will you fund yourself?' I asked at last.

'I have quite a sum of money saved,' Mary said with a slight grimace. 'From my previous employment. And Mr Benbow has agreed me a loan. It wants only the final signatures.'

'So I am to return tonight with a baby virtually tucked under my arm?' I said, and they nodded, just a brief uncertain glance passing between them.

If Mary and Benbow's request was shocking to me, it was as nothing in the face of Harriet and Grace's response. Not trusting the impulse of my own heart, I'd decided to place the decision with them. So after breakfast the next morning I called them, somewhat formally, into the dining room.

Seeing nothing to be gained by preamble, especially as Harriet's face was creased with worry, I launched straight in. I told them of my summons last night to Benbow's studio, of Mary's baby and of her ambition. I did not tell them of my outburst.

'Does she look well?' Harriet asked me, her voice strained.

'She looks tired,' I answered. 'And she longs to see you.'

Then I told them of Mary's request, and asked them, regardless of the difficulties that might be involved, whether they thought the baby should be brought to our house.

Grace spoke first.

'Of course, he must,' she said. 'And Harriet will become his mother.'

She didn't say any more, but took up a pencil and began to draw flowers on a piece of paper, for all the world as though there were no more to say or to do.

'Has he a name?' Harriet asked, and I was forced to shake my head and say that I didn't know. She was silent some minutes then, while Grace drew and I stared beyond the window at the warm rain that was falling steadily out of a bright sky.

'Do you wish the baby to come here, Mr Ransome?' Harriet asked me then, and I could not pretend to her.

'Yes,' I answered, and silently to myself, I added, 'with my whole heart.'

'I will give you my answer when I have seen Mary,' she said finally. 'I cannot decide without her.'

'But you don't think I am deceiving you?' I said, and she shook her head.

'No. But I must see her, and hear her first,' and she spoke with such grave authority that I felt no presumption at being addressed in this way by one who was, for all that I felt for her, no more than a flither-lass.

Mary came to see Harriet later that day, her baby in her arms, and what was said between them, I do not know, for I made sure to be in my room, though I could hear the baby's wail and wondered whether this was a sound that would become familiar to me. And when Mary left finally, I didn't need Harriet to tell me, because her decision was written into her every movement.

'He is to be called Jonah,' were her first words.

'Jonah?' I said.

'Yes. Because of his strange rescue.'

'And did you decide on this?' I said.

'No. It is Grace's name.'

So it happened that this scrap of a baby, this Jonah, became part of our household, became our child. All of ours. But that would be another tale, and could have no place in this one without producing some late and unseemly bulging. I would need to begin again to tell of his childhood, his adventures and escapades and his growth into manhood, this son of mine who was not my son but who became mine. And this story, the one already told, is coming to an end.

It was perhaps two or three weeks after Mary's visit, two or three weeks after Jonah's arrival, that William invited me to join him for dinner.

'Mr William?' Harriet said.

'Yes, so I won't be here for dinner,' I said. Harriet looked at the ground, looked down so hard I could see the soft hairs at the nape of her neck.

'There's a thing I want to ask you,' she said.

'Of course,' I said.

'I'd like you to read me Thomas's letter.'

'You're sure?' I said, and she nodded, her eyes not meeting mine, but staring somewhere out beyond the window. So I went and found it and brought it back to the drawing room. Then I took out the pages, opened them, and began to read. Weeks earlier I had sought to protect Harriet from such knowledge. Now I knew she needed the knowledge more than she needed any protection.

I read out all the detail. The visits to London to buy recipes, information, anything that might further the cause of the perfect cocoa, or the perfect pastille. The codes used in letters, the payment to doctors, whose testimonials, casting doubt over the purity of competitors' products, could be printed in advertisements and Thomas's forays into other men's factories. I read the whole right through without stopping, and she made not a single sound. Once or twice I looked up at her, but her face was impassive, impossible to gauge.

'Now read this,' she said when I had finished and she handed me two more sheets of the same paper, written in Thomas's hand.

'It is possible that you are now wife to an imprisoned man', I read. 'It is possible, though I shudder at the thought, that you are my widow. All that I am I owe to the Wetherbys. When all others had given up on me, they took me in and gave me a place in their household and in their factory. They have encouraged me to be the man that I am, and I have repaid them in doing this work to the best of my ability, work vital to the success and progress of the company. For this reason you must make your claim upon Mr William. You must make known to him your status, whether as my wife or my widow. He is a strict man, but fair. He will see the justice of it and will take the necessary care.'

Then I turned to the last page. 'Good bye my darling,' I read out, 'I will always love you. Thomas.'

I looked across at Harriet. She had sat now on a chair, stiff-backed, her lips tight. Her body was like a spring, arms, legs, neck, fingers tensed. Everything in me longed to hold and comfort her. I took only a single step towards her, and not to embrace her, for I would not have dared, but only to offer whatever comfort she might have allowed. But even at this I could see her coil tighter, so I went and found Grace and asked her to do the thing I wished to do, which I believe Grace knew, for she kissed me on the cheek as though to comfort me.

Although there was rain in the air that evening, I didn't ride, but walked the mile or so to William's house, needing time for my thoughts. I wondered whether I had built for myself an ivory tower, which kept me free from the mess of capitalism. Although it was the source of my wealth, my hands were clean of the tannery, my nose rarely afflicted with the smell of its pits, whereas William's hands were covered with the mess of cocoa, the stickiness of gum, the glaze of sugar. But the smell of his business was no sweeter than mine. Even as I read Thomas's letter, I knew I must act upon it now. Not for his sake, but for Harriet's. I thought it unlikely I would discover more about the precise circumstances of Thomas's death, but it was as clear to me as to Harriet that Wetherby's was responsible for it, and I couldn't bear any longer not to speak to William of it. The thing I dreaded above all was his denial, for after all how could he sit in Meeting week after week as he did, and act the part of moral arbiter and Quaker as he did if he had not also denied to himself responsibility in Thomas's death. And if he did so also to me, I was not sure I would be able to command either my words or my deeds.

William's dinner invitation had come in quite the usual way, and there had been nothing untoward in its wording. But though I had said nothing of it to anyone from Meeting, I was sure that he must have heard about the recent changes to my household, and so I prepared myself inwardly for a fight. A Quaker fight, but no less deadly for that. Harriet had given me weapons, and I would use them.

His house was quiet when I arrived, none of the usual sounds of family life. I rang the bell, and William answered the door.

'Welcome, cousin,' he said, and we embraced as usual. He looked pale, as if recovering from an illness.

'Are you quite well?' I asked.

'Well in the body, thank you, if disturbed in the mind,' he said as he showed me into the dining room.

'It's very quiet,' I said. 'Where have you put the children?'

'They are gone with their mother to Jane Kingscup for the evening. She has long been wishing for the visit.'

'So you and I will dine alone,' I said.

'Yes,' he said. 'There is much to talk about, and I thought it would be easier if we had not the usual distractions.'

We sat down, and though the table had been laid with the usual care, it was a poor meal, and it crossed my mind that even this William had engineered for some purpose, for his wife was nothing if not a generous hostess, one who believed in both nourishing and well-cooked food, and she would never have allowed the serving of such a dinner to her guests, whether they were family or no.

There was first a thin soup, closer to hot water than to broth, which I pitied the maid ladling, for, understanding more of how such girls reacted than my cousin, I could see that she was made uncomfortable by the situation. After this William himself brought in a piece of fish that had, I would guess, been boiled, for there was a quantity of surplus water pooled about it. Neither herbs, nor any sauce were produced to charge up such insipid flavour as it had, and the vegetables, like the fish, were but pallid specimens of their original selves.

William himself had fallen into what I can only describe as a sulk. His brow was lowered, his shoulders hunched and he would make no conversation except that necessary to avoid downright rudeness. Our meal was punctuated by the 'tac, tac' sound of his nail, tapping upon the rim of the side plate.

Determined to offer no grounds for an outburst, either by action or word, I ate the meal silently and with apparent good grace, making small observations occasionally on the weather, or the state of the Liberal Party. I enquired about each member of his family, and received cursory replies. I remarked upon the improved state of the railways, and again received only a monosyllabic grunt. As a final testing of the waters, I asked after the factory, and when he would not speak on this either, this project which he held closer to his heart, I sometimes thought, than his very children, but gave only a short sentence in reply, I fell silent. Not since we were boys had I known him as surly as this, a mark, I guessed, of what he felt to be the gravity and offence of my situation.

The argument, when it came, was short. William had taken me into his study and, after shutting the door carefully, had immediately come to the point.

'You are on a short road, Samuel,' he said. 'And it leads nowhere but to your own downfall.'

Although I was expecting something of this kind, still I was chilled at such harsh words from my own cousin. I made no reply, but waited to see what would come next.

'You know the words of Paul,' he said to me. 'That it is better to marry than burn. And you know, too, that as the head of the household, you bear absolute responsibility towards those beneath you, be they sisters or servants.'

'I hold my responsibility gravely, cousin,' I said, at which careful remark he became as I had never seen him before, a man at the outermost limit of his own control. Rising from his chair, he paced the two steps to the left and two to the right that the room afforded him, while across his face ran a series of emotions, so clear that I could read each there: rage, fear, love, disappointment, confusion. At last he stopped his pacing and, with his back to me, spoke again.

'I must be blunt. You have living in your house a girl who is, if I understand correctly, neither servant nor member of the family.'

'I do. She is companion to Grace.'

'But she is a working class girl, she is not a Quaker, indeed I fear she may not even be a Christian and for all these reasons and more, she is not suitable as chaperone for your sister, whom, I need not point out, requires most painstaking and experienced care. Not only this, but she is an ex-Wetherby's girl. Checking my wages books, I have established, as my informant had told me, that she used, until recently, to work in my packing rooms and sorting rooms. She has no education, I doubt she can read or write . . .'

'Barely, it is true,' I said, unable to keep a slight smile from my lips, which fortunately William did not see, and he carried on as though I had said nothing.

'And what is more, she is the girl we used for our first, and most successful poster campaign. She is a girl whose face has been visible all over the walls of the city . . .'

'Of the country even,' I could not help saying, provoking a glare.

'Indeed,' he went on, 'she has been stared at by anybody and everybody and she has almost certainly, and despite my best efforts, gained ideas above her station.'

William paused here to gather breath, and I asked him, in as conversational a voice as I could manage, who had given him his information.

'It is no business of yours,' he said. 'Enough for you to know that it was a Friend most concerned for the state not only of your soul, but of all those in your household.'

'Indeed,' I said, but William didn't notice the irony in my voice.

'To return to what I was saying, it is bad enough that this girl should be living in your house, and quite enough to provoke a visit from the Elders, which is indeed being arranged even as I speak, though I have requested not to be one of that number. But now I have heard that this unmarried girl has a baby, living with her in the house. And that Grace is playing a part in the child's care. What is this, Samuel? What kind of unnatural affair is this?'

'Did the girl leave Wetherby's on account of a pregnancy, then?' I said.

'How should I know?' he answered angrily. 'I do not investigate the state of health of all the girls who come and go.'

'But I should imagine that you have checked in this case, William,' I said calmly, though an anger was building in me too now, an anger which produced in me a stillness which was the counterpart to William's violent movements.

'Well, no, she was not pregnant,' he admitted. 'Mrs Flint believes she left for a different job.'

'She left to come into my employ,' I said. 'And, as you have just acknowledged, the baby is not hers, not in the biological sense. Since you do not know whose baby it is, nor what Harriet's purpose is in looking after him, then I think you have no right to comment.'

'And you think that a proper state of affairs?'

'It is my business, before God, how I conduct my affairs, William,' I said.

'No!' He interrupted me. 'It is not only yours, for if you bring shame upon yourself, you bring shame upon the family, and upon the Society of Friends. We can't allow you to do this, not if you are to remain a part, an organic part, of our Meeting.'

'I know where there is tending,' I said quietly. 'I must caution you from interfering in something about which you know nothing. And I will not be ruled upon it by the Elders, whatever the consequences.'

'I know nothing!' William exclaimed, his voice thick with anger. 'I was her employer for more than a year. Since she came to York, if I am correct.'

'And what do you know of her situation?' I said. 'Or of mine?'

'You are expecting me to become intimately acquainted with the lives of all the hundreds of girls and men in my employ?'

'No, I am not. But I think it no more your right to instruct them how to conduct themselves than it is theirs to instruct you,' I said.

426 THE SWEETEST THING

William was, by now, so maddened by my words, that like the proverbial bull, he threatened indiscriminately to trample on and destroy the ornaments and books in his study, his arms sweeping dangerously close as he visibly battled with the urge to strike me. But I continued with what I was determined to say, for I was as intent as he on giving my anger vent.

'Is it not strange' I said, 'that Quakers encourage their own women-folk to travel far from their families, to other Quaker Meetings in other towns, sometimes in other countries. If a Quaker wife is called as a Minister, she might leave her children and household behind for weeks, even months at a time, and you approve of this. You would approve, I presume, if it happened that your own dear wife Rachel had a calling for this work?'

William nodded grudgingly.

'And yet you will not let a girl, upon being married, children or no children, continue in your employ? But she must leave Wetherby's and never work a day more for you once the priest has declared her married.

'No matter that her family might already be living in poverty. No matter that she will likely be driven into badly paid work, perhaps dangerous work, or work that she must do in her own, ill-lit, badly-heated, badly-ventilated home. No matter that, just when a young couple most need both incomes, to prepare as best they can for the children they will likely have and the expense of it, no matter that at just that moment you deprive the young woman of her livelihood, and, what is more, you do it in the name of charity . . .'

Here I ran out of breath, and William, whom I think had been taken aback by the fervour of my speech, took the opportunity to interrupt.

'I do not know what your harbouring of this girl has to do with my factory practice, but I take exception to you, cousin or no, telling me how to conduct my business affairs. However, since you have raised this question, I will tell you that investigations carried out have shown that when married women are employed, then their husbands use this as excuse to loaf about doing nothing and are content to live on the wages of their wives.'

I had held off till now, carrying the words of Thomas's letter behind my eyes, at the back of my throat, in the base of my skull, where they pounded my senses and demanded a voice. Now it was time to speak.

'Harriet was married,' I said. 'And do you know who she was married to? You do not and could not, because she was driven by you, by your factory practice, to a secret marriage. She needed to keep her job, William. Now shall I tell you who her husband was? Her idle husband who wanted only to loaf about? Can you guess, William?'

I paused, impressed, despite myself, by my unaccustomed oratory. William was standing stock-still, his back to me once again, and he made no remark before I continued.

'Her husband, whom she loved as much as any wife could, who loved her as dearly as anybody could wish for, her husband was Thomas Newcome.'

'Thomas!' William said, and he sank to the ground, as I could never have imagined him doing, quite as if he were a character in some tuppenny melodrama.

'Thomas Newcome,' I said. 'The man who died, mysteriously I believe, not just in your employ but on your business. What was he doing, William? Was it inside the Richards' factory, or outside that he died? Did he fall, perhaps, jumping twelve feet into an alley from a factory window? Or was he caught in flagrante, wrench in hand, carrying out your dirty business? Because he left a letter for his wife that leads one to suspect the worst.'

'He left a letter?' William said from the floor.

'A letter describing his activities for Wetherby's,' I said. 'He makes not a single criticism of you, indeed he is proud of having done you such service, feeling himself so much in your debt. But it does not reflect well upon you.'

I paused again, this time to give more weight to my next remark.

'You would want to make some kind of restitution, a pension even, I presume, to his widow?'

'I loved Thomas,' he said from the floor.

'So honour his wife,' I said, all sympathy for him pushed from my heart. And then I told my only untruth of the evening, the most important lie of my life.

'You are right that the baby is not Harriet's,' I said, 'for she never had the chance to have his child. The baby is her sister's.'

I did not know before I arrived that I would say this. I didn't know I could. But suddenly, standing on my cousin's drawing room carpet, so much was at stake, so much entrusted, and I knew that this was my life's portion. That I would do all within my power to protect those I loved. Harriet, Grace and the baby boy entrusted to us all, Jonah. There was a heat inside my head and my hands that would have burned anything that stood in the way of their safety, that would have burned up my cousin, had I needed to, and I knew too that this lie had broken something between William and me. I went on.

'She was taken advantage of by a rich man, and after giving birth in the Home for Unfortunate Young Women, proved unable to care for him. So the baby has been given into Harriet's care. Now do you have the story you wished for?'

William groaned and attempted unsuccessfully to rise. I took hold of him beneath the arms and pulled him towards an armchair. For such a slightly built man, his body was heavy as lead. Somehow I managed to seat him in it, his arms dropped like plumb lines over each side, his head resting against its back. Bending over him, I spoke close to his ear.

'Will you tell the truth?' I said. 'Or shall I?'

He groaned again, and I let myself out of the room, closing the door behind me.

Standing in the hall, I pulled the bell for the maid, and after several minutes one appeared, bleary-eyed and without apron. I had forgotten entirely the lateness of the hour, and apologised for rousing her, to her apparent discomfiture.

'I wouldn't have woken you,' I said, 'except that Mr William is suffering slightly. The aftermath of the dinner, I expect. He's in his study, and may need some assistance shortly, though he wishes none from me right now. I must go home, so I thought it best to warn you of his trouble.'

The maid nodded, and opened the front door for me. I stepped out of the porch and the fresh night air was sweet, a balm to my senses.

I didn't walk straight home, but took a meandering route through the city with no particular thought as to where I was going. It was about the hour that the taverns emptied themselves and the streets were here and there thronged with lurching figures, some clutching at one another for support, others retching into doorways. But somehow in the warmth of this summer night I was not repelled, and returned beery greetings with good cheer.

I walked down Fossgate and was crossing the bridge when I halted. It was here, little more than a year and a half before, that I had first met Harriet. Here that this new passage of my life had begun. The water caught the gleam of the gaslight and showed off a murky brown, green slime shining on the brick-work above. The river was rich with effluent from the gas works and glue factories, the pig market and the flour mill, and above all from the people who lived crammed in all around, and it stank, the warm air breathing rank life into it. How strange to think that only last summer my house had smelt of Mother's dying. And now it was full of life. I walked back up the hill, back the way I had come, back towards home.

Harriet

It wasn't so long after I'd moved in to the house and all of us still finding our feet, that Grace got me into Mr Ransome's room.

At first I almost wished myself back at the factory, and it wasn't that I wanted to be working there. It was only that it filled the hours, so as you'd no need to think and no time to feel and by the end of the day you were weary enough that you might get some sleep. I missed the noises, too. Not of voices, because there wasn't any talking allowed, not during work hours. But there was all the noise made by the business of making things: cocoa, pastilles, creams, whatever, the machine noises, the sorting and the packing, and all of that kept the sounds inside my head away.

But now I was living in this vast house, everything done for me, the place so quiet you could hear a pin drop and half a dozen clock ticks, one against the other, and my only job to be alongside Grace, and that only some of the day. Now I'd too much room to think and too much time. Too much time to miss Thomas. So when Grace said she'd a task she'd to do, and would I come with her, I was pleased. And when she said she'd to blindfold me first, I let her. It wasn't much more than a few weeks and I'd got that used to Grace's ways that a blindfold didn't seem a strange thing.

I knew what it was went round my eyes. It was the shawl Mr Ransome had put about me all that time ago when we went to see the acrobat. I hadn't seen it, but I could tell from the touch, and the smell of it.

She pulled it so hard, it hurt me.

'Grace! Don't do it so tight,' I cried out.

'You mustn't see,' she said.

'I won't look,' I said, 'not till you say so,' but she kept the shawl wrapped round.

She'd covered my eyes in the hall, so then she took my hand and tugged me the way we were to go, which was first up the stairs, me fumbling at the corner, tripping over her cat, and her laughing, and next along a corridor. She stopped me once and twirled me round.

'So you don't know where you are,' she said, and I didn't.

We stopped again and I heard her turn a door handle.

'Your room?' I said, but she didn't reply, just pulled me in. I tripped on the edge of a rug and near enough fell headlong, except that Grace caught me.

'Stand,' she said, 'and don't move.'

I heard her shut the door and open the curtains. Even though I couldn't see, the dark got a bit brighter. Then she turned me a last time, just a half turn so I was stood in a certain direction, and took off the shawl.

I knew it must be Mr Ransome's room. There was his bed, his wash things, his desk, with papers and pens, his clothes still over a chair which surprised me, because he seemed such a neat man, his books on shelves.

'He's out, is he, your brother?' I said. She'd blindfolded me because I'd not have come in otherwise, which she knew, but why had she brought me in here?

'Here you are, Harriet,' Grace said. She was crouched just behind me, so I turned my head to see her, and there at her feet, and spread all over the floor behind, were photograph albums. There must have been a dozen of them, more. And they were open, all of them, and even before I bent down, I could see that all of them were showing girls.

Grace had her finger on one of them and I knelt to see it properly. It was me, and Mary too, in our flither-lass gear. I looked at it a long time, at my face which looked so young, and Mary's. I shut my eyes and I could hear Mary's voice, singing something.

Now her ghost wheels its barrow through streets broad
    and narrow,
Crying 'Cockles and Mussels, alive, alive-oh.'

'Sweet Molly Malone', I said. 'That's what you sang that day.' I began to flip through the albums, and every one of them was full of girls, all dressed in their working clothes, some of them for real and some like they'd been got up specially for the picture. Some looked pleased as punch and some like they didn't give a monkey any more, no matter that they were being took.

'There's all sorts of us,' I said. 'All sorts of girls.' And not a one who didn't have something in her hand or at her feet. A piece of cloth, a hoe, a basket of apples, a copper pan, a bundle of chain.

I thought I knew one of the girls. She lived down the street from Mrs O'Leary. She looked out all solemn, though she wasn't.

'Did you just find these?' I said.

Grace shook her head.

'But he didn't show you them, did he,' I said.

She shook her head again.

'What he's got them for?' I said. 'Is it some special reason?' but she just stood up, brushed out her skirts and tugged me out from the room again. It was only when we were out in the garden that she spoke.

'They won't matter so much now,' she said. 'Not now.' Then she swung herself up into the tree, where I couldn't reach her, not being as nimble, and with this grin on her face she sung a rhyme I'd not heard before.

> Curly locks, Curly locks, wilt thou be mine?
> Thou shalt not wash dishes, nor yet feed the swine
> But sit on a cushion and sew a fine seam,
> And feed upon strawberries, sugar and cream.

'You'll not have learnt that from your mother, surely,' I said. But she wouldn't say any more.

I went and had another look at the albums a couple of times, just on my own, but still didn't understand what he was up to. They weren't like the pictures Mary had been doing, that men liked to look at to make themselves excited, and they weren't like my posters, where I'd to look like I wanted you to buy something, cocoa or pastilles. They were just pictures of ordinary girls, their hands in front of them, staring. That's all.

It must sound funny that Mary's baby felt like mine the first time I laid eyes on him, but it was like that. Perhaps because he was hers and she'd have done anything for me, like I would for her, perhaps that's why I felt it.

She came out of the carriage with this big basket in her arms and first thing I wanted to throw the basket away, off, so as I could see her properly. It felt like years since I last had.

She was done up in this beauty of a dress. Deep green and with brocade trimmings. Not flashy, not like she'd been keen on a while back, but classy. No other word for it. Pearl earrings, a plain silver chain round her neck and her hair up tight, caught in behind with a lovely comb.

Maybe she felt like me about the basket, because the first thing she did was to leave it set down behind her and come up and hug me.

'God, Mary, what do you smell of?' I said, because she'd this odd smell to her which reminded me of the whiff there'd be to the milk churn before Mother scorched it clean again.

'It's my bosom,' she said, and she were laughing at me. 'For feeding the little fellow.'

I blushed, to be so daft, but Mary had me by the hand and was tugging me over to the basket. And still it didn't seem real at all, but more like one of Grace's games. More like something Grace'd have made up between her and her imagined friend.

'Have a look at him, Hal. He's beautiful,' Mary said, so I looked down. He'd his head on one side so I couldn't see his face, but she was right, he was. He seemed such a separate creature from Mary, lying there tucked in and dreaming. I couldn't believe that last time he'd been inside her, not out.

'He likes the jolting,' she said. 'The coach has sent him off. But he'll wake soon enough to eat.'

I fetched an old rug from the kitchen, and we spread it in some shade, one side of the garden. Then we settled there, Mary and me, and the basket off a little ways.

'Was it very bad, the birth?' I said.

Mary made a face. 'Imagine the worst, and then some,' she said. 'That'll be about the mark.'

'And the nuns?'

'They weren't so bad. I'd got their measure by then. But after, once he was born and I'd had a day or so to get over it,

I knew if I stayed put they'd make it hard for me to get away.
To get away with him, that is. I'd heard stories.'

'Stories?' I said.

She nodded. 'From some of the lay sisters. That's the ones
as don't wear the special gear. The hat and the gown. They'd
told me the babies sometimes got sold for a pile of money. To
ladies that couldn't have their own. And the stronger you were
when you were pregnant, the more likely it was yours'd be one
that was sold.'

'But they're all adopted, a'n't they?' I said.

'Yes, but if it's by a rich lot, then they pay, and they get the
baby off of you sooner, because the rich ones don't want you
mucking up their baby with your milk. That's how they
think of it, as their baby already, the minute it's born. The
nuns don't tell you straight out, because it only makes for
trouble. So I knew I'd to get away, and I couldn't get a message to you.'

'You went to Mr Benbow's?'

Mary nodded. 'And then I came to my decision,' she said.

I looked over at the basket. 'He didn't make you?' I said.

'No, he didn't. It was me. But he knows I'd be a good photographer.'

So then I said the thing I'd been thinking, which had come
into my head since Mr Ransome told us Mary's news.

'I suppose I know it too,' I said. 'You've always had a thing
for making shapes,' and Mary looked at me with this frown in
her forehead, quizzy more than cross.

'Making shapes?' she said.

'You know, arranging things,' I said, but she was still frown-
ing, so I'd to explain more, though when I spoke it I wondered
whether maybe it didn't sound daft.

'Like in the chop house and you're moving round the cutlery
and the salt and pepper shakers and anything else you can find.
Like you're doing a picture and there's the frame on it too.'

'You're smarter than I knew,' Mary said, grinning at me and I didn't know whether to be chuffed or huffed, till she leant over and grabbed me in a hug. 'Thank God you understand, Hal . . .' and I didn't hear more because she'd her arms round my ears and all I could hear was this loud rustle of her sleeves, so I just breathed in the smell of her and wished that she'd never let go. But when she'd stopped I had to ask her, hear her say it, her own lips, her own voice. So I did quick, before my nerves returned.

'So you're sure, are you?' I said, and she understood.

'Yes,' she said. 'I love my baby. I've loved him since the moment he was born. But if I don't go, I'll always wish I had. And if he were yours, then I'd know he was safe, and loved, and that I could come back and see him. Not tell him who I was, just an aunt, maybe.'

The baby gave a wail, a sharp, high sound, and I saw a tiny hand, its fingers reaching up, above the side of the basket. Mary already had her bodice unfastened, and right there, with me watching, she lifted the baby out and set him at her breast, which was three times its normal size with a great, dark nipple.

I watched the baby feed, a muscle beneath its ear shifting with each suck. And still one hand reached into air.

'Can you bear to?' I said, because I'd never seen her face so calm. It was like the baby was feeding her with something, not sucking the milk from her.

'I won't know if I don't try,' she said. 'I'd not have dreamed of this when we first took that train, Hal. That I could do something like this. Not have a baby, I mean, but . . .'

She lifted the baby onto her shoulder and rubbed his back.

'I've never seen you so gentle with anybody,' I said.

Then she put the baby the other way about, so as he could suck from her other breast.

I looked down to the far end of the garden. Grace was there, and her black cat, doing whatever it was she did when she was alone. She had on a straw hat with a great wide brim and she was making odd steps, a few this way, and then a few that, with her head down and her hands making shapes not so different from Mary's baby.

Grace was to join us for tea at half past four. That was how she'd put it, like it was the most normal thing in the world, first off for me to be thinking of having somebody else's baby, and second for her to be talking about taking tea like it was what she did all the time, with little plates and napkins.

Mary beckoned to me with her head.

'You've not had a proper look yet,' she said, and she shifted round so as I could see him. I looked full at his face for the first time, and he looked back. He had a look of Thomas, which was maybe because I so wanted him to. Then he gave up a burp which was like a gift, something from him for me, and it was simple as that. I'd have him if she'd really let me.

We'd tea in the garden, and Grace poured. She and Mary talked like they were old familiars. I went to fetch out some more bread and butter, and when I came back, Grace said, 'Jonah.'

'Jonah who?' I said.

'Jonah will be the name for him,' and she was pointing to the basket where the baby lay asleep.

I turned to Mary, who nodded her head.

'He's the one gets rescued out of the sea,' she said, and so that's what it was and no more spoken on it.

Mary had said she'd come back tomorrow and leave him.

I knew why it was so soon. She'd risk changing her mind if she waited longer.

'I'll bring his bottles and clothes and that,' she said. I nodded. I was glad because I wanted her baby now. I wanted him so much I'd have fought her for him, scrabbled on the ground and yanked her by the hair for him, her who was my best friend, my only friend just about, now I'd left the factory. Excepting Grace, but she was a different thing.

'So you'll be gone down there soon, then?' I said.

'Sooner I start, sooner I'm finished.'

'And what about a room? Somewhere to live?'

'They've got that organised, the ones as run the course.'

'And you'll be safe?' I said, which was a bloody daft thing to say, and Mary laughed at me for it. She laughed at me and then she left, the basket under her arm. But I knew she'd not be laughing tomorrow, for all her show of it.

Ever since I'd been there, Grace had filled the house with flowers. Not just a few here and there, but great jugs full everywhere. Every room would have its own, from the drawing room and the dining room to the bedrooms, mine, hers, Nellie's, the cook's and the maid's, to the kitchen, the scullery even, which drove the maid to distraction because she'd be in danger of knocking it with a broom or a mop all the time.

Grace would go out in the morning with scissors and bring in armful after armful, spreading them all over the kitchen table till the cook would be muttering under her breath about how was she meant to feed the family, and do this and do that. But Grace wouldn't hear her. And it wasn't just flowers she brought in. There'd be branches from trees and the long grasses that grew in the meadow beyond, and the little flowery weeds and sometimes even lilies from the pond. Then she'd put them all together in jugs and vases, so as any room you went into, there'd be this great rise of colour and all those smells. Bugs too, funny little things with leaf-shaped green wings that hopped high when you put a finger near, tiny spiders that threaded about the leaves and earwigs that hid in the poppy husks and made the maid shriek.

I remember the first time she brought in the water lilies. She'd got them in a bucket of water which she stood on the kitchen floor.

'What're you going to put them into?' I asked and she didn't say anything, just left the room, and when she came back she'd a chamber pot in each hand. She'd already got them filled with water and was picking up the water lilies with that tenderness she had for plants when Nellie saw what she was doing.

'Miss Grace!' she said. 'They're not clean things. You can't put flowers in them!'

But Grace just placed the flowers in the water and twirled a finger in it, which made the lilies turn. Then she carried the pots out, one at a time, carefully, and one she put on the dining room table and the other in her own room.

'There,' she said after. 'I think Mother would be proud,' but I couldn't tell if it was a joke or not, because Grace's face always stayed the same whatever she was saying.

When Mary brought Jonah back the next day, we made a quick job of it for both our sakes. She told me how to feed him with a bottle and what to do when he cried, and cleaning him and that.

'I've written it down, as much as I can,' she said. 'Get Grace to read it for you,' and she gave me some sheets of paper, 'and ask Nellie. She'll keep you sorted out. I'll be back to visit, but I don't know when. Mr Benbow'll have my address. Write to me, or draw me a picture.'

'Mary,' I said, but she put up her hand.

'Don't say anything, Hal. Not even goodbye. Else I won't be able to. He'll become part of you soon, just like Thomas was part of you.' She kissed me on the top of my head and I held her arms and then she was away.

I'd not seen Grace all that morning, though she knew Mary was to come with the little fellow. But as Mary climbed into the trap, Grace appeared, and gave her a posy of flowers, all carefully wrapped. Didn't say anything, just handed her the flowers, and Mary was gone.

Grace taught him all the colours she could find. She took him down the garden and dandled him on her knee, told him all the plants and flowers. Before he was big enough to know what she was showing him, she'd lift a stone and there'd be all the ants and their paths, going into a blind panic, dragging their eggs to safety, or she'd turn over a piece of rotting wood and put his baby finger in amongst the woodlice.

'Touch them, Jonah' she'd say. 'They've got their armour on.'

And Mr Ransome, he'd have had Jonah fed on cream and sugar, if we'd let him. He loved him as much as he'd have loved his own blood child.

Sometimes I'd look in the crib and I'd like to tell myself I could see Thomas in that face. I was his mother now, so why shouldn't Thomas be his father. I'd dream that Thomas was here with me and that Jonah was our baby, and there was no harm done by the wishing.

Besides, it was as likely a dream as the pipe dream sort we used to have, Mary and me, sitting end to end on our bed at Mrs O'Leary's, rubbing each other's toes for ease from the cold. And who'd have thought I'd climb out of the portrait? Or who'd have thought she'd end up taking them? Then I'd sing a little, just quiet, under my breath, not loud enough to wake him.

> Rock a bye baby, thy cradle is green,
> Father's a nobleman, Mother's a Queen;
> And Jonah's a gent now, and wears a gold ring,
> And Harriet's a lady and sweetly can sing.

I didn't know I'd ever heard my mother sing, until I sang to Jonah. Then I knew she must have because there was all these songs and rhymes in my head, and as I rocked him, or stroked his downy head until he slept, I could feel my mother's fingers on my cheek, her hands tucking me and my brother tight beneath the quilt. I could hear her voice.

'I'll take you back to visit when you're older,' I'd tell him. 'My mam'll love you, little fellow, and my brother'll show you his boat and his nets. I'll show you the rope down the cliff, but you'll not climb down it, so don't go getting ideas in your head.'

He'd gaze up at me, and chuckle with the sound of my voice, and I'd remember how the sky met the sea in a line, and how you'd to be quick to surprise the limpets, and how the salt made a scurf of white on your arms and how, if the sea was high, my mother would holler to us down the lane, her voice half-lost to the wind, not to go playing too close to the water.

AUTHOR'S NOTE

This is a work of fiction and I have taken liberties with time and space. However, a small handful of books has been indispensable in the writing: *Munby: Man of Two Worlds,* by Derek Hudson (Abacus, 1974); *The Diaries of Hannah Cullwick, Victorian Maidservant,* ed. Liz Stanley (Virago, 1984); *A Quaker Business Man,* by Anne Vernon (Sessions, 1987) and *Victorian Working Women: Portraits from Life,* by Michael Hiley (Gordon Fraser Gallery, 1979). I would like to thank the staff in the Borthwick Institute and City of York Library for their assistance. I am also very grateful to my agent Clare Alexander for her support and encouragement, to my editor Lennie Goodings for a wonderful piece of editing, and to Karen Charlesworth, Louise Hoole and Hermione Lee for their acute suggestions. All factual errors and conflations, deliberate and accidental, are my own.